A Lesson in Love

A Little Village School Novel

GERVASE PHINN

A Lesson in Love

HODDER &
STOUGHTON

First published in Great Britain in 2015 by Hodder & Stoughton
An Hachette UK company

1

Copyright © Gervase Phinn 2015

A CIP catalogue record for this title is available from the British Library

Hardback ISBN 978 1 444 77935 6
Ebook ISBN 978 1 444 779363

Typeset by Hewer Text UK Ltd, Edinburgh

Printed and bound by Clays Ltd, St Ives plc

Hodder & Stoughton policy is to use papers that are natural, renewable
and recyclable products and made from wood grown in sustainable forests.
The logging and manufacturing processes are expected to conform
to the environmental regulations of the country of origin.

Hodder & Stoughton Ltd
338 Euston Road
London NW1 3BH

For Misato Phinn

I

'Thank you for coming to see me, Elisabeth.'

The Director of Education rose from behind the huge solid mahogany desk which dominated the centre of her large and imposing office at County Hall. She was a stout, rosy-faced woman of indeterminate age with pale appraising eyes and thinning grey hair tied back tightly on her scalp. Elisabeth Stirling, head teacher-designate of the soon-to-be amalgamated schools of Barton-in-the-Dale and Urebank Primary, had been summoned to County Hall towards the end of the summer holidays, 'to discuss pertinent matters relating to the new school', which would open the following September.

When Elisabeth had first met her, she found Ms Tricklebank to be a rather stern and forbidding woman, a person of strong views but of few words. However, she had proved to be a perceptive and highly competent woman for whom Elisabeth had a great deal of respect. Ms Tricklebank had visited Barton-in-the-Dale village school as the senior education officer before her promotion and had later sat on the interview panel for the head teacher's position for the new school of Barton-with-Urebank so she was fully aware of the potential problems which might arise with the merging of the two schools.

The director moved from around her desk, shook Elisabeth's hand and gestured to a chair.

'Do sit down,' she said, as she sat down herself in the adjacent chair. 'I appreciate your coming in during the summer holidays, particularly just before the weekend, but I think it is important to bring you up to speed with a few things and sort out a few details prior to the start of the new term.'

'I welcome this opportunity,' replied Elisabeth. 'There are a few things which have been on my mind.'

'I am sure there have,' agreed the director. 'Well, firstly let me congratulate you on your marriage. From what I have heard, Dr Stirling is a very able doctor and a delightful man.'

'I think so,' replied Elisabeth. She smiled, recalling when she had first met the local GP.

Michael Stirling was a tall, not unattractive man, aged forty, with a firm jaw line, pale-blue eyes and a full head of dark hair greying at the temples and parted untidily. He had been on the governing body at her interview the year before when Elisabeth had been shortlisted for the headship of Barton-in-the-Dale village school and he had voted against her appointment. It was clear that he had had misgivings about this attractive, confident and clearly very capable woman. He questioned why she should be applying for such a post when she was already a head teacher at a large and thriving primary school. There was something he felt that was not quite right about her. Perhaps, he thought, she was looking for a quiet, uneventful life in some small rural school and would be unprepared to put in the time and the effort. Had Elisabeth informed the governors at the interview that the sole reason for her wishing to move to this particular school was to be near her autistic son who had secured a place at a residential school a stone's throw from the village, Dr Stirling would no doubt have voted for her appointment. Despite his reservations about her, which were not shared by his fellow governors, Elisabeth had been offered the post and in the space of just a few months she had transformed a failing, moribund school into one of the county's most successful ones. She had also transformed Dr Stirling's opinion of her. After a shaky start, the relationship of the new head teacher and the local doctor blossomed. *Who could have imagined*, thought Elisabeth now, *that in so short a time I would fall in love with this man and he would ask me to marry him?*

'And I believe you have three teenagers to contend with?' continued the director.

'I'm sorry?' said Elisabeth, still lost in thought.

'I was saying that you have three teenage boys to contend with. They will be quite a handful I guess.'

'Oh, the boys are no trouble and, touch wood, we get on really well. James is my husband's son by his first marriage and he is very even-tempered and studious, so I don't have any difficulty with him. Then there's Danny, who we are in the process of adopting, and he is such a happy young man, so it's a lovely busy house at the moment. I taught them both at Barton actually and they move on to Crompton Comprehensive next term. As you know, my son John is at Forest View, the residential special school.'

'And how is he getting on there?'

'He's making slow but steady progress,' Elisabeth said. 'I'm told there is no disorder as confusing to comprehend or as complex to diagnose as autism and I have no idea how much John understands. The main thing is that he receives the best possible care and education and he certainly gets that at Forest View. John's teacher, Mr Campsmount, is excellent too. He's such a keen, hard-working and personable young man, and he relates well to the children. John has really taken a shine to him. I couldn't be happier.'

'That is good to hear,' said Ms Tricklebank. 'I have heard good reports about this young man too. I think he will go far. Well, down to business. Things are pretty well in hand for the proposed amalgamation, with the infant children based at the Urebank site and the juniors at Barton. The governing body is in place and parents seem very satisfied with the arrangements. Well, I've had no complaints anyway. I do appreciate that managing a school on a split-site will be something of a challenge but I am confident that you will cope very well.'

'My worries are not concerning the split-site,' Elisabeth told her. 'It's getting the teachers from the two former schools to work together which I think will be the greater challenge.'

'Well, perhaps we should discuss the staffing at the new school first then. Now, if I am correct, you and Mrs Robertshaw will stay at the Barton site and Miss Wilson will move down to Urebank to join the two infant teachers there.'

'That's right.'

'As regards the remaining staffing needs—' began the director.

Elisabeth frowned, thinking of Mr Richardson, the former head teacher at Urebank who had been offered the post as her deputy which he had accepted grudgingly. She had crossed swords with this self-important and patronising man the previous year and it was clear he was angry and resentful when she had been offered the new head teacher's position. However would she manage to work with him? Ms Tricklebank clearly noticed the knitted brows.

'Now don't look so down,' she said, smiling. 'I have some news which I am certain will not be unwelcome. Mr Richardson has secured another position. He will not be joining you in September.'

Elisabeth tried not to show her massive relief at this news but inside she wanted to jump for joy.

'Really?' she replied, trying to sound calm.

'He came to see me at the end of last term,' continued Ms Tricklebank, 'and explained that he couldn't work as your deputy head teacher in the new set-up. Having been a head teacher himself, he felt he would find it hard not being "at the helm" as he put it. I can quite understand this.' Ms Tricklebank paused for a moment as if thinking of what to say next. 'And of course, what with the troubled relationship he has had with you in the past, he felt . . . well I need not go on. Last term he started to apply for other positions and, "as an interim measure before securing another headship" – his words, not mine – he has accepted the post of Deputy Headmaster and Director of Studies at St Paul's Preparatory School in Ruston, to begin there at the start of the new term. Of course technically he needed to give two months' notice but, under the circumstances, I agreed that his resignation would take effect immediately.'

'I am very pleased for him,' replied Elisabeth. 'Things seem to have worked out well for both of us.'

'This means, of course, that there will be the appointment of a deputy head teacher in charge of the Urebank site and we will need Miss Brakespeare's replacement at the Barton site.'

Miriam Brakespeare was Elisabeth's deputy at Barton-in-the-Dale, a small, timid, bustling woman who had jumped at the opportunity to take early retirement the previous term and had moved to Scarborough.

'And will Mr Jolly be moving on to another post too?' asked Elisabeth, hopeful that the former po-faced deputy head teacher at Urebank and the teacher of the upper juniors there might have found another position as well.

'No, he will be joining you at the Barton site,' said the Director of Education.

'I see.'

Mr Jolly's name belied his character for he was, by nature, not a jolly man. In fact he was a rather sad and lonely figure. It had always been the case. As a boy he had had no friends to speak of. Other children found him strange and distant, a boy who never laughed and seldom smiled. He was never invited to be part of the laughing, boisterous crowd of boys which congregated in the school yard at break times. None of his fellow pupils called at his home, invited him to their birthday parties, asked him to join them on bike rides, go to the cinema with them, fish in the local stream or play football with them on the wreck at the weekend. Not that he was good at sports anyway. He was usually the last to be picked for any team games at school. Even Anthony Davidson – who was slow and fat and wore large round wire-framed glasses, the lenses of which resembled the bottoms of milk bottles – often got picked before he did. Despite his name and temperament, Donald Jolly was never bullied, for his peers merely viewed him as something of an irrelevance. He had been an average student, one of the unremarkable majority in the boys' grammar school which he had attended, the big hump in the academic bell, a dull, plodding pupil soon forgotten by his teachers. He achieved a moderate success in his examinations and managed to secure a place at a minor teacher-training college where he scraped a certificate in education. Then he had got a job at Urebank Primary School at a time when teachers were in demand and it was said that anyone warm and breathing could secure a teaching position. He had remained at the same school for his entire career to date. When Mr Richardson was appointed as head teacher, he immediately recognised in Mr Jolly a compliant colleague in whom he could burden all the tedious administrative duties, knowing that they would be done without complaint. Hence when the position of deputy head teacher arose, Mr Richardson was happy to put Mr Jolly's name in the frame, describing him to the governors as a most dedicated, loyal and supportive colleague. Unfortunately Elisabeth could now perceive difficulties, given the two schools had merged and Mr Jolly would no longer keep his coveted but rather undeserved position.

'I asked Mr Jolly to come in and see me at the end of last term to discuss his future,' said Ms Tricklebank now. 'He informed me that he has taught junior school-aged children for his entire career and has no experience of early years education. He would therefore wish to teach at the Barton site.'

'As just a classroom teacher?'

'That's right.'

'How does he feel about returning to be as a classroom teacher having been a deputy head?' asked Elisabeth. 'I am sure he can't have welcomed such a demotion.'

'Actually he seemed quite resigned to it,' Ms Tricklebank told her. 'I explained to Mr Jolly that I could not guarantee he would secure a senior position elsewhere in the authority. Of course, should a deputy head teacher's post come up in another school, he would be free to apply for it but it would depend on the governors of that school as to whom they appointed. I think he realised that there was little chance of him getting such a post. The school inspectors found quite a deal lacking with the leadership and management of the school when they visited Urebank and he came in for some pretty severe criticism. He is, I am sure, fully aware of his shortcomings. I explained to him that should he accept a position as a class teacher at the newly amalgamated school his present salary would be protected. Of course, if he wished, he could be redeployed as a classroom teacher to another school.'

'Well, I have to say I am rather surprised that he wants to come and teach in the new set-up,' said Elisabeth. 'I can't say I took to him when we met and it was clear to me that the feeling was mutual.'

'Mr Jolly is a pragmatist,' said Ms Tricklebank. 'As I said, I think he realised that he would not get a deputy head teacher's post elsewhere and would not wish to put himself through the ordeal of an interview. With his salary protected and his pension secured, he has little to complain about. It can't be long before he retires anyway.'

'I suppose it was too much to expect to get a teacher of the calibre of Mr Campsmount.'

'I have to admit that Mr Jolly is not the best teacher in the world,' Ms Tricklebank told her, 'but I dare say that with your guidance and encouragement he will improve.'

'I fear it may be a little late in the day for that to happen,' replied Elisabeth. 'As you say, he is nearing retirement age.'

'I imagine you felt the same way about Miss Brakespeare when you took over as head teacher of Barton-in-the-Dale and she certainly proved you wrong. I am sure that Mr Jolly, under your guidance, will do the same.'

'I hope so.' Elisabeth sounded doubtful. 'One wonders how he came to be offered a senior position at Urebank.'

'As you know, the appointment of staff is firmly in the hands of the school governors,' said the Director of Education tactfully. 'There have been a number of occasions when I have advised governors against the appointment of a particular candidate only to be ignored. It is the governors' decision who is offered the post. Education officers are there to recommend and not to decide. Fortunately when it came to your appointment for the new school they listened to what I had to say and heeded my advice, not that it was needed. As you may have gathered, the decision to offer you the post of head teacher was unanimous.'

The Director of Education rose and reached over to her desk to retrieve a plastic folder containing a number of files that Elisabeth had spied since her arrival. Sitting back down next to Elisabeth, Ms Tricklebank opened the file and continued.

'With the closing of some small schools in the county, we have a number of teachers we need to redeploy and I would like you to consider a couple I have in mind. Now, if I am correct, we have just these two vacancies at Barton-with-Urebank?'

'That's right,' replied Elisabeth. 'There's Miss Brakespeare's replacement on the junior site and now Mr Richardson's on the infant site.'

'Well we are nearly at the start of the new term,' said the Director of Education, 'so we have to move pretty quickly. We could, of course, employ two supply teachers to fill the vacancies until more permanent members of staff can be appointed, but I am hopeful that two teachers seeking redeployment might just suit.' Ms Tricklebank consulted a file. 'The number of pupils attending Tarncliffe Primary has greatly declined over the past few years and it was with regret that we have had to close the school in July. The head teacher, Miss Drayton, one of these permanently optimistic and cheerful people whom nothing and no-one seemed to dishearten or discourage, has taken early retirement as has her deputy, Mrs Standish. Both were totally dedicated teachers who ran an excellent school. It was such a pity Tarncliffe had to close. Anyhow, the remaining junior teacher at the school is a Mr Hornchurch who sounds like your Mr Campsmount. Miss Drayton describes him as dedicated, enthusiastic, full of ideas, and a most creative and considerate young man.'

'He sounds exactly what we are looking for,' said Elisabeth.

'But there is something you need to know about him,' she said.

'Oh dear,' sighed Elisabeth, 'this sounds ominous.'

'Mr Hornchurch is, well, rather different,' said the director. She thought for a moment, pondering how best to put it. 'To be perfectly blunt, he is one of life's eccentrics. He's idiosyncratic, unpredictable, untidy and sometimes, when he has a project in mind, he can be rather over-enthusiastic and not a little exasperating. Miss Drayton says in her reference that he does brilliant things – like a project on astronomy when he had the whole class and their parents sitting in the playground in the middle of the night staring up at the stars and identifying all the constellations – but then, on another occasion, he took the children on a school trip to the wildlife centre at Willowbank and failed to notice one child climbing into the pond area. After the child got home and had his tea, he was sent upstairs to get ready for bed. His mother discovered him sitting in the bath, surrounded by bubble suds, with a baby penguin paddling away merrily in there with him.' The director had a smile on her face.

Elisabeth let out a crack of laughter. 'Oh dear,' she chuckled.

'I am afraid that the parents, the governors and the wildlife centre officials did not find it quite so funny.'

'But something tells me, Ms Tricklebank, that you rather admire Mr Hornchurch's idiosyncrasies?'

'Perhaps I do. The teachers I recall with affection at school and the ones who had the greatest impact upon me were rather unconventional and unpredictable. No teacher teaches in exactly the same way. Great teachers not only instruct but inspire. In my view teaching can take any shape whatsoever provided that children come to love learning and achieve good results. Mr Hornchurch is without doubt out of the ordinary. I can't see him fitting in at some schools I could think of in the county. I guess most head teachers would find him infuriating but I feel under your direction he could be a real asset.' She waited for a reply but when one was not forthcoming she asked, 'Would you like to think about it?'

'I should really like to meet Mr Hornchurch,' said Elisabeth. 'He sounds very interesting.'

'I'll arrange it.'

'What about the other teacher?'

'Miss Kennedy was deputy head teacher at Sunnydale Infants, another school which sadly had to close. She is efficient, hard-working, experienced and, in contrast to Mr Hornchurch, perhaps a little traditional in her ways but this is no bad thing. Having heard of the possibility of a post at the new school, she is eager to be considered. I am sure she might prove to be an excellent replacement for Mr Richardson.'

Anyone would be an excellent replacement for Richardson, thought Elisabeth. 'Miss Kennedy sounds very promising too,' she said.

'Good,' said the director, smiling. 'I'll arrange for her to see you as well. If you can put your head together with your Chairman of Governors and let me know a convenient date for the informal interviews, I'll arrange for the two teachers to visit the school, meet you and look around. As I said, we are nearing the end of the summer holidays so we have to be quick.'

'I'll organise something for next week,' Elisabeth told her.

'Good,' said Miss Tricklebank, closing the folder, 'If you are happy with them and they feel comfortable with starting in September then we can proceed. I shall ask Mr Nettles, the education officer who will be your point of contact here at the office, to join you when you have fixed the date.'

Later that afternoon, Elisabeth stood by the window in the sitting room at Clumber Lodge, her home for the past year, and stared at two photographs in silver frames carefully arranged on a small inlaid walnut table. One was of Michael's former wife, a striking-looking young woman who had been killed in a riding accident. She was dressed for the hunt in a black jacket and white cravat and posed before a large chestnut horse. Another was of Michael, handsome and smiling, dressed in a dinner jacket with his arm around her. They both looked so happy. Elisabeth sometimes wondered when Michael put his arm around *her* if he would ever be as happy with her as he had been with his first wife. It was clear that he had adored her and after her death he had gone through a dark and difficult time. He had shunned the company of others, appeared sharp and bad-tempered and neglected his appearance and the state of the house.

Elisabeth looked around the room. How different it was

now. When she had first visited Clumber Lodge, she had found the sitting room cold and uninviting with its heavy fawn-coloured curtains, earth-brown rug, dark cushions and dusty furniture. Despite the housekeeper's efforts, badgering the doctor to try and be a bit tidier, it had remained cluttered. The bookshelf was crammed with books and journals and papers were piled on a sofa which had seen better days. On the large oak desk was an old-fashioned blotter, a mug holding an assortment of pens and broken pencils and more papers stacked untidily. On the walls were a few dull prints and an insipid watercolour of a mountain and a lake.

Then Danny came to live at Clumber Lodge. Dr Stirling had much to thank the boy for. After his mother's death, his son James had become unnaturally introvert, wrapping himself up in a protective shell, never speaking, never smiling. He had been like a small timid creature, deep in a world in which it seldom showed its face. His only friend had been Danny, in whom he had confided, and it was Danny – good-humoured, patient and understanding – who brought his son out of the shell. It wasn't long after Elisabeth arrived in Barton that Danny's grandfather, who had raised him, sadly died and Danny was put into care until Michael agreed to foster him. Without realising it at the time, it wasn't just an opportune move for Danny but for every one of them.

Before Danny arrived at Clumber Lodge, Michael arranged for one of the musty and unused bedrooms to be redecorated. Elisabeth and Mrs O'Connor, the housekeeper, had seen the opportunity and prevailed upon the doctor to give other parts of the house greatly in need of some refurbishment an overhaul. The sitting room had been transformed and it now looked homely and bright. The walls were painted, the wood shone, the prints and watercolours had been replaced by some large bright paintings, the faded curtains had given way to long plum-coloured drapes and a thick-pile beige carpet had been fitted. The desk had been moved out and replaced by a deep cushioned sofa. Even the large pot plant in the corner gleamed with well-being.

Just before Elisabeth and Michael were married, the two photographs in the silver frames disappeared.

'Michael, why have you moved the photographs of your wife?' Elisabeth had asked him.

'We will be starting married life soon,' he had told her. 'I just thought that when we are, you may not be too happy about seeing pictures of my first wife in such a conspicuous position.'

'Not at all,' Elisabeth had replied. 'She was such a part of your life and you loved her very much. The last thing I want is for her to be forgotten.'

So the photographs were put back on the small table next to one of Elisabeth and Michael on their wedding day. On occasion Elisabeth wondered however if Michael had been right. Sometimes their presence seemed to trouble her. Her eyes were so often drawn to the photographs of the beautiful woman with the dazzling smile and she pondered whether Michael could ever love her as much. Rousing herself from her thoughts, Elisabeth heard the front door open and a moment later Michael entered the room. He came over and kissed her on the cheek, then went to the sideboard and splashed a couple of inches of whisky into a glass.

'Drink?' he asked before taking a sip.

She shook her head. 'No thank you. It's a bit early for me.'

'It is for me really,' he said, 'but I needed this.'

'Hard day?'

'Very.' He took a sip of the whisky, flopped onto the sofa and rested his head on the back. 'It seems the entire village is down with something. So, how did it go?' he asked.

'Oh, the meeting?' replied Elisabeth sitting next to him. 'Much better than I expected.'

'That's good to hear.' He put his arm around her. 'I know this amalgamation has been on your mind lately. You've not been able to think about much else.'

'Actually I was told some good news. Robin Richardson won't be starting at the new school in September.'

'Hallelujah!' exclaimed Michael.

'He's been offered a job at St Paul's Preparatory School.'

Michael finished the whisky in a gulp. 'Well, that's a weight lifted from off your shoulders. What about the other chap, that deputy of his, what's his name?'

'Jolly.'

'Has he got another job as well?'

'Unfortunately not. He'll be with me I'm afraid.'

'Well I am sure you will win him around.' He kissed her cheek. 'You are quite a persuasive woman, Mrs Stirling. Now, no more about school.'

There was a longish silence. 'Are you happy, Michael?' she asked him suddenly. She wasn't sure where it came from but thoughts of the past and *what-ifs* were obviously playing on her mind today.

'Of course I'm happy!' he exclaimed. 'Whatever brought this on?'

'Oh, it's just I've been a bit of a pain lately, worrying about this amalgamation, complaining about things, getting so tied up with school. It's a wonder you've put up with me.'

He put the glass down on the floor. 'Look, Elisabeth,' he said turning her face to his, 'I couldn't be happier. You made me the happiest man on earth when you said you'd marry me. I like putting up with you. I love you, you must know that.'

There were tears in her eyes. She glanced over his shoulder to the photographs in the silver frames. 'And I love you too,' she said before pressing her lips to his.

Mrs O'Connor, Dr Stirling's housekeeper, bustled into the room. She was a dumpy, round-faced little woman with the huge liquid-brown eyes of a cow and a permanent smile on her small lips, both framed by a tight perm that clung to her head in all weathers. Like many of her race, she embroidered the English language with the most colourful and original axioms and expressions, most of which were throwbacks to her old Irish grandmother, who had a caustic comment, a saying or snippet of advice for every occasion.

'Hello, Dr Stirling,' she said. 'Back early for once.' Before Michael could reply, she prattled on. 'Now then, Mrs Stirling,' she said cheerily, 'I've done upstairs and finished in the kitchen. Would you like me to give the sitting room a quick going over before I go?'

'No thank you, Mrs O'Connor,' Elisabeth told her. 'You get off.'

'Well, to be honest, I do have quite a lot to do. Now that I've taken on a bit of housekeeping for Father Daly at St Bede's, I don't seem to have a minute to myself. He's a very nice man, so he is, but the state of the presbytery! You should see his study. It's like a junk shop. Full of clutter, so it is. I just don't know where to start. It was a sight worse than this room before we tidied it up. I can hardly get in for all the statues and books and candlesticks and lamps. It's the devil's own job to clean because Father Daly won't let me move things. He's so stubborn; he'd whistle a jig at a gravestone as my Grandmother Mullarkey was wont to say.' Elisabeth opened her mouth to say something but Mrs O'Conner chattered on. 'He met the new vicar last week.'

'I'm sorry,' said Elisabeth, who was not really listening. 'Who did?'

'Father Daly. He thought he'd pop round to St Christopher's to introduce himself. He's something of a cold fish by all accounts.'

'Who is?' asked Michael.

'That new vicar. Mr Sparshott. Didn't give Father Daly

the time of day evidently. The poor priest was quite put-out when he got back. Wasn't even offered of a cup of tea. Stand-offish he was, this new vicar. It'll be a while before Father Daly makes a return visit I can tell you. "Never boil your cabbage twice," as my grandmother used to say. This new chap is not like the last vicar, that friendly Reverend Atticus who was made the archdeacon and is off living in Clayton. He was a real gentleman, so he was. Always passed the time of day when he met you in the village. And I don't know how that nice young girl curate will get on with the new man. Personally I'm not in favour of women priests but having said that, the Reverend Underwood, from what Mrs Sloughthwaite in the village store has told me, she is like a breath of fresh air and Father Daly, who works with her as a chaplain at the hospital, hasn't a bad word to say about her. Gets on like a house on fire with the patients, so she does. I can't imagine her getting on with this new vicar. Mind you, I can't imagine many getting on with him from what I've heard.'

To describe the new Vicar of Barton as 'something of a cold fish' was an understatement in the view of many in the village. The Reverend Algernon Sparshott had made a very inauspicious start. In his first visit to his new parish, prior to taking up his position, to attend a musical evening in the church, an event that had been organised by the curate, Reverend Ashley Underwood, he had succeeded in annoying everyone with whom he came in contact. Asked by the curate if he had enjoyed the evening, he informed her stiffly and with alarming directness that he felt a church should be a place of worship, prayer and contemplation and not a centre of light entertainment. He then managed to infuriate the Archdeacon's wife by enquiring with equal candour when she and her husband 'would be vacating the rectory'.

'Vacating the rectory!' Mrs Atticus had repeated angrily

when she spoke to her husband later. 'Vacate it, indeed! It made us sound like squatters.'

Having learnt that the new vicar had four children, Elisabeth had assured him that they would be very happy at the village school but the clergyman had replied that the two oldest were at boarding school and he had already made arrangements for his youngest children to attend St Paul's Preparatory School in Ruston, where he felt they would be better catered for. 'I am of the considered opinion,' he had told her pompously, 'that the small independent school tends to have better discipline, smaller classes and more of a work ethic than the state school.'

'You might like to visit the village school some time, Mr Sparshott,' Elisabeth had replied pleasantly, 'and see how well behaved and hard working the pupils are.'

He had moulded his thin features into a weak smile.

No, thought Elisabeth now, recalling her first meeting with the new vicar, *the Reverend Mr Sparshott is not a man one warmed to*. She smiled. *And I wonder how he will get on with the new Deputy Headmaster and Director of Studies at St Paul's.*

2

The Reverend Algernon Sparshott, the newly appointed vicar of Barton-in-the-Dale, was not a man who possessed the social skills of those who could speak easily to people they had not met before. At first meeting he appeared a dour, self-important and humourless man but in fact he was, underneath the apparent coldness and pomposity, a shy and thoughtful person. He was also someone of uncompromising views when it came to his beliefs, something which displeased some in his congregation. His lack of cordiality and seeming intransigence had held him back in preferment within the Church. The bishop, a generous-natured and optimistic man, had however decided to support Mr Sparshott when he applied for the position of vicar at Barton-in-the Dale. He felt that the cleric, after many years of dedicated service, deserved to be given the chance of running his own parish. It was a risk but the bishop felt the clergyman could very well make a success of his new advancement.

Mr Sparshott was a tall, clerical individual with straight, colourless hair and large pale eyes set wide apart. That Sunday morning he sat in a padded leather chair, his thin legs crossed before him, with an expression of extreme sanctity on his narrow bony face. He looked ponderingly at his wife, who sat knitting opposite him. Mrs Sparshott, a square-faced woman with a head of thick mousy-coloured hair and piercing eyes, was sharing with her husband her considered opinion on the curate.

'I think you should start as you mean to go on, Algernon,' she vouchsafed. 'You are the vicar here and she is the curate.'

'I am well aware of that,' said the new vicar, exasperation obvious in his voice.

'You can't have the tail wagging the dog. It appears this Dr Underwood has been given *carte blanche* by the archdeacon when he was vicar here. Of course, he let her do as she wished. Too busy with church affairs, that was his trouble. You have to be firm, Algernon.'

'I really do not need to be reminded of the fact that I am the vicar and Dr Underwood is the curate,' replied her husband, 'and rest assured there will be no tail wagging of this particular dog, to use your unfortunate expression.'

'I'm pleased to hear it,' said his wife.

'And as for the archdeacon,' continued Mr Sparshott, 'that is what vicars do – busy themselves with church affairs.'

'My goodness, you've waited long enough to get this preferment,' said his wife. 'Now that you have your own parish you need to stamp your identity upon it. You should make it abundantly clear when she arrives. She has got too many fanciful ideas introducing all these dreadful happy-clappy hymns, using that Good News colloquial Bible, organising lectures in the church and I don't know what—'

Her husband held up a hand to stop her.

'Be under no illusions, Rosamund,' he replied. 'I intend to make my position perfectly clear when I see Dr Underwood tomorrow. Now, I have morning service so I must prepare myself.'

Later that morning, the Reverend Algernon Sparshott, swathed in priestly white, ascended the pulpit at St Christopher's. The church was surprisingly full that Sunday morning which gratified him – as the curate at St Mary the Virgin at Marfleet, he had never attracted more than a handful of worshippers. The new vicar placed his hands on the top of the pulpit and leant forward dramatically, staring for a moment at his intrigued and expectant congregation. Most of the village had turned out to hear the first sermon of the new incumbent and sat in anticipation with all eyes fixed upon him. Members of the choir in the stalls craned their necks to get a better view and Mrs Fish, seated at the organ, squinted around the panel which screened the instrument. Mr Sparshott noticed that the congregation included the archdeacon and his wife, the head teacher of the village school and her husband and Lady Helen Wadsworth, the lady of the manor, who sat straight-backed and severe-looking in her reserved pew at the front of the church. If he was nervous, the new vicar certainly gave no signs of showing it.

When the curate had delivered her first sermon at St Christopher's, Dr Underwood's theme had been about kindness, consideration and love. She had spoken of a gentle, loving Jesus who had revealed God to the world and given His life for mankind, transforming hearts and forgiving sins. She had reminded the congregation of the Christian message to love one's neighbour, even one's enemies, and to give one's heart and soul to God's service.

'For St Peter urges us to be like-minded,' she had told the congregation, 'to be sympathetic, to love one another and to be compassionate and humble. "Do not reply evil with evil", he wrote, "or insult with insult but on the contrary repay evil with blessing because to this you were called so that you may inherit a blessing".' She recalled it was Jesus who had asked those who came to hear Him preach: 'He that does not love his brother who he sees, how then can he love God whom he has not seen? He that loves God, loves his brother also.'

If those sitting quietly in the pews expected the lesson to be something along similar lines that morning, they were soon disabused of the idea.

'There is only one terrible thing in the world,' the new vicar intoned, 'and that is sin.' Several of his congregation shot upright as if prodded in the back. 'We must fight valiantly against sin and the devil and remain faithful to the Lord to the end of our lives. That is the lesson of this morning's sermon.' The new vicar paused for effect. '"They that sin are enemies to their own life," it says in the Apocrypha, Chapter 12, Verse 10. But how, I ask, do we come to an understanding of sin? How do we comprehend the very nature of sin? Sin is like a lingering disease in which the patient feels himself healthy but he is far from healthy. The disease of sin conceals itself from the perception of the patient. Only he who has revived health is sensible that he has been ill. All that makes the life of a Christian great and strong and inward and free and happy is wanting in the life of the sinner. Sin is contrary to what is good and continues to destroy what is good. Sin always says "no" to God's thoughts and to God's will and to all that is good and true and right. Sin says "no" to God because it says "yes" to the pleasures of the world and the indulgences of the flesh.' He paused again for effect and shook his head solemnly. 'Sin goes forth from unbelief and consists of egoistic pleasure,' he continued. 'It asserts itself through deceit. Look at the disobedient child, at the feckless youth falling into wantonness and dependency, at the drunkard in the centre of his worldly pleasure, at the thief blighting the lives of others, of the grey head depressed under the fear of death and impotent resignation. That we are sinners crushes out what is good in us, the very thing that makes us free.'

Nearly half an hour later, the new vicar was still going strong on the evils of sin. The congregation sat in stunned silence, many with mouths agog.

One small child in the front pew was moved to ask his mother in a whisper, 'When will they pay this man and make him shut up?'

At long last, and to everyone's relief, the sermon came to an end.

'And so in the final analysis,' declaimed the new vicar, 'we should perhaps think today of the words from Romans, Chapter 12, Verse 12: "Through one man sin entered the world, and through sin came death; and thus death comes to every man, for every man is a sinner".'

As the members of the congregation left the church, Mr Sparshott, hands clasped before him, stood by the door. Most of the people, eyes down and looking thoroughly dejected, departed hastily. Only a few shook his hand but even they moved on quickly, not wishing to engage in any conversation. Lady Wadsworth was one of the last to leave. She was not a woman to mince her words.

'Well, that was a sermon and a half, vicar,' she said with cold civility.

'Lady Wadsworth, isn't it?' said Mr Sparshott, giving a small smile and extending a thin hand which she shook half-heartedly.

'It is,' replied the lady of the manor.

'I am pleased you found my sermon thought-provoking,' he said.

'Depressing would be a better description,' she replied bluntly. 'On such a bright summer Sunday morning when one feels glad to be alive, when God's in His heaven and all seems right in the world, perhaps something a little more uplifting might have been more appropriate, particularly for your first sermon.'

'Sometimes, Lady Wadsworth, one has to say things which are unpalatable—' began the new vicar.

'Well I sincerely hope that all your sermons are not of the same ilk,' said Lady Wadsworth. 'I do not attend church to be depressed. I wish you a good morning.'

As she departed, leaving the new vicar rather unsettled, the archdeacon approached.

'A most spirited sermon,' he told the new vicar tactfully.

'But clearly not appreciated by some,' replied Mr Sparshott glancing in the direction of Lady Wadsworth, who was sweeping majestically down the path.

The archdeacon was a decent person, and although he might have agreed with the sentiments of Lady Wadsworth, he was too kindly a man to criticise the new vicar's first homily.

'*Nondum considerasti, quanti ponderis sit peccatum,*' he said.

'I'm sorry, Archdeacon,' said the new vicar. 'I am not acquainted with Latin. I never had the advantage, like some, of a classical education at Oxford.'

'Thou hast not considered what weight sin hath,' the archdeacon told him.

'I thought I had expounded the nature of sin rather fully,' replied the reverend sharply, stung by the comment.

'No, no you misunderstand me. I was translating the words of St Anselm of Canterbury which I felt to be very applicable to what you said this morning – that we should consider sin most carefully. I recall at theological college reading a treatise on the very topic about the fundamental truths of the Christian religion by a German professor who expressed very similar views to your own.'

'Ah, I see,' said the new vicar, colouring a little.

'You might have come across it?'

'Perhaps,' admitted Mr Sparshott. He had lifted the sermon from the very tract to which the archdeacon had referred.

'So tell me,' said the archdeacon, 'how are you getting along with Ashley?'

'To be frank,' replied the new vicar, 'I am bound to say that Dr Underwood and myself do not see eye-to-eye on a number of matters.'

'Oh dear. I am sorry to hear that,' sighed the archdeacon.

'I prefer the King James Bible and she the Good News, I like the traditional hymns, she favours the modern ones, she is keen on various activities – lectures and demonstrations, concerts and recitals – talking place in the church but I feel they are best undertaken elsewhere. The church, in my view, is a place of prayer, worship and contemplation and not an entertainment centre. Dr Underwood is undoubtedly a clever and a most enthusiastic and committed young woman, but I fear we disagree on these and a number of other fundamental issues.'

'I see . . .' said the archdeacon sadly and thinking how he might resolve this tricky situation.

'We must be going, Charles,' interrupted the archdeacon's wife, slipping a hand though her husband's arm. She could not resist a further comment. 'We are dining with the bishop this lunchtime.'

'I was just sharing my view of Mr Sparshott's sermon,' explained her husband, 'and enquiring how—'

'You can discuss such weighty theological matters with Mr Sparshott another time,' said his wife brusquely. 'Now, come along, we don't want to be late for the bishop.'

Mrs Sloughthwaite, proprietor of the Barton-in-the-Dale village store and post office, rested her great bay window of a bust on the counter. She was a round, red-faced woman with a large fleshy nose, pouchy cheeks and bright, inquisitive eyes. There were two customers in the shop that Monday morning: Mrs Pocock, a tall, thin woman with a pale, melancholy beaked face and hard, dark eyes, and Mrs O'Connor.

'Well I've never heard the like,' remarked the shopkeeper. 'I've heard some sermonising in my time up at St Christopher's, but that sermon I had to sit through yesterday takes the brisket.'

'Dreadful,' agreed Mrs Pocock, puffing out her lower lip. 'I mean, Reverend Atticus wasn't one for giving sermons. He could put a glass eye to sleep. But you always left the church in a good mood, despite not understanding a word he said.

This new vicar put the fear of God into everyone, standing up there all high and mighty and prodding the air with a bony finger and telling us we were all wicked. He wants to look to himself before he starts having a go at other people. Let the person who never sins chuck the first brick at the greenhouse, that's what I always say.'

'That was Jesus who said that,' remarked Mrs O'Connor nodding thoughtfully, 'and there was no mention of a greenhouse as I recall.'

'I know full well it was what Jesus said,' retorted the other customer. 'I'm just repeating Him that's all.'

'"He who is without sin amongst you, let him be the first to cast a stone" – that's what Jesus actually said,' corrected Mrs O'Connor, 'and there was no mention of a greenhouse. He was talking about a prostitute who people were going to stone to death.'

'I don't know how this conversation got on to prostitutes,' remarked Mrs Sloughthwaite.

'I was just putting Mrs Pocock right,' said Mrs O'Connor.

'Don't you start lecturing me, Bridget O'Connor!' snapped Mrs Pocock. 'I've had enough of that from the new vicar. Anyway, you weren't there so you're not in a position to comment.'

'I thought he was never going to stop,' said the shopkeeper, 'going on and on about sin. As far as some of them in the congregation, like Fred Massey for example, were concerned, the sin is not so much in the sinning but in the sin being found out.'

'As my grandmother Mullarkey was wont to say, "those who talk the most often don't have anything to say",' observed Mrs O'Connor.

'He went on for a good forty minutes and—'

'Every ass loves to hear itself bray,' said Mrs O'Connor. 'Full vessels make the most sound.'

'Do you mind, Bridget?' said the shopkeeper. 'You weren't even there.' She elevated her bosom from where it had been resting on the counter, stretched and rubbed her back. 'I mean, you go to church to be uplifted. It's beyond my apprehension that someone like that should be appointed. Coming out of church yesterday morning I felt like chucking myself down a pothole at Grassington. Everyone in the church had faces like smacked bottoms.'

'When that young curate preached,' said Mrs Pocock, 'she made you feel better. Lovely short, cheerful sermons they were. I don't know why they didn't make the Reverend Underwood the vicar. I bet you anything she doesn't get on with him.'

'You're right there,' agreed Mrs Sloughthwaite with a comical lift of an eyebrow. 'I reckon they'll be at locker heads most of the time.'

'I'll tell you this,' continued Mrs Pocock, 'it'll be a while before I set my foot in that church again if Reverend Sparshott is up there pontificating from the pulpit.'

'I was telling Mrs Stirling,' said Mrs O'Connor, 'that when Father Daly went round to the rectory to introduce himself, he got a very cold reception by all accounts. Mr Sparshott never even offered him a cup of tea. Father Daly can't have been there more than five minutes. I don't think he had time to put his holy backside on a chair.'

'Well, this new vicar has put the scuppers on those economical meetings Reverend Underwood set up with Father Daly,' said the shopkeeper, 'and that's for certain.'

'Ecumenical,' corrected Mrs Pocock. 'They were ecumenical meetings.'

'That's what I just said,' replied the shopkeeper.

Mrs Sloughthwaite was a woman of a certain reputation and famous for her bluntness, thick skin, memorable malapropisms and amazingly inventive *non sequiturs*. She was also very good-hearted, down-to-earth and had a dry wit.

'I can't see that he'll settle here in the village,' said Mrs Pocock shaking her head. 'The man has a hard, mean face.'

'My grandmother used to say that she often found good-looking people the worst and those of unfortunate appearance the best,' said Mrs O'Connor. 'Maybe deep down this new vicar is pleasant enough.'

'And maybe he isn't,' retorted Mrs Pocock.

Mrs Sloughthwaite resumed her position resting her bosom onto the counter. 'I hear he's sending his children to St Paul's.'

'Who is?' asked Mrs Pocock.

'The new vicar.'

'He's not sending them to the village school?' the customer exclaimed.

'That's what I've heard.'

'Well that won't go down well.'

'No, I should imagine that Mrs Stirling is not best pleased about that.' Mrs Sloughthwaite turned her face in Mrs O'Connor's direction anticipating a comment but the housekeeper remained unexpectedly silent.

'Has she said anything to you, Bridget?' asked Mrs Sloughthwaite probing for some information which she could circulate around the village.

The Stirling's housekeeper had learnt of old to be very circumspect when talking to Mrs Sloughthwaite, knowing that whatever she divulged in the village store would be around Barton-in-the-Dale like wild-fire. She had also taken to heart another of her grandmother's aphorisms that, 'Those who gossip with you are likely to gossip about you.'

'Oh, sure I wouldn't know about that,' she replied casually.

The shopkeeper was not one to give up so easily. She made it her business to know about everything and everybody and no customer left her premises without being subjected to a thorough interrogation.

'So she's not mentioned it to you then?' she asked.

'No, she hasn't.'

'I would have thought she'd have said something.'

'Well, she hasn't.'

'I'm sure she must have made some illusion to it,' persisted Mrs Sloughthwaite.

'She's not said a thing.'

'Do you know, Bridget,' said the shopkeeper, 'you're as close as an oyster. It's like getting blood out of a stone.'

'Seems very odd to me that there's a perfectly good school in the village and the new vicar wants to send his children to another one,' observed Mrs Pocock.

'So it does,' agreed Mrs O'Connor, patting her hair.

'And Mrs Stirling's said nothing?' persevered the shop-keeper.

'Nothing,' repeated Mrs O'Connor. She had, of course, heard Mrs Stirling being very forthcoming in her views about Mr Sparshott's decision about his children's education when discussing it with her husband but that was not for Mrs Sloughthwaite to know. When in the company of the prying shopkeeper, Mrs O'Connor had managed over the years to perfect an air of abstraction.

' 'Course, it might have been the wife who wanted the children educated elsewhere,' said Mrs Sloughthwaite, abandoning further attempts to glean information from the housekeeper. 'It's usually left to the woman to make all the decisions. It certainly was in my house. I had to do everything. My Stan, God rest his soul, rarely bestirred himself.'

'Same with my husband,' said Mrs Pocock. 'Leaves everything to me. They're all the same.'

'My old Grandmother Mullarkey always used to say that "the absence of a woman in the house brings out the very worst in men".'

'Well the new vicar's wife doesn't seem to have brought out

the best in him and that's for sure,' pronounced Mrs Sloughthwaite.

'Have you met her yet?' asked Mrs Pocock.

'No I haven't,' said the shopkeeper, 'but I reckon she'll be as hard-faced and frosty as he is.'

At that very moment the doorbell tinkled and the topic of their conversation made her entrance in a rather imperious manner. Despite the mildness of the weather, Mrs Sparshott was dressed in a most extraordinary fashion: a heavy black coat topped off with a woolly hat and fur-lined gloves. A large black handbag was draped over an arm and she carried a large black umbrella which she held in front of her like a weapon.

'Good morning,' she said stiffly, removing her gloves and digging into her handbag for her purse.

'Morning,' chorused the three women.

'The post office is open, I take it?' said the new vicar's wife, looking blankly in front of her.

'It is indeed,' replied Mrs Sloughthwaite, lifting her vast bosom secured underneath her unyielding grey nylon overall and waddling from the counter to behind the post office grill.

'I should like four second-class stamps please,' Mrs Sparshott said, placing a five-pound note before her.

'Anythink else?'

'Thank you, no. Just the stamps.'

'Anythink from the shop?'

Mrs Sparshott shook her head. 'No thank you.'

'You're the new vicar's wife, aren't you?' said the shop-keeper, passing though the stamps and the change before returning to her favoured position behind the shop counter.

'That's right,' she replied, putting the stamps in her handbag.

She was certainly not one for smiling, thought the shopkeeper, examining the stern countenance before her.

'I'm Mrs Sloughthwaite, proprietor, family grocer, purveyor

of fine foods and post mistress,' she was told. 'I do hope you will patronise my store.'

Mrs Sparshott nodded in acknowledgement and allowed herself a small smile.

'And how are you settling in?' asked the shopkeeper in a jaunty tone of voice.

Mrs Sparshott gave a rather dramatic sigh and then responded with a half-smile. She closed her eyes for a moment as if in pain.

'When the archaic heating system has been replaced in the rectory and the place decorated and all the old and scuffed furniture changed, I will feel a whole lot more settled. I mean it's not yet September and already the place is as damp and chilly as a tomb. How Archdeacon Atticus and his wife survived in those conditions, I will never know. My children are particularly sensitive to the cold.' She put on her gloves.

Over many years Mrs Sloughthwaite had managed to acquire the most intimate information about everyone and everything in the village. She had become adept at gleaning tittle-tattle from those who patronised her shop and drew them out with a little tactful questioning. The information thus disclosed was then circulated throughout the village. She knew everything that there was to know in Barton-in-the-Dale. She was not going to let the new vicar's wife off the hook so easily.

'You have four children, I believe,' said the shopkeeper.

'Yes I have.'

'Quite a handful.'

'They are well-behaved children,' replied Mrs Sparshott.

'They'll be very happy at the village school,' said Mrs Sloughthwaite, knowing full well that they would not be going there.

'They will not be attending the village school,' the new vicar's wife told her. 'We have made other arrangements.'

'Really?' said the shopkeeper.

'Rufus and Reuben are away at boarding school,' she was told. 'Ruth and Rebekah are to attend St Paul's Preparatory School in Ruston when term starts.'

'It's a very good school.'

'St Paul's?'

'No, the village school,' said Mrs Sloughthwaite. 'It has an excellent reputation.'

'I have no doubt,' said the new vicar's wife dismissively, 'but my husband and I are of the considered opinion that the small independent school tends to have better discipline, smaller classes and more of a work ethic than a state primary school.'

'I don't know about that,' said Mrs Pocock suddenly.

'I beg your pardon?' said Mrs Sparshott, swivelling around to face the speaker.

'I was a governor at the village school until recently and it's got an outstanding report from the school inspectors.'

'Be that as it may,' replied Mrs Sparshott, 'our children, we feel, will be better catered for at St Paul's.'

Mrs Sloughthwaite was irked by Mrs Pocock's intervention for there was a great deal more information she wanted to extract from the new vicar's wife. 'Of course, having Dr Underwood as the curate must be a blessing.'

'Yes it is. Dr Underwood is a most dedicated priest,' said Mrs Sparshott, who was certainly not going to discuss her husband's colleague with this nosy woman whom she had just met.

'Yes, we are very fortunate to have her at the church,' said the shopkeeper exchanging glances with Mrs Pocock.

'Indeed,' agreed Mrs Sparshott, wearied by the interrogation. She made for the door. 'I must be away,' she said. 'I will bid you all a good morning.'

'Well, what do you make of that?' said Mrs Pocock when the door closed.

'I'm lost for words,' said the shopkeeper.

'That'll be the day,' chuckled Mrs O'Connor.

Mrs Sparshott strode off down the high street with a determined step. She did not intend to miss the meeting her
husband was to have with his curate; she would be there to
make sure he made it perfectly clear who was in charge in the
parish. *Sometimes Algernon just needs a prod in the right direction,* she thought, as she passed the proud monument built in
honour of the second Viscount Wadsworth, a long-dead local
squire. The Reverend Dr Underwood took too much on
herself, bringing in the new order of service and all the modern
hymns, organising all these activities and, furthermore, spending far too much time as a hospital chaplain. Her husband
would have to leave this young woman in no doubt that he
was the vicar and she was answerable to him.

As she walked up the path to the rectory, Mrs Sparshott
caught sight of a stooping figure by one of the graves. He was a
small boy with large low-set ears and a mop of dusty-blonde hair.

'What exactly are you doing?' she asked sharply, brandish-
ing the umbrella.

''Ello, miss,' replied the boy with a disarming smile.

'I asked you what you are doing in the churchyard, young
man?'

'I comes 'ere quite regular, miss,' he told her, continuing to
smile.

'Why?'

'To look after mi granddad's grave,' the boy told her.

'Oh, I see,' said Mrs Sparshott rather taken aback. Her voice
softened. 'I thought you might be up to no good. We had quite
a deal of vandalism at our last church; teenagers pushing over
the tombstones and scrawling on the graves.'

'I'm plantin' a few flowers,' said the boy. 'I've put some
Christmas roses in. They was one of mi granddad's favourite

flowers. They bloom early an' they like t'shade. Missis Atticus, who lived 'ere before you, she telled me their real name was hellebores and she telled me this story that when this little lass went to see Babby Jesus in t'stable all them years ago she saw that t'shepherds and t'kings had tekken 'im presents. She 'ad nowt to give 'im an' began to cry. T'tears fell on t'snow an' weer they fell these pure white flowers bloomed. Them were t'hellebores. It's a champion story, in't it?'

Mrs Sparshott stared at the boy for a moment. *What an unusual child*, she thought, *so polite and interesting. If only someone could do something about his coarse accent.* 'And what are you planting now?' she asked.

'Forget-Me-Nots.'

'Now the correct name for those is *myosotis palustris*,' the vicar's wife told him. 'They happen to be my favourite flowers.'

'Crikey, that's a gobful,' chuckled the boy. 'Is there a story about them an' all?'

'I fear not,' said Mrs Sparshott.

'You're t'new vicar's wife, aren't you?' said the boy, still smiling.

'Yes I am,' replied Mrs Sparshott. 'And you are?'

'Danny, Danny Stainthorpe, miss.'

'Well, Danny Stainthorpe, I wish more people in the village would keep the graves of their relatives as tidy as you do your grandfather's.' She looked around her. 'The churchyard is quite a disgrace.'

'Aye, it's not lookin' too good, is it?' Danny sucked in his lip and shook his head. 'I try an' do a bit o' tidyin' up now an' again but it needs a fair bit o' felltlin' at this time o' year afore winter sets in. Lots of diggin' ovver an' trimmin' 'edges, weedin', prunin' an' grass cuttin' an' probably more besides.'

'I am told there is a Mr Massey in the village who is supposed to keep the churchyard tidy,' said Mrs Sparshott.

Danny grinned and shook his head again. 'Well 'e's supposed to, but as my granddad'd say if 'e was 'ere, Mester Massey in't one to frame his'sen.' Danny pointed to a mound of shattered marble in the centre of the churchyard. 'Missis Atticus asked 'im umpteen times to shift that theer dead branch from yonder oak tree when it demolished t'tomb an' telled' im to get rid of all t'rubble an' all but 'e 'asn't bothered.' The boy put his hands on his hips and smiled. 'Mi granddad used to say old Fred Massey is about as much use as an ashtray on a motorbike.'

'I see,' said Mrs Sparshott pressing her thin lips together. 'Well I shall have to speak to this Mr Massey.'

Then, seeing Ashley Underwood heading up the path, Mrs Sparshott scurried off to the rectory like a startled hen.

'Do come in, Dr Underwood.'

Reverend Algernon Sparshott raised himself slowly from his old leather armchair when Ashley entered the sitting room. The new vicar's wife had ensconced herself on the sofa by the window and had taken up her knitting so as not to appear a party to the discussion which was to ensue. Stern-faced and straight-backed, she reminded Ashley of the implacable Madame Defarge in the Dickens novel, *A Tale of Two Cities*, who clicked away by the guillotine as the heads of the aristo-crats rolled into the basket beneath. Mrs Sparshott nodded at the sight of the curate and gave a humourless smile.

'I wanted to have a word with you,' said the new vicar, 'about one or two matters which have been pressing upon my mind of late. I feel that from the outset I should make my position clear so there are no misunderstandings. Do please take a seat,' he said, gesturing to a chair.

Ashley sat uncomfortably on one of the high-backed chairs while the new vicar sat in his armchair opposite her and rested his long hands on his lap.

'To be perfectly frank, Dr Underwood—'

'I welcome this opportunity,' interjected Ashley brightly, 'for I too have a number of matters which have been pressing upon my mind.'

Mrs Sparshott gave a small cough.

'Really?' replied the new vicar, sounding surprised.

Ashley glanced in the direction of the new vicar's wife who began clacking away with her needles. 'Do I take it that our conversation this morning, Mr Sparshott, concerns church matters?'

'Indeed,' replied the new vicar.

'Then I think it will hold little interest for your wife,' she said.

'My husband discusses all matters with me, Dr Underwood,' said Mrs Sparshott. The clacking of the needles ceased and she stared boldly at the curate. 'Algernon shares his views and his concerns with me on all things.'

'I see,' said Ashley. She then addressed herself to the woman. 'Well then you will no doubt be aware that your husband and I do not share the same standpoints on a number of issues.'

'I am fully aware of that,' replied Mrs Sparshott.

'I was about to say—' began the new vicar.

'I favour a more modern-day approach in the services at St Christopher's,' continued Ashley, still addressing Mrs Sparshott. 'I like the more contemporary hymns and the bible with more accessible language, whereas your husband prefers the traditional approach. And, of course, he is not in favour of the various fund-raising activities I have organised.'

'That is what I was about to say,' said the new vicar rather feebly.

'And I believe you have expressed such views to the archdeacon,' said Ashley, turning her attention to the vicar.

'I did mention something,' said the new vicar looking somewhat embarrassed. *It was unfortunate*, thought Mr Sparshott, *that the curate had decided to sit on a chair that was rather higher than his and thus she looked down upon him.* He felt at a disadvantage in this exchange.

'The archdeacon did have a word with me,' said Ashley, 'and communicated to me your concerns.'

'Did he?' said the new vicar, rising to his feet and taking a position near the fireplace. He rested a hand on the mantelpiece.

'Dr Underwood,' said Mrs Sparshott sententiously, 'I think you will allow that my husband, being the vicar, is the one to decide on the forms of service and indeed on all matters relating to the church and that you, as the curate, must act under his direction. He does, of course, not wish to be difficult but—'

'If I might say something,' said Mr Sparshott glancing severely at his wife to shut her up.

His wife resumed her knitting with a vengeance.

'Yes, of course,' said Ashley.

'It is true that we do not seem to see eye to eye on these and other sundry issues which is most unfortunate but I do not see the problem, if I might call it that, as something insurmountable. I want to assure you that I do not wish to be obstructive in any way and I do appreciate all the sterling work you have been undertaking in the parish but, with regard to the various events you have organised, to be frank, Dr Underwood, I do feel—'

'Please do not worry about that, Mr Sparshott,' said Ashley pleasantly. 'There will be no more events at St Christopher's to which you take exception. I have made other arrangements.'

'Other arrangements!' exclaimed Mrs Sparshott.

'As you may be aware, I am assistant chaplain at Clayton Royal Infirmary,' Ashley said, turning to face the vicar's wife. 'The chaplain with whom I work, Father Daly of St Bede's, has very kindly agreed that the various activities can take place at his church.'

'At the Roman Catholic church??!' exclaimed Mrs Sparshott.

'Yes. Father Daly was more than happy to accommodate all the events which I have planned.'

'Perhaps you might have discussed this with my husband, Dr Underwood,' said the vicar's wife stiffly.

'Well, your husband made me fully aware that he was not in favour of St Christopher's hosting the events and suggested that I find an alternative venue. I think he made that very clear to me when we first met. I recall him telling me that lectures and school concerts and flower-arranging demonstrations are best undertaken in a community centre or village hall and not in the House of God.'

'Yes. I did say that,' agreed the new vicar quickly before his wife could respond.

'And I believe you shared these views with the archdeacon,' said Ashley, turning her attention back to Mr Sparshott.

'I did mention it to him, yes.'

'So I assumed you would wish me to make other arrangements,' said Ashley.

'But at the Catholic church?' said the new vicar.

'Father Daly was more than happy to host the various events.'

'It would appear very strange to many people, myself included, that fund-raising for St Christopher's roof should take place at another church and in particular, a Catholic one.'

'Very strange,' echoed his wife.

'Well yes,' said Ashley, 'I fully agree. That is why the proceeds from the lectures and recitals will be donated to the Critical Care Unit at the hospital. I assume you have no objection to this?'

'I think you are taking rather too much upon yourself, Dr Underwood,' said the new vicar's wife, ceasing her clicking. 'I think in the future you would be well advised to consult my husband before taking such precipitous actions.'

'Mrs Sparshott, I shall not be consulting your husband on any matters in the future,' replied Ashley, irritated by the woman's frequent interventions.

'I beg your pardon?' said the new vicar.

'As I have said, I welcome this opportunity to speak to you, Mr Sparshott,' replied Ashley, 'because I wish to inform you that I shall be leaving.'

'Leaving?' he repeated, taken aback.

'Yes. Having discussed my situation with Archdeacon Atticus, and he being aware of the fact that you and I disagree on so many fundamental matters and would find it difficult working together, I feel the best course of action is that I should resign as curate here.'

'This is very hasty, Dr Underwood,' said the new vicar. 'Perhaps I might have appeared rather censorious. I'm sorry if I have given that impression. I am sure that we can come to some compromise should we sit down together and discuss matters. I really am not an unreasonable man and—'

'I have given it some thought and having had a heart to heart with the archdeacon, I feel this is the best course of action,' Ashley told him.

'I see. So you have quite made up your mind?'

'I have.'

'Obviously you must stay until you find another position,' said the new vicar. One might have assumed that he would be feeling inwardly very pleased that he would no longer have this troublesome priest to deal with but, in fact, he was dismayed. At heart, Mr Sparshott, despite the impression which he might give, was not a man without feeling.

'I have been asked to accept the preferment as the bishop's chaplain at Cathedral House in Clayton,' Ashley told him.

Both the new vicar and his wife were bereft of words. They looked stunned and bewildered.

'So, if there is nothing else,' said Ashley, getting to her feet, 'I do have to be at the hospital this morning.'

3

The chairman of the newly constituted governing body of Barton-with-Urebank Primary School, Major C J Neville-Gravitas, late of the Royal Engineers, flicked abstractedly through the application forms and references before him.

'I cannot say that I am overly impressed with the calibre of these two candidates,' he huffed. He leant back in his chair and stroked his thin moustache. 'Miss Kennedy appears to me to be well past her sell-by-date and this Mr Hornchurch sounds a rum sort of character, if you follow my drift, something of a loose cannon from what it says here in his reference.'

The chairman of the governing body, Elisabeth, Lady Wadsworth, a foundation governor and Mr Nettles the education officer were in the staff room at the newly merged school, meeting as the staffing sub-committee for the informal interviews of the two redeployed teachers.

Lady Wadsworth was an extraordinary-looking woman – large, rather ungainly, with a ruddy complexion, hair the colour of brown boot polish, heavy-lidded eyes and a nose sharp and slightly hooked at the end. Mr Nettles, by contrast, was a tubby man with thick blonde hair sticking up from his head like tufts of dry grass and small steel-rimmed spectacles perched on the end of his nose. His chinless face was pasty and drawn.

'I tend to agree with the major,' said Mr Nettles, nodding in a voice with an adenoidal ring to it. 'This candidate, Mr

Hornchurch, sounds, how can I put it, a bit quirky and, in my opinion, far too over-qualified for this position.'

'Quirky?' repeated Lady Wadsworth. 'And what exactly do you mean by quirky?'

'Well, unusual, odd, unpredictable. From what it says in his reference, it has to be admitted he appears rather eccentric. He sounds to me to be a bit of a maverick.'

'In my experience, Mr Kettle,' retorted Lady Wadsworth, 'anyone who makes a difference in life tends to be a bit out of the ordinary. The two best teachers I had at the girls' boarding school which I attended were rather eccentric.'

'Actually, Lady Wadsworth,' said the education officer, 'my name is Nettles.'

'Why, Mademoiselle Dubarry was quite mad,' continued Lady Wadsworth, ignoring him, 'but she taught us how to speak French extremely well and Miss Culpepper, who frequently wore her nightdress under her gown and blew her nose using toilet tissue taken from a roll on her desk, was most forgetful but she was a brilliant teacher of mathematics.'

'Nevertheless—' Mr Nettles began.

Lady Wadsworth, something of an eccentric herself, was not at all used to being interrupted and carried on regardless.

'Throughout history there have been men and woman who have been labelled eccentric during their lifetimes who have gone on to be seen by later generations as people of great originality and vision, people such as Isaac Newton, Emmeline Pankhurst, Isambard Kingdom Brunel, Amelia Earhart, Charles Darwin, Marie Curie, Admiral Horatio Nelson and indeed my great grandfather, the first Viscount Wadsworth. It was he—'

'Nevertheless,' the education officer persisted, straining his voice to be heard, 'I think we have to be very careful in appointing a teacher who, as the major quite rightly observes, may be something of a loose cannon.'

'Mr Nettle!' snapped Lady Wadsworth, 'I am getting increasingly tired of your vexatious interruptions. Please allow me to finish a sentence. As I was saying, it was my great grandfather, the first Viscount Wadsworth, who was considered by many to be too outspoken, non-conformist and eccentric during his lifetime but who became a monumental figure in the locality.'

'Quite,' said the major when he was assured that she had finished. 'Shall we move on?'

Mr Nettles pulled a face but sat in silent indignation.

Elisabeth had little time for the education officer. He was a man with an inflated idea of his own capacities and blessed with the ability to appear to be very busy whilst actually avoiding much of the work for which he was responsible. He also liked the sound of his own voice. In her dealings with him he had proved to be evasive and ineffectual. Each time she had telephoned his office at County Hall for some advice or clarification, she had been informed by his snappish clerical assistant that 'he is tied up'. Mrs Scrimshaw had once remarked that it would be a good idea if the man was tied up permanently. Previously, Mr Nettles had been put in charge of organising the school transport and having been unsuccessful in this role he had been moved on to school meals in which capacity he had proved equally heavy-handed and inept. Now he had been given the responsibility of supporting the schools which had been amalgamated to ensure that things ran smoothly, 'to be on call', as he had explained to Elisabeth, 'for any problems which might arise'. *Small chance of that*, thought Elisabeth.

The major broke into her ponderings. 'Mrs Stirling?'

'I'm sorry?' she said.

'We were just commenting on the fact that this Mr Hornchurch seems a tad unconventional.'

'I think we should reserve any judgements until we have

had a chance to see him,' she said. Elisabeth had already had the opportunity of meeting the two teachers and found them both very personable, enthusiastic and good-humoured. She had taken to them straight away.

'Yes, yes of course,' said the major, 'let's wait until we have seen them but I have to admit this chap is a bit out of the ordinary and I'm not so sure we should have redeployed teachers foisted upon us. I can't see them being of the calibre of teachers in permanent positions. I mean, if they are up to scratch I think they should be interviewed in the normal way in competition with other candidates.'

'They are not being foisted upon us, Major,' said Elisabeth, 'and their being redeployed is hardly a fault of their own.'

'After all it was the Education Committee which decided to close the schools in which they worked,' added Lady Wadsworth.

'The chairman does have a point,' observed Mr Nettles pompously and leaning back in his chair. 'In my experience redeployed teachers do tend to be a rather mixed lot and not as good as other teachers.'

Elisabeth looked at Mr Nettles. 'But were you not redeployed yourself?' she asked pointedly.

'I beg your pardon,' he replied, puffing out his lower lip.

'You were redeployed to school transport and then redeployed to school meals and now you have been despatched to another role.'

'I was not redeployed or despatched, Mrs Stirling,' he responded indignantly. 'I was gaining experience in the different branches of the Education Department. In actual fact—'

'Look,' interrupted Major Neville-Gravitas, 'can we make a start? We'll be here all day at this rate. I do have an important meeting this afternoon.' He was to play a round of golf. 'Let's have Miss Kennedy in first, shall we?'

It had not escaped Major Neville-Gravitas's notice as he scanned her reference that Miss Kennedy was sixty-two years of age. He rather expected a tired-looking teacher with grey hair and a thin, bony face to come through the door. He was therefore startled when a tall, elegant woman with tinted auburn hair and dressed in a pale-green woollen suit entered the room. She was wearing particularly high-heeled shoes.

'Good morning,' she said in a deep, resonant voice. She approached a chair, her high heels making a clicking sound on the wooden floor. There was a waft of perfume. 'May I sit?' Without waiting for an answer, she plonked herself down, crossed her long legs and smiled widely at the major.

'G . . . good morning,' said the major, stroking his moustache. 'I am the Chairman of Governors, Major Neville-Gravitas. I believe you have met Mrs Stirling our head teacher and this is Lady Wadsworth, a foundation governor and Mr Nettles, an education officer.'

'I have not met Mr Nettles,' the woman replied, staring levelly at him, 'but I have tried to contact him on a number of occasions when he was in charge of school meals.' She continued to stare at him for a moment as if waiting for a reply. She smiled. 'It appeared you always seemed to be tied up.'

'I am a busy man, Miss Kennedy,' he retorted, stung by the remark and taking an immediate dislike to this candidate.

'As are we all, Mr Nettles,' she replied pleasantly.

Elisabeth suppressed a smile. She really did like this strong-minded and confident woman.

'I see that you've been in the job quite a while,' observed the major, staring at the papers on his lap.

'I have,' she replied without elaboration.

'Forty or more years,' remarked the major, attempting a jocular tone. 'Quite a stretch.'

'You make it sound like a prison sentence,' she replied,

smiling. Elisabeth thought she could detect a mischievous gleam in her eye. She was enjoying this exchange and thought for the moment she would say nothing.

'No, no, I'm sure it has not,' said the major defensively. 'Been a bit of a stint I mean, if you follow my drift.'

'I believe you were offered early retirement,' observed Mr Nettles.

'I was,' she replied.

'But you decided not to take it.'

'No, I didn't.'

'Most teachers, I imagine,' said Mr Nettles, leaning back in his chair, 'given the opportunity, would have jumped at the chance.'

'I am not most teachers,' she replied. 'I enjoy teaching and think I am good at it. Why should I retire?'

'Good for you,' muttered Lady Wadsworth who had taken a liking to this candidate. 'I have always been of the opinion that one is as young as one feels. I certainly don't feel my age. My great grandfather, the first Viscount Wadsworth, was active in business well into his eighties.'

'Quite,' Miss Kennedy agreed. Turning to Mr Nettles, she asked, 'Do you think that someone my age is not up to the job?' A smile flickered across her face.

'No,' said Mr Nettles, 'I was merely making an observation, that's all and . . .' He let the sentence drift away.

Major Neville-Gravitas, sensing the strained atmosphere, interjected and, referring to his papers, observed, 'I see you were trained at Bishop Grotesque College in Lincoln.'

'No I wasn't,' she told him.

'No?'

'I was trained at Bishop Grosstesste College in Lincoln.'

The major smiled uncomfortably. 'I can't say I have ever heard of bishop . . . this particular man.'

'He was a great teacher, scholar, reformer, scientist and

theologian,' Miss Kennedy informed him. 'Born in 1170, he became the Bishop of Lincoln.'

'Really,' replied the major. 'How very interesting.' He didn't sound the least interested.

'He wrote many philosophical works, commentaries, prayers, religious poems and pastoral and scientific treatises,' Miss Kennedy told him. 'He was a very unusual man, an original thinker and way ahead of his time. Some might say rather eccentric.'

Elisabeth tried to suppress another smile. Lady Wadsworth snorted.

'Shall I go on?' asked the candidate.

'No, that is quite sufficient,' said the Chairman of Governors.

'The college is regarded as one of the foremost educational institutions in the country,' she added.

'And how do you feel about starting at a new school at your time of life?' asked Mr Nettles.

Miss Kennedy smiled. 'My time of life,' she repeated quietly looking up as if considering what response to make. 'You make it sound as if I should be putting my feet up and taking up crocheting. In answer to your question I feel, even at my time of life, I should welcome the challenge and I feel I am up to it.'

'Perhaps at this juncture,' said the major, feeling increasingly uncomfortable and keen to be away to the Links, 'I might ask Mrs Stirling to ask a few questions.'

'Yes, thank you,' said Elisabeth. 'I won't ask you about your experience of working with infant children, Miss Kennedy. You are obviously very well qualified in that respect. Perhaps you might share with us your thoughts about early childhood education.'

'Of course,' the candidate replied. 'I have always found that young children are full of vigour and that they delight in activity. That is why their school environment needs to be bright, colourful and experiential – good quality displays, sand, water, toys, picture books, a table of interesting artefacts, a home corner where they can dress up. It is important for teachers to design enjoyable, varied and challenging activities for them and help children find different ways of expressing their views and relating to their experiences. Young children show great interest in their surroundings and are very curious – "How? What? Why? Where?" are probably more frequent at this phase of school life than at any other. Shall I go on?'

'Please do,' Elisabeth told her.

'I believe that we should recognise children's contributions and celebrate their achievements. I don't think all infant teachers allow children to have some control over their own learning, giving them time to ask and explore and offer their opinions.'

She answered further questions from Elisabeth fully and confidently and it was clear that she was a highly committed and enthusiastic teacher with the experience, expertise and the force of character to be a first-rate deputy head teacher. Elisabeth decided that Miss Kennedy was ideal for the vacant post. Then Mr Nettles jumped on his hobby horse.

'What about reading?' he asked.

'What about it?' asked the candidate curtly.

'I imagine that you think it is important to teach children to read.'

'That goes without question,' replied Miss Kennedy.

'Could you elaborate?'

'Getting children to read is clearly extremely important,' she told him. 'After all, reading is the fundamental tool of education, the very protein of growth in learning. However, there is no conclusive evidence that teaching reading skills early, before about six, is profitable. International studies suggest that a later school starting age, six or seven, might be beneficial, if school is preceded by high-quality pre-school provision. Research has revealed that children with good reading skills generally have access to books at home and have parents who encourage their children to read but do not pressurise them or use systematic formal approaches that are commonly used in schools. Therefore I do not pressurise children. I make reading a pleasure and not a business.'

'And what about writing?'

'Forcing handwriting skills upon children before they have the basic coordinative powers may be harmful,' she said. 'Few children will have established the skills involved in writing before the age of six or seven, no matter how good their conversational language or how exposed they are to books and other forms of writing. As with reading, I do not pressurise children into putting pencil to paper.'

When the candidate had left, the chairman turned to the Elisabeth. 'I felt as if I were a pupil in her class being lectured at. She was quite fearsome.'

'And I can't say I liked her manner,' said Mr Nettles peevishly. 'Over the top with her answers, I thought, and quite self-important and over-confident of her own abilities.'

'I disagree entirely,' said Lady Wadsworth, 'I thought she was first rate.'

'So what did you make of her then, Mrs Stirling?' asked the major.

'I thought she was very impressive and should be very happy to have her join the staff.'

Major Neville-Gravitas was very particular about his appearance. He looked every inch the retired army officer in his blue blazer with crested gold buttons, pressed cavalry twill trousers, crisp white shirt and striped regimental tie. He judged others by the way they dressed and believed that teachers should look like teachers, which meant like the masters who had taught him at the second-rate public school which he had attended. The staff at his alma mater, all male, wore almost identical outfits: tweed jackets (often with leather elbow patches) beneath black academic gowns, baggy grey flannel trousers shiny at the bottoms, white shirts, sober ties, plain socks and black shoes. He was therefore taken aback when the second applicant entered the staffroom.

Mr Hornchurch was a tall, pale-faced man in his thirties, with an explosion of wild, woolly hair and a permanently surprised expression. He was attired in a bright-pink shirt, floral tie, shapeless grey cotton trousers and white trainers. In his ear he wore a small silver stud.

'Take a seat,' said the major. Elisabeth could see from his expression that he was less than impressed with the outfit this candidate was wearing. She gave a small smile.

'It occurs to me,' continued the chairman, flicking through the application form on his knee and picking up on what Mr Nettles had said earlier, 'that you are rather over-qualified to be a teacher in a primary school.'

Mr Hornchurch blinked and scratched his woolly outcrop of hair.

'Really?' He sounded genuinely surprised.

'I should think there are few young men with first-class honours from the University of Oxford who have gone into teaching.'

'Really?' said the candidate again.

'So why did you?'

'Go into teaching?'

'Yes.'

'It's the best job in the world,' replied the candidate, leaning forward. 'It's great to be with young people all day and help them learn. "Those who take on the role of teacher take on the most important role in society." Not my words – Bishop Wilberforce.'

'Not another bishop,' murmured the major under his breath.

Mr Hornchurch leant back and crossed his long legs. 'Teachers not only reveal the world to the young but they change lives. Take Socrates, Seneca, Plato, Aristotle, the prophets of the Old Testament, Jesus of Nazareth, the Buddha, Muhammad – life-changing teachers.'

'Quite,' said the major, hoping he was not in for another lecture. He looked down at his papers. 'It says here you studied something called Greats at university. I can't say I've heard of that subject.'

'It's the name given to the *Literae Humaniores* course which focuses on the Classics – Ancient Rome and Greece, the ancient languages of Latin and Greek, philosophy, history, art, architecture, philology and classical literature.'

'Hardly a course relevant for teaching or indeed for that matter any profession,' observed the major.

'Quite the reverse,' said Mr Hornchurch, straightening his shoulders and sitting up in the chair. 'Such a wide-ranging course is very relevant to any profession. Learning the Classics teaches how to analyse, problem-solve, it encourages diligence and perseverance. Prime ministers like H H Asquith and Harold Macmillan studied Greats at Oxford, Anthony Leggett who was awarded the Nobel Prize in Physics was another. And, of course, Oscar Wilde the great playwright and poet was one of many.'

'Oh yes, Oscar Wilde,' murmured the major.

'I found Latin very tedious when I was at school,' remarked Mr Nettles. 'I couldn't see the point in studying a dead language. The teacher would shout at us in Latin. One of the few phrases I recall was what he called me: *Caput mortuum*. I never did find out what it meant.'

'Dickhead,' said Mr Hornchurch.

'I beg your pardon?' snapped the education officer.

'*Caput mortuum*. It means a deadhead, a worthless person.' The candidate smiled sweetly. 'I guess dickhead is the modern equivalent.'

'Is it really,' said Mr Nettles, clearly annoyed.

'My family motto is *Audentes fortuna juvat*,' remarked Lady Wadsworth.

'Fortune favours the daring,' Mr Hornchurch translated.

'My grandfather, the second Viscount, adopted this as the family motto. He was quite a daring man in many ways.'

'But getting back to the matter in hand,' began the major. He had heard quite enough of Lady Wadsworth's antecedents.

'Yes, of course. Quite apart from anything else,' continued Mr Hornchurch, 'a knowledge of Latin helps us gain a good command of the grammar and vocabulary of our own language. Effective communication is very important in the modern world. It's always impressive to hear English well spoken, don't you think?' He paused and looked at the major.

'Oh, undoubtedly,' grunted the chairman.

'I also believe that we have so much to learn from studying the Greeks and the Romans. Take Aristotle, for example. He wrote a great deal about logic, metaphysics, physics, astronomy, meteorology, biology, psychology, ethics, politics, philosophy and literary criticism. Then there's Plato, Juvenal, Quintillian—'

'Well I think you have more than adequately explained yourself,' interrupted Major Neville-Gravitas who, having surreptitiously glanced at his wristwatch, noticed that he was now missing lunch at the golf club.

When it came to Elisabeth's time to ask questions, Mr Hornchurch gave a series of splendid answers, outlining what he had developed at Tarncliffe Primary School, the results the children in his class had achieved, the prizes they had won and the fact that the head teacher had actively encouraged his application to this particular school where she felt he would be appreciated.

'I have to admit I did not take to this candidate,' said the major when Mr Hornchurch had left the room. 'From the looks of him, I have an idea' – he coughed – 'that he . . . er . . . bats from the pavilion end, if you follow my drift.'

'I don't see the relevance of cricket in the appointment of a teacher,' observed Lady Wadsworth giving a wry smile and feigning not to comprehend the remark.

'No, dear lady,' said the major. 'I think . . . how can I put it? . . . I have an idea that he plays for the other team.'

'Lancashire!' she exclaimed mischievously.

The major sighed. 'No, no, I don't mean that at all.'

Elisabeth considered coming in at this point but decided to let the major squirm a little. She knew that Lady Wadsworth was astute enough to know what was behind the major's implied remarks.

'Perhaps you might enlighten us, Major,' said Lady Wadsworth. 'What exactly do you mean?'

'What I mean is . . . what I mean is . . . that I think we will be taking a bit of risk with this teacher,' observed the major evading having to explain himself.

'In life, Major, we don't make any progress unless we take a few measured risks,' said Lady Wadsworth. 'The first Viscount was a great risk-taker and became very successful in life. I'm sure as a former soldier you would concur with this. Think of Wellington, Nelson, Francis Drake, General John Churchill, Field Marshal Montgomery, Napoleon.'

'Yes, well they didn't wear pink shirts and trainers,' responded the major.

'I can't say I took to the man,' remarked Mr Nettles. 'Far too airy-fairy.'

'I liked him,' said Lady Wadsworth. 'What do you think, Elisabeth?'

'I would like Mr Hornchurch and Miss Kennedy to be offered the positions,' she replied.

'Very well,' agreed the major, sighing. 'It is you, after all, who will have to work with them.'

'Dickhead indeed,' muttered Mr Nettles as he left the room.

'I don't like the idea of this,' said Mr Gribbon the caretaker leaning idly against the door frame of the school office and jangling the large bunch of keys in his overalls pocket. He was a tall, gaunt man with a large nose and the glassy, protuberant eyes of a large fish. Brusque and tetchy in his manner, he seemed to spend most of his life regaling those whom he managed to corner about the countless ailments he had to endure and the prodigious amount of work he had to undertake.

'I'm not psychic, Mr Gribbon,' replied Mrs Scrimshaw, the school secretary, shuffling the papers on her desk and pursing her lips. She looked up and peered over the top of her unfashionable horn-rimmed spectacles and brushed a strand of mouse-coloured hair from her forehead. 'You don't like the idea of what?'

'Teachers and governors coming into school during the holidays,' he told her gruffly.

'They are interviewing for posts in the new school for your information,' the school secretary told him. She was used to the caretaker assaulting the ear with some wearisome tale of woe.

'I can't see why they can't do it in term time like what happens in other schools.'

'Because the teachers have to be in post at the start of the new term,' Mrs Scrimshaw told him.

'When the last head teacher was here there were no meetings in the school holidays.'

'Yes well, Mrs Stirling isn't Miss Sowerbutts, is she?'

'You can say that again,' agreed the caretaker. 'She's never out of the place. Spends most of her life here. I thought when she got married to the doctor she wouldn't be coming in so often but no chance.' The caretaker shook his head like a tetchy little dog.

The school secretary sat stiffly at her desk hoping that the caretaker would depart. She was keen to make a start on the mountain of work on her desk; the caretaker was far from keen to start the cleaning. Mrs Scrimshaw looked up at the clock on the wall and made a small clucking noise with her tongue.

'Anyway, I can't see how having interviews in the school holiday affects you,' she said.

'Oh but it does,' he replied. 'It's a lot of hard work for me having to come in and open up the school and make sure everything's ship-shape. You know what a stickler Mrs Stirling is for neatness. Then there's the cleaning up after them. They'll have been walking all over my polished floors and leaving dirty cups in the staffroom.' The caretaker stretched theatrically. 'My back's playing me up again. It's not been right since I moved them bins. I should have some assistance.' He sniffed noisily. 'Another part-time cleaner, that's what I need.'

'The less said about part-time cleaners the better,' said the secretary airily. 'We all know what happed to the last one.'

The caretaker coloured up. 'Look, there was nothing going on between me and Mrs Pugh,' he blustered.

'That's not what her husband said when he came into school that time. It's a good job you made yourself scarce otherwise you'd have more to complain about than a bad back.'

'He got the wrong end of the stick,' protested the caretaker. 'Anyway, I don't want to discuss it.'

The previous term Mr Gribbon had become rather too friendly with the part-time cleaner, so 'friendly' in fact that her husband, hearing of the caretaker's unwelcome advances to his wife, had arrived at the school to 'sort the Casanova out'.

'That Gibbon man,' he had told Elisabeth angrily, 'can't keep his hands to himself, making suggestions, brushing against her when she's wiping the surfaces and touching Bronwyn when she's buffing the floors. He's got hands like the tentacles of an octopus. She'll not be coming back to this school so long as that sex maniac is here.'

Elisabeth had tried to conceal the smile. *The phrase 'sex maniac',* she thought, *was the very last one to describe Mr Gribbon.* 'Well, unfortunately, Mr Gribbon is indisposed today,' she had lied. 'It's his bad back. It's always playing up.'

'I'll give him more than a bad back if I get hold of him,' Mr Pugh had said.

'So that motley pair what was being shown round the school was here for a job then, were they?' asked the caretaker now.

'Yes, they were.'

'Well they must be scraping the barrel that's all I can say. One's an OAP and the other some sort of sloppy Bulgarian.'

'Bohemian.'

'What?'

'You mean Bohemian,' the secretary told him.

'Whatever,' said the caretaker. 'Long hair, hippy clothes and an earring in his ear. I ask you? What's teaching coming to when they start having body piercing? It'll be rings in their noses and tattoos next.'

'He seemed a very nice man,' remarked Mrs Scrimshaw.

'I don't know how them two will take to the head teacher,' the caretaker went on, 'and I can't see them getting on with Mrs Robertshaw. I mean she could freeze soup in pans that woman and—'

'Shouldn't you be getting on with something?' interposed the secretary with some severity.

'Do you think they got the jobs?'

'I don't know why you're asking me this,' said Mrs

Scrimshaw crossly. She stifled a yawn. 'I suggest you go and ask Mrs Stirling if you're so bothered. She's still in the staff-room. Now, could you let me get on, please?'

The caretaker ambled off jangling his keys and mumbling something to himself.

'So did you appoint them?' Mrs Scrimshaw asked Elisabeth later when the candidates had departed.

'We did,' replied Elisabeth, 'and I think they will be real assets.'

'If my opinion is anything to go by,' said the school secretary, 'I think they will fit in really well. I liked both of them. They seemed very friendly and had a lot about them.'

'They did,' agreed Elisabeth.

'It will be a testing time this amalgamation but I feel very optimistic.'

'So do I.'

'Anyway, you get off home, Mrs Stirling,' said the secretary. 'You've had a hard day. Are you doing anything nice this weekend?'

'Saturday is when I see my son,' Elisabeth answered.

'Oh yes, I forgot. How is he getting on?'

'Pretty well. Progress is slow but he's happy and settled at Forest View and he has an excellent teacher. Now, don't you stay too late.'

'It is quite remarkable,' said Mr Williams, resting his elbows on the desk and steepling his fingers. He was a small, dark-complexioned, silver-haired Welshman with shining eyes. 'Over the years I have seen the progress of children with autism but your son's improvement is quite extraordinary.'

It was the following morning and Elisabeth was sitting with the head teacher at Forest View Residential Special School in his study. 'When John started here,' continued the head teacher, 'he had all the classic indicators of a severely autistic child. He tended to be fiercely independent, liked his own company and was obsessive about routine. He coped as well as he could. But he was content in his own world and not really aware of what was going on around him. Recently, however, he has shown real signs of understanding, reacting to words and pictures, mixing with the other students and has become far less preoccupied with routine as you will see. Of course, much of this improvement I put down to the patience and dedication of his teacher. Mr Campsmount is one in a million.'

Elisabeth found her son sitting at his favourite table by the window staring intently at a set of large coloured cards. She watched him from the door unobserved. *He is such a good-looking twelve-year-old*, she thought, *with his large dark eyes, long lashes and curly blonde hair.* She approached slowly and looked over his shoulder. The cards on which he was concentrating showed pictures of everyday objects: a kettle and cutlery, cups and plates, hats and coats, chairs and tables, mirrors and table lamps. He was so involved in the activity of matching the words to the pictures, something she had never seen him do before, that he was unaware of her presence. His forehead was furrowed with concentration. She sat next to him. He turned, smiled and hugged her – something else he had never done before. Then he returned to sorting out the cards. Tears blurred Elisabeth's eyes. She took his hand in hers and pressed it gently. He glanced around and smiled.

'Hello, Mrs Stirling.' John's teacher, a young man with a wide smile and china-blue eyes, came to join her. 'What about this, then?' He beamed.

'Oh hello, Mr Campsmount,' she replied, wiping a tear from her cheek. 'I can't believe what I am seeing.'

'Remarkable, isn't it. It just sort of happened since your last visit,' he told her. 'He's starting to recognise words, which is a real breakthrough. As I said to Mr Williams, there's been a much greater level of understanding lately.'

'That is so good to hear,' said Elisabeth.

'And something else,' said the teacher. 'Now you know as well as I that John's always been a quiet, gentle-natured lad, no trouble at all and a pleasure to teach, but he has not been one to interact with the other pupils. He has always liked his own company. Well, lately he's been taking a real interest in what others are doing, joining in some of the activities and going out of school on trips. I think one of our classroom assistants, Mr Pugh, has told you that he sometimes takes John down the Miners' Welfare Club. I try and take him out of school to the park once a week and he seems to really enjoy it.'

'I just can't believe the change that has taken place in John,' said Elisabeth. 'You've worked magic, Mr Campsmount. I cannot tell you how grateful I am.'

The teacher coloured up. 'Just doing my job,' he said diffidently. 'Now, there is something I want to ask you.'

'Of course,' replied Elisabeth, 'how could I refuse after what you have done for my son?'

'How would you feel about John coming home with you for a day?'

'Coming home!' she cried.

'I think he's about ready and so does Mr Williams. His doctor, who I think you know, also thinks it's a good idea.' He winked. 'We thought one Saturday. You could collect him and return him later that day.'

'Michael knew about this?' she asked, incredulous.

The teacher nodded and grinned. 'It was Dr Stirling who suggested it when he last called in to the school.'

'He never mentioned anything to me,' she said.

'I guess he wanted it to be a surprise,' said the teacher.

Elisabeth began to cry. 'In my wildest dreams,' she sniffed, 'I never thought this would ever happen. John coming home.'

That evening, snuggled up on the sofa with Michael, she glanced over to the photographs in the silver frames of her husband's former wife. It had been so thoughtful of him to suggest a visit of her son, that small touch of kindness which meant he thought a lot about her, that he really did care, that he truly loved her. And at that moment, as she sat nestled in his arms, any doubts that she had entertained about how he really felt about her vanished.

'Thank you,' she said quietly.

'For what?' asked Michael.

'For everything,' she replied, kissing him on the cheek. 'I really do love you, you know.'

4

Mrs Underwood lived in a small block of exclusive apartments in the centre of Clayton overlooking the river and the
towering cathedral. The lounge in her apartment was clinical
in appearance, rather like the waiting room of some swish
medical consultant's practice – expensively equipped but cold
and featureless. The cream-painted walls were unadorned
save for a couple of insipid canvases splashed indiscriminately
with splotches of colour (modern art apparently); there was a
sofa and matching armchair upholstered in an off-white material, plain light-brown curtains, a pale-tan carpet and a
glass-topped coffee table on stainless steel legs. In a corner
there was a small television hidden in a cabinet. There were no
photographs or ornaments.

Ashley tried to see her mother every month but never
enjoyed the visits. Over the years Mrs Underwood had become
an increasingly petulant and ill-tempered woman for whom
nothing in the world seemed to be right. Her parents had had
an unhappy marriage; as a child Ashley had never seen them
show affection or compatibility or even consideration for each
other. Long and successful marriages often have some rough
waters, but her parents' marriage seemed to be one long
raging sea. All she seemed to recall as a small girl at home
were the arguments and simmering silences between her
parents. Then, one hot summer day, it had come to a head
when her father had left home. Dressed in an expensive linen
shirt open at the neck, a pair of pale-yellow chinos and canvas

deck shoes, he was trying to appear younger than he was. His packed suitcases were at his feet. Her mother, her arms folded tightly over her chest, barred his way, looking angry and tense.

'So you're going then?' she asked in a brittle tone of voice.

'Look, Ruth, I know this is hard for you—' her father began.

'Please don't!' she snapped, raising a hand. There was a cold, contemptuous look on her face. 'You'll only sound pathetic. Twenty years of marriage and it has to end like this with you running off with a woman barely older than your own daughter.' There was a tremble in her voice.

Her father let his breath out in a weary sigh. 'We've been through all this,' he began. 'Don't start all that again.'

She smiled with her mouth but her eyes were hard as flint. 'With a woman half your age,' she scoffed. 'Well, don't come running back to me with your tail between your legs when it doesn't work out.'

'I won't be coming back,' he said with a tone of finality. 'Look, I have to go. I wanted to say goodbye to Ashley but I can't find her. Would you tell her—'

'I shall tell her nothing.'

'I had better go,' he said, his voice sounding careful, as if he were controlling himself.

'And what am I supposed to do?' she asked, blocking his way.

'Do?'

'Yes, what am I supposed to do now?' She sounded bitter.

'I'm sure any advice I could give would be wasted on you,' he replied.

'Well indulge me,' she said. 'What am I expected to live on? What about the house? What about Ashley's school fees?'

'For God's sake, Ruth, don't play the martyr. You'll be comfortably off. You'll get a generous allowance, half the proceeds of the house when it's sold and of course I'll continue to pay Ashley's school fees.' Then, picking up his suitcases and moving around his wife, he added as a parting shot, 'And you could always get a job.' Before she could reply he was out of the front door.

It was usually in bed at night when Ashley could not sleep that she recalled the time when her father had left home and ceased to be a part of her life. He had written to her for a few weeks and then the letters stopped arriving and she had never heard from him again. A cousin later told her that he moved to Canada, that he had remarried and had another family.

Following her parents' acrimonious divorce, Ashley had gone to live with her mother in a small modern terrace, leaving the large detached house and the attic bedroom she so loved. 'Home' became nothing except complaints and reproaches, no saving moments of laughter or shared pleasure. Nothing she did seemed to please her mother. She tried to love her mother but it didn't work; she couldn't love her father for she never saw him. And so she learnt to hide her feelings and conceal her thoughts. She became an angry child, suspicious of adults, and felt miserable and lonely, believing that neither parent really loved her. It took a long time for her to learn to love. Then a new teacher came to the convent school she attended. She was a small, round-faced nun with tiny, dark, darting eyes and a sharp little beak of a nose. Sister Augusta Maria looked like a small, hungry blackbird out for the early worm. Inspired by this brilliant teacher, Ashley blossomed in her studies. When the nun praised her for her work, singling her out and reading aloud her poems and extracts from her essays as an example for others, Ashley would blush and inside felt a warmth and a contentment she had rarely felt. She would run a finger over the uplifting comments on her exercise book written in a careful copperplate hand.

It was Sister Augusta Maria who introduced Ashley to the world of literature, her escape, and she threw herself into her studies, spending hours in the local library. She found the visits to the local church and the sympathetic priest a great comfort and then she found the Bible. It told her that if she was not loved on earth there was a God in heaven who did and she learnt to love the gentle, forgiving, benign figure who stared down from the cross above the altar. And it was this that drew her to the ministry.

But home always remained a grim and cheerless place. There were no fulsome congratulations when Ashley brought home her outstanding school report where the head mistress had written that 'here was a gifted student who sets the standard by which the remainder is judged'. When Ashley was accepted to study at All Souls at Oxford, her mother could barely bring herself to commend her clever daughter. Neither parent attended the degree ceremony, it was Sister Augusta Maria who sat amongst the parents. Seeing all her fellow students surrounded by proud, happy mothers and fathers, Ashley had felt that deeply.

'I thought you might have called in last week,' her mother said now. Mrs Underwood was a slight, thin-featured woman with a finely boned face and lifeless mousy-brown hair. She wore little make-up apart from a dab of lipstick. Stern-faced, she was rarely provoked to smile and even less to laugh.

'I've been pretty busy,' replied her daughter.

'Aren't you always.'

'Actually, I've got a new job,' her daughter told her, trying to sound cheerful. Her mother didn't reply. 'I shall be moving into Clayton and the work I am doing will be very different.'

'Are you giving up the church then?' asked Mrs Underwood. 'It's about time you got a proper job.'

'No, I won't be giving up the church. I am to be the bishop's chaplain.'

'And what, pray, does a bishop's chaplain do?'

'It involves lot of administrative work. There are his letters and reports and—'

'It's a sort of secretarial job then is it, this bishop's chaplain?'

'A bit more than that, Mother.'

'I would have thought that with more degrees than a thermometer you could have done better in life than end up as some sort of glorified clerical assistant. All that time you've spent in education, all that studying at Oxford and look where it's got you. Your nose was never out of a book.'

Ashley didn't reply. Her books were her friends, her escape from a dour and lonely life. It was fruitless for her to explain exactly what her new role involved so she changed the subject.

'So I shall be leaving St Christopher's in a couple of weeks.'

'You have hardly been in your present job above five minutes,' said her mother. 'Why ever do you want to move?'

Ashley considered telling her mother about the differences she had with the new vicar but merely smiled weakly. 'It offers a new challenge,' she said simply.

'I can't see being a secretary offers much of a challenge but what do I know? You've always been a headstrong girl.'

'And how have you been keeping?' Ashley asked, keen to move on to another topic of conversation. Of course, she might have predicted her mother's reply.

'Much the same,' Mrs Underwood replied. 'There's nothing for me to do except read and do the crossword. There's very little on the television I want to watch – all silly quiz shows, food and antique programmes and dreadful American films full of violence and bad language.' She leant back in her chair with an affected air of weariness. 'Of course, there's nobody in the block to have a decent conversation with. The young couple who live above rarely give me the time of day.'

This came as no surprise to Ashley. Following her mother's constant complaints about the noise from the upstairs neighbours, it was a wonder they spoke to her at all.

'You want to try and get out a bit more,' Ashley suggested.

'What, walk into Clayton? I wouldn't feel safe.'

'You could join a club. I am sure there are lots of activities at the local church.'

'I'm not one for joining a group of gossipy women and I'm afraid I don't share your religious convictions,' replied her mother.

They sat in silence for a while.

'I wondered if you might like to go out today,' suggested Ashley. 'It's such a bright, sunny day. We could perhaps have a meal down by the river.'

'No I don't want to go out,' replied Mrs Underwood. She sounded like a petulant child. 'I've never been one for public houses and it will be crowded on a day like this.'

'I had a letter from Sister Augusta Maria last week,' said Ashley struggling to find something to say. 'She's moved to a convent in York. Evidently she's been very ill but keeps cheerful and optimistic.'

'Was she the old nun with the moustache?'

Ashley smiled, recalling the old bent nun who pottered around the school. 'No, you're thinking of Sister Protase. Sister Augusta Maria was my English teacher. She was the one who encouraged me to try for Oxford.'

'Oh yes, I remember her. You were her blue-eyed girl, weren't you? I can't for the life of me understand why a young woman would want to give everything up and live with a lot of other women locked up against the outside world in a convent. There's something not quite right about it.'

'They aren't locked up, Mother,' her daughter told her. 'It's their choice. Actually they have very fulfilled and contented lives.'

'They should be married, not confined to a nunnery. Not that my marriage was anything to write home about.'

'I thought I might visit her,' said Ashley quickly to preclude her mother regaling her, yet again, with how badly she had been treated by a feckless husband. 'She was very good to me.'

'Who was?'

'Sister Augusta Maria.'

'She probably gets more visits from you than I do,' said her mother, twisting her thin mouth into a crooked smile.

There was another silence.

'So will you be moving house?'

'No, I'll travel into Clayton each day. There's a pretty good bus service.'

'I've been thinking,' said Mrs Underwood suddenly. 'Now that you have left the rectory and have a place of your own—'

'I'm renting the cottage,' Ashley told her, wishing at that moment she had never mentioned the fact she had moved into Wisteria Cottage when Elisabeth got married and had gone to live with Dr Stirling at Clumber Lodge. She could predict what was coming.

'Well it's the same thing,' said her mother sharply. 'I've been thinking,' she continued, 'that I could come and live with you. It would be much more economical. I mean, there's nothing to keep me here.'

'I don't know whether or not the person I'm renting the cottage from would altogether approve of that,' said Ashley evasively. It was, she knew, a rather feeble excuse.

'I don't see why she should have any objection. I'm not going to trash the place.'

'It's a very small cottage, Mother.'

'There is another bedroom I take it?'

'There is but it's used as my study with my desk and all my books. Anyway, I think you would be very lonely in Barton-in-the-Dale. You wouldn't know anyone.'

'I don't know anyone here,' retorted her mother.

'And I would be out all day and most of my evenings are taken up with various church functions and activities.'

'I can see that you don't want me to come and live with you,' said her mother peevishly.

'It's not that—' began Ashley.

'It sounds like it.'

'It's just that I don't think it would work out.'

'I see.'

'You would be stuck in the cottage all day with nothing to do.'

'I'm stuck here in this apartment all day with nothing to do,' replied Mrs Underwood.

And whose fault is that, thought her daughter. She had advised her mother not to move out of the small terraced house away from the few friends she had but her opinion was, as always, ignored.

'It's just the cottage is fully furnished and there wouldn't be room for all your things,' she said.

'There's nothing in this place I have any fondness for,' said Mrs Underwood.

'I don't think it would work, Mother.'

'I see. Well, I know where I stand now, Ashley,' replied Mrs Underwood. 'You read of all these ungrateful children but I never thought my own child would be so in want of feeling, particularly someone in your position, who stands up in a pulpit and tells everyone to cherish their parents and love one another.'

Ashley sighed. She could have reminded her mother how lonely and unloved she had felt as a child but she remained silent. She was just grateful she wasn't that same girl any more.

'Well I'm sure you've got lots of things to do,' she said. 'I wouldn't want to keep you.'

Ashley got up. It was pointless to continue the conversation. 'I'll try and call in next week,' she said.

'As you like,' replied her mother, before adding pointedly, 'I'm not going anywhere.'

★　　★　　★

Emmet O'Malley was a tall, broad-shouldered young man with a mass of unruly black curls and a wide-boned weathered face the colour of a russet apple. Dressed in a tailored tweed suit and mustard-coloured waistcoat and sporting a pair of smart brogues and brown kid gloves, he strode down the high street looking to the entire world like a prosperous farmer and not the traveller he had once been. He cut a very different figure now from when he had first appeared in the village the previous year. With his young daughter, Roisin, he had arrived at Elisabeth's cottage looking for somewhere to park his caravan. Then he had been wearing a heavy, thick close-fitting jacket, shapeless corduroy trousers worn at the knees and black boots which had seen better days. Around his neck was wound a colourful kerchief and an earring was fastened to his ear like a small gold manacle. He looked like the illustration of a gypsy one might see in a child's picture book.

Having charmed Elisabeth into letting him set up his caravan in her paddock at the rear of the cottage, he had told her that he was not a conventional traveller but more of an itinerant.

'I'm not a gypsy or a tinker,' he had said, 'and I have no Romany blood and I don't travel around with others. It's just that I've never been one to settle. I like to be on the road. I'd feel cooped up in a house. I like the open spaces, the changing countryside, the freedom to go where I want and stop where I want and move on when I want.'

After a few weeks in Barton-in-the-Dale, however, he knew that this was a place where he wanted to stay for a while. The village with its surrounding scattered conifer plantations, pale stone and pantile-roofed cottages, the old walls of greenish white limestone enclosing the solid Norman church with its spire spearing the sky, had a timeless quality about it. The villagers were friendly too and there were plenty of odd jobs to be done. More importantly, his young daughter, who had sometimes had a difficult time in the past with her schooling, had settled very well at the village school and begged him to let them stay. Then he was offered a job as a handyman-come-gardener at Limebeck House, the imposing home of Lady Wadsworth, so he decided to put down roots. Emmet proved to be good-humoured, honest, hard-working and efficient and before long Lady Wadsworth was so impressed with his work that she made him her estate manager. There was, of course, another more pressing reason why he wished to stay and that reason was Ashley Underwood.

He had first met the curate when she had visited Limebeck House. She arrived on a bicycle and after the meeting with Lady Wadsworth, she discovered that she had a punctured tyre. Emmet had mended it for her and they had struck up a conversation. They discovered that they both loved folk music. Later, meeting again by accident at a folk concert in Clayton, Emmet, spurred on by his young daughter, had invited Ashley to join them for a drink. As they sat at the inn by the river he told her about his ambitions and his dreams, something he had never done with anyone since the death of his wife. Ashley had smiled and listened and Emmet had been smitten by this strikingly beautiful woman with the stunning smile and the gentle nature. The feeling had been mutual: Ashley, looking into long-lashed blue eyes, had never met a man who touched her emotions so quickly.

That morning Emmet called into the village store to place Lady Wadsworth's weekly order. He found Mrs Sloughthwaite at her usual place behind the counter. She beamed widely as he stepped through the door.

'Well now, Mr O'Malley,' said the shopkeeper. 'You look fine and dandy this morning. You're like a man out a-courting.'

'No such luck, I'm afraid,' he told her, flashing a set of straight white teeth.

'Get away with you, a good-looking young fellow like you. I bet the girls are queuing up.'

Emmett coloured. 'Foot loose and fancy free, that's me, Mrs Sloughthwaite,' he told her.

'Let's see what it says in your stars,' said the shopkeeper.

'My stars?'

'Your horoscope.' She reached under the counter for a newspaper and began flicking though the pages until she came to the one she wanted. 'What's your star sign?'

'I'm not sure,' he told her.

'When's your birthday?'

'27th December.'

'Capricorn. Right, let's have a look.' She began to read. '"Your ruling planet is Saturn, your colour is indigo, your animal is a goat, your gem is the diamond and your beneficial food is the cabbage." '

'Cabbage!' he exclaimed, laughing. 'Sure I hate the stuff. I was brought up in Ireland on potatoes and cabbage and can't stand the sight of that particular vegetable.'

'It doesn't mean you have to like it,' explained Mrs Sloughthwaite. 'It just means it's your beneficial food. Anyway, let's see what's in store for you. It says, "judging by your planetary set-up you are in for an interesting time in the next few months regarding domestic matters but don't worry because, thanks to the expansive Jupiter and your benign ruler Saturn, things will eventually turn out for the best. You need to heed the advice of and trust in others and follow your feelings. You can deal with anything if you believe in yourself and persevere." That doesn't sound too bad now, does it?' She read on: '"A friend regards you as a reliable presence. They will find you a sympathetic shoulder to cry on. Friendship might blossom into something more. You are a fiercely independent person but you cherish a close relationship and true love will come your way when—"'

The shopkeeper stopped reading and looked up as the shop bell rang and Ashley entered.

'Oh, hello, Reverend Underwood,' she said.

'Hello, Mrs Sloughthwaite,' Ashley replied. She turned to Emmet and smiled. 'Hello,' she said.

'Good afternoon,' he replied, looking self-conscious.

'I was just telling Mr O'Malley here what's in store for him,' said the shopkeeper.

'I'm sorry?' said Ashley, looking puzzled.

'What's in his stars.'

'Oh I see. I'm afraid I take horoscopes with a pinch of salt.'

Mrs Sloughthwaite leant on the counter and smiled. 'Oh, you would be surprised how accurate they can be.' There was a twinkle in her eye. 'It says here that Mr O'Malley should cherish close relationships and that true love—'

'I think I've heard quite enough about what is in store for me, Mrs Sloughthwaite,' Emmet interrupted. 'I think I would rather not know.'

'You look very smart this afternoon, Emmet,' said Ashley. 'Are you going somewhere special?'

'I have some business to do for Lady Wadsworth in Clayton,' he told her. 'That's why I'm in my Sunday best. It's back to the old work clothes when I get home.'

'Well, what can I do for you, Dr Underwood?' asked Mrs Sloughthwaite.

'I'd like to place an advertisement in the shop window please.' She passed a small card over the counter which Mrs Sloughthwaite read.

'You're selling your bicycle?' asked the shopkeeper.

'That's right. I don't really have any more use for it,' said Ashley.

'Really?'

'I suppose it will be common knowledge soon enough,' said the curate. 'I am leaving St Christopher's to work in Clayton at Cathedral House to be the bishop's chaplain. It will be the bus for me from now on.'

'Well, what a pity you're leaving,' said the shopkeeper. 'You've been like a breath of fresh air in the village. Wouldn't you say so, Mr O'Malley?'

'Yes, yes indeed,' he readily agreed.

'I guess it must have been difficult getting on with the new vicar,' said Mrs Sloughthwaite, hoping to prompt a comment. She waited for a response but when one was not forthcoming, she continued. 'He's a very different kettle of fish from Mr Atticus, rather stern and serious, isn't he, that Mr Sparshott?'

She waited a moment, hopeful of a reaction but Ashley remained silent. Mrs Sloughthwaite was the last person in the village in whom she would confide anything regarding the new vicar's treatment of her.

'That sermon of his on the first Sunday he preached at St Christopher's was all hellfire and damnation,' continued the shopkeeper. 'Mrs Fish nearly fell off the organ stool in a dead faint. Mrs Pocock was only saying the other day how your sermons were much more positive, Dr Underwood. You make people feel better and have a lovely manner.'

'That's very kind of you to say so,' said Ashley.

'Don't you think so, Mr O'Malley?'

'Pardon?'

'That Dr Underwood has been like a breath of fresh air in the village.'

'Yes, she has,' agreed Emmet.

'Of course, to be the bishop's chaplain is an opportunity I couldn't really turn down,' Ashley told her.

'Well you will be greatly missed, won't she, Mr O'Malley?' said the shopkeeper looking at him and giving a small mischievous smile.

'Yes she will,' he said, feeling uncomfortable by Mrs Sloughthwaite's constant reference to himself.

'I'm not leaving the village,' Ashley said. 'I shall still rent Wisteria Cottage from Mrs Stirling so you haven't got rid of me.'

The shopkeeper looked at Emmet again and smiled. 'Well I'm sure everyone will be very pleased to hear that. Am I right, Mr O'Malley?'

'Yes, you are right, Mrs Sloughthwaite,' he replied.

'Now, how much do I owe you?' asked Ashley.

'That's all right, Reverend Underwood,' said the shopkeeper. 'Have this on the house.'

'Thank you, that's really ever so kind of you,' said Ashley. 'Well, I'll be on my way.'

As Ashley made for the door, Emmet pushed a list across the counter. 'I'll just give you Lady Wadsworth's order and collect it later,' he said.

'Right you are,' said the shopkeeper, the mischievous smile still etched on her face as he shot out the store.

Mrs Sloughthwaite, with remarkable agility for one so large, skirted the counter, waddled to the shop window and peered after the couple walking down the high street together. Having remained there for a minute, she returned to the counter and scrutinised the newspaper again. *You should cherish close relationships and true love will come your way.*

'I shouldn't be at all surprised,' she said.

'Are you in a hurry?' asked Emmet when he caught up with Ashley.

'No, not at all,' she replied.

'Do you fancy a coffee?'

'Do you know, I'd love one.'

They sat at the table by the window in the Rumbling Tum café. Ashley, Emmet thought, looked particularly weary and sounded out of sorts that afternoon. He remembered when they had last sat at the window table in the café and how pretty she had looked with the sun shining on her soft golden hair. He had stared at her deep-set blue eyes, the high cheekbones, small nose and curve of her lips. It was then that he had started to fall in love with her.

Bianca, married to the put-upon nephew of the now infamous Fred Massey, a rather morose-looking young woman with dyed-blonde hair, came over to the table to take their order.

'Hi,' she said, placing a hand on her hip.

'Hello, Bianca,' said Ashley. 'You are looking well.'

'Mustn't grumble,' replied the girl.

'I thought you'd given up your job in the café when you and your husband moved into the farmhouse with Mr Massey?' said Ashley.

'I did, but I just couldn't stand it being cooped up like one of Fred's chickens,' she said. 'I do a bit of part time here. It gets me out of the house. My mam looks after our Brandon.'

'And how is that baby of yours?' asked Ashley.

The girl's sullen expression suddenly disappeared and she broke into a great beam of a smile. 'Oh he's growing real fast. He'll be walking soon.'

'It doesn't seem long since I christened him,' said Ashley.

'No, it doesn't. It were a lovely service. Didn't he cry when you poured that cold water on his head. Yeah, it were a lovely service. Anyway, what can I get you?'

'Just a coffee please,' said Ashley.

'And the same for me,' said Emmet.

When the waitress had gone he leant over the table. 'You look tired,' he said.

'I am,' replied Ashley, brushing a strand of hair from her eyes.

'Is something wrong?' he asked.

'I just need someone to talk to,' she said quietly.

'I'm all ears.'

'It's just that . . . well . . . I feel pretty down at the moment,' she told him.

'Is it this new job?' he asked.

'No, no, I'm really excited about starting work at the cathedral. From the start I seemed to have been on a collision course with the new vicar and our recent meeting was pretty dispiriting. It became impossible for me to work with him. I feel quite sad about that.'

'But you're leaving,' said Emmet. 'You won't have to work with him.'

'Yes, I know, and I'm looking forward to working with the archdeacon again. It's my mother who is really on my mind at the moment. I've just been to see her and things didn't go at all well. In fact, they never do. To be honest, I dread going. She lives in a fancy apartment in Clayton overlooking the river and the cathedral and really has nothing to complain about; she's comfortably off and is in good health but she is someone for whom nothing seems to be right. And I'm afraid I don't feature well in her books. I always leave her feeling thoroughly depressed. I'm afraid we just don't hit it off. We never have. She's quite a demanding woman and she always manages to make me feel guilty and selfish.'

'I can't imagine a least selfish person than you,' said Emmet.

'My mother wants to come and live with me,' Ashley told him, 'but I know in my heart that it just wouldn't work out, we'd be at loggerheads all the time.'

'I can't imagine you being at loggerheads with anyone,' said Emmet. 'You're the kindest, most even-tempered person I know. You get on with everybody.'

'Not with my mother, I'm afraid.' She sighed.

'She sounds a difficult woman.'

'She is, yes,' agreed Ashley, 'but I do feel sorry for her and wish we could have a closer relationship. I have tried. When my father left her for another woman she became very bitter and bad-tempered and I grew up being constantly criticised. "You're getting more like your father every day," she used to throw in my face when she found fault with me. Nothing I did as a child ever seemed right. I'm afraid nothing has changed. It's a terrible admission for a daughter and a priest to make, but I just can't bring myself to love her.'

'Oh it's not that uncommon for a child to stop loving a parent,' replied Emmet, thinking of something within his past.

Tears welled up in her eyes. 'You're a good friend, Emmet,' she said, 'listening to all my troubles.'

I wish I could be more than a friend, he thought.

'I just don't know what to do,' sniffed Ashley, her face crumpling as she said the words.

'Hey, hey,' said Emmet reaching across the table, taking her hand and squeezing it gently.

Mrs Pocock, on her way to the village store to catch up on the local gossip, observed the two people at the window table in the Rumbling Tum café, heads close together and holding hands.

'Well, well, well,' she said out loud. 'Who would have thought it?'

John's visit to Clumber Lodge was not the success Elisabeth had hoped for. James and Danny had been well prepared for the event because Elisabeth and Michael had described the characteristics of autism: how John might appear rather remote and unapproachable, how he liked precision and order, that he might find the new surroundings disconcerting at first. They were told not to make a fuss of him, try to engage him in conversation or get him to play games with them.

'Just take it very slowly,' Michael had told them. 'John will be a bit nervous and unsure at first but when he gets used to the room and to us he'll feel more at ease.'

Michael was wrong.

Elisabeth started to have reservations about the wisdom of taking John out of school as soon as he got into the car. He sat in the back seat rocking backwards and forwards, plucking anxiously at the seat belt and looking distressed. At the house it took a great deal of patience and many gentle words of encouragement for him to get out of the car. In the sitting room his anxiety increased and he sat hunched up on the sofa. Despite Elisabeth's soothing efforts to interest him in some coloured blocks of different shapes and sizes, John rocked and whimpered. Danny and James could only stand by the door looking helpless.

After an hour, Michael put his arm around Elisabeth's shoulder and said he felt John should go back to school.

At Forest View, Mr Williams was pragmatic. 'It perhaps didn't work out this time,' he said, 'but I don't think we should give up. Social interaction is very important to try and develop.'

'But Mr Campsmount said John has got used to people more and is happy going out of school,' said Elisabeth. 'I don't understand why this visit was so upsetting for him.'

'Strange surroundings, different sounds and smells, a lot of new faces – these can all disorientate someone like John,' said Mr Williams. 'Maybe we were being a bit over optimistic. I wouldn't get too down about it. It was worth the attempt. I have always thought that unless we take a few measured risks in education, as indeed in most things in life, there can be no progress.'

Elisabeth thought of Lady Wadsworth's words when she heard this.

'So let's give it time,' said Mr Williams. 'We'll continue to work with John and have another go in a few weeks.'

Before she left, Elisabeth went to see her son. Back in the environment he knew, he was a different boy and was happily rearranging the coloured cards and smiling. She kissed his cheek, he hugged her and she left feeling downhearted.

5

The week before the beginning of the new term, Mrs Stirling and the teachers met in the staffroom, formerly the head teacher's room in the time of Miss Sowerbutts.

'Good morning, everyone,' said Elisabeth cheerily. She could feel her stomach churning nervously and there was a slight tremble in her hands but she hid her uneasiness as best she could and hoped she looked confident and business-like for this first staff meeting. If it did not go smoothly it would not bode well for the future. She was determined to try and make this amalgamation work, but she had her reservations. She could, of course, rely on Mrs Robertshaw with whom she had worked before. Shrewd, good-natured, blunt-speaking and hard-working, she was a real asset. But the other two teachers were unknown quantities; one disillusioned and resentful, the other idiosyncratic, unpredictable and untidy.

'I hope you all had a well-deserved rest over the summer,' she continued, 'and are ready for what promises to be an exciting and challenging term.' She looked around the faces before her: a smiling Mrs Robertshaw, a stern-faced Mr Jolly and an expectant-looking Mr Hornchurch. 'I won't keep you too long because I am sure you will want to get to your class-rooms to prepare them for next week. I just wanted to welcome you all to our new school and say I am really looking forward to working with you this term. We travelled through some pretty stormy waters last term with the amalgamation, the redundancies and the uncertainty.'

'We did indeed,' agreed Mrs Robertshaw.

Mr Jolly nodded. *At least we could agree on that*, Elisabeth thought.

'But thankfully that is behind us now,' Elisabeth carried on, 'and we can look forward to some stability.'

There was a knock at the door and Mr Gribbon and Mrs Scrimshaw entered.

'You wanted to see us, Mrs Stirling,' said the caretaker looking grim. He was dressed in a new grey nylon overall and held a great bunch of keys.

'Ah, Mr Gribbon, Mrs Scrimshaw,' said Elisabeth. 'Thank you both for coming to see me. I just wanted to introduce you to the staff. You know Mrs Robertshaw, of course, and I think you met Mr Hornchurch when he came for an interview earlier in the holidays. Our fourth member is Mr Jolly who joins us from Urebank.'

Nods and hellos were exchanged.

'I also wanted to say a big thank you to you both,' continued Elisabeth, 'for all your hard work during the holidays in getting the school looking so clean and bright and ready for the new term.'

The caretaker's countenance changed suddenly. He grinned and rubbed his jaw. 'A pleasure, I'm sure,' he said. 'I think the kids deserve a nice environment in which to learn,' he added, echoing the words of Mrs Pugh, the former part-time cleaner.

'Thank you, Mrs Stirling,' said the school secretary. Then, not to be outdone by the caretaker, she added, 'I'm pleased to say that everything's in order in the school office.'

'Perhaps you both might like to join us for coffee later this morning and you can get to know one another a little better.'

When the caretaker and secretary had departed again, Elisabeth gave each teacher a folder.

'I have put together a few things which I hope you will find useful: the school development plan, an outline of the curriculum with some guidelines, health and safety details, notes of children with special needs, holiday times etc. You can read these at your leisure. It just remains for us to decide who will take which class. We have four very manageable classes of roughly the same size – just less than twenty children in each. That means two upper and two lower juniors.'

'I would like to stay with the lower juniors if possible,' said Mrs Robertshaw quickly before anyone else could make a bid. 'All my prepared materials are targeted for this age group.'

'Mr Jolly?' asked Elisabeth. 'Have you a preference?'

'I should prefer to teach the younger junior children too,' he replied.

'Mr Hornchurch?'

'I'm easy,' he replied, leaning back in the chair and clasping his hands behind his head.

'Then that seems pretty much settled,' said Elisabeth, pleased it had gone so painlessly. Mrs Robertshaw and Mr Jolly with the lower juniors, Mr Hornchurch and myself with the upper juniors.'

'You intend to teach?' enquired Mr Jolly sounding genuinely surprised.

'Yes, I do,' replied Elisabeth.

'Full time?'

'I shall be spending an afternoon a week down with the infants on the Urebank site,' Elisabeth told him, 'and on those occasions a supply teacher will be taking my class. A newly appointed colleague, Miss Kennedy, has been given the position of deputy head teacher and will be in charge of the Urebank site on a day-to-day basis but I will have overall responsibility.'

'I should think you will have quite enough on, Mrs Stirling,' he observed. 'At Urebank Mr Richardson did not teach a class.'

'So I believe.' The last thing she wanted was reminiscences from him about Urebank. 'Let's move on,' she said quickly.

'I understand that Robin Banks will be in the school,' said Mr Jolly.

'He will be,' replied Elisabeth, 'but his name has been changed. He is now Robin Hardy, known as Robbie.'

'I sincerely hope that he will not be in my class,' said Mr Jolly.

'No, he will be in an upper junior class.'

Mr Jolly addressed his colleagues. 'We had this boy for a short time at Urebank until he was expelled before the end of last term and he was uncontrollable. I have never in all my experience had to deal with a child so wilfully ill-natured. We couldn't do anything with him and Mr Richardson suggested that a disturbed boy like that would be better catered for at a special school for disruptive children.'

'He bit you, didn't he?' said Mrs Robertshaw with a trace of a smile in her lips.

'He did indeed,' replied Mr Jolly, rubbing his hand. 'I had occasion to chastise him for refusing to do his work and when I pointed to his book he bit my hand. Feral, that's what he is. I have never in all my years as a teacher met such a difficult, disruptive and downright dangerous pupil.'

'Robbie has had a difficult life,' said Elisabeth. 'He's had a great deal to put up with at home. One can understand why he sometimes reacts as he does.'

'Be that as it may, Mrs Stirling,' Mr Jolly responded, 'but the boy is rude and wilful and quite unteachable.'

'Well Robbie will be with us,' said Elisabeth simply.

'Mrs Stirling, if I might—' began Mr Jolly.

'I really feel very strongly that no child should be written off,' she said, interrupting. 'I don't expel children. Robbie is, without doubt, a difficult child but as I have said he has had a great deal to put up with. From what I can gather his step-father had little time for the boy, he used to hit him and verbally abuse him and Robbie's mother appears a sad and weak character who does exactly what her husband tells her to do. It is no surprise that Robbie is mixed up.'

'It is a characteristic of damaged children to display anger,' ventured Mr Hornchurch.

'Indeed,' agreed Elisabeth. 'Robbie is a disturbed, troublesome, unhappy boy with a feeling of being unloved and—'

'With respect, Mrs Stirling,' interrupted Mr Jolly, 'that is all very well but I still feel he would be far better catered for at a special school.'

'I have to say that I agree with Mr Jolly on this,' said Mrs Robertshaw. 'As you know, I tried to teach Robbie last term and I just could not manage him. I do feel that the boy needs specialist help. His poor behaviour will have a negative effect on the other children in the school.'

'Elsie, I think you have known me long enough to be aware of my philosophy,' replied Elisabeth. 'I am not prepared to give up on a child. I think you will agree there has been some improvement in Robbie's conduct during the time he has been with us. I am optimistic that things will improve further. He is with foster parents at the moment and seems settled and they are keen that he stays here.'

'Actually I think the term now used is foster carers,' Mr Hornchurch told her. 'The boy has parents you see and—'

'Well whether they are called foster parents or foster carers,' remarked Mr Jolly, 'they will certainly have their work cut out for them with that boy, that I can say. I certainly wouldn't want to teach him.'

'I shall have Robbie in my class,' said Elisabeth.

'I don't mind taking the lad,' said Mr Hornchurch, sitting up.

'I think he might be better with me,' Elisabeth told him. 'Robbie can still be quite a handful.'

'We could give it a go,' suggested the teacher. 'I quite like the challenge of a difficult pupil. You know what they say: "Many an unruly colt makes a noble horse".'

'Well whoever said that was a fool,' rejoined Mr Jolly.

'Actually, I think it was Socrates who said it,' Mr Hornchurch told him, 'and he was no fool.'

'Whatever,' muttered Mr Jolly. 'You are welcome to have the boy in your class. If I were you I would keep my distance.' He rubbed his hand again. 'He has sharp teeth.'

'All right,' said Elisabeth, 'we shall see how Robbie gets on in your class, Mr Hornchurch, if you are sure.'

'I say, Mrs Stirling, might I make a suggestion?' he said.

'Yes, of course.'

'Could we dispense with all this Mr and Mrs malarkey? It sounds so stuffy. What about using first names?'

'Good idea,' agreed Mrs Robertshaw. 'I'm Elsie. I do so hate the name but I'm stuck with it.'

'I'm Rupert,' he told her. 'What about you, Mr Jolly?'

'I'm Donald,' he replied rather sullenly.

'Do you like to be called Don?' he was asked.

'No, I certainly do not!'

'And what about you, Mrs Stirling?' asked the young man.

'You can call me Elisabeth,' she replied. 'I am sure I have been called worse. Oh, I nearly forgot, there are just a couple more things. Mrs Robertshaw has agreed to act as assistant head teacher here at Barton and also volunteered to become the teacher representative on the new governing body, unless of course anyone else is interested.'

'I'm certainly not,' said Mr Jolly, thinking he was spending enough time in the school already. In his entire teaching career he had never given up part of his summer holidays to go into school. The last thing he wanted was his evenings taken up endlessly discussing education with a group of interfering school governors.

'I'm very happy with that,' said Mr Hornchurch. 'I'm pretty hopeless at meetings.'

As the teachers left the staffroom, Elisabeth breathed out in relief and rested her head on the chair back. The meeting had gone well, better than she had expected. *Let's hope the new term will go as smoothly*, she thought to herself.

Mrs Scrimshaw was tidying her desk later that day before departing for home when Mr Gribbon arrived at the door of the school office. He was red in the face and jangling his keys testily.

'Have you seen what that new teacher's doing?' he asked angrily.

'I've not got telescopic eyes, Mr Gribbon,' she told him, straightening a folder. 'What new teacher?'

'That hippy chap – Hornchurch. He's cluttering up the classroom with all sorts of rubbish – piles of books and plants and pictures and bloody statues and stuffed animals and I don't know what. It's beginning to look like a junk shop. I can't be doing with this. I shall have to tell Mrs Stirling. It'll be a hell on earth trying to keep that place clean.'

'Well I suggest you do that, Mr Gribbon,' said the school secretary with practised indifference when listening to the caretaker's frequent grumbles and gripes. 'I want to be on my way.'

'It's a liberty, that's what it is,' whinged the caretaker, thrusting out his jaw. 'I shall refuse to clean his room.'

'I wouldn't do that if I were you,' advised the secretary, putting on her coat.

'I'm within my rights.'

'No, Mr Gribbon, you are not,' she told him. 'You are employed to clean the school. You start making waves and complaining and they might just think you're not up to the job.'

'Not up to the job!' he exclaimed. 'Who says I'm not up to the job?'

'I didn't say you were not up to the job but if you start being difficult they might just appoint somebody else, somebody who is quite happy to clean the room.' She smiled mischievously. 'You never know, they might replace you with Mrs Pugh.'

'Well I don't think it's right,' grumbled the caretaker.

'I must be off,' said Mrs Scrimshaw. 'I have the Women's Institute meeting this evening. A Mrs Delamare from *Needlework Monthly* is speaking on "Picture Your Pet Cat in Cross Stitch" and I don't want to be late.'

'I didn't know you had a cat,' said the caretaker.

'I don't,' replied the school secretary.

Mr Hornchurch appeared at the door of the school office, beaming widely. He leant casually on the frame.

'Hi there,' he said.

'Oh hello,' grunted the caretaker.

'Hello, Mr Hornchurch,' said the school secretary.

'I wonder, Mr Gribbon, if you could be a good chap and give me a bit of a hand to get this old display cabinet the museum was getting rid of into my classroom? I'm going to display my fossils in it. I have it in the back of my car but it's a bit heavy for me to shift by myself.'

Mrs Scrimshaw could not contain a smile.

It was a bright early September morning when Elisabeth arrived for her first day as the new head teacher of Barton-with-Urebank Primary School. She had arrived early to walk around the building to make sure everything was neat and tidy. Mrs Robertshaw's classroom looked particularly attractive with vivid displays on the walls, neatly stacked books, a writing area, colourful drapes at the windows and the bookcase full of glossy-backed paperbacks. Elisabeth was pleased to see that Mr Jolly had made some effort to make his class-room bright and orderly. She arrived at Mr Hornchurch's classroom. The teacher had been in several times since their meeting the previous week to prepare for the new term. Elisabeth sighed when she opened the door to his room. It was like a cluttered attic. There were boxes and stacks of books in a corner, and tables covered in a variety of objects: birds' skulls, a stuffed rabbit, old tins, bits of pottery, coins, little brass figures, curiously shaped pebbles, fossils and shells, faded feathers, dried flowers, rusty keys, a chess set, a cricket bat – a fascinating pot-pourri of objects. She smiled and shook her head. She had been warned by Ms Tricklebank that the man was untidy but she hardly expected this. She determined to have a word with him but not for the moment. She had enough on her mind today.

On her way down the corridor she was confronted by a scowling Mr Gribbon.

'Can I have a word please, Mrs Stirling?' he said, jangling his keys.

Elisabeth could predict what he was about to say. 'Mr Hornchurch's classroom?' she asked.

'It's like a junk shop in there,' grumbled the caretaker. 'I've never seen anything like it. It looks as if a bomb's hit the place. I just won't be able to cope with this, Mrs Stirling. I mean, think of the dust. You'll have to have a word with him.'

'I intend to, Mr Gribbon,' she replied, 'but for the moment let's let things be. I have enough on my plate this morning with it being the first day of term.'

'Yes but—' began the caretaker.

'Leave it with me, Mr Gribbon,' interrupted Elisabeth, holding up a hand. 'Please. Let us get today over first.'

As she passed the small school library, she caught sight of one of the pupils poring over a large book.

'Hello, Oscar,' she said cheerfully. 'My goodness you are here bright and early.'

'Oh good morning, Mrs Stirling,' replied the boy, closing the book with a snap. 'To be honest I am pleased to be back. I've been pretty bored over the holidays. It's been frightfully dull these last few weeks what with my parents being both at work and my grandmother coming to look after me. She tends to sleep a great deal and doesn't have much in the way of conversation. Of course it comes to us all, old age, doesn't it?'

Elisabeth smiled. Oscar was, without doubt, one of the most interesting, intelligent and old-fashioned children she had ever taught. When she had first met him, this rosy-cheeked child with bright-brown eyes and hair cut in the short-back-and-sides variety, with a neat parting in his hair, spoke and acted like someone well in advance of his nine years. Dressed in short grey trousers, a crisp white shirt, striped tie, a hand-knitted grey pullover, long grey stockings and sensible shoes, he looked like a product of the 1950s and resembled a char-acter straight out of an Enid Blyton story.

The boy was now dressed rather differently. Gone were the short grey trousers and knitted pullover. They had been replaced by long flannels and a red sweatshirt. Instead of the sensible shoes he now sported a pair of colourful trainers.

'I'm pleased to hear you're so keen,' said Elisabeth. 'And I see there's been a change in your wardrobe.'

'Beg pardon?'

'The way you are dressed.'

'Ah yes,' said the boy. 'Well I thought that now I am in the top class it's about time I should "get with it" as they say. I've had a bit of a makeover.'

'You look very smart,' said Elisabeth.

'And so do you, Mrs Stirling,' replied the boy.

*   *   *

The caretaker was striding down the corridor, grumbling to himself, when the school secretary approached.

'Might I have a word, Mr Gribbon?' she asked.

'Well, make it quick,' he said abruptly, 'I'm a bit busy at the moment.' Then he added, 'And I'm not in the best of moods. I've just seen Mrs Stirling about Hornchurch's classroom.'

'It's the cockroaches I wish to speak to you about,' she told him.

'Oh yes?'

'Must you put that dreadful white powder all down the corridor and attract these dreadful insects? It's most unpleasant every morning having to tiptoe through all these horrible creatures wriggling and writhing on their backs in their death throes.'

'Ah well,' the caretaker told her, 'that's the poison I put down.'

'I am well aware of that,' the secretary snapped. 'You may recall that when we had the school inspection back in Miss Sowerbutts's time, the inspectors made comment on this and recommended it be discontinued. They found it most unpleasant having to run the gauntlet down the corridor when they arrived on the Monday morning.'

'I didn't expect the inspectors to arrive so early,' replied the caretaker. 'They were here at the crack of dawn, like the Gestapo, creeping in unannounced like that in their black suits and faces like death masks. I always have this entire corridor clear of cockroaches by eight, before most people arrive. They were here at the crack of dawn.'

'I arrive sometimes before eight,' she told him. 'It's a good job Mrs Stirling arrived after you had swept the creatures up this morning, otherwise she would most certainly have said something. Why can't you just leave the cockroaches alone? They don't do any harm.'

'That's where you're wrong, Mrs Scrimshaw,' he told her. 'They are nasty, devious, dirty little creatures and need exterminating. Once they get a hold there's no getting rid of them. At this very moment they'll be under them skirting boards breeding like there's no tomorrow. I mean, if I didn't get rid of them you'd be infested in your office with them crawling all over your desk and getting into your drawers.'

'Actually, that's not likely,' came a voice from behind the small bookcase in the school library. Oscar appeared.

'Oh, it's little Lord know-it-all,' grumbled the caretaker. 'What are you doing earwigging on private conversations?'

'I just thought you ought to know that cockroaches are nocturnal, Mr Gribbon,' the child informed him. 'That means they come out at night. They run away if exposed to light.'

'I am aware what nocturnal means,' replied the caretaker angrily.

'They like the dark and the warmth,' continued Oscar, undeterred by the caretaker's sharp manner. 'They come out at night scavenging for food.'

'And if you kids didn't drop your crisps and crumbs all over the floor, they wouldn't come out scavenging for food, would they?'

'There are about thirty species of cockroaches,' said the boy. 'Did you know that?'

'No I didn't and I'm not interested,' replied the caretaker.

'They have a very high resistance to radiation so if there was a nuclear war they would probably survive.'

'Look, I am not interested to hear a lecture from you about cockroaches!' exclaimed Mr Gribbon. 'Now get on with what you were doing and mind your own business.'

At this point Mr Hornchurch arrived ambling down the corridor whistling merrily.

'Lovely morning,' he said in a loud and cheerful voice. 'Makes one glad to be alive, doesn't it?'

The caretaker looked as if he were about to explode.

★   ★   ★

Oscar, always inquisitive, followed the new teacher and stood at the door of his classroom. He peered inside through his large coloured-framed glasses.

'Golly!' he exclaimed.

'Hello,' said the teacher.

'May I come in?' asked Oscar.

'Yes of course,' said Mr Hornchurch.

'My goodness,' said the boy looking around him in wonder, 'it's like Aladdin's cave in here. It's quite amazing.' He looked at one of the objects on a table. 'May I?' he asked.

'Yes of course,' said the teacher, thinking the young man an unusually polite pupil.

Oscar picked up a skull and held it out before him.

'What creature is this?' he asked.

'That is Renard, the fox,' the teacher told him. 'See the sharp teeth. Beautiful creature, the fox, but vicious. They can kill a whole coop of hens by biting off their heads. Have you ever seen a fox pouncing on its prey?'

'No I can't say I have,' replied Oscar, stroking the smooth white surface of the skull.

'It's very interesting,' said Mr Hornchurch. 'Its movement is very characteristic of the fox. It's called the mouse-jump.' The teacher put both his hands before him as if to demonstrate. 'The fox leaps, stiffed-legged, high into the air, arches its back and, keeping its eyes on the target, comes down with a smack, pinning its victim to the ground. The leap may carry the fox as much as ten or more feet in the air.'

'Wow!' exclaimed Oscar, wide-eyed.

'The mouse-jump is used against small animals such as mice and voles which are hidden in the grass. The fox seeks them out by listening for any faint rustlings or watching for any slight movement. It can't see its prey and has no idea what it has caught. It just sort of takes pot-luck. This explains why foxes leave shrews.'

'Why do they leave shrews?' asked the boy, fascinated.

'They don't like the taste of shrews which have a rather unpleasant smell,' answered the teacher.

'That's very interesting,' said Oscar. 'I do like to read up on facts.'

'I am not surprised,' said the teacher. 'A very famous writer called Oscar Wilde said, "young boys have a disgusting appetite for facts".'

'You know about Oscar Wilde?' cried Oscar.

'I do. He is one of my favourite writers.'

'He's my mother's very favourite writer. I was named after him. I love his stories.'

'So do I,' said Mr Hornchurch, 'and his plays and his poems. Have you read *The Ballad of Reading Gaol*?'

'No,' said Oscar. 'I haven't.'

'I shall have to lend you a copy. You can tell me what you think of it.'

'You're Mr Hornchurch the new teacher, aren't you?'

'I am,' he replied, 'and I gather you are Oscar.' He had been told by Elisabeth about this very unusual boy.

'I'm very pleased to meet you,' said Oscar. He held out a hand which the teacher shook.

'And I'm very pleased to meet you too, Oscar,' said the teacher.

'To be honest, I was hoping that I might be in Mrs Stirling's class this year,' said Oscar, 'but having met you I think I should rather prefer to be in yours. I think we could get on famously, don't you?'

'I most certainly do,' said Mr Hornchurch smiling. 'And you *are* in my class. I noticed your name on my list of pupils.'

'Gosh, how super!' cried Oscar.

At that moment another boy appeared at the door. His hands were dug deep in his pockets. He was a small twig of a child with shiny chestnut-brown hair cropped as close as a doormat, a pale freckled face and a small upturned nose. He studied the teacher for a moment with large watchful eyes then scowled and walked away.

'That's Robbie,' explained Oscar in a confidential tone of voice. 'He can be very rude and disobedient and caused quite a lot of trouble last term. I do hope he is not in your class. My mother – she's a qualified psychotherapist and counsellor – knows quite a bit about mixed-up children. She says that boys like Robbie must have a troubled childhood and that they need lots of understanding and patience.'

'That sounds very sensible,' agreed the teacher.

'It's very difficult though, Mr Hornchurch,' sighed Oscar, adjusting his glasses, 'to be understanding and patient when that person calls you a four-eyed git and tells you to bugger off!'

Later that morning, when she saw the rest of the parents arriving with their children, Elisabeth walked slowly down the school path to meet them. She had dressed for the occasion in a smart pale-grey suit, a pearl-coloured silk blouse, plain black stockings and grey patent leather shoes. She had tied her hair back into a neat little bun and wore the minimum of make-up and no jewellery. She wanted to look capable and professional.

It was an unusually large turnout of mothers and fathers standing at the gate that morning. No doubt those from Urebank were intrigued to see the new head teacher about whom they had heard a great deal. Elisabeth smiled and greeted each parent with a friendly 'Good morning'. Most nodded and smiled but stood shyly at the gate.

'Do come through,' Elisabeth told them. 'You can see your children into school if you wish.'

'Mr Richardson liked us to say goodbye to the children at the gate,' said a tall, gaunt woman dressed in tight-fitting jeans.

'Well, I like parents to come into the school,' Elisabeth told her. 'You are all very welcome.'

The woman turned to other parents hovering at the gate. 'That makes a change,' she said and she then walked up the path followed by two pale-faced, nervous-looking boys.

In assembly that morning the children sat cross-legged on the highly polished floor in the school hall. Elisabeth moved to the front and surveyed the faces before her. They were indeed a mixed group: large gangly boys, fresh-faced boys, lean bespectacled boys, chubby boys, girls with long plaits, girls with frizzy bunches of ginger hair, girls thin and tall, dumpy and small. They filled the hot and stuffy room.

'Good morning, children,' she said pleasantly.

'Good morning, Mrs Stirling,' chorused the pupils.

Those who had joined the school from Urebank were silent and wary, staring at her as if she were some rare specimen displayed in a museum case.

Elisabeth introduced herself and said how much she looked forward to getting to know all the new pupils. She then introduced the teachers, the school secretary and the caretaker and described the various exciting activities which hopefully would be on offer that term. She finished by asking the children who lived in Barton to make the new pupils from Urebank feel very welcome.

The morning passed without incident. The children moved around the school in an orderly way, they appeared happy and looked very much at home and when in class were busily occupied. Elisabeth felt well-satisfied. Most gratifying was to see a cheerful countenance on the face of Mr Jolly.

He was on duty in the playground at lunchtime when she approached him.

'And how are things going, Donald?' she asked, rather expecting some negative comment in response.

'Not too bad, not too bad at all,' he said. 'Of course at Urebank where I was the deputy head teacher . . .' he began.

Oh here we go, she thought, *here come the unfavourable comparisons.*

'. . . I had a class of thirty-five,' he continued. 'Of course Mr Richardson, unlike you, did not teach. Had he chosen to do so my class would have been considerably smaller. I must say that here, twenty pupils are much more manageable. They also seem very well-behaved. Of course things might change once they have settled in.'

'And do you miss the responsibility?' asked Elisabeth.

He looked startled.

'What, of being a deputy head teacher?!' he exclaimed. 'Not at all. There was all the paperwork and administration and difficult parents. Mr Richardson tended to ask me to deal with all that. No, I am quite happy to leave all the responsibilities to others. I thought perhaps I might like a senior position again but I am quite contented.' He smiled and wandered off.

Oscar came up, a large book tucked underneath his arm.

'Hello, Oscar,' said Elisabeth brightly. 'And how are you?'

'Oh I'm tip-top, Mrs Stirling,' he replied.

'That's good to hear. And how are you getting on with your new teacher?'

'Oh very well,' replied the boy. 'He is a most fascinating man is Mr Hornchurch. He knows a great deal about many things you know. A bit of a walking encyclopaedia to be honest. We have had a most interesting conversation at morning break about cockroaches.'

'Cockroaches!' exclaimed Elisabeth.

'Yes, he was telling me the word comes from the Spanish *cucaracha* and there were cockroaches fifty million years ago. Fancy that.'

'So what has brought on your interest in cockroaches?' she asked.

'Mr Gribbon,' replied the boy.

'Mr Gribbon!'

'I happened to overhear Mrs Scrimshaw complaining to him about the cockroaches which live behind the woodwork. Mr Gribbon kills them with this white powder which he sprinkles down the corridor at night when the cockroaches come out. It poisons them. Mrs Scrimshaw sometimes arrives at school early, before he has chance to sweep up all the bodies. She doesn't like to see all these dead and dying insects.'

'Ah yes,' said Elisabeth, 'Mrs Scrimshaw has mentioned this to me. I must have a word with Mr Gribbon.'

'Well Mr Hornchurch says there is a better and much cheaper way of killing them than by using poison.'

'Really?'

'You see, you get this large jar and put some food inside and place it with the top touching the wall so the cockroaches can climb up to reach the opening. Once inside they can't get out because the sides of the jar are slippery. You can smear some margarine on the inside of the jar for extra slipperiness. An inch of water in the bottom of the jar will make sure the insects drown. Beer tends to attract the cockroaches more than water so I'm told. It's quite ingenious, isn't it?'

'It is,' said Elisabeth.'

She caught sight of a lonely figure sitting on the wall.

'If you will excuse me, Oscar, I want a word with Robbie,' she said.

'He's been quite well-behaved this morning,' Oscar said confidentially. 'Let's hope it continues.' He then walked away whistling to himself.

'How are you, Robbie?' Elisabeth asked, sitting next to the sullen-faced boy on the wall.

'OK.'

'And how are you getting on with your foster carers?'

'OK.'

'Just OK?'

'I like it there.'

'I'm pleased to hear it. Mr and Mrs Ross are a nice couple, aren't they?'

'Yeah.'

'And do you see anything of your mother?'

The boy looked up at Elisabeth and glared. 'Yeah, I see her sometimes.'

'Don't be too hard on her, Robbie. I'm sure it was a difficult decision for her to put you into care. She still loves you, you know.'

'No she doesn't,' he retorted. 'She chose him before me.'

'I know you didn't get on with your stepfather but—'

'I hate him,' said the boy vehemently. 'It was all right before he came to live with us. She does everything he tells her. He told her it was either him or me and she chose him. End of story. I don't want to see her. It's only because Mrs Ross says I have to.'

'Well perhaps when you get a bit older you'll change your mind.'

'I won't.'

A sad, mixed-up little boy, Elisabeth thought as she heard the bell for the start of afternoon lessons and saw him wander off, hands in pockets and a grim expression on his face.

At the end of the day, when the teachers were meeting in the staffroom, Oscar arrived at the school office to find Mr Gribbon sitting on the corner of the desk jingling his keys and complaining as usual to the school secretary. The caretaker's face dropped when he saw the boy. His eyes narrowed and he looked at him as one who had spotted a slug which had slid out from under some lettuce.

'Hello, Oscar,' said the school secretary. 'And what can I do for you?'

'Oh hello, Mrs Scrimshaw,' said the boy in a cheery, sing-song tone of voice. 'Actually, it's not you I wish to speak to, it's Mr Gribbon.'

'Me?' growled the caretaker. His glance was like the sweep of a scythe. 'And what would you be wanting with me?'

'I've been speaking to Mr Hornchurch.'

At the mention of the name a muscle in the caretaker's cheek jumped and his scowl deepened.

'Oh, have you indeed?' he barked.

'About the cockroaches,' explained the boy.

'What about them?' demanded the caretaker.

Oscar produced a large jar from behind his back and held it up.

'I think we have found the answer to your cockroach problem,' said the boy, 'without using poison.'

The caretaker breathed in noisily though his nose like a horse and gripped his keys tightly.

'Shall I show you what to do with this?' asked Oscar cheerfully.

6

'I don't see why you should have to go and see her,' said Mrs Sparshott in a brittle tone of voice. She was ensconced on the sofa by the window in the rectory sitting room with her knitting upon her lap. 'These titled people think everyone should be at their beck and call. Gone are the days when clergymen owed their livelihoods to these people and had to kowtow to the lords of the manor to secure a living. Why couldn't she bestir herself and come to the rectory if it was so important for her to see you?'

Lady Wadsworth's butler had telephoned the day before making an appointment for his mistress to see the cleric at Limebeck House that morning.

'I have nothing pressing to attend to this morning,' Mr Sparshott told her. 'It's not such a great inconvenience for me to see her and the fresh air will do me good. Quite apart from that, I am quite interested to see Limebeck House.'

'Of course the invitation did not extend to myself,' said the vicar's wife sounding peeved. 'As I have said, if she wanted to see you, why couldn't she bestir herself and come to the rectory?'

'She is quite an influential person, my dear Rosamund,' said her husband.

'Eccentric rather than influential I should say,' ventured Mrs Sparshott, picking up her knitting and clacking the needles.

'I own she is a somewhat eccentric woman,' the Reverend

Mr Sparshott told his wife. 'You may recall she introduced the musical evening we attended, the one arranged by Dr Underwood.'

'I do,' replied his wife, recalling the occasion when Lady Wadsworth had made her grand entrance into St Christopher's for the organ recital. The lady of the manor, a gaunt and rather ungainly woman, had dressed for the occasion in her brightest summer ensemble – a shapeless multi-coloured cotton tent of a dress, a huge red hat with a feather and spotless white gloves. She had been liberally bedecked in an assortment of heavy, expensive-looking jewellery. With the wave of bright russet-coloured hair and the lipstick as thick and red as congealed blood, she had looked like some large exotic bird.

'What does she want to see you about anyway?' asked the new vicar's wife, ceasing her clacking.

'I have no idea,' replied her husband.

'Of course she's not of an old family,' remarked his wife. 'I gather that her great grandfather, the first viscount, purchased the title and then married some rich American heiress.'

'So I believe,' said the new vicar. 'Well I had better be off.'

'The Reverend Mr Sparshott,' announced the butler, showing the new vicar into the library at Limebeck House.

The lady of the manor rose regally from a huge plum-red, upholstered armchair to greet her visitor. At her feet a small bristly haired terrier scurried around her, gave a rumble like a distant train and displayed a set of sharp teeth. The new vicar remained at the door and eyed the dog suspiciously.

'Mr Sparshott,' said Lady Wadsworth, extending a hand, 'do come in.'

She shook her visitor's hand which she found to be disconcertingly moist.

The dog growled ominously.

'Don't mind Gordon, he's all bark and no bite.' She chuckled.

The butler gave a small cough.

'Well, he did bite the postman once but he is not keen on anyone in uniform.' The dog raised its head, yapped and then growled threateningly. 'Be quiet, Gordon! He was a rescue dog, an unwanted Christmas present and thrown in the river in a sack. Can you conceive of anyone being so cruel? Having been treated thus he is very suspicious of people and particular about whom he likes and whom he doesn't.'

The dog cocked its head and looked at her as if understanding what was being said. Then it gave a low growl again. It was clear to Lady Wadsworth that the dog did not like this particular visitor.

'Thank you for coming to see me,' said Lady Wadsworth. 'Do take a seat.' She gestured towards a chair and sat down.

The new vicar perched on the edge of a small French gilt chair carved in an ornate style, placed his hands together on his lap and looked around the room. It was far too ostentatious for his liking with its imposing carved marble fireplace, bearing the Wadsworth coat of arms, the heavy burgundy velvet drapes and the huge patterned Persian silk carpet.

Lady Wadsworth put on a pair of small gold-rimmed spectacles and observed her visitor for a moment. She noted that his eyes were drawn to the enormous portrait in oils which dominated the room. It was of a portentous-looking individual attired in scarlet robes. He stared from the canvas sententiously and bore an unnerving resemblance to the lady sitting before him.

'My grandfather, the second Viscount,' Lady Wadsworth told him.

'Really.'

'You will no doubt have seen his statue in the centre of the village.'

The cleric had indeed seen the pretentious edifice which dominated the high street. It was impossible for anyone to miss it. The great dull-bronze figure of the peer attired in military uniform stood on a large plinth enclosed in fancy black iron railings.

'The second viscount had great influence in the area,' continued Lady Wadsworth, 'and was involved in local and national politics and the church. It was he who decided which clergyman should have the living on the estate. He even controlled admissions to the hospitals and workhouse. He endowed the village school which was originally intended for the children of the estate workers. The school was given over to the Local Education Authority in the 1920s.'

'Really.'

'He was something of a writer too, as indeed were several of my forebears. A distant cousin was a bishop of some remote outpost of the Empire and was a most prolific essayist. Bishop Thaddeus Pratt. You may have come across his work.' She gestured to a wall lined in highly polished mahogany shelving and crammed with leather-bound books. '*The Sunny Side of Bereavement, Flashes from the African Pulpit, Highlights of the Reformation.* Do they ring any bells?'

'Sadly, I am not acquainted with those works,' admitted the cleric.

'How he found the time to write I do not know,' observed Lady Wadsworth.

'If one wants anything done,' said the new vicar, giving a small humourless smile, 'one should always ask a busy man.'

'Or a busy woman,' said Lady Wadsworth. She turned to the butler. 'Watson, you may bring us some coffee now please.'

The butler nodded and departed.

'And how are you settling in at St Christopher's?' she asked.

'It is early days,' the new vicar replied, 'but I am sure my wife and family will get used to village life in time. At Marfleet, where I was the curate, the parish was much larger.'

The butler arrived with a silver tray on which had been arranged an elegant silver coffeepot, two delicate china cups and saucers and a silver jug, sugar bowl, tongs and spoons. On a large china plate was a selection of biscuits and a solid block of fruit cake.

'Ah, the coffee,' said Lady Wadsworth. 'Do you take sugar?'

'Thank you, no,' replied the new vicar.

'A biscuit, a piece of cake?'

'Thank you, no.'

Watson poured the coffee, gave a slight bow and departed.

'I am sure you are very sorry to have lost your curate. I heard just this morning that she is leaving.'

'Dr Underwood will be working at Cathedral Close for the bishop. She is to become his chaplain, a post for which she will be eminently qualified,' said the clergyman, reaching for a cup and saucer. 'I think that line of work will suit her admirably.'

'I am sure you are right. Someone of her undoubted talents is able turn their hand to anything.'

'Indeed.'

'Milk? Sugar?' asked Lady Wadsworth.

'Thank you, no. I take it black without sugar,' she was told.

'Dr Underwood will be greatly missed,' said Lady Wadsworth, helping herself to a coffee. She lifted the delicate china cup between forefinger and thumb and took a sip. 'She has made a great impact in the short time she has been with us; a most personable and hard-working young woman. Of course some of the changes she introduced at St Christopher's did not go down too well with myself and a few of our older members of the congregation.' Lady Wadsworth took another sip of her coffee, before selecting a biscuit which she crunched noisily.

The Reverend Mr Sparshott placed his cup and saucer on a small table next to him. He sat up in his chair and looked interested.

'Really?'

It was the first occasion he had heard anyone voice a criticism of the former curate. It seemed the entire village had nothing but praise for her. After a while it had become rather tiresome.

'I was not in favour of her introducing the modern hymns, the new order of service and the use of a contemporary bible,' Lady Wadsworth told him. 'I make no apology when I admit to being a traditionalist. I appreciate Dr Underwood was endeavouring to attract some younger people to the services but I tend to be very traditional in my views and dislike change.'

'Well on that we can agree,' said the new vicar, suddenly becoming animated and with a determined gleam in his eye. 'I am not in favour myself of modern hymns and the contemporary bible and intend, as long as I am vicar here, to honour the long-established and time-honoured Protestant traditions and services of the established church. I have a great admiration for the immense courage of the Protestant reformers such as Calvin and Luther. In my view, the Reformation revealed the true path to Almighty God. There is no necessity for a priest to intervene when communicating with God, no need for churches dripping with gold and garish coloured statues and prelates in their rich vestments. I have no time for bells and incense for, to be frank, I eschew all ostentation in church. I am in favour of the plainness and the modesty of nonconformity and—'

'My goodness, you do feel very strongly about things, Mr Sparshott,' interrupted Lady Wadsworth, thinking the man sounded rather deranged. She was certainly not going to submit herself to one of his interminable sermons like the one she had endured at his first service. She quickly changed the subject.

'I have not invited you here to talk about such matters, thought-provoking as they may be. The reason I asked to see you was with regard to the window.'

'The window?' said the cleric, looking puzzled.

'The proposed stained-glass window to be installed at St Christopher's.'

'I am afraid I know nothing of a proposed window at St Christopher's,' he replied. He leant forward and looked at her enquiringly.

'Dr Underwood didn't mention it to you?'

'No, she didn't.'

'Well, let me explain,' said Lady Wadsworth. 'I was minded to have a plaque placed in the church – a brass tablet in the nave or the chancel commemorating my brother who was killed in the last war. I did mention on several occasions to the archdeacon my desire to have such a memorial in St Christopher's, but he was so very busy and we never got around to it. I broached the matter with Dr Underwood.' She stood and walked to the fireplace where she pointed to the coat-of-arms. 'I originally thought a plaque with the Wadsworth crest and motto and with some appropriate words would be in order. But then Dr Underwood suggested something she felt would be much more fitting: a commemorative stained-glass window in memory of my brother. I thought it an excellent idea and readily acquiesced. It would be called the Wadsworth Memorial Window.' She went to a small gilt desk with gold tasselled drawers, produced a folder and returned to her chair. 'Now I have had an artist come up with what I consider to be a most impressive design—'

'One moment, Lady Wadsworth,' the new vicar cut in. 'I have not been acquainted with this.'

The lady of the manor looked over her small gold-rimmed

spectacles and observed him for a moment. It was evident from the severe expression of irritation on her face that she was not pleased at being halted mid-sentence.

'I am acquainting it with you now,' she replied rather sharply. Her heavy-lidded eyes were intent and shone with derisive appraisal. She was not used to being interrupted and certainly not in her own house. She continued to fix the new vicar with a piercing stare.

'To be frank I am not in favour of stained-glass windows any more than coloured statues and bells and incense,' said the Reverend Mr Sparshott. He tilted his head to one side and pressed his fingertips together. 'As I alluded to earlier, I favour a plain church.'

'You mean austere and dull,' she remarked. The edge in her voice was evident.

'I should prefer to say unadorned,' replied the cleric with a dry little smile.

A look of distaste passed carefully across Lady Wadsworth's features. She bristled with indignation. Her jaw was rigid. She shut her eyes for a moment, as if composing herself before she spoke.

'So I take it you are opposed to my memorial window?' she asked.

With the small down-turned mouth of a peevish child, the new vicar nodded.

'I am afraid so,' he replied.

'Are you telling me, Mr Sparshott, that you will not allow me to have a memorial window in memory of my dear brother who gave his life for his country?' Her face was tight and angry.

'I must remain true to my principles, Lady Wadsworth,' the new vicar informed her haughtily and laying himself open to a crushing rejoinder. 'To be frank, I feel the money you would expend on such a memorial might be better used to help pay for the leaking roof at St Christopher's.' He couldn't help overhearing some local gossipers talking about some statues that Lady Wadsworth had found that had ended up earning her a tidy sum and hoped her revived tenacity for the scheme was not down to that.

'How I spend my money, Mr Sparshott,' replied Lady Wadsworth, making a supreme effort of self-control, 'is up to me.'

'Of course and—'

'And I do not need you to advise me on how to spend it.' The vicar did not respond. 'So I take it you will not sanction my window?'

The atmosphere was heavy with resentment.

'No, I am afraid I will not,' the new vicar replied.

Lady Wadsworth thumped the folder down on the small table beside her and picked up a small brass bell which she rang vigorously

'Well, there is nothing more to say,' she said, giving him a glare of Gorgon ferocity.

They sat in strained silence until the arrival of the butler.

'Mr Sparshott is going,' said Lady Wadsworth. 'Please show him out.' The new vicar stood, gave a slight bow and wished his host a 'Good afternoon'.

Lady Wadsworth responded with a slight nod of the head.

Fred Massey, a stocky, heavily wrinkled farmer with a ruddy complexion and a mane of thick, ill-cut hair beneath a greasy cap was herding his cattle down the well-trodden track by the side of St Christopher's church. He was a tight-fisted, bad-tempered old man disliked by all in the village for he rarely had a good word to say about anyone, constantly moaned and groaned about how badly he had it in life and never missed the opportunity of making as much money as he could with the least amount of effort. Most of the work on his smallholding, where he kept cattle and a few sheep, and the odd jobs which came his way in the village – repairing walls, pruning trees, killing vermin, clearing blocked drains – he delegated to his long-suffering nephew, Clarence. That morning Fred was in a particularly ill-tempered mood because Clarence and his young wife Bianca had taken their little baby Brandon to the doctor for his injections and he had been compelled to herd the cattle to the field behind the church himself.

Fred urged the sluggish cows down the rough track shouting and cursing. The animals jostled and pushed at each other, lowing in complaint at the narrowness of the road. A black and white sheepdog ran at their heels, snapping and plunging to keep the bumbling beasts going forward.

The new vicar, on his way back from Limebeck House, approached Fred with a determined step, his countenance dramatically tight-lipped and solemn.

'Might I have a word?' asked Mr Sparshott.

'Aye, you can,' replied Fred. 'Are you the new vicar?'

'I am indeed.'

'I thought you were. What is it?' asked Fred.

'I take it these are your cows?'

'They are.'

'Are you are aware that this track is church property?'

Fred's eyes narrowed and his forehead furrowed.

'I am. What about it?'

'Who gave you the permission to use it?' he was asked.

'Reverend Atticus, who was vicar here afore you, let me bring my beasts down the track to yon field what I own at the back of the church.'

'Are you unable to take your animals by another route?' asked the vicar.

'No.'

'Well I am not happy about you bringing them down here.'

'Not happy!' repeated Fred stridently.

'Not happy at all,' said Mr Sparshott. 'The animals are not only very noisy and disturb my wife who is a very light sleeper but they are extremely smelly and attract a great many flies. They also leave behind a . . . a . . . most unfortunate ordure.'

'A what?'

'Manure, dung,' explained the new vicar.

'Cows can't help that, Vicar,' replied Fred. 'They're God's creatures, as I'm sure you don't need reminding. Animals don't use flushing lavatories as you well know.'

'Indeed I do know,' said Mr Sparshott. 'The smell is very obvious and obnoxious. Now, as I have told you, I am far from happy about you bringing your cows down this track.'

'Beg pardon?'

The vicar sighed. 'Look, Mr . . . ?'

'Massey. Fred Massey.'

'Look, Mr Massey, I do not wish to debate this any further. I am extremely busy this morning.'

'I'm busy as well,' said Fred crossly, 'so I'd best be getting on.' He turned to go.

'One moment, Mr Massey, I have not finished,' said the new vicar. 'As I have just said, I am not happy about you bringing your cows down this track so in future would you desist from doing so.'

'Desist?'

'Refrain from using the track as a thoroughfare.'

'Refrain!' repeated Fred. 'Not bring my beasts down the track?'

'That is what I said. I should prefer that in future you do not bring your cows down there.'

'Not bring my cows down there,' he repeated loudly, sounding like an echo. 'I've allus brought my beasts down there. Reverend Atticus had no problem with me using the track.'

'Archdeacon Atticus is no longer the vicar here. I am.'

'I don't believe what I'm hearing,' growled Fred.

The new vicar, observed by his wife from the rectory window, turned to go.

'Hang on, hang on, vicar!' exclaimed Fred. 'If you think you can come here into our village and start laying down the law, then you've another think coming. You may try and rule the roost in that church of yours telling people what are in your congregation what to do but you're not getting away with it with me. I've lived in Barton-in-the-Dale man and boy as have my ancestors and no off-comed-un's telling me what I should and what I shouldn't do. I shall carry on using that track and grazing my cattle and my sheep on yon field as I've done before and nobody will stop me.'

'I think you will find, Mr Massey,' the new vicar informed him sternly, 'that they can and they will. Since you have brought your cows here today you may use the track this once but in future they are not to be brought here, and if you continue to trespass on church property I shall have to resort to taking legal action to prevent you from doing so. And another thing, I believe you are responsible for the rubble in the churchyard and you have been asked to remove it. Please do so. Good day to you.'

'You've not heard the last of this!' shouted Fred, stabbing a bony finger at the departing figure. 'Not by a long chalk.'

The following week, a wet and unusually chilly autumn day, a tall gangly lad with long, thin arms, long, thin legs and wild, woolly red hair appeared at the end of the track by the side of the church behind a herd of cows. This was Clarence, Fred's forbearing nephew, described by Mrs Sloughthwaite in the village store and post office as 'a nice enough lad, but limp under the cap'. He was whistling to himself as he prodded the cows gently with a stick. Suddenly the creatures came to a halt. Investigating, Clarence found ahead was a new heavy metal gate stretched across the top of the track, a long chain and two substantial padlocks. Displayed on the front was a large sign which stated in black lettering **PRIVATE! CHURCH PROPERTY**.

'I do not know who you are,' said Mr Sparshott, striding purposefully toward him and pointing a long finger, 'but remove those animals from the track immediately.'

The new vicar's wife, on the lookout at the rectory window, had seen the progress of the animals as they approached the church and had quickly summoned her husband from his study.

Mr Sparshott, with his narrow bony white features and large, pale penetrating eyes, looked to the startled Clarence like a character from a horror film. He had emerged from behind the tombstones in the churchyard dressed in a long flowing black cape; the clergyman looked like Count Dracula himself. The boy jumped and fell back onto the ground.

'Did you hear me, young man?' asked the new vicar. 'Remove those animals at once.'

'I...I...I've come to take the beasts into the field,' Clarence stuttered.

'Can you not read?' demanded the cleric.

'P...pardon?'

'There is a sign on the gate which states quite clearly that this is private property.'

'I...I...I've come to take the beasts into the field,' Clarence repeated. 'I've been told to by my Uncle Fred.'

'Well, you can't,' the new vicar told him.

'P...pardon?'

'I am assuming that your uncle is Mr Massey?'

'Y...y...yes, he is.'

'Well you can remind him that this track is private property.'

'P...pardon?'

'It is off limits.'

'M . . . my Uncle Fred said I had to bring them . . .' stammered Clarence, now getting to his feet and brushing down his soiled blue overalls.

'Well, you can't. Your Uncle Fred has been informed he no longer has access via this track. He had no business sending you with these animals.'

'I . . . I have to put the beasts in the field,' said Clarence. He looked desperate.

'Did you not hear what I said, young man?' snapped the new vicar. 'I have just told you that this track is inaccessible for him and his cows.'

'B . . . but . . . m . . . my Uncle Fred told me to do it.' He swallowed nervously, his gullet moving up and down like a frog's.

'I really do not care what your Uncle Fred has told you to do, young man, I am telling you to take your animals elsewhere.'

'I'm bringing the sheep down later on,' said Clarence.

'You are most certainly not!' exclaimed the new vicar. 'Now take these animals away and tell that uncle of yours not to bring them back.'

'H . . . H . . . He'll not like it,' muttered Clarence. 'He'll not like it at all.'

'He's only put two big bloody padlocks and a chain on the gate to my field!' cried Fred, red in the face with anger.

The old farmer was propping up the bar in the Blacksmith's Arms at lunchtime the following day and regaling the landlord and anyone else in hearing distance with an account of the altercation he had had with the new vicar and how his nephew had been turned away from the rectory.

'But it's not your property, Fred,' the landlord told him.

'Neither is it his,' retorted Fred. 'It belongs to the church.

He doesn't own it. He's been in the village no time at all and he's laying down the law. Anyway, I shall take a pair of bloody big bolt-cutters and make short work of those padlocks and chain. He can't stop me using the track.'

Major Neville-Gravitas, sitting on a stool at the end of the bar, nursing a glass of malt whisky, was enjoying Fred's discomfiture. He found the old farmer an insufferable man.

'I think he can,' he said casually.

'What's that?' snapped Fred.

'I said that I think the new vicar, as the custodian of church property, is quite within his rights to prevent you using the track,' the major told him, 'and I think it very inadvisable to remove the locks and chain. That would be construed as a wilful act of vandalism and if you used the track without permission, that would be construed as trespassing.'

'Who asked you for your opinion?' barked Fred.

'Just giving you the benefit of the facts. The vicar is responsible for church property and as such is quite within his rights to stop people trespassing upon it.'

'For your information I'm not trespassing!' cried Fred. 'I've a right to use that track.'

'I think you will find you do not,' the major informed him.

'Yes, well let him try and prevent me. What's he going to do – stand in the middle of the track all day barring my way? And if he does try and stop me, he'll soon shift himself when a herd of hungry cows come galloping towards him.'

'You'll receive a summons,' the major told Fred, 'and you will be required to appear in the County Court and no doubt be fined or even imprisoned.'

'I don't recall asking for the advice of some barrack-room lawyer like you,' Fred told him angrily. He took a gulp of beer.

'Just acquainting you with the consequences of flouting the law,' said the major, finishing his tipple.

'If I was the vicar I wouldn't object to somebody using the track,' Fred told him.

'But you are not the vicar,' retorted the major, 'and it is easy to be generous with other people's property, not that you know the meaning of the word generous.'

'Another top-up, Major?' asked the landlord. He too was enjoying Fred's tribulation.

'Just the ticket,' said Major Neville-Gravitas, 'and make it one for yourself too, my good man.' He stroked his moustache and looked around smiling.

'Thank you kindly, Major,' said the landlord.

'And how are you, landlord, on this bright summer day?' asked Major Neville-Gravitas.

'I'm fine, thank you, Major. How about you?'

'Tip-top.'

Fred scowled, downed the remains of his pint and, grumbling to himself, slid off the bar stool and left the pub.

'It does one's heart good to see the old curmudgeon get his come-uppance,' said the major when the farmer had banged out of the door.

Fred, still grumbling to himself, made his way down the high street to the village store. His eyes were puffy and bloodshot. He threw open the door, jangled the bell nosily and strode towards the counter smelling of slurry and wood smoke.

'Give us twenty of them tipped,' he said glumly, thrusting out his obstinate jaw and pointing to the display of cigarettes behind the counter.

Mrs Sloughthwaite folded her arms across her ample bosom and adopted a face as blank and stony as a sphinx. 'And the magic word?' she asked, sounding like a teacher speaking to a naughty child.

'What?'

'There is such a word as "please",' she told him. 'I've told you before, Fred Massey, if you can't be better-mannered then I shall not serve you.'

'Look, just give us the fags,' chuntered Fred and then added, 'if you please. I'm not in the mood for small talk.'

The shopkeeper reached for a packet of cigarettes and placed them on the counter. Fred snatched them up and thrust them in the pocket of his overalls. Then he poured out the contents of a battered purse and counted out the money in silver and copper coins.

'You're in a right old mood this morning and no mistake,' said the shopkeeper. 'You've got a face like a smacked bottom as my mother would say and what's wrong with your eyes? They look as if they've been stung by a flock of bees.'

'I *am* in a right mood,' said Fred. 'You're right there. And I don't feel well at all. I didn't get a wink of sleep last night what with the baby bawling its head off. Got some sort of reaction to the injections it's had. Then Bianca told our Clarence he had to go with her to the doctor's and then into Clayton this afternoon to help with the shopping. Under her thumb is the lad. Then I've had another skirmish with that new vicar.'

'From what I hear, a lot of people have had entretendes with him,' said the shopkeeper. 'You're not alone in that. So what was it about, this altercation?'

'Puffed up like a Christmas turkey,' seethed Fred. 'Tells me I can't take my beasts down yon track by the church. Put a big bloody notice up on the gate saying it's church property and two big bloody iron padlocks and a heavy chain. Then, when Clarence went there yesterday, he found the gate locked and bolted and the vicar gave him a right old earful. I'm not having it. I shall go and see Archdeacon Atticus and the bishop and take it all the way to the pope in Rome if I have to.'

Mrs Sloughthwaite gave a deep, throaty laugh. 'I should imagine the pope in Rome has enough on his plate without trying to sort out the problems with your cows and, anyway, he has no jurisprediction in England, something you would know, Fred Massey, if you ever set foot in St Christopher's.'

The doorbell rang and Ashley entered the shop.

'Good morning,' she said brightly. 'What a lovely day.'

'I don't think Fred here thinks it's a good morning, Dr Underwood,' said Mrs Sloughthwaite, 'or a lovely day, do you Fred?'

'Oh dear,' said Ashley, looking at the scowling face of the farmer. 'What's upset you, Mr Massey?'

'I'll tell you what's upset me,' he told her angrily. 'It's that sidekick of yours.'

'My sidekick?'

'That there new vicar.'

'And how has Mr Sparshott upset you?' she asked, exchanging a glance with the shopkeeper and resisting the impulse to smile.

'He's stopping me taking my beasts down that track by the rectory to my field at the back of the church,' Fred told her. 'Reverend Atticus had no problem with it but this new chap says I can't. He's put a big iron gate up with a chain and padlocks.'

'Isn't there another access to your field?' she asked.

'Aye, there is by that cottage what you're renting off of Mrs Stirling but *she* won't let me use that track either.'

'Why is that?'

'It's because she parked her car there,' said the farmer. 'I couldn't get my beasts down that track with her car in the way and if I could she said she wouldn't want all those dirty smelly creatures trampling in the mud and leaving a mess.'

'I don't have a car,' said Ashley.

'Beg pardon?' said Fred.

'I said, I don't own a car.'

'So what are you saying?'

'I wouldn't object if you wanted to use the track. Of course

I should have to ask Mrs Stirling if it would be all right but I'm sure she wouldn't mind. You would need to clear up any mess though.'

Fred's face lit up with a smile. 'Well could you have word with her?'

'I'll ring her when I get back.'

'If you weren't a woman of the cloth I'd kiss you,' said Fred in uncharacteristic good humour.

Ashley looked at the heavily wrinkled face, the discoloured teeth and the week-old stubble on his chin as grey as smoke and was relieved he made no move to do so.

'So you won't be getting in touch with the pope then, Fred?' asked Mrs Sloughthwaite, leaning on the counter.

7

On Friday afternoon Elisabeth decided to visit the Urebank site to see how Miss Kennedy and the staff were getting on.

'I'll see you tomorrow morning, Elsie,' she told Mrs Robertshaw at lunchtime. 'You know where I am if you need me but I can't imagine there will be any crisis.' In this, she was proved to be very wrong.

At Urebank Elisabeth was well pleased with what she saw. The walls were resplendent with the pupils' paintings, sketches, drawings, poems and stories, all of which were carefully double-mounted and clearly labelled. Shelves held glossy-backed picture books, small tables had vases of bright flowers, and there were corners which had little easy chairs and large fat cushions where children could relax and read.

'My goodness, Moira,' she told the deputy head teacher as they toured the building, 'you've done marvels in such a short space of time.'

'I can't take the credit for this,' Miss Kennedy told her. 'All the staff have got involved. I do think a bright and colourful environment is so important.'

'Well it's looking wonderful,' Elisabeth told her.

The deputy head teacher looked pleased with the compliment.

At the sight of a small thin-faced woman with purple-tinted hair who was busy dusting the shelves on the corridor, Miss Kennedy said loudly enough to be overheard, 'I must say we have Mrs Pugh to thank as well for getting the school so ship-shape.'

'Oh,' said the caretaker, swivelling around.

'Hello, Mrs Pugh,' replied Elisabeth brightly. 'The school does indeed look spick-and-span.'

'I like things tidy,' said the caretaker quietly before resuming her dusting.

It had been a difficult time the previous term for Mrs Pugh. As a part-time cleaner at Barton, she had complained about the unwanted attentions of Mr Gribbon and her husband had arrived at the school 'to punch the man's lights out'. It had been decided that for all concerned she should move well away from Mr Gribbon and a positive of the amalgamation was that she was able to work at the other site.

'We've made a real effort to make the school look cheerful and welcoming,' said Miss Kennedy, 'for the visitation next week.'

'The visitation?' repeated Elisabeth looking puzzled.

'The dreaded school inspector. The district HMI is paying us a visit next Thursday.'

'Ah yes,' said Elisabeth. 'I did receive a letter informing me that Mr Steel would be calling. Evidently the inspectors have been asked to report on early education and reading in particular.'

'I can't say that I am looking forward to that,' said Miss Kennedy. 'In my experience, inspectors are very good at criticising and not very good at advising. The head teacher I worked with at my last school compared them to savage and tenacious Rottweilers, the only difference being that the Rottweiler eventually lets go.'

'I think you will find Mr Steel is not at all like that,' Elisabeth told her. 'I have found him to be very accommodating and supportive. In fact he has been most helpful to me in the past and when he sees what you are achieving here I am sure, like me, he will be very impressed.'

'I hope so. Do you wish to come down when he's here?' enquired Miss Kennedy.

'No, I think I'll pass on that,' replied Elisabeth, 'unless of course you particularly want me to join you.'

'I am sure I can manage,' said the deputy head teacher.

She was pleased that Elisabeth had enough confidence in her abilities to let her take charge. It was clear that the head teacher was not one to interfere if things were going well.

On a tour of the school, Elisabeth asked Miss Kennedy how the teachers were getting on.

'Very well, all things considered,' she was told. 'Miss Wilson is excellent and Mrs Ryan and Mrs Hawthorn are pleasant and willing enough, if a little old-fashioned. I've just about managed to persuade them to abandon the dreadful old reading scheme. It's a pretty solid team and we all get on well.'

'That's good to hear,' said Elisabeth, feeling relieved.

'And how are things at the Barton site?'

'Pretty much the same. Everything seems to be going smoothly.'

Had Elisabeth known what was occurring at the other site at that very moment, she would not have ventured such an opinion.

Miss Wilson was delighted to see her when Elisabeth entered her classroom.

'Now, children,' said the teacher, 'here is Mrs Stirling, who teaches at the big school and has come to see us.'

'Good morning, Mrs Stirling,' chanted the children, 'good morning, everybody.'

'Good morning,' replied Elisabeth. 'What a lovely welcome.'

'Would you like to see what we are doing?' asked Miss Wilson.

'I should love to,' Elisabeth replied.

The children were busily engaged in a range of activities.

Some were reading on a small carpet in the corner of the room, others painting at their desks and several were in the 'Home Corner' wearing different dressing-up costumes.

Elisabeth joined a six-year-old girl. Her hair was raven-black and she had the bluest eyes Elisabeth had ever seen – large, open, honest eyes, with long, dark lashes.

'Hello,' she said.

'Hello,' the child replied.

'And what's your name?'

'Poppy,' said the girl. 'I'm six, going on seven. I'm big for my age.'

Elisabeth smiled. Children of this age were so forthright and friendly.

'Would you like to hear me read?' asked the child.

'I should like that very much,' replied Elisabeth.

'I'm a very good reader, you know,' she said. 'I use expression.'

'Do you?'

'And I can do different voices.'

'Really?

'I'm on free readers now,' said the girl. 'I used to be on the Rectum Readers when I was in Mrs Ryan's class but I didn't like them. You started on Rectum Red Book One and ended on Rectum Violet Book Ten. They seemed to go on for ever and ever. I was glad to be off the Rectum Readers and get on to proper books.'

'Actually I think they're called the Spectrum Readers,' Elisabeth told her, smiling.

'Whatever,' said the child. 'They were really really boring. Miss Wilson thought they were boring as well and she's put them away in her storeroom. These books are much better. More interesting.'

'So what is the book about that you're reading now?' asked Elisabeth.

'It's called, *When I Grow Up*. Shall I start?'

'Yes please.'

The girl gave a small cough and began to read:

> '"When I grow up," Elizabeth said, "a princess I will be,
>   with a crown on my head and a cloak of red.
>   And the crowds will stare at me.
>   But I am rather shy," she said with a sigh,
>   "So that won't do for me."'

'My name's Elisabeth,' the child was told, 'and when I was a little girl, I dreamt of being like the princess in the fairy story.'

'I don't want to be a princess,' said the girl, shaking her head.

'And what would you like to be when you grow up?' asked Elisabeth.

'Oh, I want to be a teacher,' said the child with a smile on her face, 'so I can boss people about.'

Elisabeth was pleased to see that the two former teachers at Urebank, Maureen Hawthorn and Margaret Ryan, had settled in so well. They were making a clear effort to get on with Miss Kennedy and embrace the changes that were taking place and seemed very happy with the new set-up.

Elisabeth had held certain reservations about the two infant teachers when she had first met them at a meeting at County Hall to discuss the amalgamation. They had sat together, cradling large imitation-leather handbags on their knees and said very little. They looked so different from Miss Wilson the infant teacher at Barton-in-the Dale; Rebecca Wilson was a slim young woman with short raven-black hair, a pale, delicately boned face and great blue eyes. These two women were of indeterminate age and remarkably similar in appearance. Both had short steely-grey hair and wide faces and both were dressed in brightly coloured floral dresses and cardigans and wore beads and matching earrings. Elisabeth imagined that these two teachers would be very traditional in their teaching and rather set in their ways. When she came to Urebank before the amalgamation to speak to the parents however, she found to her surprise that the two women were friendly and good-humoured. Their classrooms were the brightest and tidiest in the school and Elisabeth was impressed with the quality of the work the children had produced. She knew she would get on with them.

On the way to assembly that morning, a small girl with wide, cornflower-blue eyes and a mass of blonde hair which was gathered in two large candyfloss bunches approached Elisabeth.

'Hello,' she said.

'Hello,' replied Elisabeth.

'Are you coming into our assembly?' asked the child pertly.

'I am.'

'My name's Paige Cosgrove,' said the girl, 'and I have a brother at the big school. His name's Barnabas. Do you know him?'

'Yes I have met him,' said Elisabeth.

'We sing hymns in assembly,' said the girl.

'And what are you going to sing today?'

'"The Damp Settee."'

'I don't think I know that one,' said Elisabeth.

'Oh I thought everyone knows "The Damp Settee",' said the girl before skipping off.

In assembly the children, silent and smiling, sat cross-legged on the highly polished floor in the school hall. Miss Kennedy introduced the new head teacher who she said was based with the older children at Barton. Elisabeth said how much she looked forward to getting to know everyone.

Miss Kennedy turned to the teacher perched on the piano stool.

'Now let's have our hymn please, Mrs Ryan. Stand up children, nice and smartly, deep breaths and let's show Mrs Stirling how well we can sing.'

Elisabeth was intrigued to hear a rendering of 'The Damp Settee'.

And the children began, with Paige on the front row, singing with great gusto.

'. . . I am the Lord of the damp settee,
   And I'll lead you all wherever you may be,
   And I'll lead you all to the damp settee.'

In the staffroom at morning break the teachers chuckled when Elisabeth related what the child had said.

'I remember,' said Mrs Ryan, 'that when I was a girl we would deliberately sing the alternative words to the carol "While shepherds watched their flocks by night" as "While shepherds washed their socks at night". Sometimes, however, we would genuinely mishear the words of the carol. We used to sing "Get dressed ye married gentlemen, let nothing through this May" and "Good King Wences' car backed out on the feet of heathens".'

'Your story of "The Damp Settee" reminds me of one my father told to me,' Miss Kennedy told Elisabeth. 'He was a teacher in a primary school in Wetherby, West Yorkshire. It had a great musical tradition and one year the choir won the National Schools' Singing Competition. They had a visit from a very important school inspector called Mr Clarke, a lovely man with a great sense of humour and a deep knowledge of music. Now I should tell you that many of the children and the head teacher, having lived all their lives in the county, had strong Yorkshire accents.

"What are the children going to sing for me?" the visiting HMI asked the head teacher.

"Wetherby Socks," came the reply.

"Ah, a traditional Yorkshire folk song?" asked the visitor.

"Naw," said the head teacher. "It's a reight famous un. I'm surprised tha's not 'eard on it."

Then the children sang the well-known setting of the Shakespeare song, "Where the bee sucks".'

Elisabeth left Urebank well pleased with what she had seen and heard that morning.

At Barton things were not going so smoothly. Just after Elisabeth had left, Mr Gribbon informed Mrs Robertshaw that he had closed the boys' toilets because a blockage had caused a minor flood. The boys would have to use the girls' toilets for the time being. Chaos ensued.

'Another bloody blockage,' the caretaker grumbled as he made his way down the corridor wielding a large plunger.

Then Mrs Scrimshaw refused to go back into her office until Mr Gribbon got rid of a pile of dead cockroaches which had been swept into the corner by her office and been forgotten about. When Mr Gribbon had disposed of the insects and sprinkled his poisonous white powder generously over the office floor, the telephone rang shrilly and Mr Nettles the education officer announced down the line that he would be calling into school that afternoon to monitor how things were going.

'Not today thank you!' snapped Mrs Robertshaw thumping down the receiver.

Now weary and harassed, the assistant head teacher returned to her classroom for the start of afternoon lessons to find one of her fussiest pupils awaiting her.

'I've got tummy ache, miss,' the child whimpered.

Barely had she sat the child down and given her a glass of water when another child appeared at the classroom door with a nosebleed.

'Mr Hornchurch said, have you any tissues, miss?' asked the boy sniffing nosily.

Feeling increasingly beleaguered, Mrs Robertshaw rootled in her desk drawer in search of the tissues. Then the caretaker made an appearance.

'You had better come, Mrs Robertshaw,' he announced, shaking his head grimly.

'I'm in the middle of a lesson, Mr Gribbon,' she replied tersely, 'and I am trying to deal with two poorly children.'

'It's a bit of an emergency.'

The teacher sighed. 'Another one!'

'Can you come?'

'Oh, very well.' She fixed her class with an icy stare. 'Not a word when I am out of the room. Get on with your work quietly. Is that understood?'

'Yes, miss,' chorused the children.

Accompanied by the nosebleed and the tummy ache, she followed Mr Gribbon down the corridor. 'Now, Mr Gribbon, what is this emergency?' she asked

'A silly lad in Mr Jolly's class has swallowed a marble,' he told her.

'He's done what?'

'Swallowed a marble,' repeated the caretaker. 'Mr Jolly's in a right state. I could hear him ranting and raving down the corridor. I thought I ought to fetch you.'

'Well what am I supposed to do?'

'I've no idea but you're in charge while Mrs Stirling's out of school.'

Mrs Robertshaw strode on down the corridor, followed by the caretaker close at her heels jangling his keys noisily. She found an exasperated Mr Jolly outside his classroom wringing his hands and berating a small boy.

'Whatever made you do such a stupid thing?' the teacher demanded in a high, querulous voice.

'I was pretending it was a sweet,' moaned the child.

'You could have choked to death,' the teacher told him angrily.

'Mr Jolly,' said Mrs Robertshaw taking charge. 'Shall we just keep calm?'

'This silly child,' he told her red in the face, 'has swallowed a marble.'

'So I have been told,' she replied.

'Last week it was a rubber!' exclaimed Mr Jolly. 'Now it's a marble. Whatever next?'

'He swallowed a rubber?' asked Mrs Robertshaw.

'No, no,' said the teacher, 'he pushed the rubber tip at the end of his pencil in his ear. It was the devil's own job to get it out.'

Mrs Robertshaw turned to the boy. 'Now, it's Norman Stubbins, isn't it?' she asked.

'Yes, miss,' replied the boy and then burst into tears.

Mrs Robertshaw turned to the teacher. 'I shall deal with this, Mr Jolly,' she said. 'You may return to your class. They are getting very restless.'

'I am quite capable of—' he began.

Mrs Robertshaw held up a hand. 'Please let me deal with it.'

'Very well,' he snorted. 'Stupid boy,' he mumbled as he turned to go.

'And will you look after these two children until I've sorted this out?' She turned to the nosebleed and the tummy ache. 'You two stay with Mr Jolly for the time being,' she told the children.

'And you can be about your business too, Mr Gribbon,' she told the caretaker.

Shaking his head and grumbling to himself, the caretaker departed.

'Now, young man,' said Mrs Robertshaw, placing a hand on the boy's shoulder, 'come with me and don't look so worried.

It's not the end of the world.' In the staff room she gave him a glass of water and a tissue.

'I'm sorry, miss,' the boy wailed. 'I was pretending it was a sweet. Mr Jolly shouted at me and I swallowed it. It might never come out. I might have to go to the hospital and be cut open.'

Mrs Robertshaw could have enquired what he was doing pretending to eat a sweet in Mr Jolly's lesson but she resisted, seeing how distressed the child had become.

'Let me tell you something, Norman,' said the teacher, putting her arm around the boy's shoulder. 'When my son Graham was a bit younger than you he swallowed a plastic counter from one of his games.'

The boy stared up at her with wide eyes. 'What happened miss?'

'In a few days' time it reappeared.'

'How, miss?'

The teacher thought for a moment of the best way to describe this particular bodily function.

'Well, what went in one way' – she pointed to her mouth – 'came out the other.' She pointed downwards.

'How, miss?'

'When he went to the toilet,' she told him bluntly.

The boy suddenly understood.

'I see,' he murmured.

'I shall give you a note at home-time to tell your mother what has happened and suggest to her that it might be a good idea for her to take you to see Dr Stirling to be on the safe side. I don't imagine there is anything to worry about. I think he'll do what the doctor told me to do when my son swallowed the counter – give you a good dose of liquid paraffin.'

'Yes, miss,' said the boy, giving a small smile. 'Thank you, miss.'

'And, Norman?'

'Yes, miss.'

'No more putting marbles in your mouth.'

'No, miss.'

'Or rubbers in your ear.'

'No, miss. Thank you, miss.'

'Now back to your lesson.'

At lunchtime Mr Jolly approached Mrs Robertshaw. 'I could have dealt with it,' he told her stiffly. 'There was no necessity for the caretaker to fetch you.'

'He felt you were in need of some help,' she replied.

'Well I wasn't,' he told her peevishly. 'I had the situation well under control.'

'Mr Gribbon heard you shouting.'

'I was angry with the boy,' said Mr Jolly. 'Who wouldn't be? I would appreciate that in future you do not see fit to interfere when—'

'I'm on yard duty,' Mrs Robertshaw cut in, 'so if you will excuse me?'

'I certainly do not want to be a head teacher,' Mrs Robertshaw told Elisabeth at the end of school as they sat in the staffroom. 'Far too many problems to deal with and so many pressures.'

'It's not all blocked toilets, sick children, nosebleeds and swallowed marbles, Elsie,' Elisabeth told her. 'Most of the time it's very satisfying and things run pretty smoothly.'

Mr Gribbon appeared at the door of the staffroom looking aggrieved. 'The boiler's on the blink,' he said bluntly, 'the toilets are still blocked and there's that education officer waiting to see you in your classroom.'

Mrs Robertshaw raised her eyebrows and smiled but said nothing.

'I just wanted to touch base with you prior to the governors' meeting this evening,' said Mr Nettles. 'I was intending to throw a few ideas into the ring with you before tonight but gather you were out of school.'

'I was at the other site,' Elisabeth told him.

'And how are things going?' he asked. 'Is everyone up to speed?'

Of late the education officer had started to use fashionable jargon. His conversations were now peppered with trendy words and phrases which he had presumably picked up on the courses on which he had been sent. Elisabeth winced when she was exhorted to 'run it up the flagpole', 'bounce ideas around' or 'suck it and see'. She imagined that Mr Nettles, by using such management speak, was attempting to sound up to date, something of a specialist. Sadly for him it had the very opposite effect. It made him sound rather shallow and silly.

'Oh, we are all on board, bright-eyed, bushy-tailed and pulling in the same direction,' she told him, 'running that extra mile you know and giving it one hundred and ten per cent.'

The irony was lost on Mr Nettles, who smiled like some wide-mouthed frog. 'I am so pleased that things are going swimmingly,' he said.

The full governing body of the newly amalgamated schools convened in the staffroom for the first meeting. Those present were the chairman, Major C J Neville-Gravitas, RE (Retd); Mrs Stirling, the head teacher; Mrs Cosgrove, the parent governor; Lady Wadsworth, the foundation governor; Mrs Robertshaw, the teacher governor and Councillor Wayne Cooper, the Local Education Authority representative. Mr Nettles, the education officer, representing the Director of Education, was there in his capacity of adviser.

'Now, the first item on the agenda,' said the major, 'is the Instrument of Government.'

'And what is this?' asked a dumpy, vigorous, red-faced woman with a powerful stare.

'If you could be a little patient, Mrs Cosgrove,' said the major, 'Mr Nettles is about to explain.' He could see that he would have trouble with this rather strong-minded parent.

'Thank you, Mr Chairman,' said the education officer. 'The Instrument of Government is the means by which a school is managed and governed. All governors need to be fully conversant with it. So, if I might read what it constitutes.'

'Please go ahead,' said the major.

Mr Nettles cleared his throat and read in a high voice:

'In pursuance of section 4(3) of the Education Act of 1980, this Instrument shall have effect subject to any provision in the regulations from time to time in force under 4(1) of the Education Act of 1980, and any reference in this Instrument to the Regulations so in force. Any reference in this Instrument to a paragraph is a reference to that paragraph thereof and any reference in a paragraph to a sub-paragraph is a reference to a sub-paragraph in that paragraph. The Instrument of Government—'

'May I stop you there,' interrupted Lady Wadsworth, brushing the education officer's words aside. 'Perhaps you might like to translate that into plain English.'

'Well it means,' said Mr Nettles, struggling to find the words, 'that we ... er ... we must ... er ... adhere to the provisions of the Education Act.' His voice squeaked like a reedy instrument.

'Which are?' pursued Lady Wadsworth.

'Which are outlined in the Education Act.'

'And they are?' she persisted.

'They are ... er ... set out in the document,' replied Mr Nettled getting flustered.

'Which document?'

'The Education Act.'

'Is it me?' asked Mrs Cosgrove. 'I've not understood a blind word what's been said.'

'Neither have I,' agreed Major Neville-Gravitas. He turned to the extremely thin, big-nosed individual who sported a shock of frizzy ginger hair. 'Perhaps the councillor here can help.'

'No,' replied Councillor Cooper. 'I'm afraid not. It's all gobbledegook to me.'

'Did you understand this, Mrs Stirling?' asked the major.

'Not a word,' replied Elisabeth.

'And I don't think Mr Nettles did either,' remarked Lady Wadsworth. 'Can we move on?'

'Can I take it then that we are conversant with the Instrument of Government?' asked Mr Nettles.

Lady Wadsworth gave a hollow laugh. 'None of us understands what it means so we are not likely to be conversant with it, are we?'

'Let's move on,' said the chairman. 'We can't waste any more time trying to decipher this mumbo-jumbo. Next item on the agenda is a report from the head teacher on how things are going.'

'Before she does,' said the parent governor, 'I just want to say something.'

Oh dear, thought the major. 'Yes, of course, Mrs Cosgrove,' he said.

'I have two kids, one at this school and one on the other site. I just wanted to say they are both very happy and are doing well and I am very satisfied with how things are going. Paige's reading has come on a treat and Barnabas can't wait to get to school in the morning. Those parents who I have spoken to are very pleased as well. I just wanted to say that and have it put on record.'

'That is very heartening to hear,' said the major. 'Shall we hear from the head teacher now?'

Clearly cheered by this testimonial, Elisabeth thanked Mrs

Cosgrove and then delivered a very positive and optimistic report.

Having discussed a number of further issues regarding resources, staffing and the anticipated visit of the school inspector, they arrived at Any Other Business.

'The governing body is a member short, Mr Chairman,' announced Mr Nettles. 'With the resignation of the Reverend Mr Atticus following his translation to archdeacon, we need to co-opt his replacement.'

'Ah, now then,' said the major, 'I have the very person in mind. I think we would all agree that the Reverend Mr Atticus was a most valuable and highly respected member of this governing body. Would you agree, Mrs Stirling?'

'I most certainly would,' said Elisabeth.

'Well I am minded to ask his successor at St Christopher's—'

'Sparshott!' exclaimed Lady Wadsworth. 'You are suggesting Mr Sparshott?'

'Well yes,' replied the major. 'Do you have some objection?'

'I most certainly do!' she said. 'The man is totally unsuitable. I could not endure his presence.'

'Oh dear,' said the major. 'I gather you have had some unpleasant dealings with the gentleman?'

'I have indeed,' replied Lady Wadsworth, 'and very disagreeable they were. He has vetoed the stained-glass window to be put in St Christopher's in memory of my brother killed in the last war defending his king and country.'

'If I might come in here,' said Elisabeth, 'I think the parents too might have an objection to the appointment of Mr Sparshott as a governor.'

'Really?' said the major. 'Why is that?'

'To have a member of the governing body who lacks the confidence to send his own children to the school might be viewed as rather regrettable.'

'I wasn't aware of this,' said the major.

'Mr Sparshott has seen fit to send his children to St Paul's Preparatory School in Ruston,' he was informed.

'I see.'

'I would agree with Mrs Stirling,' said Councillor Cooper. 'It would appear rather strange.'

'Might I suggest an alternative?' asked Elisabeth.

'By all means,' said the major.

'What about Dr Underwood?'

'Is he a local man?' asked the parent governor.

'Dr Underwood is a woman,' said Elisabeth, 'and until recently she was a curate at the church. She is now the bishop's chaplain. She lives in the village and is very able and well liked.'

'I would certainly fully endorse that,' said Lady Wadsworth. 'She's a delightful young woman, very personable and highly intelligent and would be a great asset. It was Dr Underwood who suggested the stained-glass window at St Christopher's, the one the new vicar has seen fit to proscribe.'

'Well, if there are no objections, I think we should ask Dr Underwood to be co-opted onto the governing body,' said the major. He glanced around the room. 'Any objections? Good. Then perhaps Mrs Stirling might like to approach her and invite her to join us.'

'And if she's as clever as you say,' observed the parent governor, 'she might make some sense of that gibberish we heard earlier.'

'Now if there is no other business,' said the chairman, looking at his watch.

'Might I raise something?' asked the young councillor.

'Yes of course,' said the major, sighing inwardly and hoping it wouldn't take too long. *It was high time*, he thought, *that I was in the Blacksmith's Arms before last orders.*

'The county is promoting, through the School Library

Service, a Poetry and Prose Recitation Competition,' said Councillor Cooper. 'Schools are to be invited to enter pupils of older primary and secondary school age to deliver a piece of verse or an extract from a story. I do hope that this school will take part.'

'Of course,' said Elisabeth.

'I think it's a damn good idea for children to learn poems,' said the major. 'I can still recall the poems I learnt as a boy in Nobby Clark's English class.' He recited:

'If you can keep your head when all about you
Are losing theirs and blaming it on you,
If you can trust yourself when all men doubt you,
But make allowance for their doubting too.'

'Wonderful stuff Kipling, you know. Those words have stood me in good stead throughout my life.'

'I think it a very good thing that children should learn poetry,' said Lady Wadsworth. 'In my view it is an excellent way of encouraging clear speech. And I fully agree with you, Major. I too loved Kipling.' She then began to pronounce:

'Our England is a garden that is full of stately views,
Of borders, beds and shrubberies and lawns and avenues,
With statues on the terraces and peacocks strutting by;
But the Glory of the Garden lies in more than meets the eye.

'You know the great man once visited my grandfather who maintained that Kipling wrote that particular poem "The Glory of the Garden" about Limebeck House. Of course, in those days there were peacocks on the lawn and—'

'I have to say,' remarked Mr Nettles, rudely interrupting Lady Wadsworth and raising a hand to his head and scratching his scalp, 'that I question the value of children having to learn things by rote. It seems to me to be a rather old-fashioned notion. I am very much in favour of exploration and—'

'May I come in here,' said Mrs Robertshaw who had felt up until this point it would be diplomatic to remain unobtrusive at this, her first governors' meeting. Hearing the inane comment of the education officer, however, she felt compelled to speak.

'Yes, yes, of course,' said the major with a sigh and a surreptitious glance at his watch.

'The value of learning and reciting poetry, Mr Nettles,' she said, 'is great.' Her voice sounded careful, as if she was controlling herself. 'The merits of learning poetry are that it develops children's memory and gives them a greater awareness of the rhythms and rhymes of verse. Poetry is not to be read, it should be lifted off the page and heard out loud.'

'I appreciate that,' began Mr Nettles, 'but—'

'Might I finish!' Mrs Robertshaw cut him off. 'Performing poetry in front of an audience develops children's communication skills and their imagination and creativity; it increases their self-confidence and instils a love of literature and drama. It also stresses, as Lady Wadsworth has pointed out, the importance of using clear English. And thinking of the twaddle we have heard at the beginning of this meeting with regard to the Instrument of Government, it is perhaps something of which you might be mindful.'

'Perhaps at this juncture,' said the major, rising from his chair, 'I can call a close to the meeting.'

8

Ashley sheltered in the bus shelter. Driving rain teemed down from a grey sky and fell slantways across the pavements. Cars and vans, their bonnets steaming beneath the downpour, rushed along the deserted high street and lumbering lorries shuddered past throwing up waves of dirty water. Gutters gurgled, rooftops glistened and trees bent and swayed in the blustery wind. She was cold and wet and on such a dreadful Thursday had considered giving her monthly visit to see her mother a miss. *No*, she told herself, she had to see her. What she had decided had to be said.

A Land Rover pulled up. The passenger door was flung open and Emmet shouted to her to get in.

'I'm going to Clayton,' Ashley told him. 'Is that where you're headed?'

I am now, he thought to himself. 'Come on, jump in.'

'You're not going out of your way for me, are you?' she asked.

'No, no, I was headed for Clayton myself,' he fibbed. 'Get in, you're getting soaking wet.'

Ashley climbed into the Land Rover.

'Well, if you're sure. It's such a horrible day,' she said clambering into the vehicle and slamming shut the door. She shivered, wiped her wet face with a handkerchief and shook her wet hair.

'I must look like a drowned rat.'

'You look lovely,' he said before he could stop himself. 'I . . . I . . . mean you look fine.'

'I'm sure I don't,' she said laughing.

'Yes you do,' he replied.

He thought for a moment of stopping the Land Rover and telling her how he felt about her, how he loved her company and thought about her every day but no doubt she would feel embarrassed with such a declaration, smile and say she was flattered but theirs was nothing more than a friendship.

'I'm off to see my mother,' Ashley told him.

'Pardon?'

'I said I'm off to see my mother.'

'Oh right. I'm sorry, I was miles away.'

'Thinking about what?' she asked.

'Oh nothing really important.' He changed the subject. 'It's not the best of days to go out visiting.'

'I've decided that I'm prepared to let her come and live with me,' Ashley said. 'I'm going to tell her.'

'I see.'

'She can come and live with me at Wisteria Cottage. I can't imagine it will be easy but if that is what she wants. I feel it is a daughter's duty.'

Emmet didn't reply. He kept his eyes on the rain snaking down the windscreen.

'Do you think I'm wrong?' she asked.

'It's not really for me to say,' he told her.

Were he to give his opinion he would have told her not to do it, that she would be making a big mistake, that she should not have to put her life on hold for a mother who, from what he had been told, was a most difficult and demanding woman. He would have told her that parents do not have a God-given right to be cared for by their children. However, he said nothing and concentrated on his driving.

'I thought I'd see how it goes,' said Ashley, trying to sound cheerful. 'If it doesn't work out then we can always think again.'

'You have an affectionate and gentle heart,' Emmet told her. People take advantage of people like you, he was minded to add, that no daughter after the way that she had been treated would consider having such a disagreeable parent living with them, but he said nothing.

'So what's your business in Clayton?' she asked.

Emmet was not on his way to Clayton. He was heading back to Limebeck House when he saw her at the bus stop. Giving her a lift was just a chance of seeing her again. The question took him by surprise.

'Oh, just to sort out a few things for Lady Wadsworth,' he replied.

'She relies on you quite a bit, doesn't she?'

'She's a grand old lady and has been very good to me and Roisin. Salt of the earth, she is, as my mother would say. She's not a happy woman at the moment. The new vicar has put a block on her stained-glass window.'

'Yes,' sighed Ashley. 'I heard from the archdeacon that Mr Sparshott is not in favour of it. He likes a plain church. I guessed he would take exception to it.'

'Well Lady Wadsworth has certainly taken an exception to him,' Emmet told her, 'and I wouldn't like to cross her. She's pretty influential in these parts. I think your bishop will be hearing from her.'

He already has, thought Ashley.

'Thank you for listening to me the other day in the café,' she said, changing the subject. She had heard enough about the new vicar. 'It was good to talk to somebody.'

'We must do it again,' said Emmet.

'That would be nice,' she replied, smiling.

When they arrived at her mother's apartment block the rain had stopped. The dark clouds had passed overhead, a bright sun shone in the clear sky and the pavements steamed.

Here was the opportunity, thought Emmet, *to ask her out.*

'I was wondering—' he began.

'Oh look,' said Ashley, 'there's my mother at the window, looking out for me. I had better rush. Thanks for the lift, Emmet.'

'No problem,' he muttered sadly. 'What time will you be ready to go back?'

'Oh, I can get the bus,' Ashley told him. 'It's stopped raining now.'

'No, I'd like to collect you. I can do a bit of shopping in Clayton.'

'Well, if you're sure. I'll be a couple of hours I guess. About eleven o'clock?'

'That's fine,' he said, smiling.

How handsome he looks, thought Ashley, *with his open sun-tanned face and dark eyes*. She was falling in love with this softly spoken Irishman.

Ashley's mother was surprised to see her daughter.

'I should have thought you'd have given it a miss in such awful weather,' she said. 'You look soaked. Hang your coat up in the hall, it's dripping on the carpet and put the kettle on. I'm sure you could enjoy a cup of tea. I certainly would.'

Ashley bit her lip. Her mother was in the habit of speaking to her as if she were a small child. 'Yes, Mother,' she replied. She hung up her coat and went to make the tea.

'Actually I got a lift,' she shouted from the kitchen.

'I can't hear you,' said her mother tetchily. 'You know I'm going deaf in one ear.'

Ashley came in the room. 'I said I got a lift. The estate manager at Limebeck House dropped me off.'

'Yes, I saw him from the window. He's quite a striking-looking man. He's an estate manager, is he?'

'Yes, he works for Lady Wadsworth, a Mr O'Malley. He went out of his way to drop me off. It was very good of him, wasn't it? He said he would collect me in a couple of hours.'

'My goodness, you are mixing with the great and the good. Chauffer driven.' There was a hint of sarcasm in her voice.

Ashley sat next to her mother.

'I'll make the tea in a minute,' she said. 'I want to talk to you about something first.'

'Oh yes?

'I've been thinking about what you said.'

'What I said?'

'About coming to live with me.'

'And?' Mrs Underwood gazed steadily at her daughter.

'If you really want to move in with me, then I am happy for you to do so.'

'You didn't sound all that happy on your last visit when I broached the matter,' said Mrs Underwood.

'Well, I've had time to think about it.'

'And what has occasioned this change of heart?' asked her mother.

'As I've said, I have had time to think about it,' replied Ashley. 'I can see that you would be less lonely and happier and probably see a lot more people.'

'Really?'

'We can see how it goes. Of course there will have to be some give and take. We have not always seen eye-to-eye and—'

'Let me stop you there,' interrupted her mother. 'I too have been doing some thinking and I have come to the conclusion that it wouldn't work. I don't think I could live with you.'

'Pardon?'

'I said it wouldn't work,' repeated her mother. 'You are quite right that we rarely see eye to eye. We would probably be at each other's throats. I have always found you impetuous, Ashley, strong-minded and a bit too clever by half. I'm sorry to have to say it, but it's true. You take after your father in that. I can't say that we have a great deal in common to be frank. I won't say that you are a disappointment to me, that would be too harsh and unfeeling. But I do feel that after all your education and the opportunities which were afforded you in life you could have done a whole lot better than becoming a clerk to a bishop. But that is by the by. And, of course, should I come to live with you I suppose I would be expected to keep house. So, you see, I think things should be left as they are.'

'Well, if you're sure,' said Ashley, greatly relieved.

'I'm quite sure.'

'And what made you change your mind?' she asked.

'I have become quite friendly of late with one of the residents in the block, a Miss Sowerbutts. She moved here during the summer. She had intended to move earlier but altered her plans. She had a cat and they don't allow pets, you see. Anyway, when the animal died, she decided to sell her cottage in Barton and buy the apartment next to mine. We have met for coffee a few times and I find that we get on very well. She is a most refined and educated woman and we have a great deal in common. I believe you have met her. She was the former head teacher at the village school in Barton.'

Ashley had indeed met Miss Hilda Sowerbutts. New to the village and in an attempt to get to know the residents, she had called upon the woman in question and found her less than welcoming. The door of her cottage had opened and there stood a sour-faced woman dressed in pleated tweeds, heavy brogues and bullet-proof stockings.

'If you are selling anything I do not require it,' Miss Sowerbutts had told her crossly, 'and if you are canvassing for a vote I know for whom I shall vote already and if you are in the hope of converting me you are wasting your time.'

'I'm the new curate at St Christopher's,' Ashley had explained, rather taken aback by the brusque manner of the woman. 'I'm doing the rounds of the village to introduce myself.'

'I am not a member of your congregation,' Miss Sowerbutts

had informed her, 'and to be quite frank I don't agree with organised religion.'

'Well, if there is anything I can do for you,' the new curate had said, 'if I can be of any help—'

'No thank you. I am quite self-sufficient,' she had been told. 'Anyway, I shall be moving to Clayton in the near future.' With that she had closed the door.

'Yes, I remember her,' said Ashley to her mother.

'She was telling me she was treated quite appallingly by the powers that be in education,' said Mrs Underwood, 'and virtually pushed out of her position as the head teacher of the village school. The governors forced her to take early retirement and replaced her with a young woman with all these trendy methods and modern ideas.'

Ashley, of course, knew different. The school had been a moribund place under the management of Miss Sowerbutts and the school inspectors' report had been highly critical, particularly of the leadership. Under Elisabeth's firm and decisive direction, the once dark and neglected premises had been transformed into a bright, cheerful and welcoming place and within a term the school had become one of the most successful and popular in the area.

'I was telling Miss Sowerbutts,' continued Mrs Underwood, 'that I was minded to come and live with you but she advised against it. She said I would be unhappy living in Barton-in-the-Dale which she said is an insular and parochial place where everyone knows your business. She said I would get no privacy and lose my independence. In a flat of my own, she told me, I have the freedom to do exactly as I please with no-one telling me what to do or making demands upon me. There is a great deal of sense in what she said.'

'I see,' said Ashley. *Thank you, thank you, Miss Sowerbutts,* she said to herself.

'So I have decided to stay where I am,' said her mother.

Ashley felt a great wave of relief coming over her. 'Well if you're sure,' she said, trying to sound not overly pleased.

'Miss Sowerbutts goes on these cruises,' continued Mrs Underwood. 'She has always gone alone in the past but a cabin has become very expensive and the cost is much reduced if she has someone to share. She has asked me if I would like to go with her on the next cruise. It's to the Baltic.'

'I think that is an excellent idea,' said Ashley.

'I'm considering it,' said Mrs Underwood. 'I shall have to look at the brochure but I'm warming to the idea.'

'I'll make the tea,' said Ashley, going into the kitchen with a spring in her step.

'You might like to invite this estate manager in if he gives you a lift again,' said her mother. 'I should like to meet him.'

Emmet was waiting for Ashley outside the flats. The pavements steamed following the heavy rain and a bright sun made an appearance in a blue sky.

'Now then, Emmet,' said Ashley, jumping into the Land Rover and giving a great smile. 'I am going to treat you to afternoon tea. I've just received some very welcome news and shall tell you all about it if you would care to join me at the Rumbling Tum café next Saturday afternoon.'

'I'd like that very much,' replied Emmet.

'Then it's a date. Now, I need to call in at Clumber Lodge if you wouldn't mind dropping me off there. I have to see Mrs Stirling about something.'

'You must be psychic,' said Elisabeth when she found Ashley on the doorstep. 'I was intending to call around and see you this evening. I have a favour to ask. Come on in. I'll put the kettle on. You go through.'

In the sitting room Ashley found the two boys playing chess.

'Hello,' she said.

'Hello, Dr Underwood,' they replied in unison.

'So who is winning?'

Danny shook his head and sighed.

'James of course,' he said. ''E's better than me.'

'Yeah, but you're better than me at other things,' said James generously. He was a small, pale-faced boy with curly blonde hair and a ready smile.

'And how are you two liking it at the big school?' asked Ashley

'It's OK,' replied Danny, 'but not as good as t'village school. It's too big, there's all these different teachers, lots o' lessons an' we 'ave loads of 'omework.'

'I'm afraid that's the way it goes,' said Ashley smiling. 'We have all had to go through school.'

'Aye, but you were dead clever,' said Danny. 'I'm not. I'm in one o' t'bottom groups. Book learnin' isn't for me. I likes to be out an' about.'

'Book learning isn't all that's it's cracked up to be,' said Ashley. 'Take my word for it. You just follow your dream, Danny. Do what you really want to do in life.'

'You sound like mi granddad, miss,' replied the boy. 'That's what he used to say.' The boy thought for a moment. 'I reckon I'd like to do what Mr O'Malley does – 'edging an' ditchin' an' plantin' an' lookin' after a big estate, being outdoors all day.'

'Yes, that'd suit you,' said Ashley quietly and thought of Emmett again. 'And have you been up to the rectory recently?' she asked. 'I know you like to go up there to look after your grandfather's grave.'

'Aye, I was up at t'churchyard last week,' Danny told her. 'I've met t'new vicar's wife.'

'Oh yes,' said Ashley. She could picture Mrs Sparshott striding down the rectory path and shooing the boy away.

'She's dead nice,' said Danny smiling.

'Nice?' repeated Ashley. It was not a word which readily came to mind.

'Yea, we 'ad a natter about plants an' that. I said I'd tidy up t'graves for 'er.'

'Well that's very good of you, Danny,' said Ashley. *This young man*, she thought, *has a way with people. He could melt an iceberg with that smile.*

Elisabeth came in with the tea tray. 'Would you two finish the game upstairs, please?' she said to the boys. 'Dr Underwood and I have something to talk about.'

When the boys had left, Elisabeth poured the tea.

'Now what is it you wanted to see me about?' she asked.

'You first,' said Ashley.

'Well at the last governors' meeting at the school, it was unanimously decided that we should ask you to join us on the governing body, to co-opt you as a member.'

'Gosh!' said Ashley. 'I'm very flattered.'

'We all felt you would be a real asset. You would be taking the place of Archdeacon Atticus.'

'Perhaps it might be more appropriate to ask Mr Sparshott,' suggested Ashley.

'His name was mentioned but the governors were not in favour of asking him. So how about it?'

'Well, in that case, I should be delighted.'

'That's splendid. I'll send you all the details. Now, what is it you want to see me about?'

'Fred Massey.'

'Oh dear, what has he been up to?'

'To be honest, Elisabeth, I feel rather sorry for the man.'

'I think you must be the only person in the village to feel sorry for Fred Massey,' remarked Elisabeth. 'He's a very disagreeable old man.'

'The thing is,' Ashley told her, 'Mr Sparshott has barred him from using the track down the side of the rectory. Mr

Massey takes his cattle down there and into his field behind the church. The vicar's put up a big notice saying it's private property and he's locked the gate. The only other means of access for Mr Massey is down the side of Wisteria Cottage.'

'Yes I know,' said Elisabeth. 'When I first bought the place we had a falling-out about that.'

'I can understand that if you park a car on the track it would be very inconvenient to have cattle using it but—'

'You don't have a car,' interrupted Elisabeth.

'No I don't.'

'And you would like Mr Massey to use the track?'

'It wouldn't worry me,' said Ashley, 'but of course if you object . . . '

'If you are happy to let him use it, then it is fine by me, until such a time as the person living in the cottage gets a car.'

'We will make a very bad-tempered old man extremely happy,' said Ashley. 'Thank you.'

'So how do you like working for the bishop?'

'Very much,' replied Ashley. 'Bishop William is such a dear man and an easy boss to work for and of course I see Archdeacon Atticus and his wife regularly and we get on really well.'

'Unlike the incumbent at St Christopher's,' said Elisabeth. 'I believe like most in the village you didn't see eye to eye with him?'

'Sadly, Mr Sparshott and I didn't get on,' said Ashley. 'He has very fixed ideas. I am sure at heart he is a dedicated and compassionate man but he finds it hard to see the other person's point of view. He is something of a zealot, I'm afraid.'

'Well if he is not careful he will lose the small congregation that he has,' said Elisabeth.

'Maybe,' replied Ashley, not wishing to discuss her former colleague any more. 'Let's change the subject. I was thinking about one of your pupils today – that poor little boy called Robbie. I was wondering how he is getting on.'

'What made you think of him?'

'I've been to see my mother which I find something of a trial and I remembered when I was Robbie's age and how, like him, I was miserable at home. The boy came into the church. I mentioned it to you at the time. He reminded me so much of how I felt growing up in an unhappy household and feeling the pain of being a child not really wanted. Like him I was a bit of handful, troubled, lonely and unhappy, angry with the world and suspicious of adults. And so I learnt to hide my feelings, conceal my thoughts. Young Robbie reminded me so much of myself in many ways. Every time I see my mother, I recall my childhood. I'm afraid it was far from happy.'

'There's been no miraculous change in the boy,' Elisabeth told her, 'but he's certainly less aggressive and rude as he was when he first came to the school. He's being fostered by a really nice couple, a Mr and Mr Ross who live on a farm. Robbie's still a lonely child and very uncommunicative but he's not the boy he was. Anyway, now you are a governor you can see for yourself how he is getting along.'

'I have to thank a very unlikely source for my mother's change of heart,' Ashley told Emmet.

They were in the Rumbling Tum café, sitting by the window the following Saturday afternoon.

'Do tell me,' he said. 'I'm intrigued.'

'One of my mother's neighbours, a Miss Sowerbutts, some-one of like mind and from what I can gather equally complaining and irritable as she, has put her off the idea. Miss Sowerbutts has convinced my mother that she would be better staying where she is.'

'That must come as a great relief,' said Emmet.

'It does. I really don't know how I would have coped had she moved in with me.'

'You know you were saying how you found it hard to love your mother?' asked Emmet.

'I do and I feel bad about that.'

'And I said it wasn't that unusual.'

'You did, but—'

'Just listen a moment, Ashley,' interrupted Emmet. 'You shouldn't feel bad about it. Parents need to earn the love of their children. They shouldn't want to live their lives for them. Some parents cast long shadows over their children's lives. You remember when we met at the folk concert in Clayton and we sat by the river?'

Ashley nodded and sensed there was some personal suffering behind Emmet's words. She recalled the evening well. 'I do,' she said.

'Do you remember I told you about my wife and how Rowena's parents wouldn't even speak to her when she married me, that they disowned her. She really tried her best to build bridges with them but they had none of it. They wouldn't see her. Do you know, they never came to her funeral when she died.'

'How they must regret that now,' answered Ashley.

'No, I don't think they do. If there is any regret they would surely want to see their granddaughter, but they want nothing to do with Roisin despite my writing to them. They slammed the phone down when I used to call. So I have given up. They are stubborn and strong-willed and I guess have become sad and lonely people in their draughty old castle. When Rowena was having the baby she told me how she hoped that seeing their new grandchild would melt her parents' hearts, that she would be reconciled with them and they would come to accept me.' He sighed. 'It wasn't to be.'

Ashley took a sip of coffee and thought for a moment. 'You must miss your wife a great deal,' she said.

Emmet smiled ruefully. 'Oh, I do, I miss her terribly. Never a day goes by when I don't think about her and particularly when I look into Roisin's face. I see her there.' He gazed into Ashley's eyes. 'When Rowena died I never thought that I would ever feel the same way about anyone else, that I could love anyone quite the same.' He took a deep breath. 'But over the past few months I have—'

'Not interrupting anything, am I?' Major Neville-Gravitas stood before them smiling widely.

'Well actually we were just—' began Emmet, clearly irritated by the interruption.

'It's just that I wanted a quick word with Dr Underwood,' the major rattled on regardless. He turned to Ashley. 'I saw you from the street and thought I'd take this opportunity of speaking to you about the service on Remembrance Sunday.'

'Perhaps it might be more convenient for you to call round to the cottage later today,' Ashley replied.

'I'll only be a minute,' said the major.

'Very well,' said Ashley.

He sat down. 'It's early days I know to be thinking about the remembrance service, but I'm the sort of chap who likes to organise things well in advance.'

'So what was it you wanted to see me about?' asked Ashley, keen for the major to make his departure.

'Mr Sparshott, the new vicar, has been most uncooperative,' he explained, 'and wants a small, modest remembrance service in the church and nothing at the war memorial. Now we have always had a parade from St Christopher's to the memorial but he's dead against it. He told me he doesn't "go in for anything showy" as he puts it. As I told him, it's not a carnival, it's a commemoration in honour of those who gave their lives for their country, a tribute. I told him that I have arranged for the Dunkirk Veterans to join the Royal British Legion this year. Personally, I find the man a very difficult sort of cove and can't for the life of me see his objection. Anyway, I thought that you, being in the same line of work as he is, if you follow my drift, might prevail upon him to change his mind.'

'I'm afraid I'm the last person to prevail upon him,' Ashley told him. 'Mr Sparshott is a man of determined views and is very unlikely to change his mind.'

'I see,' said the major, rising to his feet and stroking his moustache. 'Then I shall have to resort to contacting the bishop and see what he has to say about it.'

'I suggest you do that,' Ashley told him.

'Oh, righto, I'll do that,' said the major, sounding deflated. He gave a slight bow. 'Well, I shall wish you good day and I apologise for intruding.'

'As I was saying,' said Emmett as the major strode for the door, 'over the past few months I've realised that I—'

'Have you done?' Bianca, arms folded over her chest, stood at the table. 'It's just that being a Saturday, there's a queue waiting for the table.'

'Yes,' sighed Emmet, 'we've done.'

It was something of a coincidence that Elisabeth came upon Robbie that afternoon when she went shopping in Clayton. She caught sight of the boy with his foster-carer sitting outside a café on a table by the river. Mr Ross was a burly man with a thick head of woolly hair and copious white whiskers which gave him the appearance of a benevolent, sleepy old lion. He was doing all the talking in a deep, voluble voice and it was clear that Robbie was listening intently. The boy's small face reminded Elisabeth of a pointer, nose pressed forward, alert, ready to flush out some game bird hidden in the undergrowth.

'Hello,' she said brightly, approaching them.

'Good afternoon to you, Missis Stirling,' said Mr Ross, rising from his chair. He patted Robbie on the shoulder. 'Say 'ello to your teacher, Robbie,' he told the boy in a good-humoured tone.

'Hello, miss,' muttered Robbie. There was not a trace of a smile on the sharp little face. How his countenance had changed since she first caught sight of him listening so attentively to Mr Ross. He looked at her now with that melancholy expression habitual to those who feel themselves badly done to in life.

Elisabeth was amused to see that both man and boy wore almost identical outfits: shapeless blue overalls beneath wax jackets with corduroy collars, tweed caps and sturdy brown boots.

'Would yer care for a cup o' coffee?' asked Mr Ross, resuming his seat.

'No thank you,' she replied, 'but I'll join you for a moment if I may?' She pulled up a chair.

Robbie continued to look at her with bright watchful eyes. Elisabeth thought for a moment. What a difficult child he had been when he had started at the school – angry, resentful, insolent – but she had recognised the unmistakable flash of distress in those bright-green eyes. She knew that beneath the child's apparent sharpness and bluster there was a sad and lonely little boy from a desperately unhappy home. His behaviour had not improved markedly since the start of the new term but he was certainly less difficult and disrespectful.

'Don't come too close,' warned the farmer now. 'Neither of us smells that 'eavenly. We've bin muckin' out this morning an' then bin to t'Clayton Auction Mart. We're a bit ripe.'

'You look quite the part, Robbie,' said Elisabeth, 'quite the young farmer.'

'I kitted 'im out last week.' Mr Ross told her. 'T' lad's got to look t'part. Can't 'ave 'im standin' there at t'Auction Mart amid all them farmers in 'is Sunday best.'

When Robbie had first arrived at Treetop Farm, Mr Ross had taken him on a tour of the smallholding.

'I shall 'ave to get thee sooarted out wi' some proper kit,' the farmer had told the boy. 'Can't' ave thee wearin' other folks' cast-offs.'

Robbie had looked a comical figure dressed in the farmer's old waxed jacket, greasy flat cap and Mrs Ross's Wellington boots, two sizes too big.

'It stinks a bit, dun't it,' said Mr Ross.

Robbie nodded but didn't say anything. Three collie dogs followed him at his heels. He bent down occasionally to stroke them.

'They've tekken to thee, them three,' said the farmer.

Robbie nodded. He was listening carefully.

''Course you get used to t'smell. It's a good, honest farming smell that's what I think. Some o' t'kids what we've looked after din't like it.'

'I don't mind,' muttered Robbie.

Treetop Farm was extensive with sheds, stone outbuildings, huge metal silos and cattle stalls. In one field was a rusting tractor and the remains of an excavator, broken and corroded, a mountain of tangled scrap metal and mounds of stone. In shed after shed were pigs of every size and colour, kept in clean, spacious pens with thick plastic slatted floors, squealing and snuffling.

'Cleanliness is reight important,' the farmer told Robbie. They were walking along the path by the side of the huge pens. Nettles and willowherbs sprouted from the cracks in the concrete. They stopped by a heap of wet leaves.

'Keep 'em well-fed, well-wattered, warm an' clean, an' theer's less chance of 'em gerrin diseases. Course they all get injected when they come which teks a bit o' time. You've also got to keep 'em interested. Yer see yer pig is an inquisitive an' intelligent creature an' likes to play, that's why there's them balls on ropes for 'em to play wi'. It keeps 'em 'appy. If a pig is stressed tha can taste it in t'meat so you 'ave to avoid gerrin 'em anxious. If they get bored an' nervous an' unhappy they nibble at their tails – bit like people bitin' their nails.'

Robbie looked at his own badly bitten nails.

'We dock t'tails o' t'piglets soon after birth,' the farmer rattled on. 'In t'past they were kept on straw an' mucked out every week.' He chuckled. 'There was this massive muck 'eap what rotted throughout t'year an' was then spread on t'fields – free fertiliser. Now we keep t'pigs 'ere in these pens an' all pig muck gus down between them slats an' gets collected at t'bottom. Then it's cleaned out, purrin a slurry tank an' then gus onto t'fields.' The farmer stopped and looked at the small figure in the oversize clothes. 'Tha dun't say much, lad, does tha?' he asked. 'Tha's as quiet as a bee in a bottle.'

Robbie didn't reply.

'Aye well, 'appen tha an't got owt to say,' said the farmer good-humouredly. 'There's summat to be said for keeping thi gob shut. I reckon all this is new to thee. Well, let's get back. Missus has cooked summat special toneet.'

They stopped at the door of the farmhouse. Mr Ross put his hand on the boy's shoulder.

'Does tha reckon tha could live 'ere then, Robbie?' asked the farmer.

'Yes,' answered the boy. He looked up to where a clamouring flock of rooks cawed above the treetops. 'Yes, I could.'

'We was minded to buy a few sheep this mornin',' said the farmer to Mrs Stirling now, 'but they were a bit pricey for my pocket so we din't bother. I don't keep many sheep. I 'ave mostly pigs on mi farm. I don't breed 'em, just fatten 'em for market. Bed an' breakfast I calls it. We gerrem two weeks after they're born.'

'That's very soon, isn't it,' said Elisabeth.

'Nay, Missis Stirling,' said Mr Ross. 'They get good rations, a mixture of proteins an' vitamins an' dried milk an' they put on weight like nob'dy's business.' He looked at Robbie. 'I'm minded to give Robbie 'ere a bit o' their rations an' purra bit o' flesh on 'is bones.'

Robbie's brow furrowed.

'I'm kiddin', lad,' laughed the farmer. 'My missus's meat an' taty pie'll soon fatten 'im up in no time.'

'So when do the pigs go to market?' asked Elisabeth.

'Come on, Robbie, speak up, lad. 'As t'cat got thee tongue? When do we send 'em to market?'

'When they weigh about 220 pounds,' said the boy.

'I'm tekkin' t'lad 'ere to see a pal o' mine this afternoon to show 'im a couple o' boars.'

'Boars?' repeated Elisabeth.

'Aye, male pigs.'

'You mean hogs?'

'Nay, Missis Stirling. You better put yer teacher reight 'ere, Robbie,' said Mr Ross. 'What's t'difference between a boar an' an 'og?'

'A boar is an uncastrated male pig fit for breeding and a hog is a castrated male,' said Robbie, repeating almost word for word what the farmer had told him earlier.

'I see,' said Elisabeth.

''Course they don't use many boars for breedin' now. Too much bother,' said the farmer. 'It's mostly done through AI. That's artificial insemination.'

'Yes, I'm familiar with that term,' said Elisabeth smiling.

'And you know what it means an' all, don't you, Robbie? I was tellin' ya last week.'

'It's when the farmer does it instead of the boar,' said the boy.

'Aye, summat along those lines,' laughed the famer. 'Do

you know, Missis Stirling, this lad 'ere 'as a way wi' mi beeasts. 'E's a natural. T'wife an' I 'ave fostered many a lad ovver t'years but none of 'em 'as shaped up like Robbie when it comes to mi animals.'

Robbie remained quiet but it was clear he was taking in every word.

''E knows nearly as much as I do abaat pigs. In't that reight?' said the farmer.

The boy nodded. There was a ghost of a smile on his lips.

'Tell Missis Stirling what sort of pigs we 'ave. Go on, lad, you've got a tongue in yer 'ead.'

'Large whites, middle whites, some ginger, some spotted but mostly what Hamish, that is Mr Ross, calls hand-over-fist, a sort of mix of breeds.'

'I tell you, Missis Stirling,' said the farmer wearing a broad smile, 'he's as sharp as a tack. There's nowt much this lad dun't know abaat pigs.'

Mr Ross asked Robbie to take the empty cups and plates back into the café which the boy did dutifully. When he had gone, Mr Ross rubbed his beard.

'T'lad 'as 'ad a lot to put up wi', Missis Stirlin',' he said.

'Yes, I know,' she replied.

'I mean 'ow would any of us feel to 'ave a violent step-father who 'ad no time for yer an' med it clear, who told yer yer were a waste o' space? That man beat down t'lad's self-esteem, told 'im 'e were useless an' took a strap to 'im an' all. First night wi' us Robbie wet t'bed. Never said nowt. Slept in t'wet sheets for t'next few days until mi missus discovered 'em. I reckon 'e thowt we'd send 'im back or 'it 'im. When 'e wet t'bed at 'ome he told us 'e were smacked on 'is wet skin. Then 'e was med to sleep in t'bath. Asked if 'e should do that at our 'ouse from now on.' He shook his head. 'What some adults do to kids is scandalous. It's no wonder t'lad's screwed-up. I tell yer, Missis Stirling, 'e's got good reason to be 'ow he is. 'T'wife an' I 'ave fostered loads o' kids in our time but we've never come across a child who is in more need o' lovin' care. Kids aren't born bad, Missis Stirling. It's how they're brung up.'

Robbie returned.

'Now then, young Robbie,' said Mr Ross, getting up from his seat and putting his arm around the boy's shoulder. 'Let's go an' see abaat these boars.'

''Course I could have predicted it,' said Mrs Sloughthwaite smugly.

The shopkeeper was giving her two friends the benefit of the latest gossip. When not behind the counter, Mrs Sloughthwaite took up her position by the window to watch the comings and goings in the village. That afternoon she had seen Ashley in Emmet's Land Rover and had smiled to herself. The occasion when they had been observed together in the Rumbling Tum café had been relayed to her by Mrs Pocock which only went to confirm the shopkeeper's suspicions that 'something is going on between them two'.

'Sure, he's a fine doorful of a man is Mr O'Malley, so he is,' observed Mrs O'Connor, 'and she's as pretty as the day is long. They make a lovely couple but I guess there's probably nothing in it.'

'Oh no, Bridget,' said the shopkeeper. 'I'm very perspicuous in these matters. I think I have a touch of second sight. Anyway it's writ in the stars and once the planetary path is set, it cannot be altered. It's fate. It said so in his horoscope.'

'You're not still reading that rubbish,' snorted Mrs Pocock.

Mrs Sloughthwaite reached beneath the counter and produced the local newspaper.

'He's a Capricorn, she's a Virgo,' said the shopkeeper. 'Their star signs have an affinity.'

'How do you know she's a Virgo?' asked Mrs O'Connor.

'I happened to notice that she had some birthday cards on August 24th which makes her a Virgo,' said Mrs Sloughthwaite, opening the paper.

'You don't miss much, do you?' observed Mrs Pocock.

The shopkeeper licked her index finger and began flicking through the pages.

'Now it says here, "Virgos are the most educated, spiritual, cultured and elegant of the zodiacal characters." Now that is Dr Underwood to a tee. This is Capricorn: "Those born under this star sign are practical, home-loving and outgoing. They are creative individuals, even-tempered and are sensitive to the needs of others." Now isn't that Mr O'Malley?'

'It doesn't say anything about romance,' remarked Mrs Pocock.

'Hold your horses,' said Mrs Sloughthwaite. She read on. '"Those born under the star sign of Capricorn show understanding of other people's points of view and try to resolve any differences by compromise. They are romantic and their marriages are likely to be successful."'

'They've got it wrong there,' said Mrs O'Connor. 'Mr O'Malley's marriage can hardly be described as successful. His wife died, didn't she?'

'Now, here it is,' said the shopkeeper, ignoring the interruption. '"You who are born under this sign can look forward to a dramatic change in lifestyle in the winter when a romantic involvement reaches fruition and a new and exciting event impacts on your life." Now then, what do you think of that?'

'Rubbish!' exclaimed Mrs Pocock. 'I don't believe a word of it.'

'Well you can be septical about it,' replied the shopkeeper, leaning over the counter, 'but the horoscopes have foretold lots of things which have come true for me.'

'Guesswork,' said Mrs Pocock.

'And the psychotic I consult,' announced the shopkeeper,

'has told me things about myself that nobody but me would know.'

'The what?'

'The medium who I've been to see.'

'You go to a medium?' asked Mrs O'Connor.

'I do and you wouldn't believe the things she told me.'

'No I wouldn't,' said Mrs Pocock, 'not a word of it.'

'What things?' asked Mrs O'Connor, intrigued.

'About when I was little and the things I got up to.'

'What things?'

'All sorts of things.'

'Yes, but what?'

'I'm not telling all and sundry about personal matters,' said the shopkeeper, puffing out her chest like an overfed pigeon. 'Suffice it to say, she was very convincing.'

'Well they always *are* convincing, these fortune-tellers,' said Mrs Pocock, 'but what they tell you is only what you want to hear. I never ever make forecasts, especially about the future.'

'I once had my tea leaves read by a gypsy fortune-teller in Whitby, so I did,' announced Mrs O'Connor.

'You've told us before,' said Mrs Pocock, sniffing.

'Everything she said would happen, did.'

'Nonsense!' snapped the other customer.

'It did, as true as I'm standing here,' said Mrs O'Connor, nodding like a toy dog. 'She said I'd be travelling across water and the following week didn't I have to take the Holyhead ferry to Ireland for my cousin Moya's funeral? And what about my nephew Tom?'

'What about him?' asked Mrs Pocock.

'The gypsy told me that someone close to me would be having an accident and didn't Tom end up at Clayton Royal Infirmary the following week with a dislocated shoulder?'

'Coincidence,' said Mrs Pocock dismissively. 'It's all twaddle this fortune-telling lark, all hocus-pocus.'

'And she told me that Tom would have to give up his sport and he has done. He's going to train to be a teacher, so he is.'

'More fool him,' said Mrs Pocock. 'I wouldn't want to teach kids these days.'

'Actually, the lady I see is not a fortune-teller,' said Mrs Sloughthwaite, 'she's a mystic and a clairvoyant with psychotic powers. She has the gift of extra-century perception.'

Mrs Pocock responded with a curt laugh. 'Huh, they're all the same – con-artists and frauds. Psychic powers my foot.'

'Well why don't you come with me and have a reading?' asked Mrs Sloughthwaite. 'You'll soon change your mind when she tells you things that only you could know – well apart from her that is.'

'Me?!' exclaimed Mrs Pocock with a hollow laugh. 'Come with you to see some hoaxer? No chance. Waste of time and a waste of money.'

'I don't mind coming,' said Mrs O'Connor.

'I'm having another psychotic plenum next Thursday,' said the shopkeeper.

'A what?' snapped Mrs Pocock.

'It's what she calls her spiritual confrontations,' Mrs Sloughthwaite told her. 'She's going to try and get through to the other side at my next one.'

'The other side of what?' asked Mrs Pocock.

'To contact those who have passed over.'

'You mean dead?'

'Mrs Wigglesworth never uses that word. She talks of those who are no longer earth-side as having passed over and being on the other side.'

'Is that her name?' asked Mrs Pocock. 'Mrs Wigglesworth? Doesn't sound very mystical to me.'

'Mediums and psychotics aren't all called Gypsy Rose Lee you know,' said Mrs Sloughthwaite. 'They're not all old and wrinkled and wear silver hoops the size of onion rings in their ears and live in booths at the quay in Whitby. Ordinary people can have second sight you know. As I said, I think I've got a touch of it myself.'

'And what happens when she gets through to the other side?'

'The spirits of those who have passed over tell you things.'

'What things?' asked Mrs Pocock.

'About things that happened long ago.'

'What things?'

'All sorts of things.'

'Yes, but what?'

'Different things to different people. You should come with us and then Mrs Wigglesworth will tell you. She lives in Marfleet.'

'Go on, come with us,' urged Mrs O'Connor. 'It'll be an experience, so it will.'

'No,' replied Mrs Pocock firmly. 'It's not my cup of tea. The very idea of someone's dead relations floating about and watching everything you do is just plain silly.'

'What are you afraid of?' asked the shopkeeper.

'Nothing,' replied Mrs Pocock. 'It's just that I take all this psychic stuff with a pinch of salt.'

'Suit yourself,' said Mrs Sloughthwaite.

Mrs Pocock thought for a moment. 'Well if I do come with you,' she replied, 'it'll only be to expose this Mrs Wigglesworth as a charlatan.'

9

Major C J Neville-Gravitas breezed into the Blacksmith's Arms one Saturday lunchtime and made his way purposefully to the bar, smiling widely and rubbing his hands together. He was dressed in a dinner jacket which sported several miniature medals.

'Good morning, landlord,' he said cheerfully.

'Morning, Major. Your usual?'

'Just the ticket,' he said, 'and make it one for yourself, my good man.'

He passed a crisp ten-pound note over the bar.

'Thank you kindly, Major,' said the landlord.

Major Neville-Gravitas stroked his moustache and looked around smiling. When he caught sight of Fred Massey perched on a stool propping up the end of the bar, his smile widened.

'I take it the gate is still chained and bolted?' he asked Fred with the air of one who had unadmitted pleasure in the contemplation of another person's misfortune.

'What?' snapped the farmer.

'The gate on the track by the rectory,' said the major. 'I take it you have not managed to induce the vicar to let you take your cows down there.'

'None of your business.'

The major, enjoying the farmer's discomfiture, persisted. 'I thought not,' he said before taking a sip of his whisky. 'I am afraid, Mr Massey, you are one of those people who are all words, who threaten to do something and in fact do nothing at all.'

Fred took a gulp of his beer, then wiped his mouth with the back of his hand.

'If you say so,' he said.

'*I shall take a pair of bolt-cutters,*' said the major, repeating the farmer's words, '*and make short work of the lock and chain.*' He chuckled. 'Idle threats. A certain proverb comes to mind when I think of you, Mr Massey: "A man of words and not of deeds, is like a garden full of weeds".'

'For your information I didn't need to do anything,' said Fred, 'so keep your clever comments and your proverbs to yourself.'

'So you managed to persuade the vicar then, did you?' asked the landlord.

'I didn't need to,' Fred told him. He turned to the major. 'Here's a proverb for you to stuff in your pipe and smoke, Major-know-it-all: "When one door shuts, another opens." I'm taking my beasts by another route. Reverend Underwood, who has more Christian kindness in her little finger than that new vicar has in the whole of his body, is letting me use the track down by Wisteria Cottage.'

'Mrs Stirling will soon put a stop to that,' said the major. 'As I recall, she prevented you doing that when she first bought the cottage.'

'Yes, well she's changed her mind,' Fred told him.

'I'll say this for you, Fred Massey,' said the landlord, 'you can fall in a heap of manure and climb out smelling of roses.'

'Pity he has to climb out,' said the major under his breath.

'Aye, well it's my charming and persuasive nature what does it,' Fred told the landlord, grinning and showing a set of discoloured tombstone teeth.

The major gulped down the remainder of his drink.

'Another tot of whisky please, landlord,' he said glumly,

disappointed that he could no longer gloat at Fred's misfortune.

'You look very smart today, Major,' said the landlord. 'Going somewhere special?'

The major brightened. 'Army Benevolent Fund charity luncheon at the Masonic Hall in Clayton. I'm the treasurer of the fund-raising committee and we have some big brass brigadier speaking this lunchtime. I guess he'll bore the pants off us but one has to show willing for such a worthy cause.'

'That's the pot calling the kettle black if ever I heard it,' said Fred Massey.

'Did you make some observation?' asked the major.

'You could bore for Britain,' said Fred.

The major decided to ignore the comment, not wishing to enter into an argument with his nemesis. He turned his back on Fred and continued to address the landlord.

'As I was saying before I was so rudely interrupted, this dinner is quite a big do and—'

'You put your foot in it good and proper when Mrs Stirling's brother was in here,' interrupted the farmer with a gravelly laugh.

'I have no idea to what you are referring,' replied the major, feeling uncomfortable. He knew very well to what Fred was referring and his face became flushed with anger and embarrassment. He did not wish to be reminded of that occasion.

The major had been holding forth in the public house on his pet subject – the British Army. He had been telling the landlord that standards had dropped, how, in his day, they didn't have the equipment they had now and all the sophisticated weaponry and body armour. 'I'm not saying it's not still a dangerous job,' the major had remarked, 'but soldiers these days have a much easier time of it.'

Not long after she moved to the village, Elisabeth's brother Giles came to visit her. Unbeknown to the major, he was a serving army officer who had been awarded the Military Cross for conspicuous bravery and he had taken great exception to these remarks and given the major a piece of his mind. 'What you have just said is a load of bloody nonsense!' he had exclaimed before leaving the pub.

'Yes,' chuckled Fred now. 'You were certainly given a good dressing down and no mistake.'

'Look, Fred Massey!' exclaimed the landlord. 'You've been warned. Another word out of you and you can take your custom elsewhere.'

'I shall bid you good day,' said the major angrily and, gulping down his drink, he scooped up his change from the bar and strode for the door.

'Bemedalled ass,' said Fred. 'Another pint down here, landlord, if you please.'

Having consumed a further three pints, Fred emerged from the Blacksmith's Arms worse for drink. He hiccupped nosily, steadied himself on the door frame and peered down the street, blinking and trying to focus on a dark shape that was heading his way. He squinted and then recognised the figure.

'Bloody Nora,' he muttered, 'it's her.'

'A word, Mr Massey, if you please!' said Mrs Sparshott, approaching him with an intimidating look on her face.

'Ah 'tis the vicar's wife, to be sure, to be sure,' he slurred in a mock Irish accent and attempting to stand upright. 'Sure and begorra what can I do for you?'

'What you can do for me, Mr Massey, is remove the unsightly mound of rubble from the churchyard,' she told him.

Fred tried to focus on the pinched face with his pale, watery eyes. He abandoned the Irish brogue.

'And what rubble would this be?' he asked, feigning ignorance.

'You know perfectly well what rubble,' said Mrs Sparshott. 'All the remains of the tomb which make the churchyard so unsightly. You were responsible for it, I believe, when you cut down that large branch from the oak tree which destroyed the ancient and impressive mausoleum of the Reverend Joseph Steerum-Slack.'

'Mrs Atticus didn't like it,' Fred told her. He hiccupped. 'She hated the sight of it and was glad to see it go. She said it was an eyesore.'

'That is of no consequence,' said the vicar's wife. 'Now, when are you going to remove the rubble?'

'When hell freezes over,' Fred told her.

'I beg your pardon?'

'I don't intend to touch that rubble of yours. Since I've been barred from church property by that husband of yours, I shall not be coming anywhere near the church or the churchyard in future and if you want that rubble shifted then I suggest you shift it yourself. Good day to you.'

Fred lurched off, leaving Mrs Sparshott open-mouthed.

As the major waited for the arrival of the brigadier at the Masonic Hall in Clayton and Fred Massey staggered up the track to Tanfield Farm, three women stood at the gate of La Chaumière Rose, a small honey-coloured stone cottage with a thatched roof and crazy-paving path. The garden, which had a wishing well and an assortment of brightly painted plaster gnomes, was immaculate with a small healthy-looking lawn, neatly trimmed hedges and carefully tended flowerbeds.

'Is this it?' asked Mrs Pocock, pulling a face.

'This is it,' replied Mrs Sloughthwaite. 'Mrs Wigglesworth is expecting us. I told her I was bringing two friends along with me.'

The door, with its brass knocker in the shape of a grinning pixie, opened before the women had reached it.

Mrs Sloughthwaite gave a small smug smile. 'Telepathetic,' she whispered to her companions.

'She saw us from the window,' replied Mrs Pocock under her breath. 'I saw the curtains move.'

Mrs Wigglesworth was a dumpy, round-faced little woman. Her heavily made-up face was pale and powdery, her glossy lips the colour of crushed raspberries and her eyes a bright and startling blue. She wore a vivid pink and amazingly tight-fitting woollen two-piece suit which emphasised her heavy hips and wide shelf of a bosom and she sported a long rope of artificial pearls and matching earrings. There was a waft of lavender cologne.

'Welcome to "Roselea",' she said to her visitors, her round face wreathed in smiles. 'Do come in.'

The three women were shown into a small tidy lounge where virtually everything was coloured pink: walls, curtains, carpet. Even the two prints above the fireplace depicted a pink sunset and the artificial silk flowers on the small occasional table were pink roses.

'Do sit down and make yourselves comfy,' trilled Mrs Wigglesworth.

The three women sat on a sofa upholstered in a thick rose-coloured material with matching cushions.

'Now, first things first. I've popped the kettle on. I am sure you would all like a nice cup of tea.'

'Could I have coffee?' asked Mrs Pocock

'No dear, not coffee,' said Mrs Wigglesworth, waddling off to the kitchen. 'It has to be tea without milk and sugar so I can read your leaves.'

When the clairvoyant had disappeared, the three women sat for a moment in silence on the edge of the sofa. Then Mrs Pocock whispered, 'Did you ever see the like? I've never set eyes on so much pink in all my life. It's like sitting in a big cloud of candy floss.'

'It is a bit overpowering I have to admit,' agreed Mrs Sloughthwaite in a hushed voice.

'I like pink,' said Mrs O'Connor, 'in moderation that is. It's a colour that raises one's spirits, so it does.'

'Well it helps.' Mrs Wigglesworth, having overheard the comment, had returned unobserved.

'I'm sorry?' said Mrs O'Connor.

'Raises the sprits, dear,' said Mrs Wigglesworth. 'That's what I do.'

'Oh, I see.'

Mrs Pocock pulled another face.

Their host was carrying a tray on which were three pink gilt-edged bone china cups and saucers, a matching creamer, three delicate silver spoons, a strainer and a big silver-plated teapot.

'Pink,' she confided as she poured the tea with the fixed smile cemented on her face, 'is such a warm and comforting colour and creates the right ambiance which emboldens the spirits to make contact.'

'So they can recognise colour then these spirits?' ventured Mrs Pocock.

'Oh yes, dear, they can see and smell and feel a great deal.'

'Are they here now?' asked Mrs O'Connor in a hushed voice.

'Yes, dear,' replied Mrs Wigglesworth. 'They are always with us.'

Mrs O'Connor gave a small shudder and looked around.

When the visitors had finished their tea, Mrs Wigglesworth cleared everything away except one cup and saucer. She then draped a fringed pink velvet cloth over the table.

'I was telling my friends about you being a clairvoyant,' began Mrs Sloughthwaite.

'Amongst other things, dear,' said Mrs Wigglesworth. 'I combine the mystical powers and secrets of palmistry, tarot, clairvoyance, astrology and face reading. Born gifted with spiritual powers, I can help and advise my clients on their problems.' She looked searchingly at Mrs Pocock. 'And I can see you have a problem, dear,' she added.

'Me!' exclaimed Mrs Pocock.

'I can read it in your face, dear. Would you mind coming to sit over here with me?' she asked. 'I need you to be near to me when I read your leaves.'

'Why have you picked my cup rather than the others?' she asked apprehensively.

'Because you are in need of greater help, dear.' Mrs Wigglesworth fluttered her false eyelashes and put her hand on Mrs Pocock's arm in a reassuring way as her client sat in the chair. 'You see, I was born with second sight, an extrasensory gift and I see people's thoughts in their eyes, know the secrets from what is written on their faces and feel their hopes and fears by touching them.' She looked down at the saucer. 'And the leaves also tell your story. I can't control the leaves. The leaves say it all.'

Mrs Pocock was lost for words.

The clairvoyant swirled the remains of the cup around before upturning them on the saucer, which she placed in front of her on the table. Her eyes took on an eager glint as she peered at the tea leaves as if scrutinising a specimen under a microscope and her forehead creased in concentration. The three women leant forward expectantly.

There followed a long silence.

'Cancer!' exclaimed Mrs Wigglesworth suddenly.

'What?' cried Mrs Pocock, jumping up in her seat as if she had been doused in icy water.

'Your star sign. I see that yours is Cancer. Am I right, dear?'

'I've no idea,' replied Mrs Pocock. The colour had drained from her face. 'I don't read horoscopes.'

'When is your birthday, dear?'

'The twenty-fourth of June,' replied Mrs Pocock, sounding agitated. She sat down.

'I thought so. You're the crab.'

'A crab?'

'Your star sign, dear. Like the crab I can see you are strong and tenacious, tucked away between the cracks in the rocks. If you feel strongly about something you don't let go, you hang on. You're a dogged and determined person.'

'That's spot on,' observed Mrs Sloughthwaite from the sofa. 'When she's got a bee in her bonnet she won't let it lie.'

'Please!' said Mrs Wigglesworth sharply. 'No interruptions. It disturbs my psychic concentration.' She looked down again at the tea leaves and then gave Mrs Pocock a studying look, neither friendly nor unfriendly. 'You have a hard shell but inside there is a softness. Of course, if you are challenged you can be very tough and stubborn and make use of those sharp pincers.'

Mrs Pocock looked down at her hands.

Mrs Wigglesworth continued. 'I can see that you are a troubled person, that life has not treated you all that well and that some people misunderstand you.'

Mrs Sloughthwaite and Mrs O'Connor, sitting mesmerised on the sofa, exchanged looks.

'You don't feel that you've achieved your true potential. Am I right, dear?'

'Well yes, I mean no, I do sometimes feel like that,' murmured Mrs Pocock, spellbound.

'Taken for granted, dear,' sighed Mrs Wigglesworth.

'Well, yes, I sometimes feel like that,' agreed Mrs Pocock.

'Things will improve. I see a brighter future here, greater happiness and fulfilment.'

Mrs Wigglesworth suddenly drew in a huge slow intake of breath. She pressed her fingertips together and closed her eyes in a prayer-like attitude. 'I'm getting some strong psychic vibrations. Someone's coming through,' she murmured.

'Who?' asked Mrs Pocock, leaning forward.

'It's a woman. Her name's Betty.'

'I don't know a Betty.'

'It could be Peggy. She passed over into the spirit world a long time ago.'

'I can't be doing with this,' said Mrs Pocock, half rising from her chair.

'Or Connie.'

Mrs Pocock sat back down with a jolt.

'My mother was called Connie,' she said.

'She says don't worry about the sixpence.'

'Sixpence?' Mrs Pocock twitched nervously.

'You kept the sixpence. She knew you had taken it. She says it doesn't matter.'

Mrs Pocock held her hand to her throat.

'Good Lord!' she muttered.

'She says little Vicky's with her.'

'That was my sister.'

'She passed over when she was young, didn't she, dear?'

Mrs Pocock nodded.

'She knows you often think about her. Well, she wants you to know that she's happy and says not to grieve your heart for her.'

Mrs Pocock felt her chest tighten and tears springing to her eyes.

'I was thinking about her only today,' she said, sniffing.

'I can see a wardrobe,' intoned Mrs Wigglesworth.

'A wardrobe?' repeated Mrs Pocock.

'With a door that won't close. He doesn't want to be in there, dear.'

'That'll be my father,' said Mrs Pocock. 'I've got him in the wardrobe.'

'Jayus, Mary and Joseph,' muttered Mrs O'Connor, making the sign of the cross.

'I keep his ashes in the wardrobe,' said Mrs Pocock. 'He's on a shelf at the back.'

'He doesn't want to be in there,' repeated the medium. 'It's dark in there. He wants to be free. He wants to be scattered on the ocean, dear,' said Mrs Wigglesworth, 'and carried away on the currents of time.'

'But he never liked water,' said Mrs Pocock. 'He got sea sick on the boating lake at Blackpool.'

'Your father has an important piece of information for me to impart to you,' continued Mrs Wigglesworth. She produced a small lacy handkerchief from up her sleeve and dabbed the perspiration which had gathered on the tiny wisps of white hairs across her upper lip. 'He says to tell you that you must visit the doctor. He says you need to know that.'

'What is it?' implored Mrs Pocock. 'What does he think is wrong with me?'

Mrs Wigglesworth opened her eyes and blinked rapidly.

'He's gone,' she said cheerily. 'Short and sweet. It sometimes happens like that. Some don't hang about.'

Mrs Pocock sat bolt upright in the chair, too stunned to speak.

'Can you do me now?' Mrs Sloughthwaite asked the clairvoyant.

'Not today, dear,' replied Mrs Wigglesworth. 'I've expended all my psychic energy. I'd be happy to arrange another consultation for next week.' She looked at Mrs Pocock but continued to address Mrs Sloughthwaite. 'I think your friend is in need of some TLC,' she whispered. 'It sometimes comes as a bit of a shock when the spirits come through.'

Later, as she headed for the door with her arm around Mrs Pocock who still looked dazed, Mrs Sloughthwaite was approached by the clairvoyant.

'There is the little matter of my professional fee, dear,' said Mrs Wigglesworth in a hushed voice.

'Oh yes,' said Mrs Sloughthwaite opening her handbag and feeling rather aggrieved that she should have to pay. *After all,* she thought, *it was Mrs Pocock and not herself who had got through to the spirit world*. It would be an expensive cup of tea.

'Thirty-five pounds,' said Mrs Wigglesworth smiling and then added, 'plus VAT.'

Mrs Pocock was uncharacteristically quiet on the bus home.

'I thought,' said Mrs O'Connor, speaking in a low whisper as if there had been a death, 'that when she said she had an important piece of information for her to impart, that she would tell her where some hidden money was stashed.'

Mrs Sloughthwaite wasn't listening for she was still smarting from having to part with her money.

'I don't think we should have brought her,' continued Mrs O'Connor. 'I blame myself for persuading her to come. She's in a state of shock.'

Yes, thought the shopkeeper. *I'm in a state of shock having to fork out thirty-five quid plus VAT.*

Major Neville-Gravitas stood in the entrance at the Masonic Hall, awaiting the arrival of the distinguished guest. He was in a rather ill-tempered frame of mind for he had arrived at the function to see he was the only one in a dinner jacket and wearing his medals.

'It was agreed at the committee meeting, Cedric,' said a small slight man of about sixty with sparse mousy hair and a long, inquisitive nose.

'I certainly did not agree,' said the major peevishly.

'We decided that it should be an informal affair.' He was dressed in a blazer with a regimental badge on the breast pocket, baggy grey trousers and shiny black shoes.

'I don't recall anything of the sort!' snapped the major. 'I understood it would be a formal occasion.'

'Well, you missed the last meeting. I guess nobody thought of telling you. They just assumed you knew.'

'I'm not a mind-reader!' retorted the major.

'These things happen,' said the small slight man feebly.

'These things should not happen,' replied the major, still speaking in a petulant tone of voice. 'As the treasurer, I would have thought it right and proper that I was informed. I feel such a fool being the only one in a dinner jacket.' He started to unfasten his medals.

'I can only apologise, Cedric,' said the small, slight man. 'I guess it's too late for you to go back home and change.'

'Out of the question!' exclaimed the major. He stuffed the medals in his pocket.

'I'm sorry for the mix-up.'

'And I know nothing about this Brigadier Carstairs who's speaking. Since I am the one to introduce the man it would have been helpful for me to have his CV.'

'It was a last-minute change. The speaker finder arranged for the MP, Sir Toby Fratton-West, to speak but he was called back to the Commons for some important vote.'

The major looked at his watch.

'So what's this brigadier like?' he asked.

'I don't know,' said the small, slight man. 'We asked for a speaker from an agency and this retired brigadier was suggested. He seemed ideal for the occasion. Although they hadn't got him on their books or heard him speak themselves, they said that that he comes with a strong recommendation. Evidently quite an excellent raconteur, very amusing and with some wonderful anecdotes about life in the army and he would not be charging a fee. He seems perfect for the occasion.'

'Something of an unknown quantity then,' observed the major. 'Well I hope he doesn't drone on. In my experience, brigadiers can be very boring people. Anyway, when is he arriving?'

'Any minute now I should imagine,' said the small, slight man.

'I've been standing out here awaiting his arrival for the last ten minutes.' The major looked at his watch again and sighed. 'I must say that when I was in the army punctuality was extremely important and if I was late on parade—'

He stopped mid-sentence as he caught sight of a tall, elegant, middle-aged woman who had been standing nearby. She was dressed in a stylish grey silk suit, pink blouse and extremely high-heeled shoes and was regarding him levelly.

'I'm sorry, madam,' he said, moving forward, 'this is a private function.'

'So I believe,' she replied smiling.

'It's for members only,' said the major. 'We're waiting for our speaker, the brigadier.'

'I'm the brigadier,' said the woman, patting the major on his arm, 'and I promise I won't drone on for too long.'

The surgery was particularly busy that morning. When Michael popped his head around the door of the waiting room he found the place so full some patients were standing. They were coughing and sneezing, sniffing and wheezing.

'Good morning,' he said cheerfully.

'Morning, doctor,' came a subdued chorus from the ill and the infirm.

'I shall be with you in a minute,' he told them, thinking to himself that he would not be getting home for quite some time.

His first patient, Mrs Pocock, looked as if she had the weight of the world on her shoulders. She had had a series of sleep-less nights thinking of what Mrs Wigglesworth had divulged at the psychic consultation and, although she had been in perfect health for many years, she decided to visit the doctor to put her mind at rest.

Dr Stirling, however, did not put her mind at rest.

'I am very glad you came to see me, Mrs Pocock,' said Dr Stirling having given her an examination.

'Is something wrong?' she asked.

'Your blood pressure is abnormally high,' said the doctor.

'What does that mean?' she asked anxiously.

'It means,' replied Michael, 'that we need to bring it down. I shall prescribe some tablets and we will monitor it over the next few weeks.'

'So is it serious?'

'No, I don't think so, not if we control it, but I would like to see you next week to do a blood test and I need a sample of urine.' He gave her a small tube in a plastic bag. He looked at the tragic expression on the patient's face. 'I don't think there is anything to worry about but just to be on the safe side we will run a couple of tests.'

'Thank you, doctor,' she said, getting to her feet.

'It's very lucky that you made an appointment to see me. You say you have not been feeling unwell?'

'No, I just thought I'd have a check-up. I mean you never know, do you?'

'Well it is just as well that you did.'

The second patient of the morning gripped his stomach dramatically as he entered the consulting room.

'I think I'm being poisoned, doctor,' he groaned.

'And what makes you think that, Mr Massey?' asked Dr Stirling, trying to conceal a smile. He knew from experience what a malingerer this patient was and how melodramatic he could be when describing his aliments.

'I've had no trouble with my belly up until my nephew Clarence and his wife and baby moved in with me. I've had terrible pains since then.'

'For how long?'

'On and off for three weeks.'

'And you think someone is poisoning you?'

'I reckon it's Bianca, she's my nephew's wife. I think she's putting something foreign in my food.'

'And why should she be doing that?' asked the doctor.

'To get my money, that's what,' whined Fred. 'When I kick the bucket, Clarence will inherit the farm and everything. I reckon that wife of his can't wait to be rid of me and get her hands on it.'

'Or it could be that it's something you ate which didn't agree with you,' said the doctor.

'I think she might be slipping in a poisonous variety of mushroom into my meals – Death Cap or something like that. I wouldn't put it past her. You hear about this sort thing all the time in the papers. Relations wishing to get their greedy hands on the money of them what are old and helpless.'

'Well let's have a look at you,' said the doctor. 'Just lie on the couch and lift up your shirt please . . . OK, so tell me what it feels like,' said Dr Stirling, kneading the patient's stomach.

'Just a heavy, dull, excruciating pain,' moaned Fred.

Following the examination, Dr Stirling washed his hands. 'I'm sending you to the hospital for some tests,' he said. 'I am pretty certain, Mr Massey, that no-one is trying to poison you. I think you may be intolerant to certain foods.'

'Aye, well we'll see what they say at the hospital,' replied Fred, making for the door. 'I never had any trouble before Clarence and his family moved in with me.'

The next patient of the day was Mr Gribbon, who entered the consulting room bent-backed and exhaling loudly.

Another malingerer, thought the doctor.

'I see it's still the back,' he said.

'Terrible, doctor,' complained Mr Gribbon, screwing up his face as if in pain. 'I can hardly move.'

Having observed the caretaker cycling at speed down the towpath by the canal, running for a bus, digging his garden and carrying heavy bags at the supermarket, Dr Stirling knew for a fact that there was nothing much wrong with this patient's back.

The doctor examined the patient, then sat behind his desk and took out a notebook. 'I think this has gone on long enough,' he said.

'What?' exclaimed the caretaker.

'You've been having trouble with that back of yours for some time. Something needs to be done.'

'That's why I'm here, doctor,' said Mr Gribbon, nodding. 'A few days' rest in bed at home will do me a power of good. If you could just give me a sick note . . . '

'Oh, I think something more drastic than that is needed,' he was told.

'Drastic!'

'I have mentioned this before when you have been to see me,' said Dr Stirling. 'I'm going to refer to you a specialist at the hospital. I think an operation may be in order. You might be laid up for quite some time but in the long run it will sort out your back problem.'

'Operation!' interrupted the caretaker. 'Oh I don't like the sound of that. I don't like hospitals.'

'I'll make an appointment for you at Clayton Royal Infirmary.'

'No, no, don't do that, doctor,' said the caretaker. 'I'm sure a few days' rest will sort me out.'

'I'm afraid it won't, Mr Gribbon,' replied Dr Stirling. 'If you don't keep moving, your back might seize up. So, what about the hospital? Shall I make that appointment for you?'

'No, don't do that.'

'Of course the job of work you do cannot help your condition,' said Dr Stirling. 'All that heavy lifting and stretching, bending and sweeping. Perhaps you ought to consider changing to something more sedentary.'

'Sedentary?'

'So you wouldn't have to do all the heavy work. You could have a word with my wife. Obviously she would be sad to see you go but under the circumstances—'

'No, no, doctor,' spluttered the caretaker. 'I'm not the sort of person to complain. I'll put up with it.'

'I'll prescribe some painkillers.'

'And you won't mention anything to Mrs Stirling about suggesting I get another job?'

'Of course not, Mr Gribbon,' replied Michael, smiling. 'Everything said inside this room is strictly confidential.'

On leaving, Mr Gribbon moved rather quicker than when he had entered.

The last patient of the day was Robbie's mother. It was clear that Mrs Banks was not at all well. Her face looked an unhealthy shade of grey and there were dark shadows under her eyes.

'I have a lump, doctor,' she said.

On most Saturdays Danny liked to be out in the open air. He was a country lad at heart and loved nothing better than to roam the outdoors. That afternoon he decided to go down to the woods and headed for the millpond by a narrow muddy path, dark beneath a canopy of spreading branches thick with leaves of russet and brown. At the millpond he sat on a dead tree trunk, his legs stretched out before him, and looked out across the oily black water. Then he stared up at the clear blue sky. A hawk rode the air currents, sweeping in wide circles above the trees. He could feel the warmth of the mellow afternoon sun on his face and caught a waft of wild garlic. His granddad had once told him that things in life generally work out for the best and in this, as in most cases, he had been proved right. On these occasions, when he was alone, Danny liked to remember the old man who had brought him up. He could picture the weathered face the colour of bruised parchment, the grizzled, smoky-grey hair, the untidy beard and the smiling eyes resting in a net of wrinkles. He could see him in the clean, long-sleeved, collarless shirt, open at the neck, baggy corduroy trousers and heavy boots. When his grandfather died, Danny felt his world was falling apart. Then he had been fostered by Dr Stirling and went to live at Clumber Lodge. The doctor married and the new Mrs Stirling moved in. He had come to love them both. They were like the mum and dad he had never known.

After a while Danny reached into his pocket and took his pet ferret Ferdy out of his coat; he had smuggled it out of the cottage without anyone seeing. He put one hand under the creature's stomach and gently stroked the sleek body with the other.

There was crackle of twigs behind him and, turning, Danny saw a small hunched figure approaching.

'I thought you'd be down here,' said Robbie.

'Eyup,' said Danny, moving along the trunk to let the boy sit down.

They sat there in silence.

'It's champion 'ere, i'n't it?' said Danny after a while. 'Dead peaceful. I reckon there'd have been a reight racket when t'mill were workin'.' He looked at Robbie when the boy didn't answer. 'Does tha want to 'old mi ferret?'

'No, I'm not bothered.'

''E won't bite.'

'I know. I just don't want to hold him.'

'Suit thissen.'

There was another silence.

''Ow's t'fosterin' goin' then?' asked Danny.

'It's OK,' replied Robbie, picking up a pebble.

'Where are yer livin'?'

'Treetop Farm.'

'I'd love to live on a farm. It's not that I'm un'appy weer I am, but I'd love to live on a farm wi' all them animals.' He put the ferret back in his pocket. 'Are they all reight?'

'Who?'

'Them who are fosterin' ya.'

'Yes they are.' Robbie hurled the pebble into the water.

In truth, his foster carers were more than allright. After some initial wariness, Robbie was beginning to like them and to trust them. Mr and Mrs Ross had fostered many children over the years, sometimes taking into their home those difficult and demanding children who were hard to place. They knew from experience that adult–teenager conflict was often par for the course and had learnt ways of dealing with it in a calm and patient manner, never losing their tempers and helping those in their care to express their feelings and deal with those moments of frustration that could so easily have become full-blown tantrums. They recognised in Robbie a child who was hurt and lonely, a boy who felt unloved and unwanted. From the start, Mr Ross had treated Robbie as a young adult and in doing so the boy had begun to respond and act more responsibly. Mrs Ross listened, on the few occasions when Robbie opened up, to what he had to say to her and acknowledged his feelings. Both Mr and Mrs Ross knew that children like praise and that Robbie had received precious little in his young life. They knew that a little praise went a long way. They didn't judge the boy's mother and could understand that she had felt vulnerable and under pressure from a dominating husband until she was unable to cope.

'Tha dun't say much, does tha?' said Danny now. 'It's like gerrin blood out of yon pebble.'

'I want to ask you something,' said Robbie.

'Oh aye?'

'How do you get adopted?'

'I don't reightly know,' Danny replied.

'But you're being adopted, aren't you?'

'Aye I am. I suppose it's for kids who don't 'ave a family. I 'ave a grandma but we din't gerron an' I don't see much of 'er. Anyroad, she dun't want me livin' wi 'er.'

'My mum doesn't want me living with her,' said Robbie. His mouth was a tight little line.

''Ow come?'

'When my dad died she married again and now she doesn't want me any more. It's because of him. I hate my stepfather. I can't stand him. He said to her that it was either him or me. And she chose him.'

'I've never 'ated anybody,' said Danny, scratching his hair. 'There's them as I dunt like but I can't say I 'ate 'em.'

'Well you'd hate my step-father. When he first came to live with us everything changed.'

Immediately after Robbie's step-father had moved in, he put his stamp on the house. The place smelt of him. He got rid of most of the things that had belonged to the boy's father, keeping only those items that he wanted for himself – the fishing rods, tools, the motorbike and the big leather armchair in the lounge. Every time Robbie saw his step-father sprawled in the chair smoking and guzzling a can of lager, he felt incensed and hatred caught in his throat like a solid lump. Then the shouting had started and the violence.

'So I wasn't wanted,' said Robbie.

'That's pretty rotten,' said Danny.

'So how do you get adopted then?'

'Well it starts off with yer goin' to live wi' somebody an' if tha gets on wi 'em then they sometimes adopt ya. That's what Dr and Missis Stirlin' are doing wi' me. It teks a long time an' you' ave to see a social worker an' there's loads o' questions to answer an' papers to sign.'

'And if you're adopted will you be able to live with them for good?' asked Robbie.

'Yeah, that's the idea.' Danny knew how difficult Robbie could be. He had been a pupil at the village school and had witnessed the boy's outbursts, his anger and his insolence. 'T'thing is, Robbie, thy 'as to behave thissen. If tha starts kickin' off an' answerin' back an' bein' a pain in t'bum an' causin' trouble, then they'll not want thee an' tha'll be sent back an' tha'll end up in one o' them children's 'omes. If tha likes it weer thy are an' gerron wi' them what fosters you, then thas got to keep tha nose clean otherwise there's no way they'll adopt thee.'

Robbie nodded.

'Now does tha want to come an' see a badger sett?'

10

Each lunchtime Elisabeth made a point of touring the school. She knew of head teachers who closeted themselves in their rooms for most of the day; she resolved not to be one of these. She wanted the teachers and the children to see a lot of her. That lunchtime, as she walked along the corridor and visited each classroom, she felt justifiably proud. The building was immaculate: clean, tidy, bright walls, highly polished floors and displays of work well mounted. Children's paintings and poems, posters, pictures and book jackets covered every available space. Shelves held attractive books, tables were covered in shells, models, photographs and little artefacts and there were coloured drapes at the windows. But there was something missing. The school was unusually quiet. She decided to put an item on the agenda at the next staff meeting to get volunteers to organise some extracurricular activities for lunchtimes and after school.

When she had been appointed as head teacher of Barton-in-the-Dale School, Elisabeth had asked the children how they felt the school might be improved. The answers had been predictable. Many of the children had bemoaned the fact that there was little happening out of lessons, no sports teams or after school clubs, lunch-time activities and trips out of school, needs that Elisabeth had identified herself and which she was determined to meet. When she had suggested that they might provide some lunchtime and after school activities, the teachers were keen to be involved. Mrs Robertshaw soon recruited a good number of children for the drama club, Miss Wilson organised a rounders' team and held practices, for boys and girls, at Friday lunchtimes and Miss Brakespeare, the deputy head teacher, started a craft group.

Elisabeth had then enlisted the support of people in the local community. Mr Atticus had been delighted to be asked to take the assembly now and again and start a chess club and his wife, a very fine artist, had agreed to take an art class. Mr Parkinson, the scout leader, had coached the boys and girls at football practice each Thursday after school and Mr Tomlinson, who played the organ in the chapel, had supervised the choir which, at its first performance, had delighted the minister and the congregation at the Methodist chapel.

During the weeks which followed, the school had become a hive of activity at lunchtimes and after school. The clubs and extra classes, the sports activities and the music had taken off to such an extent that Elisabeth started to receive many positive comments from parents at the school gates about how pleased they were with these initiatives.

With the start of term at the new school, things had changed in that many of the clubs and activities were no longer on offer. Miss Brakespeare had married Mr Tomlinson and they had retired to Scarborough, Miss Wilson now taught at the Urebank site and Mr Atticus, recently translated to archdeacon, and his wife had moved to Clayton. *Yes*, thought Elisabeth now, *we need to organise some more activities*.

Elisabeth arrived at the library. Originally a dark, unused corner near the toilets, the area had been transformed into a small but pleasant space with a carpet and cushions, a small table and chairs and a good selection of books. A small girl with large wide-set eyes and long rust-coloured hair, curly and shiny, sat reading.

'Hello, Roisin,' said Elisabeth.

'Oh hello, Mrs Devine. I mean, Mrs Stirling. I keep forgetting you got married.'

'I've not had much of a chance to speak to you since we started school this term,' said Elisabeth. 'How are things?'

'Just grand,' said the child. 'My daddy and me have moved into the gate lodge at Limebeck House.'

'A bit different from the caravan I guess.'

'I liked the caravan,' said Roisin, thoughtfully, 'but having a room of my own is better. I've never had a room of my own.'

'And how is your father getting on up there at the big house?'

'Just grand,' replied the child. 'He's been given a new job. He's now an estate manager. He says it's just a fancy name for being the odd-job man.' She giggled. 'He has to shave every day and he's had his hair cut and sometimes he has to get all dressed up.'

'Well you give him my best wishes,' said Elisabeth.

'I will.'

'Now, I've been asked to enter some children for a competition. It's to perform a poem or an extract from a story. Might you be interested?'

'I don't know if I could stand up in front of a lot of people,' said the child.

'You did when you took the part of the wicked witch in *The Wizard of Oz*. You have a strong clear voice and I think you would do very well.'

Roison thought for moment. 'Well, I suppose I could. I do like poetry and I do know some poems by heart. Daddy taught me them.'

'I think that's pretty much settled then,' said Elisabeth. 'We will decide on what you might perform later on.'

'I know someone who would do really, really well when it comes to performing,' said Roisin.

'Oscar?' said Elisabeth.

'Oscar,' repeated the girl.

'Well I'm up for it,' said Oscar when Elisabeth found him and told him about the competition. 'It sounds frightfully exciting and I know just what poem to recite. I've started learning it already.' He was sitting on the wall in the playground having been told by Mr Hornchurch to vacate the classroom.

'He's telling off two of the boys,' Oscar said confidingly. He looked peeved. 'I had to leave off what I was doing and come outside. It's very inconvenient you know, Mrs Stirling. I was in the middle of writing an entry in my journal.'

'Who were the boys?' asked Elisabeth, fearing the worst.

'Robbie, of course,' Oscar told her, 'and Barry Biggerdyke. They've been fighting.'

'Oh dear,' she sighed. 'Do you know what about?'

'Something and nothing I guess,' replied the boy, sounding very old-fashioned. 'Violence is never the answer, is it, Mrs Stirling?'

'No, it isn't, Oscar,' she replied.

Elisabeth arrived at Mr Hornchurch's classroom and looked through the window in the door. The teacher was sitting on his desk, his legs dangling down. He didn't look like someone remonstrating with two miscreants. He looked as if he was engaged in some casual conversation.

Standing before him were the two boys.

Elisabeth popped her head around the door.

'Is everything all right, Mr Hornchurch?' she asked.

'Everything is fine, thank you, Mrs Stirling,' he replied.

'Is there anything I can do?'

'Nothing,' he said smiling. 'All is in hand.'

Both boys looked at her sheepishly.

'I don't think we need to bother the head teacher,' Mr Hornchurch told the boys when Elisabeth had gone. 'To involve Mrs Stirling makes it all the more serious and we wouldn't want that, would we? If we did see Mrs Stirling about this, I suppose she would probably want to contact your parents or guardians, ask them to come into school, threaten you with suspension, keep you in at breaks, stop your football practice – all sorts of dire punishments. So, as I said, you wouldn't want that, would you?'

'No,' replied Robbie under his breath.

The other boy gave a non-committal grunt.

Barry Biggerdyke was an unfortunate-looking child with his pasty complexion, crooked teeth and large protruding ears. His large moon face was half hidden behind a fiercely cut gingery fringe.

'What was that, Barry?' asked the teacher calmly. 'I didn't quite catch what you said.'

'No!' said the boy loudly. He stared at the teacher. There was a wary and resentful look in his eyes.

'So,' said Mr Hornchurch, meeting the boy's challenging glare, 'let's get to the bottom of this, shall we? Who started it?'

'Him. He punched me,' said Barry in the petulant tone of the aggrieved. He rubbed his chest.

'For what reason?'

'I said something.'

'And what did you say?'

'I said he stinks and he does.'

Robbie remained silent. He balled his fist with fury. His lips were pressed together in a tight thin line and his eyes were like arrow slits. He was trying hard to control his anger.

'And how do you think that makes someone feel, Barry, to be told they stink?' the teacher's tone was enquiring rather than reproachful.

'I don't know,' replied the boy sullenly.

'I mean if someone were to say something unpleasant about you, make some hurtful comment, how would you feel?'

'I don't know,' repeated the boy.

'Oh I think you do, Barry. You would be very upset wouldn't you, possibly very angry?'

'He shouldn't have punched me,' said the boy, rubbing his chest again for effect.

'You are quite right, he shouldn't. I am not excusing Robbie in all this but you must understand that if you decide to make some wounding comment about someone then you must expect the consequences.' The teacher then leant forward on the desk. 'Don't you think?' he asked, challenging the boy to disagree.

Barry gnawed at his bottom lip. 'I suppose,' he said.

'So, it won't happen again, will it?'

'No,' mumbled Barry.

'And, Robbie,' said Mr Hornchurch, 'violence solves nothing. If someone says something unkind to you it is best to ignore it, just put it down to the comments of a sad and stupid person who has nothing better to do than hurt other people's feelings. There's an old rhyme which goes, "Sticks and stones may break your bones, but calling names never hurts me".'

Robbie remained silent with his head lowered. Of course, he knew different. Sticks and stones may break your bones, but calling names can break your heart. He knew from experience that cruel words, like those he had received from his step-father, unlike bruises and cuts, never heal.

'So we will leave it at that,' said Mr Hornchurch, jumping down from his desk. 'So no more name-calling, Barry, and, Robbie, in future, no lashing out. Is that understood?'

Robbie took a little breath as if he was about to speak but he didn't say anything. He just nodded.

Later that afternoon, as Mr Hornchurch was on his way to the staff meeting, he saw Robbie lingering in the entrance hall.

'Still here?' said the teacher.

'I'm getting a lift home,' Robbie told him. The boy edged closer.

'Was there something else?' asked the teacher.

'Are you going to tell Mrs Stirling?' asked Robbie.

'About what?'

'About me hitting that lad?'

'Didn't I say we didn't need to bother the head teacher?'

'Adults say a lot of things they don't mean,' said the boy.

'Well I don't. I mean what I say. OK?'

Robbie nodded and headed for the door but turned and, as an afterthought, said, 'And anybody would stink if they landed in three feet of pig shit.'

'I'm telling you, Mrs Scrimshaw, that I heard these footsteps coming down the side of the school by your office and when I went out to investigate there was no-one there. Whoever or whatever it was disappeared into thin air. It made me go cold all over.'

It was later that afternoon and in the small school office the caretaker, perched on the corner of her desk and leaning closer, was telling the school secretary about what he described as 'a supernatural occurrence'.

Mrs Scrimshaw caught a strong whiff of floor polish and disinfectant and wrinkled her nose.

'Come on, Mrs Scrimshaw,' he said. 'What do you make of that, then?'

The secretary removed her glasses and placed them carefully on the desk. She looked up at the caretaker. 'What do I make of it?' she told him. 'I reckon you were imagining it, that's what I reckon.' She replaced her glasses and looked down at the pile of papers before her.

'I was not imagining anything,' replied the caretaker. 'I heard them as clear as anything. I'd just finished buffing my floors and turned off all the lights and then I came in your office to empty the bin and heard them, these footsteps on the path down the side of the school, big clomping footsteps they were.'

'You have already told me,' she said, sounding irritated. 'Well I've not heard anything and I'm in the office all the time.'

'It always happens at night when you've gone home,' the caretaker told her.

'Really, Mr Gribbon,' she told him impatiently, 'I have far more important things to think about than imaginary footsteps. I have all these papers to staple together for the staff meeting after school so can you let me get on, please?'

'Really loud they were, as if someone was wearing heavy boots.'

'Mr Gribbon,' replied the school secretary sharply, 'as I've just said, I have better things to do this afternoon than listen to you romancing about some imaginary footsteps.' She shuffled in her chair and picked up a stapler.

'Well, I reckon there's something very peculiar going on,' he persisted, rubbing his chin thoughtfully. 'I tell you this, it fair put the wind up me hearing these footsteps and then whoever or whatever it was disappearing into thin air.'

'Well if it's bothering you that much,' she replied, 'I suggest you have a word with Mrs Stirling. She'll perhaps put it on the staff meeting agenda under "ghosts". Now I must get on.'

Oscar appeared at the door. 'Excuse me, Mr Gribbon, I'm sorry to interrupt your conversation but I couldn't help overhearing what you were saying.'

The caretaker turned and grimaced. 'Well you shouldn't be earwigging,' he snapped. 'You should be getting off home. You hang about the place like a bad smell.'

'Hasn't your mother arrived to collect you yet, Oscar?' asked the school secretary.

'No, not yet, Mrs Scrimshaw,' replied the child cheerfully, 'but I am sure she will be here directly. She has a great many commitments on Fridays and said she would be a little late.'

'Perhaps I ought to give your mother a ring,' she said.

'She'll be on her way,' the child told her casually. 'I wouldn't trouble yourself.'

'Anyway, what do you want, Oscar?' asked Mrs Scrimshaw.

'I couldn't help but overhear what Mr Gribbon was saying,' said the boy. 'You were talking very loudly. I could hear you down the corridor.'

A vein in Mr Gribbon's temple stood out and throbbed angrily. 'And?' he demanded.

'I've heard those footsteps too.'

'You have?' exclaimed Mr Gribbon. 'When?'

'Last week,' the boy told him. 'I was waiting to be collected by my mother but she was running a little late again and I was getting a bit worried. I came into the office to ask Mrs Scrimshaw to phone my mother but she had gone home. That's when I heard them.'

'The footsteps?' asked the caretaker.

'Yes. First of all I heard the gate open and then close with a bang and there followed these footsteps. They were really loud and echoey. I thought it might be you wanting to lock up so I looked out of the window to see.'

'And?' asked the caretaker.

'There was no-one there.'

'What did I say, Mrs Scrimshaw!' Mr Gribbon exclaimed gleefully. 'I wasn't imagining it.'

'Of course, there must be some logical explanation,' announced Oscar. 'Personally I don't believe in ghosts myself. People don't just disappear.'

'It's about time you were disappearing,' said Mrs Scrimshaw, 'so off you go back and wait for your mother in the entrance. I am sure she won't be too long now.' She glanced at the caretaker who was rubbing his chin and looking thoughtful. 'And you can disappear as well, Mr Gribbon. I've wasted enough time this afternoon.'

★   ★   ★

'The first item on the agenda this afternoon,' said Elisabeth at the staff meeting, 'is to say thank you to you for all your hard work and for making these first few weeks of the new school term go so smoothly.'

'Apart from the boy swallowing the marble,' muttered Mr Jolly.

'Apart from the marble,' repeated Elisabeth smiling. 'I hope you all feel as optimistic as I do about things. The children have settled in well, I have received some very complimentary letters from the parents and the new governors are a keen and committed team. All in all, I think we have made a really good start.'

'I think things have gone extremely well,' said Mrs Robertshaw. 'I expected a few teething problems but as you say, Elisabeth, it's been incident free.' She glanced over at Mr Jolly and could not resist a further comment. 'Apart from the episode with the marble that is.'

Mr Jolly grimaced.

'I think we have heard enough about the marble,' said Elisabeth. 'Let's move on. Now at the governors' meeting Councillor Cooper mentioned the county Poetry and Prose Recitation Competition. Schools are to be invited to enter pupils to deliver a piece of verse or an extract from a story and I think we should take part. If there are some children in your class who you feel might enjoy competing and are in with a chance then do let me know. I've already mentioned it to a few pupils and they seem very keen. Elsie, perhaps you could do a bit of coaching?'

'Of course,' replied her colleague.

'Now this brings us on to extracurricular activities,' said Elisabeth. 'I am hoping we can offer a range of clubs and sports for the children at lunchtimes and after school. I know it is a lot to ask of you. I appreciate that you need a break at lunchtime and after a hard day's work you might not be inclined to stay after school, but I do feel it is important that we can put some things on. Several people in the village have agreed to come into school and help. Mr Parkinson, the scout leader, has agreed to continue to coach the football team and Dr Underwood, the bishop's chaplain, who used to be the curate at St Christopher's, has agreed to be a governor and said she would be delighted to take some assemblies. I was wondering if—'

'Underwood?' interrupted Mr Hornchurch. 'Ashley Underwood?'

'That's right,' replied Elisabeth.

The teacher's face lit up. 'Well, well, well.'

'Do you know her?'

'Know her? I was at Oxford with Ashley,' he told her. 'We were both students together at All Souls. I knew her really well.'

'It's a small world,' observed Mrs Robertshaw, wondering just how well he had known her.

'So she became a priest after all,' said Mr Hornchurch. 'She always had a leaning in that direction.'

'So you will be seeing a lot more of her,' said Elisabeth.

'Well I never,' said Mr Hornchurch, shaking his head. 'Fancy Ashley ending up in the same place as myself.'

'It might have been preordained,' remarked Mrs Robertshaw smiling.

'Well you can catch up with Ashley when she comes into school next week,' said Elisabeth. 'Now, how do you all feel about taking on some of these activities?'

'I'm happy to give up a couple of lunchtimes,' said Mrs Robertshaw. 'I can continue with the drama group and will take on the choir if no-one else is interested.'

'Thank you, Elsie,' said Elisabeth. 'We had a thriving art class and the chess club too. I would be sorry to see these stop. Would anyone be prepared to take these on?'

'Oh, I can manage those,' said Mr Hornchurch, 'and I would like to offer an astronomy club and a natural history society as well. They were very popular at my last school.'

'It's rather a lot,' said Elisabeth.

'I like to keep busy at lunchtimes,' said Mr Hornchurch. 'And maybe Ashley could give me a hand.'

Mrs Robertshaw exchanged a look with the head teacher.

'Now what about you, Donald?' asked Elisabeth, turning to a somewhat disenchanted-looking Mr Jolly. 'Is there anything you can offer?'

'Actually not a lot,' he replied. 'I'm afraid that I have very few interests outside school although I have taken up one activity which might appeal to the children and I suppose I could offer it as a lunchtime activity.'

'And what is that?' asked Elisabeth.

'Line dancing,' replied Mr Jolly.

No-one said a word but there were quite a few smiles at the revelation. All tried to imagine the teacher stepping out onto the floor in denim jeans, cowboy boots and a Stetson.

Elisabeth approached Mr Hornchurch as he put on his coat ready to leave.

'Could I have a quick word, Rupert?' she said.

'Yes of course.'

'What was the problem with Robbie?' she asked.

'The problem?' He looked puzzled.

'I noticed you were telling him off earlier today.'

'It's sorted,' the teacher told her.

'Well would you like to tell me what the matter was about?'

'No, I don't think there is any need to bother you with it.'

'I beg your pardon?' Elisabeth was taken aback by the bluntness of his reply.

'I have dealt with it,' he told her. 'It was nothing serious and I did promise both boys that it would go no further. I think if you were to become involved it would make me appear to have gone back on my word.'

'I'm not saying that I want to be involved,' said Elisabeth, rather irritated. 'I would just like to know what it was all about.'

'The two boys had a bit of a spat that's all,' replied the teacher, 'as boys often do and, as I have told you, I have dealt with it.'

'Very well,' said Elisabeth, thinking there was more to meet the eye with this particular teacher. 'So on the whole Robbie is behaving himself, is he?'

'He's a strange boy,' said Mr Hornchurch. 'A bit of a dark horse. He's uncommunicative, a loner and not really interested in anything we do in class. He won't contribute in lessons, is brusque and at times he can be rude but I've taught children like him. In my experience behavioural problems at school are often a symptom of being upset or frustrated about something – it's not always about attention-seeking or disobedience.'

Elisabeth nodded, thinking she could not have expressed her views any better. 'Yes, I think you are right,' she said. 'So you are happy that he should stay in your class?'

'Of course,' replied the teacher. 'I believe, with a bit of patience and perseverance, in time Robbie will turn out all right. I just need to get him interested in something. The main challenge I have is to get the boy reading. He never settles down to a sustained read but just flicks through the book looking at the pictures.'

'I might have the answer there,' said Elisabeth.

'Really?'

'Are you going into town at all this weekend?' she asked.

'Well yes, I intend to,' he replied.

'Call in at the White Rose Bookshop in the market square and speak to Sue, the owner. She knows more about books than anyone I know. I want you to buy a couple of books. I'll settle up with you on Monday. Ask her if she has any books about pigs.'

'Pigs!'

'Pigs,' said Elisabeth. 'Robbie has become very interested in pigs.'

Monday morning just before break was the period for silent reading in Mr Hornchurch's class. This gave the teacher the opportunity of selecting some children to hear them read, talk about what they were reading and suggest books in which they might be interested. Robbie, who was sitting, as usual, at the back of the class flicking though a picture book, was the last to be called to bring his reader up to the teacher's desk. He did so grudgingly. He was minded to refuse but then thought of the consequences. He could not afford to get into any more trouble at school. He knew that too much depended on him behaving himself. He perched stiffly upright on the end of the chair by the side of the teacher's desk and supressed a sigh of weariness. Mr Hornchurch smiled. He detected the faint smell of wood smoke and dung clinging to the boy.

'Now then, Robbie,' said the teacher cheerfully, 'let's see what you're reading, shall we?'

The boy slid the book across the desk and looked at the teacher. His green eyes were as hard as enamel, his mouth pinched and sullen. 'Ah, a book about sailing ships,' said Mr Hornchurch. 'Are you interested in books about the sea?'

'Not really,' muttered the boy.

'Would you like to read a little to me?'

The boy felt instantly defensive. 'I don't want to,' he said. 'I'm crap at reading.'

'Just read a few lines for me,' persisted the teacher.

'I told you I'm crap at reading. I don't want to.'

Some of the children looked up from their books wondering what the teacher would do next.

'OK,' said Mr Hornchurch nonchalantly. He could see the futility of trying to pressure the boy into reading. 'Maybe next time.' He reached into his desk drawer and produced a couple of books which he placed before the boy. Robbie leant forward and there was a glint of real interest in his eyes as he scanned the covers.

'I thought you might be interested in these,' said Mr Hornchurch casually. He tapped the first book with a finger. 'This one is about breeds of pigs and how to rear them. I had a look at it at the weekend. I never realised there were so many breeds and how clever and inquisitive these animals are.' He pointed to the second book. 'And this is a story about a very crafty pig which evades being sent to market. Would you like to borrow them?'

'You got them for me?' asked the boy.

'Yes,' replied the teacher. 'I called into the bookshop in Clayton on Saturday. I thought you might be interested in them.'

Robbie nodded. 'I am,' he said.

'And next week maybe we can talk about them and you might read a little to me.' The bell rang for break. 'OK, everyone,' said the teacher to the class, 'books away, chairs underneath the desks and you can go out quietly.'

Robbie stayed seated for a moment. He clutched the books to his chest possessively, as if they were some precious objects about to be taken from him. Then he said under his breath, 'Thanks.'

On his way to the staffroom Mr Hornchurch heard a commotion coming from the school hall. He found a boy sitting on the floor surrounded by a group of noisy children and a red-faced Mr Jolly, hands on his hips, shaking his head angrily.

'You silly, silly boy!' exclaimed the teacher.

'A problem?' asked Mr Hornchurch.

''E's gorr 'is finger stuck,' said a mop-headed boy with a feathery fringe.

'This stupid child, Norman Stubbins,' explained Mr Jolly, red in the face and breathing out noisily, 'has managed to get his finger stuck down this hole in the floor. Not content with swallowing a marble and pushing a rubber in his ear, now he's got his finger jammed.'

The hole in question was for securing the wall bars when they were pulled out from the wall.

''E might never gerrout,' said the mop-headed boy.

Norman began to wail.

'I think it would be a good idea if your class went into the playground, don't you, Mr Jolly?' suggested Mr Hornchurch. 'Then we can try and extricate the boy's finger without an audience.'

'Yes, yes,' agreed the teacher and, waving his hand in the air, dismissed his class.

When the children had departed, the teacher shook his head. 'I really do not know what gets into this silly boy,' he explained. 'He attracts accidents like a magnet attracts iron.'

Oscar appeared at the door. 'Something wrong?' he asked.

'This is no concern of yours,' Mr Jolly told him. 'Go away.'

'Actually he can be of help,' said Mr Hornchurch. 'Go to the staffroom please, Oscar, and ask for the bottle of washing-up liquid by the sink. Tell Mrs Robertshaw it is for me and I will explain later.'

'Righty-ho,' said the boy chirpily and trotted off.

Norman began to wail again.

'Now don't worry,' said Mr Hornchurch, putting a hand comfortingly on the boy's shoulder. 'Just stop tugging at it. We will soon have your finger out.'

'He should not have put it in!' snapped Mr Jolly.

'No he shouldn't,' replied Mr Hornchurch calmly, 'but these things do happen.'

'They seem to happen to this boy far too often,' grunted Mr Jolly.

Oscar returned with the bottle of washing-up liquid. Mr Hornchurch squirted a few generous drops around the boy's trapped finger.

'Now very gently wiggle it about,' he told Norman.

'Wiggle what about, sir?' asked the boy.

'Well he doesn't mean your bottom, you silly boy,' said Mr Jolly crossly. 'Wiggle your finger about.'

'Very gently,' said Mr Hornchurch.

'I once got my big toe stuck up the tap in the bath,' remarked Oscar. 'It was quite an ordeal. My mother used some soap and it soon came out. It was rather embarrassing sitting in the bath with nothing on and—'

'Depart immediately!' ordered Mr Jolly. 'I am not the slightest bit interested in your mishap.'

Oscar looked at the crimson-faced teacher. 'My mother, you know, always says that in a crisis it is best to keep calm and collected and to decide on a clear plan of action. Getting in a panic doesn't help.'

Mr Hornchurch tried to stem a smile.

'I am not bothered with what your mother has to say,' mouthed Mr Jolly. 'Now do as you are told and go away.'

Norman's finger slid out. 'I'm free!' shouted the boy. 'I'm free!'

'There, you see?' said Mr Hornchurch.

'Thank you, sir,' said the boy, beaming widely. He rubbed his finger and jumped to his feet.

Mr Gribbon appeared at the door, keys a-jangling.

'What's going on here then?' he asked bullishly. He spied the drops of washing-up liquid on his prized parquet floor. 'Who's done this?' he demanded, stabbing at the floor with a finger.

'I'm afraid we have had a bit of an accident,' explained Mr

Hornchurch. 'This young man got his finger stuck. I was using some washing-up liquid to make it slippery.'

'Got his finger stuck!' echoed the caretaker.

'In this hole,' said Oscar.

'What was he doing putting his finger in the hole?' asked Mr Gribbon.

'Being silly, that's what,' said Mr Jolly.

'Look at the mess on my floor!' exclaimed the caretaker. 'It's just been buffed.'

'I think it would be a good idea, Mr Gribbon,' said Oscar looking up at the bad-tempered face of the caretaker, 'if you were to put something over the hole to stop this happening again, maybe to use some sort of stopper such as a cork. Don't you think?'

Two small red angry spots appeared on the caretaker's cheeks. If looks could maim, Oscar would at that moment be on crutches.

'What's up wi 'thee toneet?' asked Mr Ross.

Robbie sat at the large pine table in the farmhouse kitchen poking the meat on his plate. His face had an all-too-familiar downcast expression.

'Nothing,' mumbled the boy.

'Now come along, Robbie,' said the farmer, patting the boy on the arm, 'there's summat up wi' thee. Tha dun't say much at t'best o' times but toneet tha's not strung two words together.'

'Leave the lad be, Hamish,' said his wife. 'Mebbe he doesn't feel like talking.'

Mrs Ross was larger than life: a round, red-faced, jolly woman with long grey hair gathered up untidily in a tortoise-shell comb and large friendly eyes behind enormous coloured frames. She wore a shapeless pink cardigan and bright tartan skirt.

'I can see there's summat up,' persisted the farmer. 'We've fostered enough kids in our time for me to know that there's summat on t'lad's mind. Best gerrit off of tha chest, Robbie.'

'You'll be mad,' mumbled Robbie.

'Mind-reader then are tha?' asked the farmer. 'Come on, lad, tell us what's up.'

'I've been in trouble at school,' the boy muttered.

''As tha?' asked Mr Ross. 'So what 'as tha bin up to?'

'I punched a kid.' The boy's voice was flat and drained of feeling.

'Oh, Robbie!' said Mrs Ross. 'You shouldn't have done that.' The boy hung his head and said nothing.

'Hitting somebody is not the answer,' said Mrs Ross gently.

'He said things about me.' Robbie's voice, when it came, was small and far away.

'Hitting somebody never solves any problem,' she said.

'What did t'other lad say?' asked Mr Ross.

'He said I stank.'

'Well happen I would 'ave smacked him one if he told me I stank,' said the farmer.

'Don't you go saying that, Hamish Ross!' exclaimed his wife. 'He shouldn't have hit him.'

Robbie rubbed his eyes with his fists. 'Are you going to send me back?'

'Send you back?' repeated Mrs Ross. She looked across the table at the small, pale, resolute face wet with tears. 'Whatever put that idea into your head?'

'For being in trouble,' said Robbie.

''Course we're not goin' to send thee back,' said Mr Ross. 'Stop yer mitherin'. I used to gerrin a reight few scrapes when I were a young 'un,' he said, chuckling. 'It's what lads do. Thy 'as to stick up for thee sen.'

'Don't you go excusing Robbie,' said his wife. 'It was wrong for him to hit somebody but, having said that, the other boy shouldn't have said he stank. Mind you, when you two came in after that carry-on in the piggery last week you both reeked to high heaven.'

Mr Ross laughed. 'Aye, we din't smell too 'eavenly, did we, Robbie? That were a reight do, an' no mistake.'

'He shouldn't have been helping you in all that muck,' said the farmer's wife. 'I wasn't happy with you, Hamish, expecting the lad to do it.'

'I didn't mind,' mumbled Robbie.

The slatted floor of the piggery had collapsed and four of

the pigs had fallen through and into the slurry. It was a dirty, smelly job for Mr Ross and the boy to liberate the creatures. Having waded through several feet of the stinking sludge, they had managed to rescue the pigs and had arrived back at the farmhouse only to be met at the door by Mrs Ross who wouldn't let them enter until they had stripped to their underwear. After a bath and several showers, the smell still clung to them.

'I'll tell thee what,' said the farmer, patting Robbie's arm, 'I couldn't 'ave managed on mi own gerrin them pigs out.'

'Don't you go changing the subject,' said the farmer's wife. She turned to Robbie. 'So what did Mrs Stirling say? Was she mad with you?'

'She didn't say anything,' replied Robbie.

'She must have said something.'

'It was my teacher who told me off. He said he wasn't going to tell Mrs Stirling. It might have got me into more trouble.'

'Well that was very good of him,' said Mrs Ross. 'I reckon you would have been in a lot more bother if he had sent you to the head teacher.'

'Seems to me,' said her husband, 'it were six o' one an' 'alf a dozen of t'other. Now then, Robbie, get that meat-and-tatie pie down thee, lad. Elspeth's not been slavin' away cooking ovver t'Aga all afternoon for thee to leave an empty plate.'

Major Neville-Gravitas walked briskly through the door of the village store and reached in his jacket for his wallet. 'Just a packet of my usual Panatelas please, Mrs Sloughthwaite,' he said cheerily. He turned to the other two customers. 'Good morning, ladies.'

'Morning,' replied Mrs Pocock and Mrs O'Connor in unison.

'How did the first governors' meeting at the new school go?' asked the shopkeeper as she passed him the cigars and he handed her a crisp ten-pound note.

'Extremely well,' replied the major. 'Mrs Stirling has certainly got a handle on things.'

'She's a sight different from Miss Sowerbutts,' ventured the shopkeeper, affording the major the opportunity to share his views on the former head teacher of the village school. She passed him his cigars and change. 'Thin and sharp as vinegar, she was.'

'Indeed,' agreed the major. 'Miss Sowerbutts was, to put it mildly, a difficult woman at the best of times, a woman of strong views and one who was not afraid of expressing them.'

'She should have been got rid of years ago,' said Mrs Pocock. 'It was only the inspection which pushed her into retirement. She was about as much use as a chocolate fire-guard. When I was on the governors board there, I was always complaining about her, not that anyone listened.'

'That's all water under the bridge now,' the major told her.

The shopkeeper leant over the counter. 'Miss Sowerbutts used to come in here with a face like the back end of a late-night bus on a wet weekend making insinuendos about the quality of the food what I sell. Mrs Lloyd was telling me she's finally sold up and moved to Clayton into one of them fancy flats by the river. She said her cottage has been sold.'

'I wouldn't know,' said the major, pocketing his change.

'I thought she'd decided not to move,' said Mrs O'Connor.

'Well she must have changed her mind,' said Mrs Sloughth-waite. 'Anyway she'll be missed about as much as an ulcerated tooth.'

'Well I will wish you ladies a good morning,' said the major, making for the door.

'I don't see why I got kicked off the governing body,' said Mrs Pocock who had been standing with arms folded during this conversation but wasn't going to let the major escape so easily before she had her say.

'You were not kicked off,' said the major, stopping in his

tracks. 'You were deemed ineligible to be a governor at the new school. Since you no longer have a child attending there you cannot sit on the governing body as a parent governor.'

'I didn't miss a meeting when I was a governor,' she said, sounding peeved.

'Couldn't you squeeze her on?' suggested Mrs Sloughthwaite. 'I mean, she might be illegible but I'm sure you could pull a few strings, you being the chairman and all.'

'That is out of the question,' replied the major.

Not one of the world's most tactful people, he then informed those present that Dr Underwood had been approached to be a co-opted governor and they now had a full complement.

'I could have been co-opted,' said Mrs Pocock peevishly. 'Dr Underwood hasn't got kids at the school as far as I know and she's not been in the village two minutes.'

'You are quite correct,' agreed the major. 'Dr Underwood does not have children at the school but she was deemed to be more suitable than any other person.' With that he strode out of the door.

'Well I never,' exclaimed Mrs Pocock, 'did you ever hear the like?' Her face was flushed with anger.

'You want to calm down,' said Mrs O'Connor, smoothing an eyebrow with a little finger. 'Remember, you're not to get excited what with your blood pressure.'

'And you'd have never known about that,' said Mrs Sloughthwaite, 'if you hadn't been to see Mrs Wigglesworth. It was her who told you what was in store for you when you had your cyclical confrontation. She told you to go and see the doctor and when you did Dr Stirling put you on those blood pressure pills.'

'You don't need to tell me what I already know,' said Mrs Pocock. 'I was intending to go to see the doctor anyway,' she added untruthfully, 'because I've not been feeling myself lately.'

'But it was Mrs Wigglesworth who prompted you to do so,' said the shopkeeper. 'She told you to go and see a doctor, didn't she?'

'Yes, she did, I'll grant you that,' replied Mrs Pocock. 'I must admit there were things she told me that made me think but I'm still not convinced she's all that she claims to be.'

Unbeknown (or so she thought) to Mrs Sloughthwaite, her friend had seen the medium again and had become so intrigued by Mrs Wigglesworth's pronouncements that she had booked a further consultation.

'Has your mother been through?' asked Mrs Sloughthwaite.

'Been through? Been through what?' asked Mrs Pocock.

'Been through from the spirit world?'

'How would I know?'

'Well I know for a fact that you've been to see Mrs Wigglesworth again.'

'Who told you?' asked Mrs Pocock, put-out.

'She did. I went for a cyclical confrontation myself yesterday.'

'She had no business telling you other people's private business,' said Mrs Pocock crossly.

'Well has she been through then, your mother?'

'No she hasn't.'

'What about your father?' asked Mrs O'Connor. 'Has he been through?'

'As a matter of fact he has,' Mrs Pocock told her. 'He came through again and said he was happy that he's not still in the wardrobe. I sprinkled his ashes on the railway line at Clayton Junction because he worked on the railways.'

'I was booked in for another spiritual confrontation next week,' said the shopkeeper, 'but Mrs Wigglesworth has had to cancel due to unforeseen circumstances.'

⋆   ⋆   ⋆

With a heavy heart Ashley walked slowly up the village high street to the rectory, anticipating another disagreement with the vicar. The Reverend Mr Sparshott had telephoned her the previous day asking her to call in to see him when it was convenient. *Better get it over and done with,* she thought, so that bright Saturday morning she steeled herself for the inevitable confrontation and set off for the interview.

'A penny for them,' came a voice behind her.

'I'm sorry?' said Ashley. Turning, she found Elisabeth.

'Your thoughts. Penny for your thoughts. You were in another world.'

'Yes, I guess I was,' replied Ashley. 'I was wondering what the new vicar will have to say to me. I'm on my way to visit the rectory. I have been summoned.'

'Oh dear,' said Elisabeth, 'that sounds a bit inauspicious.'

'We'll see.'

'I'll walk with you if I may.'

'Of course.'

'So how are things going at the cathedral?' she asked.

'Fine,' replied Ashley. 'I'm really enjoying the work. You don't get to meet many folk when you're a curate, just the same old faces in the congregation, but at the cathedral there are so many new people with whom you come into contact.'

'I believe one of my teachers has been in contact with you?'

'Oh Rupert Hornchurch? Yes, he gave me a ring. It's quite a coincidence both of us ending up in the same neck of the woods.'

'It is,' agreed Elisabeth. 'He's a very good teacher and quite a dynamo. He never seems to sit down. He's so full of energy.'

'Yes, when he was at college he was one of the star students. Ended up with first-class honours.'

They walked in silence for a while.

'I received a letter from my brother yesterday,' Elisabeth told her. She knew she was being indelicate but she couldn't resist – when her brother had come to stay with her last year when she first moved to Barton-in-Dale, he had taken such a shine to the new curate at the church and Elisabeth had never seen him like that before so she just had to say something. 'Giles was asking after you.' When Ashley didn't reply, Elisabeth continued. 'He has been posted to some faraway place in the Middle East. He doesn't tell me where. I don't suppose he's allowed to.'

'It must be very worrying for you,' said Ashley.

'It is, but the army is the life he chose. He asked how you were getting on.'

'That was nice of him.'

'You know he became very fond of you when he was here on leave. Perhaps more than a little fond.'

Ashley coloured a little. 'I do hope he will take care of himself,' she said.

'I know this might sound rather intrusive but he was asking if there is anyone you are seeing at the moment. I know it is none of his business really, nor mine if it comes to that, but he was thinking of asking you to go out for a meal when he's next on leave. I sound like a matchmaker, don't I? He didn't want to put his foot in it if there was someone . . . you know what I mean.'

'Well,' replied Ashley stopping, 'to be honest, Elisabeth . . . there is someone. I'm very fond of Giles but I really wouldn't want to raise any hopes that we might . . .' Her voice tailed off.

'Ah, I see,' said Elisabeth. 'You are a dark horse and no mistake. I won't pry. Anyway, do call into school when you can.' She then hastened off.

Ashley sat on the bench facing the village green to think for a moment. A lone lazy-looking sheep looked up from cropping the grass and stared at her. There *was* someone she had fallen for. She had liked him since their first meeting over a year ago now when she was visiting Limebeck

House and found that her bicycle had a puncture. A tall
good-looking young man had appeared from around the
side of the building. She watched him as he fixed the puncture, listened to his soft Irish brogue and was captivated.
His voice, smooth and melodious, was impossible to with-
stand. She pictured him now: the tanned face, shiny black
curls, the winning smile and the eyes long-lashed, warm and
dark. She had never met a man so gentle and kind. Emmet
was always the perfect gentleman, attentive, generous, good-
humoured . . . but he had never asked her out. After their
meeting at the folk concert the previous year, she had the
feeling that he wanted to, but he had said nothing and there
had been several opportunities for him to do so. Perhaps he
didn't feel for her what she did for him. Perhaps he just saw
her as a friend, someone he could talk to and nothing more.
At the Rumbling Tum café he had told her how he missed
his wife terribly, that he felt he could never feel the same
way about anyone else, couldn't love anyone quite the same.
And yet it was the way he looked at her . . . There was something in his look which told her he enjoyed being in her
company, that he found her attractive. And wasn't he about
to say something in the café before the major so rudely
interrupted them? She was confused. Until she knew
whether Emmet felt the same way about her as she felt about
him, she couldn't contemplate going out on a date with
Elisabeth's brother. She sighed, stood up, and carried on
her way.

In the churchyard Ashley found Danny and Robbie vigorously chopping and digging away with gusto.

'Hello, you two,' she called.

Both boys stopped what they were doing. Danny waved
and Robbie wiped his brow with the back of his hand. 'Oh
hello, miss,' Danny called back.

'Busy at work I see,' Ashley said.

'We're fettlin' t'churchyard,' said the boy, coming to join her, 'but it's a big job.'

Robbie followed but remained a few yards away.

'It's ovvergrown wi' nettles an' tares an' teasels an' docks,' Danny said. 'That corner's full o' thorns an' brambles. It's like a jungle. An' there's all this rubble from that smashed tomb.'

'It is a bit of an eyesore,' said Ashley.

'It is, in't it,' agreed Danny. 'Mester Massey was supposed to gerrit shifted but he's not got around to it an' knowing 'im, 'e never will.'

'It's a while since I saw you, Robbie,' said Ashley. 'How are you getting on?'

'All right,' muttered the boy. He looked at the ground.

Suddenly a head appeared from behind a large gravestone. 'Good morning, Dr Underwood,' said the Reverend Mr Sparshott with uncharacteristic good humour. Dressed in a shabby coat, a flat cap, rubber boots and wearing a pair of large leather work gloves, he was wielding a pair of shears. 'I do appreciate you coming to see me. I guess you are very busy with the bishop's business at the weekends.'

'Good morning,' replied Ashley. She was surprised to see the vicar, who was apparently so particular about the way he dressed, attired like a down-at-heel farmer. She was more surprised by his manner. Gone were the icy forthright demeanour and the officious bearing. 'I see you have some helpers,' she said.

'Yes, these boys are assisting me to tidy the churchyard,' he told her. 'It is good to know that not all young people are wayward and irresponsible. At my last parish we had a deal of vandalism from youngsters: overturned gravestones, smashed windows and graffiti.'

'Danny is a regular here, aren't you, Danny?' Ashley said, smiling at the boy. 'He tends his grandfather's grave.' She put a hand on his shoulder. 'He's a good lad.' Then she added, 'And so is Robbie.'

'Yes indeed,' said the vicar. 'Mrs Sparshott has quite taken to the boys.' He pointed to a large pile of rubble. 'A Mr Massey was supposed to see to this debris, for which he was entirely responsible I may add, but he is by all accounts a lazy and feckless man.'

'Mi granddad used to say that Mester Massey was abaat as much use as a one-pronged pitchfork,' said Danny shaking his head.

'Exactly,' said the vicar. 'So, I shall have to get someone else to remove it. It is such a blot on the landscape. I have written to the archdeacon about authorising its removal. He hasn't mentioned anything to you I take it?'

'No,' replied Ashley, 'but I do know he is aware of it and things, I have no doubt, are in hand.'

'Well come along into the rectory,' said the vicar, tucking the shears under his arm and removing his gloves. He shouted to Danny and Robbie. 'You are doing a fine job, boys, but don't overdo it.'

Danny smiled widely. Ashley had never seen a child more ready with a smile. What a contrast he was to his companion. Robbie, the weasel-faced little boy with the thin lips and the shiny green eyes and with that permanent expression of anguish and apprehension, looked as if he expected to be struck a blow at any moment.

Ashley was pleased to see that Mrs Sparshott was not in the sitting room.

'Now, Dr Underwood,' said the vicar, rubbing his hands, 'do make yourself comfortable. I'll just change out of these gardening clothes.'

A moment later he was back.

'Would you care for a cup of coffee?' he asked.

'No thank you,' Ashley replied. 'I had a cup before I set off.'

'I won't tempt you with another,' he said affably. 'As my wife frequently points out, too much caffeine is not good for one.'

Was this the same man who had been so distant and difficult with her in the past? Ashley asked herself. It seemed to her, observing the smiling figure before her and having seen him so good-humoured with Danny in the churchyard, that Mr Sparshott showed some human quality after all. His pompous clergyman's manner, stiff and cool, appeared to have been put aside and with it the detachment she associated with all his actions to date.

He sounded decidedly amiable.

The vicar stood by the fireplace and rested his hand on the mantelpiece. 'And how are you liking life at the cathedral?' he asked.

'Very well,' replied Ashley.

'Rather different from being a curate I guess?'

'Yes.'

'Good, good,' said the vicar. 'Well, the reason I have asked you to come and see me is I should like to ask a favour of you. Next Sunday week is the final of the county Poetry and Prose Recitation Competition at the town hall and one of my two daughters has been successful in being selected to perform.'

'Congratulations,' said Ashley.

'I was wondering,' continued the vicar, 'if I might prevail upon you to take the services that Sunday. Mrs Sparshott and I would like to be at the finals.'

'Yes, of course,' said Ashley.

The vicar rubbed his long hands. 'Splendid,' he said.

'Is that all?' she enquired, thinking that he could very well have asked her on the telephone the previous day.

'Well, to be frank, there is another matter I wish to see you about. I take it the bishop has received my letter?'

'Which would that be?' asked Ashley, feigning ignorance.

She knew exactly the letter to which he referred. The bishop had mentioned it to her.

'I thought he might have said something,' said the vicar. 'It concerns Halloween.'

'Ah, yes, I believe he did comment upon it.'

'And might I ask, was his lordship at all sympathetic to my suggestion?'

'I really think you should wait to hear from Archdeacon Atticus,' replied Ashley. 'I believe the bishop has asked him to deal with the matter. I am sure he will be in touch.'

'I see,' said the vicar thoughtfully.

'So, if that is all . . . '

'I am most concerned,' said the vicar, 'about the harmful effects of celebrating Halloween. "There must never be anyone among you," it says in Deuteronomy, "who practises divination with a soothsayer, augur or sorcerer, who uses charms, consults ghosts or spirits or calls up the dead". I shall preach on this matter as we approach All Saints' Day.'

Ashley was not minded to debate the matter with the priest, knowing it would prove fruitless and she had a busy day ahead. She would leave the response in the hands of the bishop who, at that very moment, had the Reverend Sparshott's letter in front of him.

The bishop had summoned the Venerable Mr Atticus, Archdeacon of Clayton, to the bishop's palace to discuss a number of issues which were on his mind and one of these concerned the new vicar at Barton-in-the Dale. The bishop, a round jolly-looking individual with abundant grey crinkly hair and kindly eyes, indicated a seat in front of his desk. He steepled his chubby fingers and smiled widely.

'I trust there is nothing amiss, my lord,' the archdeacon asked nervously.

'Hopefully not, Charles,' replied his lordship. He inhaled

noisily. 'I think perhaps you might like to pay a visit to Barton-in-the-Dale. I have received a number of letters which relate to your successor at St Christopher's and which are somewhat worrying.' He picked up the first letter. 'This is from a Lady Helen Wadsworth bemoaning, in quite vociferous terms, the refusal of the Reverend Mr Sparshott to countenance a stained-glass window which she wishes to place in St Christopher's in memory of her late brother who was killed in the last war. Evidently, when you were the vicar at Barton-in-the-Dale, you sanctioned a plaque to be placed in the church in commemoration but Dr Underwood, as curate, suggested a window and it was agreed. Mr Sparshott, however, has refused his consent.'

'Oh dear,' sighed the archdeacon.

'Lady Wadsworth does not mince her words,' said the bishop, tapping the letter. 'She is not at all happy about it.'

The archdeacon sighed and managed a weak smile.

'A second letter,' continued the bishop, 'is from a Mr Massey, who describes himself as a gentleman farmer with strong connections. He states that the vicar has barred him from using the track by the side of the rectory to take his cattle to his field beyond. He claims he has some entitlement dating back to the Middle Ages and threatens to take the matter up with the pope.' His lordship allowed himself a small smile. 'Perhaps he is unaware that we broke from Rome over four hundred years ago.'

'I believe that matter has now been resolved, my lord,' answered the archdeacon. 'I understand from Dr Underwood that Mr Massey is now taking his cattle via a different route.'

'I see,' said the bishop. 'Then a Mrs Fish has written saying she can no longer be organist at the church because the vicar has been critical of her playing and she has moved to the Methodist chapel where she is better appreciated, and a Major Neville-Gravitas has been in touch to say Mr Sparshott refuses to sanction a service at the war memorial on Remembrance Sunday.'

The archdeacon massaged his forehead. He could feel a migraine coming on.

'And a Mr Lloyd,' continued the bishop, 'one of the church-wardens, who describes herself as a stalwart of the church, writes that he feels he cannot work with the vicar either.'

'My lord—' began the archdeacon.

'If I may finish, Charles,' said the bishop. 'Then I have received this correspondence from the man himself.' He picked up a letter. 'Mr Sparshott suggests here that I write a pastoral letter to all the schools in the diocese informing the head teachers and the governors of' – he began to read from the letter – '"the dark origins of Halloween, the pagan symbols and rituals which are related to supernatural beings and occult forces". He goes on to remind me that the cele-bration of Halloween is in direct conflict with biblical teachings, quoting Deuteronomy and Leviticus and Galatians. He states that if head teachers and governors were made aware of these sinister origins, they would not allow their children to participate in such practices and dress up as witches and werewolves and the like. I have, of course, no intention of writing to schools.'

'I don't imagine such a letter from a bishop laying down the law,' said the archdeacon, 'would go down very well, particu-larly in the non-church schools. If such a letter were to be sent, it would be better to come from the education authority.'

'Yes, that is what I think,' agreed the bishop. 'Now, Charles, I suggest you have a word with the Reverend Mr Sparshott, pour oil on the troubled waters and smooth things over. Clearly he is a man of passionate beliefs and I am sure he works faithfully and in a dedicated manner, but I feel he needs some support and advice. He sounds a little too strident. I am certain that you do not need to be reminded that one of the functions of the archdeacon is to help a cleric see his or her shortcomings and to try and solve the problem. I have every confidence that you will be able to do this admirably with regard to a fellow priest.'

'I shall, of course, do my best, my lord,' sighed the venerable cleric.

The archdeacon contemplated his Friday evening dinner and sighed inwardly. 'Toad-in-the-hole' seemed a very apposite description of what was on the plate before him. The black, lumpy, unappetising sausage curled up on top of a flat, insipid square of Yorkshire pudding looked very much like a creature which had emerged from a pond. When Ashley Underwood lived with them at the rectory in Barton, she had taken charge of the cooking and served up the most sumptuous meals. His mouth watered at the memory of the last splendid dinner she had cooked: grilled scallop with tomato and garlic sauce followed by bread-crumbed escalope of veal with lemon and a crisp Caesar salad with golden syrup sponge with thick custard to finish. He stared down at his plate and then attempted to sever the sausage.

'So are you prepared for the meeting tomorrow?' asked his wife, attacking a sausage.

'The meeting?' enquired the archdeacon, surfacing from his reverie.

'The meeting with Reverend Mr Sparshott.'

'Oh, I haven't given it a great deal of thought,' replied her husband mendaciously.

'Well I hope you will put him straight,' said his wife.

'My dear Marcia,' said the archdeacon, giving up on the sausage, 'it is not my function to "put people straight" as you term it. My role is to advise, support and encourage, to act as a critical friend to my fellow priests and not be some sort of dictator laying down the law.'

'You are not at interview, Charles,' replied his wife. 'I am fully conversant with what the duties and functions of an archdeacon entail. As you are well aware, my late father was an archdeacon before his translation to bishop and I should add that when he *was* an archdeacon he never shied away from sorting out the troublesome priests. He was a no-nonsense sort of man and known for his straight-talking. If he saw a nettle, he would grasp it. If he detected a problem, he would face it squarely. I am afraid, Charles, that you tend to be too soft with people.'

'A soft answer turneth away wrath,' her husband uttered.

'I'm sorry?'

'It's from Proverbs, my dear. "A soft answer turneth away wrath." It is sometimes much more prudent to handle such matters gently and—'

'My father, the bishop, never minced his words,' interrupted Mrs Atticus. 'He told it how it was and he was greatly respected for doing so and I should add that had he been asked to speak to Mr Sparshott he would . . . '

Her husband ceased to listen and speared a piece of cremated sausage. Over the years he had learnt to turn a deaf ear to his wife's diatribes. He knew from past experience that it would not be long before the sainted bishop arose in his wife's conversation. He had never really got on with his wife's father. He could picture the narrow, bony face set in an expression of severe sanctity, and the wild bushy eyebrows that frequently arched with disapproval. He could hear the deep, resonant voice dripping with condescension and recall the searing blue eyes which had frequently rested upon him when they had disagreed.

'Yes indeed, my father would have sorted out the Reverend Mr Sparshott in no time at all,' Mrs Atticus was saying, scattering her husband's thoughts. 'He was very good at dealing with difficult clergy. Since Mr Sparshott become vicar of St

Christopher's he has managed to alienate everyone with whom he has come into contact.'

'I am aware of all that, Marcia,' said the archdeacon. 'I do not need to be reminded of it. Mr Sparshott, it has to be admitted, is not the most sociable of men and does hold strong views with which some might disagree but he is, no doubt, a devoted priest. In my experience, my dear, people can be very hasty in criticising others. I try and look for the good.'

'I know you do, Charles,' retorted the cleric's wife, 'and I find it a rather irritating habit. You are blind to the faults in others. The entire world is good in your eyes. I cannot recall an occasion when you have spoken ill of anyone.'

'I try not to, Marcia,' he replied, rising from the table and surveying his unfinished dinner. 'Now, I'm afraid I have quite lost my appetite.'

In fact the meeting the following Monday morning with the subject of their conversation went better than the archdeacon could have predicted. He had imagined that the vicar would not take kindly at all to any criticism, however tactfully put. He was therefore surprised and indeed gratified by the vicar's response.

When he arrived at the rectory, Archdeacon Atticus was shown into the sitting room by Mrs Sparshott, who seemed in rare good humour.

'I am so pleased to see you, Archdeacon,' she said. 'I guess you have come about the refurbishment of the rectory and the removal of the unsightly demolished tomb in the churchyard.'

'Amongst other things,' replied the archdeacon.

'Algernon is in his study,' she said. 'You know where it is. I'll put the kettle on. I am sure you would welcome a cup of coffee.'

The archdeacon found the vicar in earnest conversation with Danny Stainthorpe.

'You see, tying a fly is something of an art,' the clergyman was saying. 'The salmon is very fussy about what he goes for in my experience and will not be fooled by any old thing.'

'I trust I am not interrupting anything?' said the archdeacon, poking his head around the door.

'Not at all,' said the vicar. 'Do come in. I am showing young Danny here how to tie a fly.'

''Ello, Mester Atticus,' said Danny.

'Hello,' replied the archdeacon.

'T'vicar says 'e'll tek me fishin' one day,' Danny said.

'As a thank you for helping me tidy up the churchyard,' explained Mr Sparshott. 'Danny and his little friend have been most excellent workers and done a splendid job. I have been telling him about my passion for fishing and he has become most interested.'

'Mester Sparshott's given us a fishin' rod,' said Danny excitedly.

'It's a split cane rod,' explained the vicar. 'Nowadays they have all these fancy fibre-glass types but I prefer the old-style rods.'

'Really?' said the archdeacon. *So the new vicar had not alienated everyone in the village*, he thought.

'So you see, Algernon,' the archdeacon told the vicar later when Danny had gone home, 'I have been asked by the bishop to have a quiet word with you.' He coughed. 'You see, the thing is, he has received a few letters.'

'Indeed. I wrote to his lordship myself,' the Reverend Mr Sparshott told him sitting up in his chair. 'It was about Halloween. I do hope that he—'

'Yes, yes, the bishop did receive it,' interrupted the archdeacon, 'and he has asked me to discuss the matter with you. However, firstly I need to have a word about some other letters which he has received, letters which concern you.'

The archdeacon coughed again. 'It appears that since becoming vicar here you have, how may I put it, trodden on a few toes.'

'He's received letters of complaint about me?' asked the cleric.

'Indeed.'

'From whom?'

'Lady Wadsworth, Mrs Fish, Mr Lloyd, and others.'

If the vicar was concerned by what he had heard he certainly did not show it. 'Yes, I imagine I have ruffled a few feathers while I have been at St Christopher's,' he replied. 'I believe in speaking my mind. I am a straight-talking sort of person and if what I say does not please everyone then so be it. After all, Jesus himself made himself unpopular with some of the things he said.'

Dear Lord, save me from another straight-talking sort of person prayed the archdeacon, thinking of his dear wife and her sainted father.

'But, Algernon, might I venture to suggest that you tread a little more carefully. It is a difficult time settling into a new parish, meeting your congregation and gaining the support and respect of the villagers in such a close-knit community as Barton-in-the-Dale. In my experience, the residents of these small Dales villages take some time to get to know and are wary of newcomers. Of course, I quite understand that you are clearly a man of strongly held views and you are not afraid of expressing them but sometimes, in doing so, you perhaps have tended to rub people up the wrong way. I would urge you to be a little more accommodating.'

'Well, Archdeacon,' replied the cleric, not at all affronted by the comments, 'I readily admit that some of my views have not been welcomed in the parish and my plain-speaking has upset some people. I am the first to admit that I am not by nature a sociable person and I find polite conversation very trying. With hindsight, perhaps I may have been a little over-zealous. I shall bear what you have said in mind.'

'I am grateful for that, Algernon,' said the archdeacon. 'Now there is the matter of your letter to the bishop concerning Halloween.'

'Ah, yes,' said the vicar brightly. 'Tell me, is his lordship sympathetic to my suggestion that he contact all the schools in the diocese?'

'Well . . .' said the archdeacon, thinking of the most tactful way to tell the vicar that his lordship was not at all sympathetic. In fact he had been rather annoyed that one of his priests should take it upon himself to suggest such a thing to his bishop and quote from the Bible in doing so.

'Archdeacon?' said the vicar.

'I'm sorry?'

'You seemed miles away. You were going to tell me what the bishop thought of my letter.'

12

The finals for the Poetry and Prose Recitation Competition took place at County Hall on a bright Sunday morning. The finalists, who had been selected in the first round of the competition, numbered around twenty children drawn from the county schools. Accompanied by their teachers and parents, the young competitors walked nervously down the long, echoey corridors to the council chamber where they were to perform. The interior of the building was like a museum, hushed and cool, with high decorative ceilings, huge ornate brass chandeliers, marble figures and walls full of gilt-framed portraits of former councillors, mayors, aldermen, leaders of the council, high sheriffs, lord lieutenants, members of parliament and other dignitaries.

Elisabeth had invited Mr Jolly to take the children from the school. The teacher was surprised but clearly pleased to have been asked and he readily agreed. For the occasion he had dressed in his smartest grey suit, maroon waistcoat and he sported a large bow tie.

The three pupils who had been selected to perform from the school included Oscar and Roisin and a wide-eyed little girl of about ten with round cheeks, closely-cropped red hair and legs like pestles. The girl, called Amber, had that wonderfully fresh rosy complexion of a daughter of the Dales. Usually a reserved and quietly spoken child, she had astounded Mrs Robertshaw when she had turned up at the audition. She had performed 'The Solitary Reaper' by William Wordsworth with such power, fluency and confidence that she outshone all the other children.

The council chamber had rows of heavy dark wooden benches with padded green leather seats. They faced an imposing carved throne-like chair where the mayor would sit at council meetings. Above hung a full-length portrait of Queen Victoria, by the side of which was a dark wooden panel bearing, in elaborate gold lettering, the names of former mayors. There was a large polished oak table at the front for the three adjudicators and a rostrum where the performers would stand. The children were asked to take their seats at the front, their teachers and parents to sit at the rear.

As Mr Jolly scrutinised the programme, he was approached by an exceptionally thin and sallow-complexioned man with a thick crop of greying hair. This was Mr Richardson, former headmaster and colleague at Urebank Primary School and now the Deputy Headmaster and Director of Studies at St Paul's.

'Good morning, Donald,' he said brightly.

Mr Jolly looked up and squinted. 'Oh, hello, Robin.'

'I see you have been dragooned into giving up your Sunday.'

'Oh, I'm quite happy to do it,' said his former colleague.

'So how are you getting on in the new set-up? I guess it's pretty dire.'

'I'm getting on pretty well, pretty well.'

'I suppose you have to put a brave face on it,' said Mr Richardson in a patronising tone of voice. 'I do feel sorry for you having to work with that woman. I know I couldn't.'

'Mrs Stirling? Actually she's not too bad at all,' replied Mr Jolly.

'Really?' It was not something Mr Richardson wished to hear. He imagined that his former deputy would relate a catalogue of complaints and say how desperately unhappy he was.

'In fact, I am quite enjoying my new role,' Mr Jolly continued cheerfully.

'Enjoying it! Oh come along, Donald, I find that very hard to believe, having to kowtow to that woman with all her fancy ideas.'

'Mrs Stirling doesn't interfere with what I am doing. In fact she's been quite helpful and supportive and the teachers are pleasant enough. As you know, at Urebank I had a class of thirty-five but now I have only twenty pupils and I have to say they are much better behaved.'

'Don't you have that dreadful child we had to expel, the one who bit you? What was his name? Banks, wasn't it?"

'Yes, it's Robbie Banks,' said Mr Jolly, 'although his name has changed to Robbie Hardy now.'

'It's a pity he couldn't change his attitude. Ghastly child. He should be in a special school away from other children. Of course I've always been of the opinion that you cannot make a straight beam out of a crooked timber. He was a most unpleasant and malicious boy. I can't imagine that you are enjoying coping with the likes of him.'

'He's not in my class,' replied Mr Jolly. 'In fact, I don't have any troublesome children.' He decided to be tight-lipped about Norman Stubbins. 'The preparation of lessons and the marking have been reduced quite considerably,' he continued. 'And, of course, I don't have all the responsibilities of a deputy head teacher, the mountains of paperwork to deal with, all the administration and the tiresome bureaucracy.'

'Well, I'm pleased to hear things have worked out for you,' said Mr Richardson insincerely. He tried a different tack. 'Of course you must feel somewhat hard done by.'

'In what way?'

'Having once been in a senior position as a deputy head and now reduced to a mere classroom teacher,' said Mr Richardson.

'No, not really,' replied Mr Jolly. 'I still get paid the same.

I'm on a protected salary, you see. I find I have more time on my hands. I've taken up line-dancing.'

'Really?'

'I find it very relaxing and, of course, it's good to get the exercise.'

'But don't you feel it is a bit of a come-down?' persisted Mr Richardson.

'What, line-dancing?'

'No, having been a deputy head and being reduced to just a classroom teacher.'

'Do you?'

'Pardon?'

'Feel it a bit of a come-down? After all, you were a head-master and you are now a deputy. It's hardly a promotion, is it?'

Mr Richardson had expected his former colleague to be unhappy in his new situation and full of grumbles and griev-ances. He was disappointed to learn that he seemed, in fact, remarkably content. He was also chafed by his remark.

'Mine is a mere temporary measure until I secure another headship,' he replied defensively. 'This position is an excellent opportunity for me to gain some experience in the private sector.'

'If you say so, Robin,' replied Mr Jolly. 'Ah, I see we are about to start.'

'We have a particularly strong field,' Mr Richardson told his former colleague.

Mr Jolly smiled. 'Yes, so do we,' he replied.

The three adjudicators took their seats.

A lean man with grey frizzy hair like a pile of wire wool stood and waited for silence. 'Good morning,' he said in a nasal tone of voice. 'My name is Sebastian Fenwick and it is my pleasure to be the chairman of the judging panel. I should like to welcome teachers, parents and children to the final of the county Poetry and Prose Recitation Competition. We have had a record number of entries and the standard has been particularly high. Today we have the finalists drawn from the first round and I am delighted to see so many talented young people who will delight us with their recitations. But I mustn't twitter on. You are here to listen to the children this morning and not me.' He gave a small laugh. 'Let me first of all introduce my fellow judges.' He turned to a handsome woman with bright eyes and light sandy hair tied back to reveal a finely structured face and dressed in a pale-green silk suit. 'This is Mrs Lillian Lumsdon, a stalwart of the Society of Teachers of Speech and Drama.'

'Good morning,' said Mrs Lumsdon.

'And on my left,' he said, indicating a thin, gaunt-looking woman with waist-length sandy hair and dressed in a long, flowered-print dress, is the Dales poetess, Philomena Phillpots. Some of you might be familiar with her work.' The woman nodded and gave a thin smile. 'This promises,' continued Mr Fenwick, 'to be a most interesting and enjoyable day. I should like to congratulate all you young people who have succeeded in reaching this, the final of the competition and to wish you all the very best of luck. It takes a great deal of courage to stand up and perform in front of an audience and I am sure many of you young people are nervous. This is quite natural for we all, even the most accomplished speakers, suffer from some apprehension. I know from experience what it feels like to have your stomach doing kangaroo jumps . . .' And so he continued.

The Dales poetess sighed. One could tell from her expression that she wished he would shut up and get on with it, instead of rambling on.

'I would say to you all,' the chairman continued, well into his stride, 'take a deep breath, speak clearly and just do your best. Now a few words about the procedures.'

The Dales poetess sighed again.

'Each of this morning's participants,' he said, repeating what was already printed in the programme, 'will perform his or her poem or prose extract from the podium here at the front. Then they will explain to the judges – short and sweet, please – why they have chosen this particular piece. They will then discuss with the panel any matters arising from the presentation. They will be judged on the technique and interpretation of the selected piece and on the content of their discussion. I hope that is all clear.' He looked around as if expecting questions but when none were forthcoming he took his seat and glanced at the papers before him. 'Could I ask our first competitor, Melissa Jackson, to take the podium.'

The children from the different schools in the county then took it in turns to perform their chosen pieces. Oscar gave a most dramatic rendering of several verses of Oscar Wilde's *The Ballad of Reading Gaol*, Roisin recited 'The Lake of Innisfree' by W B Yeats in a gentle lilting voice and Amber performed 'The Solitary Reaper' clearly, confidently and with skill. Last to perform was Rebekah Sparshott, a tall willowy girl with feathery blond hair and large pale eyes between almost colourless lashes. She recited 'Ozymandias' by Percy Bysshe Shelley with grim determination and in a loud and confident voice.

The judges took a great deal of time deliberating. Finally they appeared and took their seats.

'It has been immensely difficult this morning to decide on the winners,' said Mr Fenwick. 'I know this is often what judges say but, in all truth, it was extremely hard for us to agree upon the winners. The standard this morning has been particularly high. However, we are bound to reach a decision and here it is.' He consulted his papers and after a dramatic pause announced, 'Commended for their most competent performances are Oscar and Rebekah, highly commended is

Roisin – who all receive book tokens – and, for a most powerful and poignant rendering of the Wordsworth poem, we award the winning cup to Amber.'

As Mr Jolly gathered the three children from his school to head for home, the Reverend Mr Sparshott approached him, accompanied by his daughter and Mr Richardson.

'I take it you are these children's teacher,' said the vicar.

'Yes,' replied Mr Jolly rather defensively.

'I wanted to congratulate them on their success,' said the vicar. 'I thought the young lady who recited the Wordsworth poem was a very worthy winner and the other children performed extremely well.'

'Thank you,' answered Mr Jolly, basking in the praise. He could see a brooding Mr Richardson listening but remaining silent.

'To have three winners from the same school,' continued the vicar, 'is most impressive, most impressive indeed. You must feel very proud.'

'Oh, I am,' said Mr Jolly.

'And you as their teacher must be commended for coaching these children to such a high standard.'

'One tries one's best,' replied Mr Jolly, who had taken no part at all in coaching the children.

'My daughter Rebekah,' continued Mr Sparshott, resting a fatherly hand on the child's shoulder, 'is a pupil at St Paul's. She is here with her teacher.'

'The Deputy Headmaster,' corrected Mr Richardson.

'Yes, we are acquainted,' said Mr Jolly.

'Tell me,' said the vicar, 'which school do these children attend?'

'Barton-with-Urebank Primary School,' Mr Jolly told him. 'It's in the village of Barton-in-the-Dale. Do you know it?'

'Yes,' said the Reverend Mr Sparshott, 'I have heard of it.'

*   *   *

The next Monday morning, as instructed the week before, Mr Steel arrived bright and early at the Urebank site. The senior HMI was a cadaverous man with sunken cheeks, greyish skin and with the mournful countenance of an undertaker. He was also possessed of the deep and solemn tones appropriate to a funeral. At first meeting he was guaranteed to scare the living daylights out of any teacher and frighten the children. His appearance and his voice, however, belied a warm and friendly manner. He had visited both Barton-in-the-Dale School and Urebank School prior to their amalgamation and had written detailed inspection reports on each. He had judged the former school as outstanding and the leadership and management excellent. His report on Urebank School, however, was rather different. Several areas were said to require improvement and the leadership and management of the headmaster was judged to be merely satisfactory. At a later meeting with the Director of Education, Mr Steel had fully endorsed the decision to amalgamate the two schools.

If Miss Kennedy was nervous about the visit of the HMI, she did not show it.

'Do come this way, Mr Steel,' she said, leading the way down the corridor and waving a hand theatrically in front of her. She was quietly confident that the inspector would find little to criticise for the school looked neat and bright, the paintwork sparkled, the floors shone, children's work was attractively displayed along all the walls and there was a calm and pleasant atmosphere.

As they approached the first classroom, a small girl of about six with a mass of golden curls, great wide eyes and apple-red cheeks appeared. She passed Miss Kennedy a brown paper bag.

'My daddy said to give you back your knickers, miss,' she announced.

'Thank you, Blossom,' said Mrs Kennedy without a trace of embarrassment.

'Perhaps I should explain,' she said to the inspector after the child had departed.

'There is really no need,' replied Mr Steel, holding up a hand.

'Yesterday little Blossom had an accident as some young children are prone to do,' Miss Kennedy told him. 'She wet her knickers. I always have a few spare pairs in case of such contingencies and supplied her with some.'

The inspector began to laugh.

Mrs Kennedy placed a hand on his arm. 'I wouldn't want you to think that I was having some clandestine affair with one of the parents,' she said.

The HMI met little Blossom later at morning break as he wandered around the playground chatting to the children. This time it wasn't wet knickers that distressed the child.

'Can you help me?' she moaned, running up to him, clutching her cardigan in front her. Tears bubbled from her eyes.

'If I can,' replied the HMI bending down. 'What seems to be the problem?'

'I've been sick,' wailed the child.

'Oh dear,' Mr Steel told her. 'Don't you worry. You come along with me and we'll find Miss Kennedy.' He held out a hand.

The child shook her head. 'I can't,' she replied sniffing.

'I don't bite,' said the HMI.

'I can't hold your hand,' said the girl

'Why is that?' he asked.

'Because,' she replied, looking down, 'I've been sick in my cardy!'

After break the inspector joined Miss Wilson's class. He had met this teacher before when he had visited Barton-in-the-Dale school prior to its amalgamation. In his report he

had judged her to be enthusiastic, committed and well-organ-
ised, a teacher who had an excellent relationship with her
young charges. On first meeting the inspector, Miss Wilson
had felt nervous and intimidated when he appeared at her
classroom door like a black-clad villain from a pantomime but
when she found him to be friendly, good-humoured and
supportive, she relaxed.

'Good morning, Miss Wilson,' said the HMI, entering the
classroom. 'May I join you?'

'Yes of course,' replied the teacher. 'Children, this is Mr
Steel.'

'Good morning, Mr Steel, good morning, everybody,'
chorused the children.

'Some of you may remember Mr Steel,' Miss Wilson told
the children.

A child with curly blond hair and rosy-red cheeks raised
her hand. 'He's a suspector, miss!' shouted Blossom. 'He
helped me when I was sick.'

'I hope you're feeling better now,' said the inspector to the
child.

'Yes, I am,' she said. 'I was really sick, miss, but I managed
to get it all in my cardy.'

'Thank you, Blossom,' said the teacher. 'I think we have
heard quite enough about that.'

'Miss Kennedy put my cardy in a plastic bag,' Blossom
said, undeterred, 'and told me to take it home to my mummy.'

'Well that's good. Now, Mr Steel is really interested in seeing
what we are doing this morning, children, and he would like
to find out how you are all getting on. Who will tell our visitor
what we are doing?'

A freckly-faced boy with large glasses raised a hand. 'We're
doing poems,' he said.

'About grannies and grandpas,' added another child.

'Before playtime the children wrote down everything they

could think of about their own grandparents. So if you would like to take a seat, Mr Steel, we will see what interesting things the children have come up with. Let's start with grannies.'

The children were keen to volunteer their ideas and little hands waved in the air. Their responses came so fast the teacher, who was writing down their thoughts, had quite a job to keep up. Soon the white board at the front of the classroom was full of their observations.

Grannies don't walk fast, they go slowly.
They never tell you off.
They talk all the time.
They smell of flowers.
They tell you stories and sing songs.
Grannies have white hair and wrinkly faces.
They have knobbly hands.
They have lumpy cardigans and yellow beads.
They wear brown stockings.
Grannies are fat and wear glasses.
They sit in armchairs and fall asleep.
They love children but they don't have any of their own.
They can take their teeth out.
They have bad legs.
Grannies are good for cuddles.

'My goodness, what a lot of ideas,' said Miss Wilson. She then caught sight of a small boy who had remained silent and sombre. 'What about you, Joshua?' she said. 'Can you tell us something about your grannie?'

'I haven't got a grannie, miss,' said the child sadly. Bright spots of tears appeared in the corners of his eyes and he sniffed noisily.

'Of course you have,' replied the teacher.

'I haven't, miss. I've only got a nannie.'

'But she's a grannie,' Miss Wilson told him. The boy stopped sniffing to listen. 'There are a lot of different names for grannies. You call your grannie nannie. I used to call mine nana.'

'And I used to call my grannie Flopsy Wopsy,' said Mr Steel.

'I think I'm going to be sick again,' said Blossom.

Mr Steel was well aware that handling a group of lively infant children, all of whom have their own personalities, is not an easy job. He knew it demanded a great deal of skill, expertise and patience.

In Mrs Ryan's classroom he met a small boy with a shock of ginger hair and missing his front teeth. A small green candle of mucus appeared from a nostril. The infant sniffed it away noisily but it re-appeared immediately. He eyed the inspector.

'What is your name?' asked Mr Steel.

'Who wants to know?' replied the boy.

'I'm Mr Steel, a school inspector.'

'My name's Harrison. And what do you do?' The child asked bluntly.

'I travel around the country and I visit schools,' replied Mr Steel, smiling with the frankness necessary when dealing with an inquisitive child.

'I'd like to travel around the country,' said the boy. 'When I grow up I want to visit lots of places.'

'Why, then you might like to think about a job which involves a lot of travelling,' said the inspector. 'Perhaps you might become a train driver.'

'No,' replied the child, sniffing again. 'You have to be dead clever to be a train driver.' Then he added with unconscious sarcasm, 'I think I'd rather do what you do.'

*   *   *

Mr Steel left the school impressed by what he had seen and drove slowly along the twisting ribbon of road which led to the village of Barton-in-the-Dale, enjoying the magnificent scenery which stretched out before him. On such a mild autumn day, the colouring of the scene was remarkable: long belts of dark-green firs glistening above an ocean of crimson heather, great walls of rusty-coloured rock rising into sheer russet bracken slopes, grey wood smoke rising to the pale purple of the sky. It was a bright and silent world.

As he approached the village, he caught sight of a small boy, hands stuffed in his pockets, sauntering along on the grassy verge. He was a small, thin stick of a boy with shiny chestnut-brown hair. The inspector pulled over and wound down his car window.

'Shouldn't you be at school, young man?' he asked.

The boy stared at him with large watchful eyes as bright as polished green glass. 'Shouldn't you be at work?' came the quick reply.

'What school do you attend?' asked the inspector.

'What's it got to do with you? Bugger off!'

'It has a lot to do with me, young man,' said Mr Steel. 'I'm a school inspector.'

'Well go and inspect somebody else,' said the boy.

'What's your name?'

'Mary Poppins. What's yours?'

'I shall remember your face,' said Mr Steel.

'And I'll remember yours,' replied the boy, 'in case the police are looking for a weirdo in a car talking to kids.'

Mr Steel shook his head, wound up the window and went on his way.

Things, he found, were not going too well on the Barton site. The inspector arrived at lunchtime to find the head teacher and a harassed-looking Mr Jolly in the school entrance with a whimpering boy.

'He's a very silly young man, Mrs Stirling,' said Mr Jolly crossly. 'He attracts mishaps like a jam pot attracts wasps. Accident prone, that is what he is.'

'Mr Jolly,' said Elisabeth calmly and quietly, 'it is not helping getting into a state.'

'I appear to have come at an inopportune time,' said the inspector.

'Yes,' agreed Elisabeth. 'Young Norman here has fallen from the wall bars in the hall. I don't think anything is broken but he's a bit shocked. I've asked the school secretary to telephone his mother.'

'I've chipped my tooth,' wailed the child.

'Yes, but don't worry,' Elisabeth reassured him, putting an arm around his shoulder, 'I am sure the dentist will put that right.'

Mr Gribbon appeared like the spectre at the feast. 'What's to do?' he asked.

'This stupid boy has had another accident,' Mr Jolly told him. 'He's now gone and fallen off the wall bars in the hall.'

'I've chipped my tooth,' wailed the child again.

'It's the lad who got his finger stuck, isn't it?' asked the caretaker.

'The very same,' said Mr Jolly.

'And the one who swallowed the marble?'

'The same.'

'He wants to keep out of trouble,' said Mr Gribbon.

'I've chipped my tooth!' wailed the child again.

'Yes, we heard you,' said Mr Jolly.

'You should have been more careful,' said the caretaker to the boy.

'Mr Gribbon,' said Elisabeth, 'will you please ask Mrs Scrimshaw if she has managed to contact Norman's mother yet?'

'That's what I came to tell you,' said the caretaker. 'She's tried ringing the home number and the emergency number and there's no reply.'

'Typical,' muttered Mr Jolly.

'I see.' Elisabeth thought for a moment. 'Will you explain the situation to Mr Hornchurch please, Mr Jolly,' she said, 'and ask him to look after my class while I take Norman to the hospital and Mr Gribbon, would you tell Mrs Scrimshaw to continue to try and contact the mother and let her know what has happened?' She turned to the inspector. 'I'm really sorry about this, Mr Steel,' she said. 'I'm afraid these things do happen in school.'

'They certainly happen to this boy,' mumbled Mr Jolly.

'I am quite happy to take your class while you are away, Mrs Stirling,' said Mr Steel.

'Really?'

'Quite happy. I thought I might do some poetry.'

'Well if you're sure . . . '

At this moment Robbie strolled through the door, his hands dug deep in his pockets.

'Oh, it's you!' exclaimed Mr Steel, pulling a face.

Robbie shrugged. 'So what?'

'I had occasion to speak to this young man on the way here,' he told Elisabeth, stabbing a finger in the direction of Robbie. 'When I asked him why he was not in school he was most rude.'

'Oh, Robbie,' sighed Elisabeth, shaking her head.

'When that copper came into school and talked to us in assembly,' said the boy, showing no sign of remorse, 'he told us that if a strange man in a car started to talk to us we should tell him to push off and then tell the teacher. We were told not to talk to him. Well I was approached by this bloke.' He pointed at the inspector. 'He might have been one of these weirdoes who kidnap kids.'

'I merely asked, young man, why you were not in school,' said Mr Steel, 'and I told you I was a school inspector.'

'Anybody could say that,' retorted the boy. 'I could say I was Spiderman. Doesn't make it true, does it?'

'As I recall, you told me you were Mary Poppins,' said the inspector.

'Well, there you go then,' replied Robbie.

Elisabeth could see this was getting out of hand and intervened. 'Actually, Robbie had permission to be out of school this morning, Mr Steel,' she explained. She lowered her voice. 'Robbie is being fostered at the moment and had an appointment with his social worker.' She turned to the boy. 'You might have been a little more polite, Robbie,' she told him, without raising her voice. Robbie shrugged again. 'It doesn't cost anything to have good manners.'

'So are you saying we've got to talk to strangers now?' he asked, knowing the question was rhetorical.

'No, I am not saying that,' replied Elisabeth, seeing that this discussion was getting nowhere. She quickly changed the subject. 'Anyway, now you are here, Robbie, you can be very helpful and keep Norman here company. I need to take him to the hospital.'

'What's he done?' asked Robbie.

'I've chipped my tooth,' wailed the child yet again. 'I fell off the wall bars.'

'Dozy bugger,' mumbled Robbie.

At the hospital Elisabeth, sitting waiting in A&E with the two boys, was approached by a tall, thin intense-looking woman with a face as pale as a lily and dominated by heavy black-rimmed glasses. Her iron-grey hair was parted savagely down the middle and stretched around her head in a thick plait. She looked drawn and tired.

'Hello, Robin,' said the woman, addressing the scowling figure who had seen her coming over.

'Hello,' he grunted.

'Hello, Mrs Stirling,' said the woman.

'Good afternoon Mrs Banks,' replied Elisabeth.

The woman sat on the very edge of the chair next to Robbie, her body held stiffly upright and her thin fingers locked together on her lap. 'And how are you keeping, Robin?' she asked her son.

'It's Robbie!' snapped the boy. 'I've told you before not to call me Robin. It's a stupid name.'

'Please don't speak to your mother like that, Robbie,' said Elisabeth sharply.

'So how are you keeping?' Mrs Banks asked him.

'OK,' replied the boy sullenly.

'Why are you at the hospital? You've not hurt yourself, have you?'

'I've come with him,' Robbie nudged Norman, 'and if I had have been hurt you wouldn't have been bothered.'

'That's not true,' said the boy's mother sadly. 'I care a lot about you.'

Robbie huffed.

'I've chipped a tooth,' whined the patient. 'I fell off the wall bars in the hall.'

'Oh dear,' said Mrs Banks. 'Well I hope you'll be all right.' She turned to her son. 'I do worry about you,' she said. 'I thought I might come out and visit you next Sunday.'

'Suit yourself.'

'See how you're getting on.'

'I'm getting on a lot better than when I was at home,' replied Robbie unkindly. 'I told you that the last time.'

The woman sighed. 'Could I have word, Mrs Stirling?' she asked Elisabeth.

'Yes of course.'

They stood a little away from the boys so as not to be overheard.

'I'm glad I've got this opportunity to speak to you,' said the woman. 'I was intending to call into school to ask about Robbie.'

'Well, as you can tell, he can still be sharp with people,' Elisabeth told her, glancing at the boy who sat grim-faced, 'and sometimes he can still be quite rude but, thankfully, there have been no angry outbursts, he gets on with his work a great deal better and his behaviour has improved quite a lot.' She omitted to tell her about the fight he had been in. 'I will have a word with him about his behaviour. He shouldn't speak to you like that.'

'He's got good reason, Mrs Stirling,' said the woman. 'I've let him down. I should have handled things better, stood up to my husband more.' She sniffed and reached in her pocket for a tissue.

Although Elisabeth agreed that the boy's mother could have dealt with the situation a whole lot better, she smiled and said, 'With the benefit of hindsight we could all have handled things we have done rather better, Mrs Banks. Anyway, Robbie is getting on really well and that's the main thing.'

'That's good to hear,' said Mrs Banks.

'We've been very patient with him,' said Elisabeth, 'and it appears to be working. Of course, he still has his moments. Anyway, it's pleasing to see that he seems very settled with his foster carers.'

'Yes, I've called at Treetop Farm a couple of times,' said Mrs Banks. 'Mr and Mrs Ross are good, kind people and very good with him.' She blew her nose and pushed the tissue into her pocket. Then she looked down at her hands and began twisting the ring on her finger. 'Robbie was still very short with me when I visited, hardly said more than a few words.'

'I'm afraid he's still an angry little boy,' Elisabeth told her. 'Rightly or wrongly, he feels aggrieved by what he considers the unfairness of his treatment. He still feels very hurt and resentful.'

'I hope you can understand,' said the woman sadly, 'that I felt I had to have him put in care. It really was for his own good. Life at home was impossible – all the rows and squabbling and shouting. And, of course, my husband said it was either him or Robin, that one of them had to go.' She gave a wry smile. 'It's ironic really. Frank's walked out anyway. He worked away from home on building sites and was often away for days at a time. I had my suspicions that there was someone else and I was proved right. There was another woman.'

'I'm sorry,' said Elisabeth.

'Oh, don't be. It couldn't go on as it did. Frank was a very moody and sometimes violent man. I should never have married him. The thing is, Mrs Stirling, I'd like Robbie to come back home. Now that his step-father has gone it will be a lot better and—'

'That would be Robbie's decision, Mrs Banks,' interrupted Elisabeth. 'He's of an age now when he can make up his own mind. I don't think he can be compelled to return home if he doesn't want to. He is settled and happy where he is. It might be better to leave him there, certainly for the time being. Of course, I'm not the expert on these matters. Miss Parsons of the Social Services is the best person to advise you.'

'I'm seeing her next week,' said Mrs Banks. She sniffed. 'I really would like Robin home. I do miss him. I really do.'

'Perhaps given time he will decide to return,' said Elisabeth.

'Would you have a word with him?' asked Mrs Banks.

'Me?'

'Just to raise the matter with him and explain the situation about his step-father and see if he might like to come home.'

'I think Miss Parsons might be the best person to do that,' Elisabeth told her.

'No, I don't think so,' said Mrs Banks. 'She hardly knows him and you see Robin, I mean Robbie, every day. I know that he likes you and trusts you and that he listens to what you have to say. You've been so good for him. Most teachers would have given up on him. I should be very grateful if you could speak to him.'

'Very well,' agreed Elisabeth. 'I'll have a word with him.'

'Thank you.'

'Mrs Banks, may I ask why *you* are at the hospital?' asked Elisabeth. 'You are not unwell I hope?'

'Oh, I'm sure it's something and nothing,' replied the woman dismissively. 'Your husband's sent me to have some tests. Just routine, a sort of check-up.'

She did not reveal that the specialist was not at all satisfied with what he had discovered.

13

It was another wet and windy Thursday when Ashley sheltered from the driving rain in the bus shelter. Earlier that week it had been mild and on occasions quite sunny but on Wednesday the weather had turned unusually cold for that time of year. By the Thursday a ragged grey curtain of cloud hung from an iron-grey sky and the wind drove the rain at a sharp slant.

That afternoon, as she waited for the Clayton bus, Ashley was joined by Mrs Sloughthwaite and Mrs O'Connor.

'I've shut up shop this afternoon,' explained Mrs Sloughthwaite when Ashley had asked her who was minding the village store. 'Thursday's my half-day closing.' She shook her umbrella violently, showering water in every direction.

'We're having a bit of something to eat in Clayton and then off to the cinema,' said Mrs O'Connor.

'And if we had known the weather was going to be like this we'd have stopped at home, wouldn't we, Bridget?' grumbled the shopkeeper.

'Sure I don't mind about the weather so long as it's dry,' remarked her companion.

'I've never known rain like this,' continued Mrs Sloughth-waite. 'It's been raining incestuously since I got up this morning.'

'Of course, it rains a lot in Ireland,' remarked Mrs O'Connor. 'Rains like shoemakers' knives, so it does. You get used to it. That's why everything is so green. It's not called the Emerald Isle for nothing.'

'Well it's not rained like this since we had the floods and the river broke its banks,' said Mrs Sloughthwaite.

'When I looked at the sky this rnorning,' Mrs O'Connor added, 'I could tell there was a plomp of rain a-coming, so I did. Fine day for young ducks, I said to myself.'

'And I've never known it so cold at this time of year,' said the shopkeeper.

'As my Grandmother Mullarkey was wont to say,' said Mrs O'Connor, 'it's cold enough for two pair of shoelaces.'

Mrs Sloughthwaite rolled her eyes. There were times when she could make no sense of her friend's observations, particularly when the sainted Grandmother Mullarkey was quoted.

'Mrs Pocock's not with you then?' enquired Ashley.

'No, she's at the hospital,' the shopkeeper answered. 'She's having these tests done.'

'She wouldn't have gone to see Dr Stirling if it hadn't been for the psychic who told her to go,' added Mrs O'Connor.

'The psychic?' repeated Ashley.

'Mrs Wigglesworth. We went to see this medium,' said Mrs Sloughthwaite, 'and she disclosed information to Mrs Pocock that only those who have passed over could possibly know. It quite unsettled her – Mrs Pocock that is.'

Ashley thought of the letter Mr Sparshott had despatched to the bishop liberally quoting from the Book of Samuel about the unfaithful King Saul who violated God's command not to consult spirit mediums. The vicar would have something to say on the matter should it come to his ears.

'Well I hope she's all right,' said Ashley.

'We had to laugh, so we did,' said Mrs O'Connor. 'Dr Stirling asked Mrs Pocock, so she told us, to provide a sample of you-know-what to take to the hospital and gave her this small plastic tube. She filled it up and put it in the bathroom and, would you guess, her husband only went and mistook it for shampoo and used it to wash his hair! He told her he didn't know what shampoo it was and it gave no lather at all but that his hair had never been so shiny.'

'Oh dear,' said Ashley, chuckling.

'We did laugh,' said Mrs O'Connor.

'Are you going somewhere nice then, Dr Underwood?' asked Mrs Sloughthwaite, turning to Ashley. She was eager to glean what information she could before the bus arrived.

'To see my mother,' replied Ashley. 'She moved into a new apartment last year and lives in Clayton. I try to see her as much as I can but I've been so busy lately.'

'She doesn't live in one of those De Courcey Apartments, those that overlook the river and the cathedral, does she?' asked Mrs Sloughthwaite.

'Yes, she does,' replied Ashley.

'That's where the former headmistress of the village school lives,' said the shopkeeper. 'Miss Sowerbutts was supposed to have moved there some time ago but she gave back word when she was told they don't allow pets. Anyway, when her cat died she decided to sell her cottage and move there.'

'Yes, I believe my mother has met her,' said Ashley.

'It's a small world, so it is,' observed Mrs O'Connor.

'I suppose the vulnerable keep you fully occupied,' said the shopkeeper to Ashley.

'I'm sorry?'

'The vulnerable Atticus.'

'Actually the archdeacon is called "the Venerable",' Ashley told her, 'but I guess at times he does feel rather vulnerable. It's quite a difficult job he has dealing with any problem which might arise in the diocese.'

'He wants to deal with that problem at St Christopher's,' said Mrs Sloughthwaite. 'Nobody has a good word to say for the new vicar. He's such a sour puss. I've not set foot in the church since his first service. He went on for a good hour telling us we were all sinners.'

'The worst wheel always creaks the most,' commented Mrs O'Connor. 'I recall—'

'Mr Sparshott is about as welcome as snow in harvest,' interrupted Mrs Sloughthwaite. 'It's such a pity that you had to leave. It's not the same at St Christopher's any more.'

'I'm sure in time the vicar will settle in,' said Ashley diplomatically, 'and when people get to know him they will maybe change their opinion.'

'And pigs might fly,' replied the shopkeeper.

A shiny black Mercedes pulled up outside the shelter. The window was wound down and Emmet O'Malley shouted, 'I'm going into Clayton. May I give you three lovely ladies a lift?'

The three women clambered into the car, Mrs Sloughthwaite and Mrs O'Connor in the back with Ashley in the front. On the back seat was Roisin.

'I think you know my daughter,' said Emmet as he drove off.

'Hello,' said the little girl brightly.

'Hello, darlin',' said Mrs O'Connor.

'Off somewhere nice?' asked the shopkeeper, curious as ever.

'My daddy's taking me to buy a book,' said Roisin. 'I won a book token in a competition at the Town Hall.'

'Did you indeed?'

'I had to say a poem. I got the second prize,' said the girl. 'When I've picked my book my daddy and me are going to choose some curtains and a carpet for my bedroom.'

'I can't say I'll be very good at choosing curtains and carpets,' admitted Emmet.

Mrs Sloughthwaite nudged Mrs O'Connor. 'Perhaps it needs a woman's touch,' she said archly. 'I'm sure Dr Underwood would give you some advice, wouldn't you, Dr Underwood?'

'I'm afraid my expertise doesn't run to interior design,' laughed Ashley.

'I think you have very good taste,' persisted Mrs Sloughthwaite. 'I'm sure Mr O'Malley would welcome a bit of help, wouldn't you, Mr O'Malley?'

'We're finally getting the gate lodge at Limebeck House the way we want it,' explained Emmet, feeling embarrassed. 'It was in a sorry state, cracked brick and exposed plaster, roof and windows in disrepair and open to the elements. There's still a lot to do, of course, but it's pretty much restored.'

'My goodness, you've gone up in the world,' remarked Mrs Sloughthwaite, 'a lovely new house and a fancy new car.'

Emmet laughed. 'I'm afraid I don't own either,' he said. 'I'm renting the gate lodge from Lady Wadsworth and this is her car which I am taking to be serviced.'

'You seem very settled in the village,' remarked the shop-keeper. 'No plans of moving on then?'

'No,' replied Emmet. 'I think our travelling days are over.' He glanced over at Ashley. 'There are many reasons why I wish to stay in Barton.'

'Well, we're very pleased you're staying,' said the shop-keeper. Then, with a small smile, she added. 'Aren't we, Dr Underwood?'

'Yes we are,' said Ashley.

'I have my very own room,' said the child excitedly, 'with a window that looks out over miles and miles of countryside. It has pictures on the wall and a really big bed. It's really comfortable. It will be even nicer when it has a carpet and curtains.'

'Bit different from the caravan,' Mrs Sloughthwaite remarked.

'I did like the caravan,' said Roisin. 'It was nice and cosy but I love my new room.'

'You're a very lucky girl, so you are,' said Mrs O'Connor. 'When I was a child I had to share a room with my three sisters.'

'I know I'm lucky,' said the child.

'And I can see that you're the apple of your father's eye,' said Mrs Sloughthwaite.

'You're not wrong there,' agreed Emmet.

Mrs Sloughthwaite and Mrs O'Connor were dropped off at the market cross and Ashley at her mother's flat.

'I'll collect you in a couple of hours if that's all right,' said Emmet.

'You really don't need to bother,' she said. 'I can get the bus back to Barton.'

'Not in this weather,' he told her. 'Anyway, I should like the company. Four o'clock, I'll be outside waiting for you.'

'Oh, do come up and meet my mother. She would like to see you. She gets so few visitors. It's apartment number three.'

Later that day Emmet arrived at the flat with a bunch of flowers.

'For me?' said Mrs Underwood, giving one of her rare smiles. 'How very kind.' She passed them to Ashley. 'Put them in water, will you? You'll find a vase in the cupboard. And put the kettle on while you're in there. I am sure we would all welcome a cup of tea. You'll find some orange juice in the fridge for the little girl.' She turned to Emmet. 'Do sit down, Mr O'Malley.'

'May I sit on the sofa, please?' asked Roisin.

'Of course you may,' replied Mrs Underwood. *What a pretty child*, she thought, staring at the small figure with the large wide-set eyes and long rust-coloured hair, and so polite too. She turned again to Emmet. He was a striking-looking man, tall, broad-shouldered and dressed smartly in a tweed suit and mustard-coloured waistcoat and sporting a pair of smart tan brogues. Very presentable. Ashley could do a whole lot worse than him. 'My daughter tells me you work for Lady Wadsworth at Limebeck House, Mr O'Malley.'

'Yes,' replied Emmet.

'You're the estate manger there, I believe?'

'It's rather a fancy title for a general factotum,' he told her.

'Not at all,' said Ashley, coming in from the kitchen with the tea tray. 'You're being too modest, Emmet. You run the place.'

'There is only one person who runs the place,' he said, 'and that's Lady Wadsworth. She's a very formidable woman but an excellent employer.'

'My daughter tells me you are a widower, Mr O'Malley,' said Mrs Underwood.

'Yes, that's right.'

'I am sorry to hear it. Was your wife Irish like yourself?'

'Rowena always thought of herself as Irish but her ancestors were Scottish. Her parents, Sir Eustace and Lady Urquhart, considered themselves more English than Irish. They were of an old Anglo-Irish family.'

'Oh, Sir Eustace and Lady Urquhart,' repeated Mrs Underwood, clearly impressed. 'They live in Ireland then, do they?'

'At Castle Morden by Lough Moy,' Emmet told her.

'In a castle, my goodness. And do you see much of your wife's parents?' she asked

'No, I'm afraid not,' he said.

Sir Eustace and Lady Urquhart had made it patently clear from the outset that they strongly disapproved of the association of their daughter with some sort of itinerant, fiddle-playing hippie and wanted nothing to do with the man their daughter had taken up with. They hoped for a much better match for their only child. After several heated arguments they had given their daughter the ultimatum that should she continue with the relationship, she would not be welcome in their home. They would disown her. Rowena, always strong-minded, had been defiant and left, later to marry Emmet. Neither her parents nor any of her relations had attended the wedding. Tragically, Rowena died giving birth to their child.

When Emmet called at Castle Morden shortly after his wife's death with the new-born baby in his arms, he was refused entry and turned away. Since then, apart from a couple of telephone calls when they had refused to speak to him, he had had no contact with his wife's parents.

'Not too much milk,' said Mrs Underwood as her daughter poured the tea. 'She always puts far too much milk in despite the number of times I have told her I like it strong. "Strong enough to stand a spoon up in it", as my mother used to say.'

Emmet smiled, showing a flash of white teeth. '"Strong enough to trot a mouse across it", as my grandmother used to say.'

Mrs Underwood laughed. 'They have such quaint sayings, the Irish,' she remarked. 'So how do you take your tea, Mr O'Malley?'

'Just as it comes,' replied Emmet.

'Be careful with the orange juice on the sofa, won't you, dear,' Mrs Underwood warned Roisin.

'I will,' replied the child. Then she added, 'I like your flat. It's beautiful.'

'Thank you,' said Mrs Underwood. 'I was considering moving in with my daughter,' she told Emmet, 'but decided against it. It wouldn't have worked. I do value my own privacy. There are some biscuits in the cupboard,' she told Ashley. 'Could you get them?'

When her daughter had left the room, Mrs Underwood lowered her voice. 'I rather hoped for something better for my daughter, Mr O'Malley,' she confided.

'In what way?' he asked.

'I thought with her education she might have studied medicine or accountancy or the law, something rather better than theology and ending up as an assistant priest. Of course she's very strong-minded and would go her own way.'

Emmet gave a wry smile. *Where he had heard that before*, he thought.

Ashley appeared with the biscuits. 'Did I miss something?' she asked.

Later Mrs Underwood watched from the window as her daughter climbed into the shiny black Mercedes. *Yes*, she said to herself, *she could do a whole lot worse than settling down with the estate manager at Limebeck House.*

The following Saturday the weather changed for the better and the day was sunny and windless. The trees had a golden lustre to them that bright morning, the mist had gone and the air was clear and fresh. Danny sat with the vicar on the banks of the river watching the surface of the water. They were having a rest from casting in their lines, enjoying the contented silence. When the clergyman suggested to the boy that he might like to join him on a fishing trip one Saturday morning, Danny had readily agreed. He had never been fishing before, except for minnows and sticklebacks with a net, but always wanted to try his luck for bigger fish.

'It's dead peaceful 'ere, in't it?' said Danny after a while.

'Indeed it is,' agreed the vicar. He gave a little nod of satisfaction.

'I like to sit out 'ere in t'oppen,' said the boy. 'It gives you time to think abaat things, to sooart out what's goin' on in yer 'ead, to get away from everythin' an' everybody.'

'That's very true,' agreed the cleric. 'I like to think things through, away from everyone and everything. It restores one's peace of mind. "God never did make a calmer, quieter, more innocent recreation than angling." A famous writer called Izaak Walton said that in his book *The Compleat Angler*. I'll let you borrow it if you're interested.'

'I'm not that clever at reading,' Danny told him, 'but I'll 'appen to look at t'book if tha's a mind to lend it me.'

Danny stood and sniffed the air like a hare in a field rising up on its hind legs. 'I love t'country,' he said with a sigh. 'All t'sights an' sounds an' colours an' t'smells of outdoors, to feel t'fresh earth between yer fingers. It's a special time o' year is autumn. Every plant an' tree an' woodland creature knows that summer is on its way out. They can sense it.' He looked up at the empty sky. 'See t'swallows swoopin' ovver 'ead preparin' for their long journey south. They're beginnin' to feel t'cold in t'air, that winter's on its way an' they know it's time to leave.' He looked around. ''Edgehogs'll soon be burying themselves, tucked up nice an' warm in some dry place till spring.' He pointed to a huge tree with a great thick trunk and overhanging branches. 'See 'ow t'green o' t'leaves is curlin' an' fadin' an' gerrin rusty around t'edges. Soon they'll be stripped from t'branches, fall down to become a thick red carpet under yer feet. It's like a sooart o'magic.'

'You're very observant, Daniel,' said the vicar smiling. 'Quite the poet.'

'Oh I dunt know abaat that. Mi granddad used to say that most people look at everythin' an' see nowt, they don't 'ave t'time to stand an' stare, they don't see all t'beauty what's around 'em an' to be thankful for all t'wonders o' nature.'

'He sounded a very wise man, your grandfather.'

'Oh 'e was that,' said Danny thoughtfully. 'One o' t'best. I miss 'im, I really do.'

'You were brought up by your grandfather, I gather?' said the vicar.

'Aye, after mi mam died,' replied Danny. 'She were killed when I was a babby. I never knew 'er or mi dad.'

Mr Sparshott had never really known his father either. His apparent deficiencies of character – aloofness, pomposity, gravity – were no doubt the result of his upbringing. His father was a distant, bad-tempered and domineering man who made little secret of the fact that he found his son a disappointment. His mother was a nervous, timid woman given to bouts of illness when she would take to her bed for weeks at a time. As a boy, Algernon Sparshott, an only child, had been shown little love and was despatched to a boarding school out of the way where he remained lonely and miserable for his entire school career.

'It must have been hard for you,' he said to Danny now.

'It was when mi granddad died an' I din't know what was goin' to 'appen to me. I could 'ave bin put in an orphanage or into care miles away but Dr Stirling took me on. Mi granddad used to say that people like that are t'salt o' the earth.'

They sat for a minute enjoying the peace.

'I allus thought that to catch a fish you used worms,' said Danny.

'You can use worms,' answered the vicar, 'but sweetcorn, luncheon meat, cheese, bread crumbs, wasp grubs and maggots can all be used as bait. Fish, like people, enjoy quite a varied diet you know.'

'What sooart o' fish will we catch, d'you think?'

'There is no guarantee that we will catch anything,' said the vicar. 'In this river there are dace, grayling, roach, perch, trout and salmon but I've sometimes spent all day fishing and not had a bite.'

'Salmon!' cried Danny. 'I din't know there was salmon.'

'Oh yes. You see, the salmon spend their first three years in the river in fresh water and then make for the open sea. Then they return to lay their eggs.'

'Could we catch a big salmon?' asked Danny.

'That's not very likely in this river,' the vicar told him. 'It's too small and narrow. You see, the size of the fish really depends on the width and depth of the river. The smaller the river, the smaller the fish. It's not unheard of in the largest rivers to land a ten or twelve-pound salmon. If we are lucky today we may catch a one-pound trout.'

The Reverend Sparshott, having a captivated audience, became talkative and uncharacteristically ebullient and contin- ued to tell Danny at length about the joys of fishing.

'Did yer bring your sons fishin' when they were young?' asked Danny.

'No, I didn't,' replied the vicar. 'I'm afraid that Rufus and Reuben were not very keen. They never shared my interest for fishing. They felt it to be a bit of a waste of time sitting on a riverbank watching the water.'

'I s'pose they're dead clever, your sons, aren't they?'

'Yes, I suppose they are,' replied the vicar. *Perhaps too clever by half*, he thought to himself.

'I'm not dead clever. I'm in t'bottom group at school. Most o' t'lads mess abaat in t'class an' t'teachers do a lot o' shoutin'.'

'There are different kinds of cleverness,' said the vicar.

Danny chuckled. 'That's what mi granddad used to say. "We can't all be brain surgeons," he said. Can I ask you summat, Mester Sparshott?'

'Of course.'

'Why did you send your sons away to school?'

The vicar pondered this for a moment. 'I thought they would be happier away from home and work harder. Boarding schools offer children a different sort of education. They develop self-confidence and self-reliance, teaching them to stand on their own feet, to become independent.'

'You must miss 'em.'

'I do,' he replied.

If truth be told, the Reverend Mr Sparshott did not miss his sons all that much. As they grew to adolescence they had become moody, wilful and argumentative and he wearied of the constant squabbles. When he was offered the chance of sending them to a boarding school with vastly reduced fees for the sons of the clergy, he broached it with the twins. They were only too pleased to be away from home. When they telephoned, which was infrequently, it was usually to ask for money or to seek permission to go on some trip or other. When he suggested that they might like to bring a couple of friends to stay in the holidays, they informed him quite bluntly that they would feel embarrassed having to show any of their chums where they lived. Most of the boys at the school came from very affluent backgrounds with parents who owned large houses and had holiday homes in France or Spain.

'I wouldn't like to go away to school,' Danny said. 'I'm really happy where I am.' The boy scratched his mop of hair. 'Sometimes I think just how lucky I am.'

The vicar felt suddenly moved by what the boy said and saddened too. He could not help asking himself why his own sons couldn't be as open and good-natured as this boy who radiated such goodwill and indeed why he himself seemed to be unable to do the same.

'So how are the boys liking it up at the new school?' asked Mrs Sloughthwaite.

Elisabeth had called into the village store to place her weekly order and, like all the other customers who patronised the shop, was not allowed to leave until the shopkeeper had gleaned all the latest news and relayed all the latest gossip.

'James seems very settled there and enjoys the work,' she replied, 'but Danny, as you might guess, prefers the outdoors to being stuck behind a desk all day. He isn't as keen.'

'I was never very hacademical when I was at school,' admitted Mrs Sloughthwaite. 'I could never see the point of the stuff we had to do. Neither did my father. "All la-di-da and bloody daffodils" – that's what he thought of poetry. Then there was that allergybra and trigonometry. And I couldn't cope with French. It was double Dutch to me. I was telling Mrs Pocock who called in yesterday. She was saying that her Ernest hates it up at Clayton Comp. He's been put in the bottom group and says it's terrible boring, not like when he was at the village school. She also told me that Malcolm Stubbins is making his presence known. Always in trouble is that lad.'

Elisabeth, picturing the large-boned individual with tightly curled hair and prominent front teeth, had feared that the boy's behaviour would deteriorate when he moved up to the secondary school. Her former pupil had initially been a disagreeable, badly behaved boy, not above bullying other children, but she had worked hard and his conduct had improved. His younger brother Norman was much better behaved but a magnet for accidents.

The shopkeeper shook her head. 'He's a wayward young man is that Malcom Stubbins if ever there was one and I don't think that brother of his is any better, is he?'

Elisabeth decided not to reveal the latest accident of Norman Stubbins. She knew if she did it would be around the village like wildfire. 'Oh, Norman is a biddable enough boy,' she said diplomatically.

'Evidently Malcolm was in front of the headmaster for what he said to the school inspector,' said the shopkeeper.

'Oh dear,' muttered Elisabeth.

'Apparently this inspector walks into the classroom dressed all in black and with squeaky shoes and a face that would curdle milk. "Bloody hell! It's Count Dracula!" shouts out Malcolm. Then, when this inspector asked him a question later on, he said, "Bugger off, Granddad!" You wouldn't credit it, would you? Speaking to a school inspector like that.' The shopkeeper lowered her voice as if being overheard. 'Mind you, Mrs Pocock's not a one to talk when it comes to her son. Ernest was in detention along with Malcolm for what *he* said to the school inspector.'

'Which was?' asked Elisabeth, intrigued.

'He was asked how many teachers worked at the school and the lad replied "about half of 'em". Cheeky little devil.'

'Well, thankfully James and Danny are well behaved,' said Elisabeth. 'I think they know that if they did get into trouble at school they would be in twice as much trouble at home.'

'They're good lads your two,' said the shopkeeper. 'Never an ounce of trouble. Young James is a very polite boy and Danny could charm the birds off of the trees.'

'He certainly seems to have charmed the vicar and his wife by all accounts,' said Elisabeth.

'The Sparshotts?' exclaimed Mrs Sloughthwaite. 'It'd take a cavern of witches to charm them two.'

'Danny's been helping out tidying up the churchyard and has seen quite a bit of them,' Elisabeth told her. 'He tells me that they are very nice, once you get to know them.'

'I'll conserve my judgement on that,' said the shopkeeper. 'I've never met a more straight-laced, humourless, puffed-up pair in my life.'

'Well, Danny seems to have seen another side to the new vicar. Mr Sparshott took him fishing last Saturday,' Elisabeth said. 'They seem to share an interest in the outdoors.'

'"Well, I'll go to the bottom of our stairs", as my dear departed mother used to say,' said Mrs Sloughthwaite. 'It's hardly creditable.'

'Mr Sparshott gave him a rod and all the tackle and showed him how to fish for trout. Danny was full of it when he got home.'

As if on cue, the Reverend Mr Sparshott entered the store. 'Good afternoon,' he said.

'Good afternoon,' the two women replied together.

'We were just talking about you,' said Mrs Sloughthwaite.

The clergyman stiffened. 'Really?' he asked sharply, with the defiant air of someone preparing for a confrontation

'Mrs Stirling was telling me you've got a new little friend.'

'I'm sorry,' said the cleric. 'I don't follow.'

'Young Danny. I believe you've taken him fishing.'

'Ah, yes,' said the vicar, his face softening. 'It was by means of a thank you for all the hard work he has been doing tidying up the churchyard. Daniel is a very personable young man and most polite. He is a credit to you, Mrs Stirling.'

'Oh I can't take any credit,' Elisabeth told him. 'Danny was brought up by his grandfather. Mr Stainthorpe was a remarkable man.'

'Yes, Danny speaks very highly of him,' said the vicar. 'I trust you have no objection to my taking him fishing? He assures me he did seek your permission.'

'Yes, he did,' replied Elisabeth. 'It's good of you to take an interest in him.'

'Would that all young people were so well behaved and diligent as young Daniel,' said the vicar. 'As I said, he is a credit to you and your husband. And speaking of credit, I think you might take some credit too for the performance of the pupils from the village school at the county Poetry and Prose Recitation Competition. The children from the village school did exceptionally well.'

Hearing the man now, Elisabeth was taken aback how different his demeanour was. When she had first met him at the musical evening in the church prior to his taking up the position as the vicar, she had found him dour, pompous and self-opinionated. He certainly appeared to have mellowed.

'And I believe your daughter did well too,' she said.

'Indeed, my wife and I were very proud of her,' said the vicar. 'Rebekah is a shy child at the best of times so we were particularly pleased that she was prepared to perform. I have to own, however, that the young girl who recited 'The Solitary Reaper' certainly deserved the first prize. Her rendering of the Wordsworth poem was superlative, a most mellifluous interpretation of one of my favourite poems.'

'All la-di-da and bloody daffodils,' muttered Mrs Sloughthwaite to herself.

'I beg your pardon?' asked the vicar.

'Oh nothing,' she replied.

'I am pleased to have bumped into you, Mrs Stirling,' continued the vicar. He lowered his voice and moved away from the counter. 'Might I have a quiet word with you on another matter, something which has rather troubled me?'

'Yes, of course,' replied Elisabeth.

'Following the morning service last Sunday, at which I gave a sermon on the dangers of celebrating Halloween, a concerned parent approached to inform me that her daughter, who I believe is in your class at the village school, was asked to write a poem about ghosts and witches.'

'I think she must have been mistaken,' said Elisabeth. 'I can assure you that I have not asked any children in my class to write such a poem.'

'No, I gather it was not you who took that particular lesson. I believe you were accompanying a boy who had had an accident, to the hospital.'

'Dearie me,' said Mrs Sloughthwaite who had been listening intently to the exchange and was keen to get the information before the conversation continued. 'I hope he wasn't badly hurt.'

'No, just a few bruises and a chipped tooth,' Elisabeth told her.

'The thing is, Mrs Stirling—' began the vicar.

'Who was it then?' probed the shopkeeper.

'Norman Stubbins,' Elisabeth told her. 'He fell off the wall bars in the hall. He's rather accident prone.'

'My goodness,' said the shopkeeper, 'Mrs Stubbins has her work cut out with her two lads. One in trouble at the big school and then the other leaping off wall bars and being taken to hospital.'

'If I might continue,' said the vicar, irritated by the interruption. 'As I was saying, the girl was asked to write a poem about witches by the stand-in teacher, an elderly man, I was told.'

'Ah yes, Mr Steel,' said Elisabeth, giving a small smile. 'He was good enough to step in and help out.'

'Well, perhaps you might have a word with him about the dangers of asking children to write about such an unsuitable topic.'

'I can't see any harm in it myself,' said Mrs Sloughthwaite, leaning on the counter. 'It's just a bit of fun and kiddies like hearing about witches and monsters and ghosts and they love dressing up.'

'My dear lady,' retorted the vicar fiercely, his mouth thinning with certainty, 'it is quite the contrary. There is a great deal of harm in introducing children to such things. Belief in the supernatural, the world of spirits, seers, mediums and psychics, paranormal séances and clairvoyants is quite nonsensical but can lead to untold psychological problems.'

'Oh I don't know about that,' replied the shopkeeper dismissively. 'It's just a bit of harmless fun and, anyway, such things as ghosts do exist.'

'Nonsense!' snapped the vicar.

'Well you've got a ghost up at the school, haven't you?' said Mrs Sloughthwaite addressing Elisabeth.

'I don't think so.'

'Yes, the caretaker was in here yesterday and he said you've got some ghostly presence clomping up and down outside of the school. He said he could hear these heavy footsteps as clear as day but when he looked through the window there was nobody there.'

'I can assure you, Mrs Sloughthwaite, that I have not heard anything about a ghost,' answered Elisabeth.

'Mr Gribbon reckons it could be the ghost of that little girl who fell in the mill pond and got caught up in the water wheel and drowned,' announced the shopkeeper.

'When was this?' asked Mr Sparshott.

'Oh donkey's years ago,' Mrs Sloughthwaite told him. 'She was skating on the ice at the mill pond one Christmas and went through. Mr Gribbon reckons it might be little Florence's spirit wandering around.'

'Stuff and nonsense,' retorted the vicar. 'As I have said, belief in such things can lead to countless problems.'

'What sort of problems?' asked the shopkeeper.

'Serious psychological problems,' he told her. 'In my last parish at Marfleet a woman consulted one of these supposed clairvoyants, a Mrs Wigglesworth, who lived in the village. This charlatan claimed to be some sort of mystic and said she could converse with the dead. The poor woman who consulted her started to imagine deceased relations talking to her and she ended up having a nervous breakdown. She had to consult a psychiatrist, and is still receiving treatment.'

Mrs Sloughthwaite's mouth fell open like a fish on a slab. She licked her lips nervously and became uncharacteristically silent.

'As I was saying, Mrs Stirling,' the vicar went on, 'I think you might have a word with Mr Steel.'

'Perhaps you might like to have a word with him yourself, Mr Sparshott,' replied Elisabeth. 'I am sure he would be most interested in your views.'

'I should be pleased to do so,' said the vicar.

'Mr Steel can be contacted at the central office of the Department for Education in London. He is one of Her Majesty's senior inspectors of schools.'

14

The following week Mr Steel called into school to report on his visits to the two sites.

'Before I give you the feedback,' he told Elisabeth, 'might I ask how is the boy you took to the hospital? Nothing seriously wrong I hope.'

'He's fine,' she replied.

'That's good to hear,' said the inspector. 'It is always a worry when a child in your care has an accident, isn't it? You feel somehow responsible, even though it is often the child's own fault.'

'It is,' agreed Elisabeth.

'One has to be so very careful that all the health and safety procedures are in place,' continued the inspector. He paused for a moment. 'I assume in this case they were.'

'They were,' Elisabeth answered. 'Tell me, how did you get on teaching my class?' she asked, keen to change the subject.

'Oh, it was good to get back in the classroom,' said Mr Steel, becoming animated. 'The children were most attentive and responsive and produced some excellent poetry. As it is coming up to Halloween I thought I would get them to write some poetry on the subject. The discussion we had was most wide-ranging and interesting. The little Irish girl, Roisin, gave us a most fascinating account of the Banshee, the Irish spirit of folklore whose wailing warns of impending death. The children were spellbound. I told them of the prayer my Scottish grandmother used to say:

"From ghoulies and ghosties,
    And long-legged creatures,
    And things that go bump in the night,
    Dear Lord, deliver us".'

He gave a throaty laugh. 'One boy said he thought that there
were ghoulies and ghosties in his parents' bedroom the night
before because he heard all this bumping and banging through
the wall. I decided not to go down that road. Yes, it was a most
successful lesson even if I do say so myself.'

Elisabeth decided that this was not the best time to tell him
of the vicar's disapproval and the letter which would be wing-
ing his way.

'On a more serious matter, there was something I feel you
should know about, Mrs Stirling,' said the inspector. 'I have to
admit that I was very shocked when I was told.'

'This sounds ominous,' said Elisabeth.

'When I was talking to the children,' continued Mr Steel,
'the small boy who sits at the front of the class, Bobbie I think
his name is, told me something of which you need to be aware.
I was quite taken aback.'

'About what?' asked Elisabeth.

'Something about his father.'

'Mr Marshal?'

'The boy told me he is a smackhead.'

'A smackhead!' exclaimed Elisabeth.

'I believe this to be the colloquial term for a persistent drug
user.'

'Yes, I am aware what the term means,' said Elisabeth.

'The boy was telling me he often has to help his father
because of his condition. It sounds an alarming situation.'

Elisabeth laughed.

'I hardly think this is a cause for amusement, Mrs Stirling,'
said Mr Steel sharply. 'I should have thought that you would

be as concerned as I and feel the need to refer this case to Social Services. It is unacceptable for a child to be in the house of a drug addict.'

'I can assure you, Mr Steel, that Bobbie's father is not a smackhead,' Elisabeth told him, trying to contain her laughter. 'He's an asthmatic.'

The inspector's report was largely encouraging. Mr Steel congratulated Elisabeth on her leadership and management, the smooth running of the school, the clean, bright state of the buildings, the calm and workmanlike atmosphere and the excellent behaviour of the children. He felt the amalgamation had been a great success and commended her on achieving this. The inspector had many very positive comments to make about the teaching at the infant site and he was particularly praiseworthy of Mr Hornchurch's and Mrs Robertshaw's lessons. Then came the fly in the ointment. He was less impressed with Mr Jolly.

'I have observed this teacher before,' explained Mr Steel, 'when he taught at Urebank and I have to say he is not the most inspiring of teachers. On the plus side, he had prepared his lesson thoroughly and the material he gave to the children was appropriate and to some extent interesting but his teaching could best be described as lacklustre. I have to say I did sympathise with one pupil. As we listened to the teacher he leant over to the boy sitting next to him and whispered, "Doesn't time drag when you're bored." Mr Jolly was teaching about the Vikings which is a fascinating topic and one that should have captivated the children but he made a Viking raid sound like a visit to the corner shop. His questions, I have to say, were quite bizarre.'

'In what way?' asked Elisabeth.

'Well, he asked the class what they thought Vikings came in. One child said large boats with dragon's heads on the front, another iron helmets with horns on, a third leather jerkins and boots and another child swords and shields, all of which sounded to me very reasonable but which he dismissed. "I did tell you last week," he told them, "that Vikings come in hordes." After the lesson I asked one boy what he had learnt and he replied "Not a lot". I must say I found myself in some agreement.'

'So what do I do?' asked Elisabeth. It was all very well for the inspector to tell her what was wrong, she needed to know how to put it right.

Mr Steel thought for moment. 'To be honest, there's no magic answer,' he said. 'I am inclined to the view that teachers are born. Some have a real affinity with the young and come alive in the classroom, making their lessons attention-grabbing and challenging, but I am afraid others do not. Some teachers can make the driest subject interesting and others manage to make the most exciting topic boring. My advice is to give Mr Jolly as much support and help as you can, encourage him to attend some courses to help him improve his classroom skills and let him observe the good practice demonstrated by the other teachers in the school.'

'He's a bit long in the tooth for that, don't you think?' asked Elisabeth. 'It won't be too long before he retires.'

'Well, I don't think there is much else you can do,' replied Mr Steel, 'short of going down the road of competency which is a long and arduous route. As you are aware, it is extremely difficult to sack a teacher unless he runs off with the school fund or something inappropriate occurs with a pupil. Mr Jolly has done neither. He is not the greatest teacher in the world but I have seen worse.'

After showing Mr Steel to the door, Elisabeth headed for the school office to collect her post. Despite all the many laudable things the inspector had said about the school, it was the problem of Mr Jolly which occupied her mind.

The first letter she opened that morning was from a firm of

solicitors informing her that Mrs Stubbins would be taking legal action against the school for gross negligence. The firm, which had 'No Win! No Fee!' in large type underneath its fancy letterhead, maintained that there was 'lack of due care and supervision in the PE lesson' when their client's son had fallen from the wall bars, suffering widespread bruising and severe damage to his teeth which required extensive and expensive remedial treatment.

Elisabeth sighed. She recalled the last occasion Mrs Stubbins had seen fit to complain. A round, shapeless woman with frizzy dyed-ginger hair, an impressive set of double chins and immense hips, had appeared at the classroom door the previous year claiming her elder son Malcolm was being picked on. Elisabeth had been straight with the woman, telling her that her son was lazy, disruptive and difficult; a boy who didn't like to work and would not apply himself. His behaviour, she had said, was unacceptable. Mrs Stubbins, unwilling to believe what she had been told, had moved her son to Urebank. There the boy had proved Elisabeth right and his behaviour was such that he had been promptly expelled. Mrs Stubbins had eaten humble pie and persuaded Elisabeth to take her son back on the understanding that he would behave himself. Since then the boy's behaviour had improved markedly. From what Elisabeth heard about Malcolm in secondary school, he had sadly returned to his old ways.

'Is something wrong, Mrs Stirling?' asked the school secretary, seeing the expression on the head teacher's face.

Elisabeth passed the letter over the desk. 'You had better call Mr Nettles at County Hall and ask him to call in and see me,' she said.

After school Elisabeth asked the school secretary and the caretaker to join the teachers at the staff meeting.

She spent a little time on the inspector's report, briefly

outlining Mr Steel's findings and congratulating all present on their hard work and dedication. Then, holding up the solicitor's letter, she informed them of the possible legal action. Mr Jolly sat hunched in the corner of the room like a condemned man with a tragic expression on his ashen face. Elisabeth had acquainted him with the letter before the meeting.

'Is it that daft boy who got his finger stuck in the hole in the hall, Mrs Stirling?' asked the caretaker.

'It is,' replied Elisabeth.

'The one who swallowed the marble? The Stubbins lad?'

'The same,' she said, 'and I can add a few other accidents to the list.'

'Well, if he was messing about on the wall bars and fell off, he's only got himself to blame. He's lucky he didn't break his bloody neck. Pardon my French.'

'While we might agree with you, Mr Gribbon,' said Elisabeth, 'there are those who do not share our view – this firm of solicitors, for example, who feel there is a case of negligence to answer. It is claimed there was a failure on the part of the school to exercise reasonable care, that not enough account was taken of the potential harm of children using the equipment and that there has been a breach in duty. I have spoken to Mr Jolly and am quite satisfied that the children were warned to be careful on the equipment and were fully supervised and that he had acted appropriately. It is clear to me that Norman fell as a result of his own carelessness. However, questions will be asked and we need to be prepared. I intend to interview each child in Mr Jolly's class as well as Norman to get to the bottom of this. As teachers we have a duty of care and I want to make certain that there are no loopholes.' Elisabeth turned to the caretaker. 'Mr Gribbon, I take it that the wall bars were fully secured prior to the lesson?'

'Yes they were!' replied the caretaker abruptly. 'I check them before every PE lesson and then fasten them to the wall afterwards.'

'And the floor in the hall was clean and free of anything that the children could slip on?'

'My floors are my pride and joy, Mrs Stirling, everyone knows that,' said the caretaker, stung by the comment. 'I buff them up every day. You can see your face in them.'

'Maybe you buff them up too much,' remarked Mrs Scrimshaw. 'It's like an ice rink in the hall. Many's the time I've nearly slipped.'

'The lad fell off the wall bars, Mrs Scrimshaw!' snapped the caretaker. 'He didn't slip on the floor.'

'He could have slipped when he hit the floor though,' said Mrs Robertshaw. 'I mean, I have found it very slippery in there as well.'

'Wait a minute! Wait a minute!' exclaimed the caretaker. 'I hope I'm not being held responsible—'

'Thank you, Mr Gribbon,' said Elisabeth.

'I hope I'm not being made the scrapegoat!' he cried.

'Scapegoat,' murmured Mrs Scrimshaw, shaking her head.

'Of course not,' said Elisabeth. 'As you say, the boy fell, he didn't slip on the floor.'

'Speaking of floors,' interposed Mrs Robertshaw, 'I should like to ask Mr Gribbon when he is going to deal with the cock-roaches that litter the corridor floor every morning. There's an accident waiting to happen if ever there was one.'

'Look—' began the caretaker angrily, the veins in his temple standing out and throbbing.

'Let's not get side-tracked,' said Elisabeth, cutting him off.

'I did everything I could,' said Mr Jolly in a rather pathetic tone of voice. 'It was just an unfortunate accident and if the boy had been more careful ...' His sentence remained unfinished.

'I'm sure you did what any of us would have done,' Mrs

Robertshaw reassured him. 'I don't think there is anything to worry about.'

'Life is full of risks,' observed Mr Hornchurch, leaning back in his chair. 'Accidents happen. I can't think of any adult who has survived childhood without having an accident.'

'Exactly,' agreed Elisabeth. 'I really do not think there is a case to answer.' She looked at Mr Jolly's gloomy face and prayed she was right.

The boy studied Elisabeth with large watchful eyes as bright as polished green glass as if she were an object of mild curiosity.

'So, Robbie,' said the head teacher cheerfully, 'how are things?'

The boy shrugged. 'OK,' he muttered, looking down at his feet.

They were sitting at lunchtime the following day on a low wall which bordered the playground. 'I believe you're coming along nicely with your reading. Mr Hornchurch tells me he is very pleased with your progress. I gather you have nearly finished the books he gave you.'

'They were about pigs,' muttered the boy.

'I guess you are becoming quite the expert on those particular creatures. And how are you getting on with Mr and Mrs Ross at Treetop Farm?'

Robbie kept his head down and shuffled. 'OK,' he said with a sniff.

'And I hear from Mr Hornchurch that you are keeping out of trouble. I'm very pleased with you, Robbie.'

The boy suddenly looked up. 'It's about my mum, isn't it?' he asked. 'I'm not stupid you know, miss. You want to talk to me about my mum.'

'Yes, it is,' she answered. 'I had a word with your mother at the hospital.'

'I know. I saw you,' he replied.

'She asked me to speak to you. She told me your step-father has left and he won't be coming back.'

The boy raised his little chin defiantly and stared at her. 'So?'

'She misses you, Robbie.'

'Well I don't miss her.' He hunched his shoulders and folded his arms tightly across his chest.

'She would like you to go back and live with her,' Elisabeth told him.

'Well I won't!' he shouted.

Children in the playground looked in his direction.

'She feels badly about what's happened,' Elisabeth told him.

'So she should,' he replied vehemently. 'She wanted rid of me.'

'That's not true, Robbie.'

'Then why did she put me into care?'

'Your mother felt it would be best for you to be away from home for a time,' said Elisabeth. 'Now that things have changed, your mother would like you to go back. I think the problem was with your step-father. Now that he's gone, things at home will be a lot better.'

'I don't want to go back!' cried the boy. 'I've told you, I like it where I am.'

'Try and understand, Robbie,' said Elisabeth, 'how difficult it must have been for your mother to put you into care. She felt she couldn't cope.'

'She dumped me,' said the boy sadly. 'She didn't want me any more.' Bright spots of tears appeared in the corners of his eyes.

'That's not true,' said Elisabeth gently.

'Yes it is.' He thought for a moment, studying his feet, then looked up suddenly and gave her a level stare. 'They can't make me go back, can they?'

'No, I don't think they can but I want you to think about

things. Your mother, despite what you might think, does love you and feels very sorry for how things have turned out. She misses you, Robbie. Try and make more of an effort with her. She's very unhappy at the moment and very lonely and I don't think she's too well.'

'What's up with her?'

'I don't know but she was at the hospital for some tests. I'm not sure what for. I don't think it's anything to worry about.'

'I'm not worried,' said the boy bullishly but Elisabeth could tell he was rather shaken by the news. He got up to go.

'On another matter,' she said. 'You remember when you came with me and Norman to the hospital?'

'Yeah.'

'Did he say anything to you about what happened?'

'When he fell?'

'Yes.'

'He said he was messing about, pretending to be a monkey.'

'Did he?'

The school secretary came striding across the playground.

'Mrs Stirling,' she said as she approached, 'that Mr Nettles from the Education Office has phoned. He says he'll call into school tomorrow lunchtime if that's convenient. He said "he's found a window in his diary", whatever that means.'

'That's fine, Mrs Scrimshaw,' replied Elisabeth.

'Can I go now?' asked Robbie.

Elisabeth rested a hand on the boy's shoulder. 'Will you think about what I've said?' she asked.

The boy nodded. 'OK, but I'm not going back,' he said stubbornly.

'Oh and Robbie, I would really like you to remember to call me 'Miss' like all the other children when you are talking to me. All right?'

He nodded again. 'All right . . . miss.'

★   ★   ★

Mr Nettles was waiting in Elisabeth's classroom. The situation regarding Norman Stubbins' accident on the wall bars was explained to him and he was shown the letter from the solicitors.

'Dear oh dear,' sighed the education officer, rubbing his forehead. 'This is most unfortunate, most unfortunate indeed. A state of affairs like this could reflect very badly upon the school, upon yourself as the head teacher and the Education Authority.'

'How reassuring,' remarked Elisabeth sardonically.

'Would that I could say that this is just a storm in a teacup, Mrs Stirling,' he said, the sarcasm lost on him, 'but I fear there could be some regrettable repercussions. I shall have to consult Mrs Pickering, the county solicitor, and keep her up to speed but my initial feelings are that we should try and keep this under wraps and agree to some sort of compensation. Were this claim to be contested with the ensuing court case, there could be some very unwelcome publicity. Yes, I think it would be the best course of action to settle out of court.'

'Have you quite finished, Mr Nettles?' asked Elisabeth, 'because if you have there is something I wish to say.'

'Go ahead, Mrs Stirling,' he replied.

'There is no question whatsoever of settling this ridiculous claim for compensation. To do so would admit liability. I have spoken to the boy's teacher and all the children in the class and it is clear that Norman was being silly and not taking sufficient care. To admit our culpability would mean we have accepted that we have been negligent which is certainly not the case.'

'Mrs Stirling, if I may point out—' the education officer began.

'So I suggest,' continued Elisabeth, ignoring what he was about to say, 'that you go and see the county solicitor, explain the situation and say that there is no question, no question whatsoever, of conceding and if we have to go to court then so be it. I should be pleased to speak to Mrs Pickering personally and I am sure she will want to get in touch. I have, of course, informed my Chairman of Governors and Major Neville-Gravitas is of the same opinion as myself.'

'The newspapers will have a field day if this goes to court,' Mr Nettles told her, shaking his head. 'Settling it keeps it low key.'

'I don't think you quite heard what I said,' Elisabeth told him, trying to remain calm. 'We are not, I repeat not, settling anything. Now, it is nearly time for afternoon school so if you will excuse me.'

Robbie sat in the barn nursing a weaner pig on his lap. Two collies were at his feet, curled up in the hay watching him attentively. The boy had arranged a small sick bay – some bales of hay in a half square and a trough with water and another of food. The pig, wrapped in a threadbare grey blanket, breathed nosily and looked up at the boy with small dull eyes. The farmer and Robbie had noticed the sick animal earlier that day, the way the head had hung down and how, after staggering for a few steps, it had flopped down unable to stand.

Mr Ross, wearing his old shapeless waxed jacket and greasy flat cap, came in the barn and sat next to the boy. The two dogs pricked up their ears.

''Ow's it doin'?' he asked.

'Not too good,' replied Robbie, stroking the animal's back.

'Aye, well,' said the farmer. 'Just keep it warm an' try an' gerrit to drink an' tek a bit o' food. That's abaat as much as yer can do.'

'What's wrong with it?'

'I don't reightly know,' the farmer told him. 'Could be 'owt.'

'Will it be all right?' asked Robbie.

The farmer sucked in his bottom lip. 'Can't say,' he said. 'I've seen some recover, others die. That's the way of it.'

They sat for a moment without speaking.

'You know,' said Mr Ross, 'some folk can't understand that those of us what rear these beeasts can 'ave an affection for 'em. I mean they're animals what are bred an' fattened an' then sent off to be killed an' etten but this dun't mean yer can't gerra bit fond of 'em, 'specially when they're took badly like this little 'un. Does that mek any sense to thee, Robbie?'

'Yes, it does,' replied the boy, continuing to stroke the pig.

'You like animals don't you, lad?' asked the farmer.

'I do, yes,' he replied. There was a fierce determination in his voice. 'They're not like people. You know where you are with animals. They don't mess you about. They don't tell you what to do all the time. They don't say things that they don't mean and they don't say things that will hurt you.'

'Well I'll tell thee summat,' said the farmer, 'tha'll find that I don't say owt that I don't mean and I don't say things what'll hurt thee. Thy ought to know that by now.'

'I do know,' muttered Robbie, 'You're different.'

'Any road, animals are like people, really,' said the farmer. 'Just need a bit o' TLC.'

'What's that?' asked the boy.

'Tender lovin' care,' replied the farmer, thinking to himself that the boy had probably not had much of that in his own young life. 'I reckon you've been messed abaat a bit, aven't you?' said Mr Ross.

The boy nodded.

The farmer rested a hand on the boy's shoulder. 'I hope yer don't think that me an' t'missus mess yer abaat, tell yer what to do all t'time?'

'You don't,' said the boy.

'I'm glad yer think so.' He stroked his beard and thought for moment. 'Wife's bin at me to 'ave a word wi' you,' he said.

'What about?' asked Robbie. He stopped stroking the pig and looked up at the leathery sun-scorched face. His expression was guarded and hard. He felt a nervous jump in his stomach. When people in the past had used that phrase, "I want a word with you" it had always meant he had been in some sort of trouble and was about to be told off.

'It's abaat what's goin' to 'appen to thee. Abaat your future,' Mr Ross told him.

'She wants me back!' the boy cried.

'Who wants thee back?'

'My mum,' said the boy. 'She does, doesn't she? She wants me to go back and live with her. Mrs Stirling told me. Well I won't go!' he shouted. 'I won't go!'

'By 'eck, tha's got a reight old temper on thee,' said Mr Ross chuckling. 'Calm thissen down, lad, an' 'ear what me an' t'missus wants to say to ya.'

Robbie calmed down. His small body drooped. 'Please, please don't make me go back,' he pleaded with a sorrowful look. He rubbed his eyes with a balled fist. 'I like it here. I don't want to—'

'Hey, hey,' said Mr Ross, reaching out and patting the boy's hand. 'Tha dun't need to get thissen all upset. Nob'dy's goin' to send thee back. Just listen to what I 'ave to tell thee.'

Robbie's bottom lip trembled uncontrollably.

'Now then,' said Mr Ross. 'It's true reight enough that yer mam is keen on yer goin' back to live wi' 'er but—'

'I won't go,' muttered Robbie, fighting back tears.

''Ear me out!' said the farmer. 'Yer mam misses thee, Robbie. She wants thee to go back but you don't 'ave to if tha dun't want to.'

'I don't,' whimpered the boy.

''As tha got cloth ears, lad?' asked Mr Ross. 'Did tha not 'ear what I just said?' He repeated his words slowly and with emphasis. 'Tha dun't 'ave to go back if tha dun't want to.'

Robbie looked up and sniffed. 'I don't?' he murmured.

'No, tha dun't,' said Mr Ross. 'Nob'dy's mekkin' thee do summat what tha dun't want to.'

'So can I stay here?' asked Robbie.

''Course ya can stay 'ere,' replied the farmer, 'but just keep yer gob shut for a bit an' 'ear what I 'as to tell thee. T'wife an' me 'ad a meeting last week wi' Miss Parsons o' t'Social Services an' wi' yer mam,' Mr Ross told him. 'We telled 'em we thowt tha'd settled in 'ere an' that tha was behavin' thissen an' that we was 'appy for thee to stay wi' us. Now your mam seems to me to be a reasonable sort o' woman an'—'

'But I don't—' began Robbie again.

'Just listen!' exclaimed the farmer. 'Pin tha lugs back an' keep yer gob shut an' 'ear me out. Nah then, yer mam only wants what's best for thee. Tha might not believe that now, Robbie, after all tha's been through but it's true enough. She feels reight badly abaat what 'appened an' is tryin' to mek it reight. She did say she wanted you to go 'ome where yer belong but Miss Parsons suggested that tha should stay 'ere, certainly for t'time bein'.' He gently tapped the boy's head. 'Now 'as that sunk into yer noggin yet?'

'Yeah,' replied the boy, nodding. He breathed out in relief.

'I know tha's mad wi' yer mam but she cares abaat thee. She does love thee, Robbie, whatever tha may think an' she's 'ad a difficult time of it 'erself' by t'sound of it wi' that 'usband of 'ers. Time's a gret 'ealer. Tha might one day change yer mind an' want to gu back an' live wi' 'er.'

'I won't,' muttered Robbie.

'Miss Parsons telled us,' continued Mr Ross, 'that what's reight for t'child is at t'centre of everythin' an' that tha voice should be 'eard afore anybody else's. Tha's old enough now to

know tha're own mind. She said that stability is reight important in a kid's life an' that since tha were settled 'ere an' you've
been be'avin' thaself, tha should stay weer thy are.'

'So I can still stay here then?' asked Robbie.

'Aye, tha can.'

'Can I be adopted?'

'Well, no,' replied the farmer, 'kids can't be adopted unless
their parents agree or they're med what's called wards o' court
but there's summat called special guardianship which is
between fosterin' an' adoption. This gives me an' t'wife what's
called foster parental responsibility burrit means that tha's got
to keep in contact wi' yer mam.'

'I don't want to,' replied the boy.

'Listen to me a minute,' said the farmer. 'Tha can't allus'
ave tha're own way, Robbie. Tha's got to mek a bit of an effort
thissen. Tha's got to meet us half way 'ere. Bottom line is that
nowt's gunna change for thee. Tha can stop wi' us as long as
tha wants. Me an' Mrs Ross aren't soft touches tha knows.
Tha can't allus do as tha pleases. Now, since tha's been wi' us,
tha's kept tha nose clean an' settled in 'ere gradely. I'm dead
chuffed abaat t'way that tha's tekken to lookin' after t'pigs.
Miss Parsons 'as asked to see thee an' yer mam an' me an'
t'wife next week to explain things more fully to yer.'

'I want to stay here for good,' said Robbie determinedly.

'What 'ave I just said?' asked the farmer. 'I've telled thee tha
can, but if tha does stop 'ere, there are two conditions.'

Robbie's brow furrowed and he looked troubled. 'What?'
he asked.

'Tha's got to mek an effort to be nicer to yer mam when
you see 'er.'

'And what's the other one?' asked the boy.

Mr Ross, smiling broadly, leant over to ruffle the boy's hair.
'That tha's got to keep 'elpin' me wi' mi pigs. Are tha all reight
wi' that?'

'Yeah,' said Robbie. There was a flicker of a smile.

'Good lad,' said the farmer. 'Now let's see if we can get this little fella to drink summat, shall we?'

15

Mrs Widowson shuffled into the store puffing and coughing with age and effort. She was an extremely old, wrinkled individual with a long gloomy face.

'How are you keeping?' Mrs Sloughthwaite asked the customer when the wheezing had abated sufficiently to make conversation seem feasible.

The old lady shook her head ominously. She had misery written all over her face. 'Not good, Mrs S,' she replied. 'Not good at all.'

'Oh dearie me. I am sorry to hear that. Is it your arthritis?'

'What?'

'Your arthritis!' shouted the shopkeeper.

'What about it?'

'Is that what's troubling you?'

'It's my hips,' said the old woman. 'I'm in constant purgatory. I'm a martyr to my joints. I'm tested beyond human endurance.'

Mrs Pocock sighed and shook her head. There was little sympathy coming from that direction.

'Doctor Stirling says it's a wonder I can keep upright,' complained Mrs Widowson. 'Pain is my constant companion these days I'm afraid. I shall have to have my hips done but I'm not keen on another operation at my time of life.'

Mrs Pocock, who had called in for her paper and the latest bit of gossip, viewed the aged customer before observing uncharitably, 'Well, when you get to your age you have to expect a few aches and pains.' She sniffed self-righteously. She was inclined to comment further that it is always the creaking gate that lasts the longest but, seeing the icy stare of the customer, refrained from doing so.

'That's as may be,' retorted Mrs Widowson, her voice cracking with indignation. She turned her rheumy eyes in the direction of Mrs Pocock and remarked pointedly, 'Old age and infirmity comes to us all one day, as you will soon find out. If you are digging a grave for another, be careful you don't fall in it yourself.'

'That's true enough,' agreed Mrs Sloughthwaite, nodding dully. 'It comes to us all does old age and there's a remedy for everything but death. Every door may shut but not death's door.'

'Who said anything about death?' Mrs Widowson. 'I'm not ready for my coffin just yet, thank you very much.'

The shopkeeper shifted her prodigious bulk and leant over the counter. 'Well, it was you who mentioned graves,' she said. 'Anyway, speaking of getting old, I can tell you I've been feeling my age of late. My back goes out more than I do and I feel like the morning afterwards but have not had the night before. A dripping tap makes me rush to the lavatory. And my vision's not what it was. I need my glasses to find my glasses. I'm seeing the hoptician next week. I reckon I've got one of these stigmatas in my eye and I'll need an operation.'

'It could be cataracts,' said Mrs Widowson with a baleful look. 'I've had them done. The surgery didn't work and my eyesight is worse than it was. Eye operations are very hit-and-miss.'

'So how's that grandson of yours?' asked the shopkeeper, wishing to change the topic of conversation. 'Is he a father yet?'

'No, nothing's happening,' the customer confided glumly crossing her bony arms across her chest.

'Give it time,' said Mrs Sloughthwaite.

'He's given it time,' Mrs Widowson told her. 'He's been married all of five years and nothing's happened yet and from what he says it's not through want of trying. I can't see as how anything will happen now.'

'Perhaps his wife's impregnable,' said the shopkeeper. She lowered her voice. ''Course it could be him with problems in the downstairs department. My Stan had trouble in that area and that's why we never had kiddies.'

'Too much information,' muttered Mrs Pocock.

'No, it's not our Neil,' said Mrs Widowson, sounding affronted. 'It's his wife Noreen. She's got something called a tipped womb which makes it hard for her to conceive.'

'She's inconceivable then,' remarked the shopkeeper.

'Seems like it,' said Mrs Widowson.

'Well, it's just the luck of the draw,' observed Mrs Sloughthwaite. 'I mean, some couples just can't have children.'

'And others produce them like rabbits,' added Mrs Pocock, 'and don't know when to stop. Then they live off of the state and claim all these benefits and are first in the queue for a council house.'

'She could go for that VHS treatment at the hospital,' Mrs Sloughthwaite told her, 'or, failing that, they could adopt a kiddie.'

'Huh!' huffed Mrs Pocock. 'I certainly wouldn't go down that road. Your own kids are trouble enough I can tell you without taking on somebody else's.'

I won't disagree with that, thought the shopkeeper picturing the woman's brooding, ill-humoured son.

'Well, young Danny Stainthorpe's being adopted by the Stirlings,' said Mrs Sloughthwaite, 'and you couldn't wish for a nicer young man.'

'You give it time,' remarked Mrs Pocock cynically and with a downturn of the mouth. 'When he gets to be a teenager it'll be all grunts and grumbles and moods and temper tantrums.'

Mrs Sloughthwaite was minded to say that not all young people are like her Ernest but kept her opinion to herself.

'Danny'll not turn out like that,' she said, coming to the boy's defence. 'He's a nice, well-behaved boy.'

'You mark my words,' said Mrs Pocock almost gleefully, 'he'll be difficult to handle when he gets older and Dr Stirling and his wife will rue the day they took him on.'

'Well I think young Danny deserves a pat on the back for all the work he's doing tidying up the churchyard,' said Mrs Sloughthwaite, daring to disagree.

'That's what I got when I was a girl, a good pat on the back,' remarked Mrs Pocock, 'and my father made sure it was low enough, hard enough and often enough and it never did me any harm.'

That's questionable, thought the shopkeeper.

'Yes, he's a nice young man is Danny,' said Mrs Widowson. 'He helped me take my shopping home last week. Carried my bags right up to the front door and wouldn't take a penny for doing it.'

'The new vicar's taken quite a shine to the lad, I hear,' said Mrs Sloughthwaite. 'Danny was in here yesterday and he says Mr Sparshott took him fishing as a thank you for helping him tidy up the churchyard.'

'Fishing with the vicar!' exclaimed Mrs Pocock. 'The lad wants to be careful. You hear all these stories about men taking a shine to boys.'

The shopkeeper sighed. 'You've got a very supercilious mind, you have. Not every man who is friendly with boys is a paediatric you know.'

'Well, all the same,' said Mrs Pocock belligerently, 'I don't think it's healthy and someone should say something.'

'You know, one day you'll have something good to say about somebody,' said the shopkeeper.

'You're a fine one to talk,' retorted Mrs Pocock. 'You've never been backwards in coming forwards when it comes to criticising others.'

The shopkeeper rose from the counter. 'And who pray have I passed judgement on?' she exclaimed indignantly.

'Well, you were very critical of the vicar after that sermon of his and you haven't a good word for Fred Massey for a start,' said Mrs Pocock.

'Nobody's got a good word for Fred Massey,' countered the shopkeeper. 'Cold as an axe head and as clever as the devil in brogues, that's what he is and talk about being mean. He wouldn't give a blind hen a worm.'

'I saw Fred Massey at the doctor's,' said Mrs Widowson, massaging one of her hips and wincing. 'He looked in a bad way. Face as grim as a week-old corpse he had.'

'It always looks like that,' said Mrs Pocock. 'Face like a bag of rusty spanners.'

'He's been in bed with his kidneys, so he says,' said Mrs Widowson.

'That's the drink,' said Mrs Sloughthwaite. 'He's never out of the Blacksmith's Arms. His kidneys will be like pickled walnuts the amount of beer he puts away.'

'He reckons that his nephew's new missus is putting things in his food.'

'Who, Bianca?'

'That's what he says. Was telling everyone in the waiting room at the doctor's surgery. He thinks she's trying to poison him, been putting some toadstools in with his mushrooms.'

'He's going soft in the head,' said Mrs Sloughthwaite. 'Why would she want to poison him?'

'I could think of a few that would have good reason,' remarked Mrs Pocock.

'He says she wants him out of the way so she and his nephew can get their hands on his money and the farm,' answered Mrs Widowson.

'Hot air,' said the shopkeeper. 'Mind you, she's good reason to poison him. It can't be easy living in the same house as Fred Massey.'

'He says that Dr Stirling is sending him for tests at the hospital.'

'Knowing Fred Massey,' said Mrs Pocock, 'he'll survive. It's always the worthless vessels that don't get broken.'

At that moment the subject of their discussion walked through the door.

'Speak of the devil,' muttered Mrs Pocock.

'We were just talking about you, Fred,' said Mrs Sloughth-waite brightly.

The visitor, a short, thick-necked individual with a curiously flat face and dark hair greying at the temples, was shown into the drawing room at Limebeck House.

'Her ladyship will be with you presently, sir,' said the butler.

'I see that Lady Wadsworth has put her windfall to good effect,' observed Mr Massingham, looking around.

'I beg your pardon, sir?'

'All these renovations,' said the visitor with an airy wave of his hand.

'Indeed, sir,' answered Watson, 'a great deal has been done since your last visit.'

The last time Mr Massingham of the Massingham and Makepeace Fine Arts Auction House had been shown into the room he had found it a cheerless, ill-lit and draughty chamber full of furniture draped in white dust sheets. It had been transformed. The heavily moulded ceiling had been restored to its former glory, the marbling columns and pilasters repainted, the elaborate gilt armchairs and sofas recovered, the inlaid satinwood table shone with polish, the heavy velvet curtains embroidered with gold had been cleaned and the huge crystal glass chandelier sparkled as it caught the light. *Perhaps a little overdone*, thought the art expert, *but a vast improvement nevertheless.*

Lady Wadsworth entered the room.

'Mr Massingham,' she said, extending a hand. 'It is good of you to come. I hope it will not be a wasted journey.'

'My dear Lady Wadsworth,' he said obsequiously, bowing and taking her hand which he kissed lightly. 'It is such a pleasure to see you again.' He waved a hand in the direction of Watson who stood by the door. 'I was remarking to your butler here on the changes since my last visit.'

'Indeed,' she replied. 'The money I received from the sale of the statues went a long way to pay for the much-needed renovations. Of course, there is still much to be done and everything is so very expensive. I am hoping that the two new statues which we have discovered will be of interest to you.'

Mr Massingham had been asked to visit Limebeck House the previous year to value a painting that Lady Wadsworth was minded to sell to pay for the restoration of the house. Reputedly purchased by Sir William Wadsworth, her great-great-grandfather around the 1760s, the magnificent painting of a rearing stallion had pride of place over the grand fireplace in the drawing room. Lady Wadsworth had always been led to believe that the masterpiece was an authentic work of art by the great equine artist George Stubbs. She was soon disabused of this notion.

'It's a copy,' Mr Massingham had informed her bluntly. His face had been as blank as a figurehead on the front of a ship.

But on his way out the visitor, stooping to retrieve a fallen glove, had caught sight of a shapely white marble foot poking out from under a dust sheet. He had uncovered the figure like a mortician gently uncovering a corpse. When all had been revealed he had staggered back to the door and steadied himself on the architrave. 'I think I am about to swoon,' he had murmured.

The sculpture under the dust sheet and a second one stored on the stable block were sixteenth-century studies of reclining classical figures, executed in the finest Carrara marble. They were sold at auction for a considerable amount of money.

'I have to admit to a great excitement,' confessed Mr Massingham now. He was like an eager child waiting to open his presents on Christmas morning. 'It would be astonishing were we to discover that the two statues you mentioned to me on the telephone are of the age, rarity and quality of the ones we took to auction.'

'Let us hope they are,' stated Lady Wadsworth. 'I'm afraid they've been down by the lake for a good few years so might show some signs of wear. I recall as a child my brother and I used to throw snowballs at them.'

Mr Massingham winced. 'Shall we take a look?' he said.

A young man with a shaven head and sporting a brightly coloured tattooed snake which twisted around his neck was busy at work in the kitchen garden. He was cleaning a large white statue of a naked woman with a wire brush, a bottle of bleach and a bucket of soapy water.

'Stop!' commanded Mr Massingham, rushing towards him. 'Desist! Leave off from what you are doing immediately.'

The youth addressed Lady Wadsworth. 'Mr O'Malley told me to give them a good going over,' said the youth. 'They were all mucky.'

'This is my estate manager's assistant,' Lady Wadsworth told Mr Massingham. 'Thank you, Jason, you may stop what you are doing.'

'These statues must be professionally cleaned,' said Mr Massingham petulantly. He gave the youth a savage look. 'They should not be scrubbed with a wire brush and doused in bleach! So many great works of art have been ruined by thoughtless cleaning. Such barbarism. Now move out of the way, young man, and let me examine them.'

'Sadly,' said Mr Massingham as he sat with Lady Wadsworth in the drawing room later that morning, 'the statues are crude Victorian replicas, very much worse for wear and of little value.'

Lady Wadsworth drummed her hands on the small occasional table next to her chair. 'Ah well,' she sighed, 'I suppose it was rather too much to hope that they were of any consequence. I am sorry you have had a wasted journey.'

'Maybe there is something else I could take a look at?' asked Mr Massingham.

'I fear not. There is the furniture of course, one or two paintings and some of the porcelain which may be of some value but I am loath to part with these. So many things have been sold over the years to maintain this draughty old building. I really do not wish to sell any more.'

The butler, who was standing by the door, coughed.

'Was there something you wished to say, Watson?' asked Lady Wadsworth.

'What about the etchings in the attic, your ladyship?'

'Etchings in the attic?' repeated the visitor.

'Oh those,' said Lady Wadsworth dismissively. 'I hardly imagine that they will be of any interest to Mr Massingham.'

'I should be pleased to look at them,' said the fine art expert.

'They are just a few old pictures,' Lady Wadsworth told him, 'and some of them, if my memory serves me right, are rather salacious.'

The art dealer sat up in his chair. 'Really?'

'I am sure they are not worth bothering with.'

'Nevertheless,' said Mr Massingham.

Watson was despatched to the attic to get the etchings. When he returned, a dusty leather-bound folder was placed on the small rosewood card table. Mr Massingham blew away the dust, opened the folder and examined the first picture with a small magnifying glass. Then he stood and breathed noisily through his nose like a horse. There was an expectant pause. 'These are not etchings,' he declared.

'What a pity,' said Lady Wadsworth.

'If I am not mistaken they are Renaissance chiaroscuro woodcut prints,' he stated. 'This art technique's golden age was in sixteenth-century Germany, Italy and the Netherlands and these wonderfully detailed scenes were revolutionary and became very popular at the time. This first one, for example, is very similar to the woodcuts to be found in the Albertina Museum in Vienna.' He held it up for Lady Wadsworth to view. 'This huge, naked giant with bulging muscles clubbing to death the cowering figure is probably the great Hercules.'

'It's not the sort of racy drawing one would have on the wall,' commented Lady Wadsworth. 'It's extremely ugly and off-putting and leaves little to the imagination. All those muscles and naked flesh. No wonder my grandmother consigned them to the attic.'

'No, no, my dear lady, I beg to differ. This is a wonderfully naturalistic and life-enhancing depiction of a classical theme.' He picked up another print. 'This one I think is of the great Hercules again killing another enemy with some sort of horn. It's very like the one displayed in the bishop's palace at Bishop Auckland.'

'Good gracious!' exclaimed Lady Wadsworth. 'How very singular. The bishop who purchased them must have had a very strange taste in art. I should have thought pictures on religious themes would have been more to his liking.'

'A man of discernment, I should say,' said Mr Massingham, leafing through the other prints.

'So are they worth anything?' he was asked.

'Undoubtedly, that is, if they are genuine,' replied Mr Massingham.

'And do you think they are?' asked Lady Wadsworth.

'I am no expert on this period in art history,' he answered, 'but I have seen such woodcut prints before and I am of the opinion the ones here may very well be authentic and possibly the work of the most influential engraver of his day, one Hendrik Goltzius who made classical scenes such as these first two.' He took another print from the folder and examined it closely. He raised an eyebrow and coughed. 'Goltzius's speciality, however, was in erotic prints like this one.'

Lady Wadsworth leant over in her chair to see the print better and Watson joined her. He too bent forward to get a closer look. 'I must say they are very revealing,' she said before turning to the butler. 'You don't need to ogle, Watson,' she told him.

'Indeed they are somewhat explicit,' agreed the art expert. 'May I ask from where you acquired them?' he asked.

'Well I certainly didn't buy them!' exclaimed Lady Wadsworth. 'Like the statues that went to auction, they were brought back by that ne'r-do-well forebear of mine, young Tristram Wadsworth. I think I mentioned to you on your last visit here that he was a gambler, drinker, womaniser and a thorough-going reprobate who gallivanted around the continent on the Grand European Tour and brought back all manner of statues and paintings and *objets d'art*, most of which were of an indecent nature and have been sold to pay for death duties. My grandmother, I guess, thought that like the naked statues these were shocking and might corrupt the servants.' She glanced at Watson, who maintained a dead-pan face. 'They were put up in the attic out of the way.'

'Erotic prints such as these go for a great deal at auction,' she was told. 'I feel certain that there are many collectors who would be very interested in these if they prove to be the genuine article. With your permission I should like to take the one of the great Hercules to show a colleague better versed than I in this branch of art.'

'You can take them all as far as I am concerned,' said Lady Wadsworth.

'No, I shall take just the one to be on the safe side. They might prove very valuable and I would feel most uncomfortable in the possession of the full set.' Mr Massingham carefully packed away the remaining prints and bent to kiss Lady Walworth's hand. 'I shall be in touch.'

That afternoon another visitor arrived at Limebeck House.

'The vicar's here to see you, your ladyship,' announced the butler.

'Mr Sparshott? What the devil does he want now?' Her mouth was compressed and unsmiling.

'Shall I tell him you are unavailable?'

'No, I suppose I should see what he wants. Let me go and freshen up a little. You can bring him in here and tell him I shall be in attendance presently.'

The Reverend Mr Sparshott had never courted popularity or sought approval in the parishes where he had been curate and had many times upset some of his congregation with his candid views and uncompromising sermons. However, sitting by the river bank thinking over what the archdeacon had said to him and reflecting on the dwindling attendance at his services, he determined to make more of an effort with the residents of the village and try and be more accommodating and approachable. He therefore decided to mend a few bridges. First on his list was the lady of the manor. He would tell her that he had reconsidered her proposal for a stained-glass window and, having thought the matter over, would now raise no objection should she wish to go ahead. He would, however, not countenance anything too showy.

Reverend Mr Sparshott was a man with plain tastes, one

who eschewed all ostentation at home and in the church. He therefore found the furnishings and decorations in the drawing room not at all to his liking. It was a far too garish and flamboyant room. He perched on the edge of a massive Victorian ottoman and picked up a beautifully bound and embossed leather folder which had been left on the small rosewood card table next to him. He examined the contents: drawings of hideous-looking witches boiling frogs, great naked figures wrestling in rocky landscapes, fire-breathing creatures being bludgeoned to death and lovers caught unawares by the Grim Reaper. His eyes seemed to bulge from their sockets. He had never seen anything so explicit and so shocking.

Lady Wadsworth swept regally into the room.

The cleric slammed shut the folder and jumped up as if he had been poked with a cattle prod. His face was flushed.

'Ah, Reverend Sparshott,' said the lady of the manor, 'I see you are studying my prints. Interesting, aren't they? The Bishop of Durham, I am told, has some similar in his palace at Bishop Auckland.'

The reverend gentleman, for a rare occasion in his life, was completely stumped for words. He opened his mouth as if to reply, then snapped it shut.

Ashley could tell from the solemn look on her mother's face, the straight-backed posture and by the chill formality of her welcome that something was amiss.

'So, how was the cruise?' she asked, forcing herself to sound cheerful.

'It was all right,' her mother replied indifferently. She didn't elaborate so it was obvious there was something else on her mind.

'Just all right?' asked Ashley.

'Yes, that is what I said,' snapped her mother. 'It's not something I would repeat.'

'So what was wrong with it?' asked her daughter.

'It's not something I wish to talk about.'

On the previous visit her mother had been uncharacteristically good-humoured and uncritical but that morning Ashley knew there was something unacceptable that she had done.

They sat there in silence for a moment.

'Shall I make a cup of tea?'

'No, I had one before you came,' answered Mrs Underwood. She fingered the ring on her finger. 'And have you been driven here by that Irish man who works for Lady Wadsworth?'

'Emmet?'

'I forget his name,' replied her mother, who knew perfectly well what he was called.

'No, I haven't been driven here by Emmet,' Ashley said. 'I came on the bus as usual.'

'And are you seeing a lot of him?'

'No, not really.'

'Miss Sowerbutts, who I was with on the cruise, told me he was some sort of gypsy, that he arrived in the village in a caravan and does odd jobs and as for being the estate manager for Lady Wadsworth, she said that is nonsense. Of course the Irish are great storytellers. One can never know if they are telling the truth or not. You want to be careful letting a man like that give you lifts.'

Ashley gave a small smile. 'Miss Sowerbutts is wrong,' she said. 'Emmet is indeed Lady Wadsworth's estate manager. He's really nice. I like him.'

'I hope you are not forming some sort of attachment to this man,' said her mother.

'What a strange turn of phrase that is,' replied her daughter, '"forming an attachment". It sounds as if I'm like an extension to a house or some sort of accessory.'

'Don't be silly, Ashley, you know perfectly well what I mean. Are you involved with this man? If you are, it is quite unthinkable that someone with your background and education and a position in the church should be consorting with a man like that.'

'Why?'

'What do you mean why? You know very well why. A gypsy! What would people say?'

'I couldn't care less what people say.'

'No, you never have cared what people say,' said Mrs Underwood. 'That's your trouble. Strong-willed. Well, what would this bishop of yours think?'

'I am sure that knowing the bishop as I do, he would have no objection to my seeing whomever I wished.'

'But to be connected with such a person is inconceivable, surely you can see that!' cried her mother. 'You have got to an age where I can't forbid you to see this man but I urge you to think of the consequences of associating with a person who is so very different in upbringing, education, social class and, I should imagine, religion.'

'I like Emmet, mother, I like him very much and I intend to continue to see him whether you like it or not.'

'Headstrong,' said her mother. 'You have always been headstrong.'

'Let's not talk about it any more,' said Ashley. 'We will only get into an argument.'

'I'm merely pointing it out for your own good,' persisted Mrs Underwood. 'This relationship is improper and you must not encourage this man.'

'Did you ever love my father, Mother?' Ashley asked.

Mrs Underwood gripped the arms of her chair and sat up. Love was not a word she expected to hear mentioned. 'What sort of question is that?'

'Well did you? Did you ever love him?'

'I don't wish to talk about your father. You know how it upsets me.'

'You see, as a child I always doubted that you did love him. I never saw you put your arm around him, say a kind word, smile when he came into the room. I can't remember ever seeing you kiss him.'

'I don't have to listen to this,' said her mother. 'I am not going to sit here to be interrogated.'

'But I am?'

'What?'

'Am I supposed to sit here and be interrogated?'

'I do not wish to discuss this any more,' said her mother. 'But I will tell you this, Ashley, I am bitterly disappointed in you, extremely upset that you seem to be throwing yourself away, seeing a man so well beneath you in every respect, particularly after all that has been done for you. I do not wish to hear the man's name mentioned again and he is certainly not welcome in this apartment.'

'Thank you for making your feelings clear, Mother,' said Ashley. 'Now, if you don't mind, I think I'll make tracks. I'm going to the theatre tonight.'

'And are you going with someone?'

'Just a friend,' said her daughter.

'Well I hope it's not the Irish gypsy,' said her mother disdainfully.

Mr Jolly stood at the door of the classroom. It was the end of the school day and Elisabeth was tidying up before going home.

'May I see you, Mrs Stirling?' he asked. The man looked oppressed by life.

'Yes, of course,' she replied. 'Come in.'

The teacher sat on one of the small wooden chairs used by the children, his legs pressed together, his back hunched and his hands clasped on his lap. He presented such a pathetic figure, tragic-faced and dressed in his old tweed sports coat with the leather patched elbows and wearing baggy flannel trousers. The teacher lowered his head and cleared his throat with a small cough then licked his lower lip nervously. 'I have had some time to think about the situation,' he said grimly. He paused and took a deep breath.

Following the school inspection, Elisabeth had been candid with Mr Jolly. At first she had stressed the few positive things Mr Steel had said about the lesson he had observed but then took the teacher through the criticisms as tactfully as she could. He had listened without interruption with a miserable expression, nodding frequently. She had been surprised by his reaction. Elisabeth had rather expected him to resent the comments and dispute the criticisms but he had not. He accepted that his lessons were not the most stimulating and that he was not the most interesting and motivating of teachers. He had told her that he didn't need a school inspector to tell him that. Elisabeth had been gratified to hear that he would agree to attend some courses and accept help.

'Was it about the inspection report that you wish to see me?' she asked now.

'No, no,' said Mr Jolly. 'It's about the accident. In fact, I can't get it out of my mind.'

'Well, I'm sure things will turn out for the best,' Elisabeth reassured him.

She suddenly felt very sorry for the man. *He must be feeling very down,* she thought, *having been told his teaching was wanting and now having to face an accusation of negligence.*

'I'm at a pretty low ebb at the moment, Mrs Stirling,' he said sadly.

'I can understand that,' said Elisabeth, 'but I don't need to tell you that you have my full support and that of your colleagues and the governors.'

'Thank you, I appreciate that.' He massaged his forehead and took a deep breath.

'I have decided,' he said, 'that perhaps, after all, we should not go to court over this.'

'Not go to court?' repeated Elisabeth.

'That's right. I really don't think I could face standing in a witness box with everybody staring at me and having to answer all those questions and accusations.'

'I see,' said Elisabeth in a calm and quiet voice which disguised her annoyance. She thought, having discussed the matter with him, that they had agreed that the action should be contested. 'So are you suggesting that you should admit liability?'

'I just want this to be over and done with, Mrs Stirling,' he said wearily. His features were moulded into an expression of despondency. 'It's been so very stressful and . . .' His voice cracked and faltered.

'May I ask you what has changed your mind?' asked Elisabeth. 'I thought that when we talked the matter over you agreed with me that we should refute the allegation.'

'It's just that it would save a great deal of trouble,' he answered.

'For whom?'

'Well for all of us. Mr Nettles said that—'

'Mr Nettles!' interjected Elisabeth. 'What has Mr Nettles got to do with this?'

'He called me up to discuss the situation,' explained Mr Jolly.

'Did he indeed?'

'He said that were this to go to court there could be repercussions.'

'And what did he say these repercussions would be?' enquired Elisabeth.

'That if it went to court it would be very nerve-wracking for me and that there could be much adverse publicity not only for myself but for the school and the Local Education Authority.'

'And he suggested that you admit responsibility for what happened?' Elisabeth tried to remain composed. Inside she was seething.

'Not in so many words he didn't,' said Mr Jolly. 'He said I should think very carefully about pursuing the matter. To settle out of court, he said, would keep it low-key, otherwise it would be all over the papers and that—'

'One moment,' said Elisabeth, holding up a hand. 'Could I ask you, did you give me an honest and accurate description of what happened when Norman fell from the wall bars?'

'Yes I did,' he replied in a voice hardly audible.

'You told the children at the outset of the lesson to take care on the equipment?'

'Yes, I always do.'

'And you were in the hall for the entire lesson?'

'I was, yes.'

'And did the children inform you after his accident that Norman was acting the fool on the wall bars before he fell?'

'They did but—'

'Then why do you think you should admit to being negligent?'

'I do so,' replied the teacher, 'in the hope that by not contesting this action I might be able to put the whole unhappy episode behind me. As Mr Nettles pointed out—'

'I am not interested in what Mr Nettles said,' Elisabeth cut in. 'Do you feel responsible for what happened?'

'Well, no, not really.'

'Then why should you admit that you were at fault?'

'It's just that it would be over and done with. My mother used to say that it is better to turn your back in a gale than press your face against it.'

'And my mother used to say that sometimes one has to grasp the nettle. And I shall have one particular Nettle to grasp when I speak to him. We shall fight this nonsensical action and it will be thrown out of court.'

Mr Jolly gave a mirthless smile. 'You really are that confident?' he asked weakly.

'I am,' she replied. 'Now you try and put it out of your mind and, as for me, I need to have a word with Mr Nettles.'

Elisabeth found Mrs Scrimshaw in the school office talking to Mr Hornchurch. The teacher was looking remarkably smart and was clearly in a very good mood.

'I thought you two would be away by this time,' she said.

'I've a WI meeting tonight,' replied the secretary. 'It's not worth me going home. Anyway, I've quite a lot to get through.'

'And I'm meeting Ashley and we're going to the theatre,' said Mr Hornchurch beaming. 'We're going to catch up on old times.'

'Have a lovely evening,' said Elisabeth.

'Well I must make tracks,' he said. 'It wouldn't do to be late. I'll see you both tomorrow.' He skipped out of the office.

'You don't think love is in the air, do you?' remarked Mrs Scrimshaw.

Elisabeth smiled. 'No, I very much doubt it,' she said.

'I mean they do make a nice couple, don't they?' said the secretary. 'I wouldn't be at all surprised.'

Oh, I would, thought Elisabeth.

16

'It's been really good to catch up with you again, Ashley,' said Mr Hornchurch.

He was sitting with his former college friend in the pub overlooking the river in Clayton. He had made a real effort with his appearance and was wearing a smart jacket, pale-pink cotton shirt and plum-coloured corduroy trousers.

'It has,' she agreed. 'I'm afraid I've lost touch with so many of my college friends. We all seem to lead such busy lives.'

'Quite a coincidence isn't it, that of all the places we could have ended up in, it was Barton-in-the-Dale?'

'It is,' she said.

'Perhaps it was meant to be,' he told her, smiling. 'Maybe our paths were destined to cross again. Do you believe in fate?'

'No, I don't,' she said. 'Anyway, Rupert, thank you for inviting me to the theatre. It's been an age since I was able to sit and watch a play.'

He pulled a face. 'The one tonight was a bit dark and depressing, wasn't it, but then Ibsen's dramas are never a barrel of laughs. I'm afraid the old pastor in the play didn't come out too well, did he? I don't think Mr Ibsen had a great deal of time for the clergy.' He then began to recite in a stentorian voice. '"And priests in their gowns were doing the rounds and binding in briars my hopes and desires".'

People on the other tables turned their heads in his direction.

'I hope I don't resemble Pastor Manders,' said Ashley, smiling.

'No, no, of course not,' he replied. 'You couldn't be more different. You are one of the good guys.'

'I'm pleased to hear it.'

'It's so good to see you again,' he said.

'Yes,' she replied, not really listening to what he was saying. Her mind was on Emmet. She stared out over the river to the cathedral and they were quiet for a moment.

'I'm told the new vicar is not unlike him though,' said Mr Hornchurch.

'Who?'

'Pastor Manders, in the play,' he said. 'Hypocritical, prideful, incapable of spontaneity, someone who doesn't believe in the freedom of expression. Isn't your Mr Sparshott a man of that ilk? You worked with the man, you should know.'

'I don't think Mr Sparshott is at all like that,' said Ashley, springing to the vicar's defence. 'He is rather a distant figure, it has to be admitted, and perhaps his social skills leave a little to be desired but he's not like the sort of destructive character of the clergyman in the play. I'm afraid Pastor Manders doesn't know the meaning of love.'

When Rupert went to get more drinks, Ashley looked out at the fast-flowing river. The last time she had been here it had been with Emmet and his young daughter. They had met at a folk concert and he had asked her to join them for a drink by the river. She recalled the child with eyes the colour of polished jade and the long rust-coloured hair, curly and shining, and saw how she doted on her father. It had been memorable, sitting out on that mild summer evening, such a treat for her to be away from church matters, to have a respite from talking theology with the archdeacon or education with his wife, to leave weddings and funerals and christenings and parish visits behind for a short while and to talk about Ireland and music and poetry. She thought of Emmet now.

'And how do you like the religious life?' asked Rupert, returning with the drinks.

'Pardon?' said Ashley. 'I was miles away.'

'Life in the church. What's it like being a priest?'

'I'm enjoying it and finding it very fulfilling. What about you? Do you like teaching?'

'Tremendously,' he replied. 'There is no other job like teaching. I really believe that a good teacher changes lives.'

'Well, mine certainly did,' said Ashley. 'Sister Augusta Maria changed my life.'

'My teachers too,' he said.

'You're still as passionate about everything, Rupert,' said Ashley.

'It gets me into trouble on occasions,' he admitted. 'I sometimes get a bit over-enthusiastic about things.'

'And how are you getting on with Mrs Stirling?'

'She's top drawer,' he replied. 'I really fell on my feet getting redeployed to Barton. She has a way with people. She brings out the best in the teachers and in the pupils. There's a sad, angry little boy in my class, a really mixed-up, lonely kid who seems at odds with the world. He's being fostered at the moment because his mother couldn't cope. Most head teachers would have expelled him but Mrs Stirling is determined to try and help him. He's had a pretty rough time.'

'That would be Robbie,' said Ashley. 'I know the boy. He came into the church. I was asking Mrs Stirling about him only the other day. He's in your class, is he?'

'He is,' replied Rupert. 'Having met him you will probably know he can be quite a handful at times but there is something about that stubborn and sometimes exasperating child that I like. I think beneath that hard shell of his is a sensitive little boy. I don't think the other teachers at the school feel the same. One of the teachers who was redeployed like me taught Robbie at Urebank before the lad was expelled and Robbie bit him.'

'Is that Mr Jolly?'

'That's him.'

'I met him when I came into school to take the assembly,' said Ashley. 'I believe he's going through a bit of a bad time himself at the moment.'

'You heard? Yes, a boy in his class had an accident and the parent is taking legal action. I'm afraid it doesn't look too good for the man.'

'I hope things work out for him,' said Ashley. She looked at her watch. 'I think we should be getting back. We don't want to miss the last bus.'

'There's a much more lively production in here next week,' said Rupert. 'It's Shakespeare's *Love's Labour's Lost*. I wonder if you might like to join me again and maybe have a bite to eat beforehand?'

'Thank you, Rupert, but I really am so very busy at the moment.'

'Ah well,' he said with a smile. 'Perhaps another time.'

As they stood in the bus shelter waiting for the last bus back to Barton-in-the-Dale, Emmet, driving along the Clayton Road, caught sight of them chattering and laughing. He drove past.

'If you're wanting the letters, Mrs Stirling,' said the secretary, 'I've nearly finished them.'

It was the next morning, the day after Elisabeth's conversation with Mr Jolly.

'You seem you be very clued-up with your computer,' said Elisabeth. 'I'm very impressed.'

Mrs Scrimshaw's face brightened. 'Oh it's pretty straightforward when you know how,' she replied. 'I got the hang of it in no time. I have to say that it's so much better than the type-writer. I can save documents and access them at a press of a button, amend letters and cut and paste material; it has a spell-checker and even makes sure I get the grammar right.' She had not divulged to Elisabeth that she had received a crash course after school from young Oscar as he waited to be collected by his mother. He had taught her how to plug in all the sockets, access the programs and taught her the rudiments of word-processing. Then Mr Hornchurch had given her a few lessons at lunchtimes so she now felt confident.

'I am very pleased you have taken to it so well,' said Elisabeth.

'Is there something you wanted, Mrs Stirling?' asked the secretary.

'Yes, could you get me the Education Office please? I need to speak to Mr Nettles.'

The secretary pulled a face as she dialled the number. 'I bet you a pound to a penny that he's tied up,' she muttered.

'Hello.' It was a young woman's matter-of-fact voice at the end of the line.

Mrs Scrimshaw passed over the receiver.

'I'd like to speak to Mr Nettles, please,' Elisabeth told her.

'He's tied up at the moment,' came the reply.

'Well I suggest you untie him. I need to speak to him urgently.'

'He's in a meeting.'

'This is Mrs Stirling, head teacher at Barton-in the-Dale Primary School,' Elisabeth told the speaker sharply. 'I need to speak to Mr Nettles as soon as possible. It is very important. Please tell him when he is untied to phone me back.'

'I'll tell him,' replied the young woman curtly and placed down the receiver.

It was early Friday morning when Elisabeth, sitting oppo-site Mrs Scrimshaw in the school office, managed at long last to speak to Mr Nettles. When she mentioned that she had left a message for him requesting that he return her call, he sounded breezily dismissive.

'Yes, yes, Mrs Stirling, I do appreciate that you wished to speak to me but I was in a very important meeting.'

'Which was?'

'I beg your pardon?'

'Might I ask what was so important about this meeting which you could not leave to speak to me? I did say it was very important.'

'Well it was . . . er . . . about er . . . staffing and various other matters.'

'As I did say, I wished to speak to you urgently.'

'Well, I am here now,' he said nonchalantly, 'and I am all ears.'

'Why did you see fit to speak to Mr Jolly?' asked Elisabeth.

'I take it this concerns Norman Stubbins' accident?'

'Yes it does. Why did you speak to a member of my staff without my knowledge?'

'I felt it would be useful to have a word with him,' he replied loftily.

'Why?'

'To offer my advice.'

'I gather that your advice was that he should accept liability for the accident and that things should be settled out of court.'

'That was one option I flagged up, yes,' agreed the education officer.

'It was an option you flagged up to me, Mr Nettles,' replied Elisabeth, 'and I told you very clearly that it was not one we would be taking up and that we would be challenging the action. The governing body, which of course I have consulted, was unanimous on this and if you had taken the time to speak to Mrs Pickering, the county solicitor, you would know that she too is in agreement. I spoke to her when you were tied up.'

'The thing is—' the education officer started.

'I strongly resent your interference, Mr Nettles,' said Elisabeth, 'and would appreciate it if in future you speak to me before approaching a member of my staff on matters such as this.'

She thumped down the receiver.

'That's telling him,' said Mrs Scrimshaw.

'Still here?' said the caretaker, poking his head around the office door later that afternoon.

'I've got another WI meeting tonight,' Mrs Scrimshaw told him.

'Is that why you're all dolled up?'

'All dolled up!' she exclaimed. 'You make me sound like one of these women who walk the docks at midnight waiting to be picked up by a sailor.'

'No, no,' protested the caretaker. 'I was meaning that you just look very well-turned-out, that's all.'

'I like to make an effort,' she said. 'I'm the chair again and I shall be introducing the speaker. Now, if you will excuse me, I'm putting together the agenda for tonight's meeting and have quite a lot to get through.'

The caretaker remained at the door and, despite his dismissal, he clearly had no intention of moving.

'Who have you got speaking tonight then?' he asked.

'A Mrs Wigglesworth.'

'And what's her subject?'

'If you must know, she is giving us a talk, on "Voices From Beyond the Grave". She's a medium. Now if you wouldn't mind . . .'

'A medium what?'

'She's a psychic. She gets in touch with those who have died.'

'That'll not be barrel of laughs,' huffed the caretaker.

'Not all our speakers we invite to our meetings are barrels of laughs,' retorted the secretary. 'We have some very serious talks you know.'

'I'd like to get in touch with my Auntie Nora and get her to clear up the matter of the clock,' said the caretaker, jangling his keys. 'Before she died she promised the clock to me. My sister walked off with it before the funeral and I reckon she took a set of fish knives as well. I've not spoken to her since.'

'Is there something you wanted, Mr Gribbon?' asked the secretary irritably. 'It's just I have quite a lot to get on with.'

'No, there wasn't anything in particular,' said the caretaker, remaining rooted to the spot. 'I saw your light on and just thought I'd pop in and see how you are.'

'Well I'm fine thank you.'

'I reckon Mr Jolly is up for the high jump.'

'I'm sorry?'

'Mr Jolly. He must be wetting himself.'

'And why would he be doing that?'

'Well, he's being taken to court over that kid what fell off the wall bars, isn't he? That Mrs Stubbins is claiming it was negligence and knowing what I know about Mr Jolly it's very likely he wasn't in control of the class at the time.'

'Were you there then, Mr Gribbon?' asked Mrs Scrimshaw.

'Was I where?'

'In the hall when the boy fell from the wall bars?'

'No, I wasn't.'

'Then how would you know it was very likely Mr Jolly wasn't in control of his class?'

'I'm merely surmising, Mrs Scrimshaw. The point is that that Stubbins lad has had accident after accident since he's been in Mr Jolly's class. It'll look to them at the court that that's too much of a coincidence won't it? There was the marble what he swallowed, then he pushed a rubber in his ear, then he got his finger stuck and now the accident with the wall bars. They're sure to bring all that up when he goes to court. Lack of proper supervision, that's what they'll argue. And of course Mr Jolly will go to pieces in the witness box. He could lose his job and it won't look good for the school either.'

'From what I've been told,' replied the secretary, 'it was the boy's own fault, playing the fool.'

'That's as may be,' said the caretaker, drawing in a breath through his teeth with a sort of hissing noise, 'but these lawyers are as slippery as greased eels and will have Mr Jolly tied up in knots.'

'And since when have you been a legal expert?' asked the secretary.

'I've read about cases like this in the paper,' Mr Gribbon told her, 'and I'm telling you, Mr Jolly might not be with us for much longer and, to be honest, he'll not be missed.'

'Talking of things being slippery, they might bring up your floors,' said Mrs Scrimshaw.

'Who might?'

'The lawyers representing Mrs Stubbins. I mean you buff them up so much, it's like a skating rink in there. I've nearly gone over a few times and Mrs Robertshaw's said she's slipped.'

'He didn't slip on the floor,' retorted the caretaker, 'the lad fell from the wall bars.'

'Maybe, but, as you have pointed out, lawyers are as slippery as greased eels and they might raise the matter of slippery floors. You might be called to give evidence.'

'They wouldn't call me, would they?' asked the caretaker sounding less bullish.

'Look, I must get on,' said the secretary. 'Why don't you go and investigate the phantom footsteps?'

'I've heard them again you know,' said the caretaker.

'Really,' she said, not as a question but as a way of making him shut up.

'As sure as I'm standing here.'

The secretary wished he was not standing there but getting on with the cleaning of the school.

'You could perhaps ask this Mrs Wigglesworth who it is?' he said.

'I might just do that,' replied Mrs Scrimshaw. 'Now, could I get on . . . ?'

'How long are you going to be?' asked the caretaker, jangling his keys again. 'I need to lock up.'

'I shall be as long as I need to be,' replied Mrs Scrimshaw crossly. 'If you hadn't interrupted me and kept me talking I would have been finished by now.'

'Well can you lock up?' asked the caretaker. 'I've got a darts match tonight.'

The secretary sighed loudly. 'Yes, I'll lock up,' she told him. 'Now could I get on?'

When the caretaker had gone, the building became eerily silent. During the day the school was a noisy, bustling place with the shrill ringing of bells and buzzing telephones, children singing and chattering and running, teachers calling into the office and, of course, the garrulous caretaker with the loud, grating voice who constantly interrupted her. Now all was strangely quiet. Mrs Scrimshaw suddenly felt cold and unaccountably unnerved. She glanced at the floor expecting to see an army of cockroaches marching towards her desk but there was not a sign of the insects. She had stayed late at school before and never felt uneasy about being in the building alone but that evening, for some reason, she felt agitated. She turned off the computer, quickly tidied her desk and prepared to leave. Suddenly she turned her head sharply sideways like a ventriloquist's dummy. There were heavy footsteps directly below her window. She held her breath to slow her heart and looked out expecting to see a dark, looming figure peering at her through the glass. But there was nobody. There was just the heavy clunking of feet outside.

Mrs Scrimshaw sat in frozen silence until the footsteps eventually died away. She clutched her umbrella and, pointing it ahead of her like a bayonet, tiptoed out of her room and inched her way down the corridor. A few cockroaches scurried back under the skirting boards. At the entrance to the school she fumbled in her handbag for her keys and with a trembling hand charily opened the door. She peered out. All was still. Ominous ragged black clouds hung overhead and a blustery wind fluttered the leaves on the great oak tree which towered above the school, its spreading branches like huge arms embracing the building. She looked out at the ancient Norman church, wreathed in shadow and the blackened war memorial with the stooping angel cradling the dead soldier. A lone black-faced sheep on the village green watched her and from some distant wood there came the strident cawing of the crows.

The ladies of the WI listened with rapt attention as Mrs Wigglesworth, dressed in a startlingly bright-pink woollen suit and sporting a rope of huge glass beads and long glittery earrings, described her psychic gifts and how she was in constant touch with those who had 'passed over'.

Encouraged to give a demonstration, she closed her eyes and breathed in theatrically, then exhaled loudly. There was a hush in the hall. Mrs Wigglesworth opened her eyes. 'Is there someone here tonight called Joyce?' she asked. She had reckoned that there must be someone of that name. It was a popular name in WI circles. She waited. 'It could be a Joan,' she said finally. 'Sometimes the paranormal wires get crossed. Is there a Joan in the room?'

'That's your middle name, isn't it?' asked a stout woman, looking at Mrs Scrimshaw.

'Yes, it is but I would rather not—' began the school secretary.

'Would you stand up, dear,' asked Mrs Wigglesworth.

'I'd rather not,' said Mrs Scrimshaw. She was already feeling tense after her unsettling experience earlier in the school. One supernatural encounter was quite enough for one day.

'There is someone coming through, dear,' said the psychic, 'and he wants to speak to you.'

'Well I'd rather not speak to him if it's all the same to you,' she replied.

'There's nothing to fear,' said Mrs Wigglesworth. 'He just wants to make contact. He needs to tell you something.'

'I don't really want to hear it.'

'He's very insistent, dear.'

Urged by her fellow members, Mrs Scrimshaw reluctantly got to her feet.

Mrs Wigglesworth suddenly drew in another huge slow intake of breath. She pressed her finger tips together and closed her eyes in a prayer-like attitude. 'I'm getting some strong psychic vibrations from someone called Jack,' she murmured. She opened her eyes. 'Who is Jack, dear?'

'My husband,' replied Mrs Scrimshaw.

'Has he passed over, dear?'

'Passed over?'

'Is he on the other side, dear?'

'Well he wasn't this morning,' Mrs Scrimshaw told her.

'It's another Jack,' said the psychic. 'Is there another Jack in your family who has gone to the other side?'

'It could be my Uncle Jack,' Mrs Scrimshaw told her, 'but we always called him Jacky and I didn't see much of him.'

'This must be him,' said Mrs Wigglesworth. She closed her eyes and breathed in noisily. 'Yes, I see him now. It's your Uncle Jacky. He wants you to know he's happy where he is.'

Well that's a surprise, thought Mrs Scrimshaw, *for in life her*

Uncle Jacky was a miserable and bad-tempered old man who left his wife for another woman.

'There's someone with him,' said Mrs Wigglesworth. 'It's a woman.'

'Is it his wife, my Auntie Doris?' she asked.

'It is, dear, right beside him and she's happy too.'

Mrs Scrimshaw tried to picture it. Her Aunt Doris was certainly not happy in life living with the cantankerous, tight-fisted and gloomy husband and then being deserted after thirty years of a tortured marriage. 'And is the other woman with him as well?' she asked.

'Another woman, dear?'

'A busty blond called Angie?'

'There's no other woman, dear.'

'Well, where is she, the woman he ran off with?' persisted Mrs Scrimshaw. 'Is she not up there with him as well?'

'I'm sorry, dear,' said Mrs Wigglesworth looking a little flustered. 'He's gone. Spirits are very unpredictable. They are here today and gone tomorrow in a manner of speaking. Now, is there someone in the audience called Beryl?'

'The Reverend Dr Underwood,' announced Watson, showing Ashley into the drawing at Limebeck House.

The lady of the manor rose from an elaborate French gilt armchair carved in an ornate style and smiled warmly. At her feet her small bristly haired terrier gave a rumble. 'Thank you for coming, Dr Underwood,' she said. 'Gordon, behave your-self,' she told the dog.

'It's a pleasure,' replied her visitor, looking around her. 'My goodness, what a wonderful room.'

'It wasn't,' replied Lady Wadsworth. 'It was a shambles – dark, damp and depressing. You might recall what it was like when you were last here and I gave you a tour of the house. I never spent any time in here but now, having recently had it all refurbished and restored to its former glory, I find it a most pleasant room. You may have heard that I came into quite a tidy sum of money.'

'Yes, I heard about the statues,' said Ashley.

'The money from the sale of those was swallowed up but I have had another stroke of luck,' Lady Wadsworth told her. 'I discovered these very old and valuable woodcut prints.'

The butler coughed.

'Well, Watson discovered them. They were tucked away in one of the attics. Evidently it turns out that they are by a famous sixteenth-century engraver.'

'Hendrik Goltzius,' said the butler.

'Thank you, Watson,' said Lady Wadsworth, sounding rather irritated by the interruption. 'Anyway, this man's works were collected and copied by artists across Europe and I am told some famous Spanish painter, I forget his name but—'

'Francisco de Zubarán,' the butler informed her.

'Thank you, Watson, and—'

'He used the print of *The Great Hercules* as the model for his paintings *Jacob and his Twelve Sons* which are displayed at the bishop's palace at Bishop Auckland,' said Watson.

Lady Wadsworth looked at her butler who remained standing expressionless by the door.

'Thank you again, Watson,' she said. 'I am sure Dr Underwood is not interested in hearing a lecture on art history. As I was saying, these prints were tucked away in one of the attics out of sight and one could well understand why.' She lowered her voice. 'They were, how might I put it, rather risqué illustrations and left little to the imagination and certainly not the sort of thing to have hanging on one's walls. My grandmother, I guess, thought that should they be seen they might give the servants ideas.' She glanced at Watson who maintained a dead-pan face. 'They were consigned to the attics out of the way. Anyhow, that is by-the-by. They realised

a very acceptable price at auction, enough for me to have
further resources to pay for the continued restoration work on
the house and gardens. I'm so sorry, here I am rambling on.
Do sit down.' She indicated another gilt chair. 'Watson, you
may bring us some coffee now please.'

The butler nodded and departed.

'I wanted to see you,' said Lady Wadsworth, 'to discuss the
arrangements for placing my commemorative plaque in the
church. The new vicar was initially very much against the idea
– strange man with a very odd manner – but he has had a
change of heart and is now prepared to let me go ahead with it.'

'I'm delighted to hear it,' said Ashley. Perhaps Mr Sparshott,
after all, was not quite as intransigent as she imagined.

'I think the dear archdeacon must have had a quiet word
with him. Mr Sparshott also agreed that, since you suggested
the plaque in the first place, you might like to liaise with my
estate manager and deal with the details. Of course you know
Mr O'Malley?'

'Yes I do,' replied Ashley.

'He's worked wonders since he's been my estate manager. It
was certainly a stroke of luck him coming to Barton-in-the-
Dale.'

'Yes, it was,' agreed Ashley.

'So would you be prepared to do this for me?'

'Of course.'

'I thought you would. I have told Mr O'Malley you would
be coming to see me this morning. If you could spare the
time, perhaps you could have a word with him now. He's over
in the estate office.'

'Yes,' said Ashley. 'I have the time.'

Ashley found Emmet sitting at a desk poring over a large sheet
of paper.

'Hello,' she said brightly. 'May I come in?'

'Yes, yes, of course,' he replied, getting up from his chair.

'I'm not disturbing you, am I?' she asked.

'No, no I'm . . . er . . . just studying the plans for the walled garden. Lots to be done.' He sounded awkward and looked embarrassed, like a child caught with his hand in the biscuit jar.

'Are you all right, Emmet?' she asked.

'Yes, of course,' he replied.

'Why the serious face?'

'Things to do,' he said feebly.

Ashley had rather expected to see the sunny smile and receive the usual warm welcome. Today, however, Emmet appeared as if his mind was elsewhere. He had always been so easy and unaffected but now, for some reason, he sounded cautious and reserved.

Ashley could never have guessed what was on Emmet's mind, but seeing her with another man had upset him greatly. He had entertained the hope that their friendship might blossom into something more. Now, he realised that this would never be. She was dating someone and looked so happy when he saw her at the bus stop. He had discovered that the man she was with was his daughter's teacher, and former college friend, maybe an old flame. So on this occasion he was careful not to show any sign of his affection for her and remained diffident.

'It's nice to—' she began.

'It's good of you to—' he started.

They stopped nervously as if they were meeting for the first time.

'After you,' she said.

'No, no, after you,' he replied.

'Lady Wadsworth asked me to come and have a word with you,' Ashley told him.

'Yes, she said you might be calling in.' He gave a weak smile.

'Well, here I am,' she said when it was clear he wasn't going to say anything more.

'Yes, here you are. Do sit down.'

'I've not seen very much of you lately,' said Ashley, perching on a stool.

'I've been kept pretty busy with all the renovations,' told her. He couldn't meet her eyes.

'I see.'

'There's so much to do.'

'And how's Roisin?'

'She's grand,' he replied, looking up.

'She seems to like it at the school,' said Ashley.

'Yes, she does. There's a parents' consultation meeting next week so I'll find out a bit more about how she's getting on from her teacher.'

'And how does she like Mr Hornchurch?'

'Oh . . . very much.' He looked down for a moment feeling uncomfortable at the mention of the man's name.

'You'll like him too,' said Ashley. 'He is quite a character.'

'Yes, so I believe.'

'We were at university together you know. He has a first-class brain and gave the tutors a run for their money but he is very modest with it. He got a first. I imagined he would end up in academia as a professor, not teaching young children, but he seems to have taken to it really well. I gather the children all like him and Mrs Stirling is very taken with him too.'

'It seems everyone speaks very highly of him,' said Emmet with a hint of sarcasm in his voice. They stood there looking at each other, neither speaking. 'Well,' he said suddenly, 'shall we talk about the plaque?'

Ashley felt disheartened as she headed back to the cottage that afternoon. Her meeting with Emmet had confused her. He had been so serious and distant with her, so unlike his usual friendly and ebullient self. He had spoken to her like a solicitor might talk to a client: polite, brisk and business-like. Following her visit to her mother's she had thought long and hard about Emmet and knew she was falling in love with this gentle-natured Irishman with the dark eyes. It appeared he didn't feel the same way about her.

17

It was the evening of the parents' consultation evening. Mr Gribbon, dressed in a freshly washed grey shiny nylon overall, poked his head around the school office door.

'Parents will be arriving soon, Mrs Scrimshaw,' he said, 'and it's not six o'clock yet. I've hardly had time to clean the place.' He sat on the corner of the desk and sucked in his breath. 'When Miss Sowerbutts was head teacher here she made the parents wait outside. Even when it was bucketing down or there was a foot of thick snow on the ground, she wouldn't have them doors opened 'til seven and then there was a stampede to get first in the queue to see the teachers.'

'Times have changed, Mr Gribbon,' Mrs Scrimshaw replied, pausing in her typing and peering over the top of her horn-rimmed spectacles. The secretary had worked for the former head teacher and found her difficult and demanding. Unlike the present incumbent of the post, Miss Sowerbutts had rarely visited the school office to pass the time of day and had closeted herself away in her room for most of the time. Furthermore, she had never uttered a word of thanks in all the years Mrs Scrimshaw had worked for her. 'I think opening the doors early and having this system of appointments is much better.'

'Maybe,' muttered the caretaker, 'but there's all the mess for me to clean up.'

'I thought that is what caretakers did,' responded the secretary.

'What?'

'Clean up.'

'I don't get any overtime for doing it,' he replied indignantly. 'When I had a part-time cleaner to help I could just about manage but now I never have a chance to sit down and what with my bad back and all . . . I might raise the matter with Mrs Stirling.'

'If I were you, I wouldn't mention part-time cleaners to Mrs Stirling after what happened with you and Mrs Pugh,' warned Mrs Scrimshaw.

'Nothing happened with me and Mrs Pugh!' he cried, colouring up.

'That's not what Mr Pugh thought,' said Mrs Scrimshaw, enjoying the caretaker's obvious discomfiture, 'when he stormed into the building to "punch your lights out".'

'Yes, well he got the wrong end of the stick.'

'All the same, I wouldn't go mentioning part-time cleaners to Mrs Stirling. She won't want reminding of that unfortunate incident.'

'It was just a misunderstanding,' muttered the caretaker. 'Anyway, I don't want to talk about it.'

'If Mrs Pugh had taken things further you could have ended up in court, never mind Mr Jolly.'

'Look, can we change the subject?' said the caretaker.

'Have you spoken to Mrs Stirling about the footsteps yet?' asked Mrs Scrimshaw.

'No, I haven't,' he replied, 'but I intend to mention them when I get the chance.'

'I will admit it was a bit scary,' said Mrs Scrimshaw.

'You wouldn't believe me, would you?' gloated the caretaker. '"I have better things to do this afternoon than listening to you romancing about some imaginary footsteps", you said.'

'Yes, well I will admit there was someone or something out there,' replied Mrs Scrimshaw grudgingly. 'Why don't you have a word with Mrs Stirling now before the parents arrive?'

'I might just do that,' said Mr Gribbon, jangling his keys and departing.

Mr Gribbon found Elisabeth in her classroom sorting through the children's exercise books.

'I think everything's in order around the school, Mrs Stirling,' he said, smiling ingratiatingly. 'All ship-shape and Bristol fashion.'

'It certainly is, Mr Gribbon,' replied Elisabeth. 'I've just had a tour. You've done a splendid job. The school looks particularly clean and bright.'

'I aim to please,' he said, smiling smugly and basking in the praise. 'Though I couldn't get into Mr Hornchurch's classroom to give it a going over. It's still like a landfill site in there. What parents will make of it, I don't know.'

'Don't worry about that,' Elisabeth told him.

When Mr Hornchurch had started at the school she had had some concerns about the untidiness of the teacher's classroom but having seen the quality of the work the children produced under his direction and observed the excellence of the teaching, she was prepared to tolerate the apparent clutter. On his recent visit, Mr Steel the school inspector had watched one of the teacher's lessons and initially he too had been disapproving of the visible disorder until he had spoken to Oscar.

'How can you find anything in all this jumble?' Mr Steel had asked the boy.

'What exactly are you looking for?' Oscar had replied.

'Suppose I wanted a pencil,' the inspector had said.

'What sort?' the boy had asked.

'Just a pencil.'

'There are a great variety of pencils,' Oscar had informed him. 'There's hard ones like 2H and 3H or soft like 2B or 3B.'

'Any pencil will do.'

Oscar had dug into a box by the window and produced the item. 'This is the most commonly used – the HB.'

'What about a rubber?' Mr Steel had said.

Oscar had produced this article from another box. 'They are called erasers in America.'

'Suppose I wanted a sheet of paper.'

The boy had disappeared into the storeroom and returned with a wad of coloured paper. 'Any particular colour?' he had asked.

'What about a dictionary?'

'What sort?' Oscar had inquired. 'Thesaurus, lexicon, phrasebook or rhyming dictionary? I can find anything you want.'

'But *I* wouldn't be able to find anything in here,' the inspector had told him.

'But then you are not in Mr Hornchurch's class, are you,' Oscar had responded pertly.

Mr Steel had smiled, 'Very true,' he had agreed. 'Very true.'

'There was something I think I should mention, Mrs Stirling,' said the caretaker now.

'I think I know what it's about,' said Elisabeth.

'You do?'

'It's about getting some extra help for you, isn't it?'

'No, no, I wasn't—'

'Well, you will be pleased to know, I have been on to County Hall and they are dealing with it. You will be getting a part-time cleaner before next term.'

'That's something which would be very welcome,' said the caretaker.

'I realise you have had a lot of extra work to do lately without any help,' Elisabeth told him, 'and I am very appreciative.'

'Oh you know me, Mrs Stirling,' answered the caretaker blithely, 'I'm not a one to grumble. I just get on with it.'

'And how's your back?' she asked.

'My back!' he exclaimed. 'It's fine.'

'It's just that I heard you mentioning you were having some trouble with it to Mrs Scrimshaw.'

'Oh, it's nothing to worry about,' he told her.

'Perhaps you ought to go and see my husband and let him take a look at it.'

'I wouldn't want to bother Dr Stirling,' he replied.

Having thought about what the doctor had said to him about work and considering changing to something more sedentary, Mr Gribbon had decided to keep quiet about his back. He would not like to think that the head teacher might consider him not up to the job. He was pleased Dr Stirling had not mentioned his visit to the surgery to his wife.

'So what is it you wish to see me about?' she asked.

'It's something which is very unsettling,' answered the caretaker.

'You had better tell me.'

'I think we might have a ghost,' he whispered.

'Ah yes, the ghost!' she said.

'You know about it?' asked the caretaker.

'Mrs Sloughthwaite was mentioning it when I called into the corner shop. I can't say that I have heard or seen anything unusual.'

'This is a very old school, Mrs Stirling,' said Mr Gribbon. 'Hundreds of kids have passed through them doors over the years. It's very possible that there is some sort of supernatural presence here, maybe some former pupil who had been badly treated in the past and died and now comes back to haunt the place. It could be the ghost of that little girl who fell through the ice in the mill pond. I've heard these footsteps, strange unearthly footsteps clomping down the path by the side of the school office. When I look there's no-one there. Once I heard this heavy breathing outside the window as well. I tell you, it put the fear of God into me. I've heard these footsteps a few times and I'm not alone. Mrs Scrimshaw's heard them and that Oscar as well and he never misses a thing what goes on. Mrs Scrimshaw was telling me she was speaking to this psychic after a WI meeting who told her that the spirits of the dead have been known to return to earth. It's fair put the wind up both of us.'

'And have you seen this ghost?' asked Elisabeth, resisting the urge to laugh out loud.

'No, I haven't actually seen it,' said the caretaker, 'just heard these weird footsteps, really loud and spooky, clomping down the path by the side of the school office, usually after the school has finished. I heard them again last night when I was locking up. Anyway, I looked through the window expecting to see somebody peering in but there was no-one. Then there was this unearthly breathing. Then footsteps started again. It sounded as if it was somebody wearing clogs like what the kids wore in the olden days.'

'It's certainly very strange,' said Elisabeth.

'Perhaps we ought to get the vicar in to exorcise it,' said Mr Gribbon.

'I'll think we will pass on that for the moment,' said Elisabeth. She could imagine Mr Sparshott's reaction to that suggestion, having heard him declaiming in the corner shop on the dangers of believing in the supernatural.

'It's very creepy,' said the caretaker.

'You leave it with me, Mr Gribbon,' Elisabeth told him. 'I'll look into it. I am pretty sure we do not have the ghost of some long-gone former pupil walking around the school at night.'

On her way to the staff room she heard laughter. She found Mr Hornchurch and Mrs Robertshaw sharing something which they obviously found very funny. Mr Jolly sat in the corner marking books with his characteristic gloomy expression. He looked a sad and sorry figure with his lank thinning hair and dull reddish face.

'I could hear you two down the corridor,' she told Mrs

Robertshaw good-humouredly. 'Something's obviously amused you both.'

'Rupert here was telling me about the school reports he's been writing,' she answered. 'Go on Rupert, tell Elisabeth.'

'Well,' said Mr Hornchurch, 'we've been looking at measurement in class as part of our work in maths. At the beginning of the term I measured the height of all the children in feet and inches and showed them how to convert them into metres and centimetres. I have done the same with their weights, asking them to convert pounds and ounces into kilograms. I have measured them and weighed them at different intervals and recorded how much each of them has grown and put on weight and I have asked them to do their own conversions. Of course at this age the children tend to shoot up. However, when I measured Jimmy Arnold I discovered that he had shrunk.'

'He'd shrunk!' repeated Elisabeth.

'He was two centimetres smaller than he was at the beginning of the term,' said the teacher.

'How mysterious,' said Elisabeth.

'Very,' said Mr Hornchurch.

'What has this to do with the school reports?' she asked.

'Well little Jimmy is a nice enough boy,' said Mr Hornchurch, 'but a pretty average pupil who doesn't contribute much in class. He tries hard but his work has not really improved very much. I was thinking of something positive to say on his school report so I started with: "Jimmy seems to have settled down in his new school".'

Elisabeth smiled and left her two colleagues chattering and laughing and went to join Mr Jolly.

'How are you, Donald?' she asked, lowering her voice.

'Bearing up, Mrs Stirling,' he replied disconsolately. 'Bearing up.'

'I wanted to have a word with you about tonight. It's likely that Mrs Stubbins will come to the consultation evening.'

'Yes,' he sighed. 'I thought she might.'

'If she mentions Norman's accident,' said Elisabeth, 'don't get into any discussion about it. Just say that the matter is in the hands of the county solicitor and that it will be settled in court.'

'Yes, I think that's a good idea,' agreed Mr Jolly.

'Just tell her how Norman is getting on with his school work in class and be very circumspect. I know from experience that Mrs Stubbins can be a difficult customer, so if she becomes argumentative refer her to me.'

Mr Jolly sighed again. 'I will,' he said.

In the classroom Elisabeth found Oscar's mother, an extremely thin and intense-looking woman with large eyes and greying hair caught back untidily in a black ribbon.

'Good evening,' said Elisabeth sitting at her desk. 'You are here bright and early.' She invited the parent to come and sit next to her.

'I won't keep you long, Mrs Stirling,' said the woman. 'I've got an appointment to see Oscar's teacher in a few minutes but just wanted to catch you before I see him.'

'Your son seems to be getting on very well in Mr Hornchurch's class,' said Elisabeth.

'Oh yes, very well indeed,' replied the parent. 'It's Mr Hornchurch this and Mr Hornchurch that at home at the moment. They seem to have these long conversations about all sorts of topics which Oscar finds fascinating. They also have an interest in chess. I think he's found a kindred spirit. He's been doing some advanced maths and is learning all about astronomy. He has asked for a telescope and a Latin primer for his birthday.'

'A Latin primer?'

'He's really enjoying the Latin lessons,' Oscar's mother told her.

'Latin lessons?' Elisabeth looked surprised.

'Did you not know? Mr Hornchurch is teaching him Latin one lunchtime a week.'

The teacher is full of surprises, thought Elisabeth. 'I had no idea,' she said.

'Anyway, it's about Oscar's future that I wished to speak to you,' said the parent. 'He will be leaving here next year and my husband and I have been talking to our son about which secondary school he might like to attend.'

'It's a little early to be thinking about this, isn't it?' asked Elisabeth. 'He has a couple more terms after this one here before he moves to secondary school next September.'

'Yes, but Oscar's been going on about his future. You see, some of the independent schools are already starting to inter- view prospective students. So, I thought I would ask your advice.'

'Well, let me see,' said Elisabeth. 'There is the comprehen- sive in Clayton of course, St Dominic's, the public school and Sir Cosmo Cavendish Boys' Grammar School.'

'The boys' grammar is offering scholarships,' said the parent, 'and Oscar is wondering if he should try for one.'

'Oscar will do well at whichever school he attends,' said Elisabeth. 'The grammar school has a fine academic reputa- tion as does St Dominic's and I am sure Oscar will hold his own in either. If he sits for the scholarship I have no doubt he will pass the entrance examination and the interview with flying colours. Clayton Comprehensive, however, also does well for the bright pupils. My step-son James is there and he is enjoying school, working hard and achieving good results.' *It's a pity though*, thought Elisabeth thinking of Danny, *that it doesn't do as well for the less able pupils.*

'What would be your advice?' asked the parent.

'I would suggest you look around the potential schools and see which one Oscar likes the best. Ask about the examination results, the extracurricular activities, the music and the sports on offer.'

'Oscar's not keen on anything sporty,' said the parent. 'He's not a team player. He says he doesn't see the point of chasing a ball around a field with a lot of other children. Anyway, that's what we will do, have a look around all three schools. By the way, how is the boy who had the accident? Oscar said he had a nasty fall.'

'He's fine,' answered Elisabeth, dismayed to know that word clearly had got around. 'He just had a bit of a tumble.' *The sooner this unhappy episode is over, the better*, she thought to herself.

After listening to the parents of the pupils in her class, Elisabeth cheered up and felt pleased by the many positive comments she received, especially from those whose children had been at Urebank before the amalgamation. There were some parents, however, who were less happy with one particular teacher. One was a tall, gaunt woman dressed in tight-fitting jeans and a floppy red sweater. She said her elder son, who was in Elisabeth's class, was very happy in the school and she had no complaints on that score. He enjoyed the lessons and all the extracurricular activities and the standard of his work had improved. She was less satisfied, however, with her younger son's teacher.

'Not to put too fine a point on it, Mrs Stirling,' said the parent, 'my Harry finds the work in Mr Jolly's class tedious. He's not settled and doesn't want to come to school and he told me Mr Jolly's in some sort of trouble over an accident involving one of his pupils. There's a woman I was just talking to in the corridor who says children are not safe in his class.'

'I can assure you,' Elisabeth told the woman, 'that the children are perfectly safe in Mr Jolly's class. It is true that a child did have a not-too-serious accident in a PE lesson but he is fine. Accidents do sometimes happen.'

The parent of Harry persisted. 'Could my son transfer to Mrs Robertshaw's class?'

'I will look into it but can't promise anything,' said Elisabeth. 'I will, however, have a word with Mr Jolly. Now, if you will excuse me, I do have other parents to see.'

The last to see Elisabeth were Mr and Mrs Ross.

'Robbie seems to be getting on a lot better at school,' said Mrs Ross. 'We've just spoken to Mr Hornchurch and he says Robbie's work has steadily improved and he's not as rude and uncooperative as he was. Of course he still has his moments but he seems happier in himself.'

'Yes, I'm pleased to say that there has been an improvement in his attitude and behaviour,' said Elisabeth.

'That's largely down to you, Missis Stirlin',' said Mr Ross. 'Yer never gev up on t'lad. Lots would 'ave, but you didn't.'

'I try hard not to give up on any child, Mr Ross,' she replied. 'So, how is Robbie doing at home?'

Mr Ross scratched his beard. 'T'lad's gorra temper on 'im an' 'e can be pig-headed an' moody at times but I like 'im. 'E's got summat abaat 'im. Bit o' backbone. Like a lot o' t'kids we've fostered 'e's 'ad a rough time of it but Robbie's a tough little tyke an' no mistake. Thing about 'im is 'e just needed someb'dy to tek an interest in 'im, listen to what 'e wants to say, get things off o' 'is chest. I reckon in time 'e'll turn out all reight.'

'You should see him with the animals, Mrs Stirling,' said Mrs Ross. 'He has a real affinity with them, hasn't he, Hamish?'

''E 'as that,' agreed her husband.

'I'm delighted things are working out so well,' said Elisabeth. 'It sounds like a bit of a success story to me. And how is Robbie getting on with his mother?'

'It's about his mother that we wanted to have a word with you,' said Mrs Ross. 'The thing is, we met with Mrs Banks and the social worker last week.'

'There's summat called special guardianship,' explained Mr Ross, 'which is between fosterin' an' adoption. This gives me an' t'wife what's called foster parental responsibility an' we agreed to this. It means that Robbie can stop wi' us but 'as got to keep in contact wi' 'is mam.'

'We went to the meeting expecting Mrs Banks to fight to get Robbie back to live with her but she didn't,' said Mrs Ross. 'She seemed happy with the arrangements. The thing is, Mrs Stirling, she's an ill woman. She looked as grey as slate when we saw her and had lost what little weight she had. She's to go into a hospital next week.'

'A hospital!' exclaimed Elisabeth. 'It's that serious, is it?'

'I'm afraid it is,' Mrs Ross told her.

'She told us she's not got long to live,' said Mr Ross, shaking his head.

'Poor woman,' murmured Elisabeth. 'This is so sudden.'

'The condition she's got is terminal,' said Mrs Ross. 'The doctors, she told us, have given her just a few weeks at the most. They're arranging for her to go into one of these hospices when there's room. I reckon she's known about what she's got wrong with her for some time but didn't do anything about it.'

'Does Robbie know?'

'We've told t'lad that she's ill,' answered Mr Ross, 'an' that she'll be going into a special sooart of 'ospital.'

'And how is he taking it?' asked Elisabeth.

''E seems to be copin',' answered the farmer. 'As I've said, 'e's a tough lad but 'e keeps a lot o' things bottled up an' 'e's not said much. We're tekkin' 'im to see 'is mam next week.'

'His mother asked us if we would take care of Robbie when . . . anything happens,' said Mrs Ross.

'Permanent like,' added her husband.

'To adopt him,' said his wife.

'And what did you say?' asked Elisabeth.

'We said we would. Hamish and I didn't need to talk things over and think about it as Miss Parsons suggested. We agreed there and then that it was the best thing for the boy. He needs a lot of love, Mrs Stirling.'

'You are both very special people,' said Elisabeth. She felt almost moved to tears.

'No, no, Missis Stirling,' said Mr Ross. 'Anyone else'd do t'same.'

No, they wouldn't, thought Elisabeth. Not many people would take on a child like Robbie.

When Mr and Mrs Ross had gone, Elisabeth began to tidy the room ready for going home. She imagined the long hot soapy bath, a glass of white wine and snuggling up with Michael on the sofa.

Emmet popped his heads around the door.

'Hello, Elisabeth,' he said brightly.

'Oh hello, Emmet,' she said. 'I guess you're very pleased with what Mr Hornchurch had to say about Roisin. He tells me she is one of his star pupils.'

'Ah, she's doing grand,' he said, 'just grand.' He stood there for a moment as if thinking of something to say.

'And how are things up at the big house?' Elisabeth asked.

'They're grand too,' he replied. 'Lady Wadsworth has had another bit of good fortune. She discovered these old wood-cut prints in one of the attics, a bit rude by all accounts. They gave the vicar a bit of a shock when he visited and cast his eyes on them. They were sold in London and fetched for a tidy sum. So now she can have more work done on the house and grounds. Sure it would be a wonderful thing if we could all find some hidden treasure in our attic – not that I've got an attic.'

'And how are you both liking living in the gate lodge? It's a bit different from the caravan.'

'We like it very much,' he replied.

'Well it's getting late,' Elisabeth told him. 'I should be making tracks.'

Emmet didn't move. 'He's an interesting man is Mr Hornchurch,' he said.

'He is,' replied Elisabeth. 'I've never known anyone with such a wide knowledge. He's settled in really well and the pupils like him.'

Emmet remained at the door nodding.

'Is there something particular you wished to see me about, Emmet?'

'I believe he was at college with Ashley?'

'Yes,' said Elisabeth, 'they were at Oxford together. Small world, isn't it?'

'I saw them at the bus stop last Friday,' he said.

'Apparently they went to the theatre, to some rather depressing Scandinavian drama, from what he told me.'

'I was wondering if . . . well it's difficult . . . the thing is . . . I wanted to ask you . . . '

'Emmet O'Malley,' laughed Elisabeth, 'this is the first time since knowing you that you have been stuck for words. Come on, what is it?'

'Are Ashley and Mr Hornchurch an item?' he asked.

'An item? Rupert Hornchurch and Ashley?'

'You know, are they seeing a lot of each other? Are they going out together?'

'I do know that there is someone she is keen on,' replied Elisabeth, 'but I can't imagine it's Rupert Hornchurch. I think perhaps they were just catching up on the old times they had at university together but I may be wrong.'

'But there is someone?' he asked.

'Yes, I think there is,' she answered. 'My brother Giles took quite a shine to her when he was staying with me. I mentioned to Ashley that he had written to me and said that when he was next home on leave he was minded to ask her out. He didn't want to put his foot in it if there was another man on the scene.'

'And she said there is?' he asked.

'Yes, I think so,' she said.

Emmet looked downcast. 'I see.'

'I'm sorry, Emmet,' said Elisabeth. 'You have taken quite a shine to her too, haven't you?'

'I have,' he answered. 'I thought I might have asked her out but I know I'd be punching above my weight. Ah well, it wasn't meant to be. Goodnight, Elisabeth.'

'Goodnight, Emmet.'

When the teachers and parents had gone, Elisabeth walked around the silent school as was her habit at the end of the day. She turned off a few lights in the classrooms, closed doors and picked up the odd piece of litter. She had told the care-taker, who had stood at the end of the corridor jangling his keys impatiently, that she would lock up and he could get off home. As she sat in the school office looking through the letters that she hadn't dealt with that day, she heard a noise outside the window. It was quite distinct: heavy, resounding footsteps. When she turned to look in their direction, expect-ing to see a figure outside, the footsteps stopped abruptly, then they continued again.

This is ridiculous, thought Elisabeth. She opened the window and peered out, then let out a crack of laughter as she saw the culprit.

Saturday morning found Danny in the churchyard, on his knees between the cracked and weathered tombstones poking away at the soil with a trowel, his face smudged with dirt.

'Hard at work I see,' said Mr Sparshott approaching him.

'If tha dunt keep on fettlin' it,' Danny told him, 'then t'weed'll get t'better o' ya. That 'eavy rain we've just 'ad 'as brought 'em on like nob'dy's business. All yon side by t'church wall is full o' dandelions, moss, knotgrass, cleavers, cow parsley, twitch an' I don't know what else. Thistles are t'worst 'cos they seed so much. It's like a jungle in theer.'

'I can't say I'd recognise knot grass and cleavers if I saw them and have no idea what twitch is,' replied the cleric.

'Twitch is what me granddad called that really stubborn weed. It's known as couch grass or iron weed an' it's as tough as old boots an' t'devil's own job to get t'roots out.' Danny scratched his mop of dusty hair. 'I've bin thinkin' what we might do wi' this rubble.'

'Ah yes, the rubble,' sighed the vicar. 'I must get on and have it moved. I guess Mr Massey has no intention of doing it. It really is an eyesore.'

'Missis Atticus said it was an eyesore before it got smashed,' said Danny. 'She were glad it got demolished.'

'I am inclined to agree with her,' said the vicar, staring at the remains of the Gothic mausoleum. 'These ostentatious graves are not to my taste.'

The huge and elaborate black marble tomb which had been erected in the centre of the churchyard dwarfing every other memorial, was now in ruins. The incumbent, the Reverend Joseph Steerum-Slack who had been the vicar at St Christopher's in the nineteenth century, certainly planned his tomb to be larger than life when he was dead as he was in life. He intended never to be forgotten – hence that extravagant mausoleum which he designed himself and left sufficient money in his will to have erected. The only part which had remained intact and now rested on the wall by the side of the church was the epitaph: 'Here entombed are the remains of the Reverend Dean Joseph Steerum-Slack. He was honoured and esteemed by all who knew him.' This was followed by a Latin verse.

'From what I gather of the man,' said the vicar, surveying the remains and giving a wry smile, 'Dean Slack was far from honoured or esteemed. He was quite an unpleasant and outrageous character by all accounts and devoted his time to hunting and drinking and gambling. He had been dean at the cathedral until he was removed and put out to pasture in Barton. He burnt the rectory to the ground with himself and his dogs inside in the nineteenth century.'

''Is grave's a bit ovver t'top,' said Danny.

'Rather like the man himself,' remarked Mr Sparshott. 'How the dead are commemorated can tell us a lot about the person,' he said. 'This particular clergyman clearly thought a great deal about himself in life. In contrast, your grandfather's grave, Danny, is simple and speaks of a modest man.'

'Aye, he weren't one to show off,' replied the boy. He shook his head and sighed. 'It's a pity that nob'dy comes to look after the graves o' them what died.'

'Unvisited and forgotten,' murmured the vicar. Then looking at Danny he added quickly, 'Except, of course, your grandfather's grave.'

'What abaat mekkin a rockery out of this rubble, ovver theer by yon tree?' said Danny, pointing to a patch of ground overgrown with nettles and dock leaves. 'You could plant some 'ardy shrubs an' leave that bit o' grass around it for some wild flowers – cowslips, campion, celandine, meadow grass, cornflowers, stuff like that. There's loads of wild flowers an' they'd mek a grand display. Tha could purrin some 'eartsease, speedwell, ox-eye daisy an' foxgloves an' all. I reckon it'd look reight champion.'

'It's a lovely idea,' said the vicar, 'but to move all this debris will take an age.'

'We could do it slowly bit by bit an' I reckon I could get some 'elp.'

'Let me think about it,' said the vicar. 'I shall have a word with Mrs Sparshott and see what she thinks. Now don't overdo it. I'm going into Clayton this morning but shall be back at lunchtime if anyone wants me. I'm fishing this afternoon if you would care to join me.'

'Champion,' replied the boy.

Later, when Danny was packing up his tools, he was approached by a portly individual. The man's round red face was half hidden beneath a large Panama hat.

'Hi there, young fella,' he said.

''Eyup,' replied Danny.

'You're doing a mighty fine job there.'

'Aye, it needed doin'. Danny put his hands on his hips, cocked his head and studied the visitor. 'Tha're an American.'

'I sure am,' said the man, smiling widely.

'I'd love to go to America,' said Danny.

'One day, you must. Now tell me, do you know all the graves in the churchyard here?'

'Most of 'em.'

'Well you can maybe help me find a grave.'

'I'll try. What's t'name?' asked Danny.

'The Reverend Joseph Steerum-Slack. Quite a mouthful, eh? He was an ancestor of mine and was the rector or dean or something like that. He lived here a good few years ago. I'm doing some research into my family history. Could you point me in the direction of his grave?'

Danny glanced at the mound of rubble underneath which the bones of the man in question were buried and smiled uneasily.

Fortunately the epitaph was well out of sight. 'I can't be reight sure,' he lied. He pointed to a large tilted and moss-covered sandstone slab, the lettering on which had been worn away over the years so the name of the person who was interred underneath was too eroded to make out. 'I think it's mebbe that one over theer.'

The man put on a pair of small spectacles and walked over to the gravestone. He then stooped and examined it, running a finger along the gouged lettering

'I can't make anything out,' he said. He stood up and shook

his head. 'I figured it would be bigger and more elaborate than this, him being such an important man and all.'

'There are lots o' tombs inside t'church,' said Danny. 'Mebbe' e's in theer.'

'I'll take a look,' said the man, 'and then I'll speak to the vicar. Maybe he can help and tell me something about my ancestor.'

''E's out at t'moment an' not likely to be back for some time,' Danny told him.

'Pity, I should have liked to have seen him,' said the man. 'I'm afraid I can't stay that long.' He reached into his bag for his camera and took a photograph of the worn gravestone. 'Anyway, young fella,' he said, 'thanks for your help.'

18

'Is it sometimes OK to tell a lie?' Danny asked the vicar.

They were sitting on the river bank that afternoon having just cast in their lines.

'I think it is always best to tell the truth,' replied Mr Sparshott.

'Even if it upsets somebody?'

The vicar looked solemn and thoughtful for a moment. 'Yes, even if it upsets somebody,' he replied.

Mr Sparshott had never been one to dissemble. He had always told it as it was and, in doing so, many times he had upset and even offended those who had sought his advice. He said what he felt needed to be said, never tempering it out of politeness or the wish to please and sometimes would tell people what no-one else would. He was never reticent in expressing his firmly held views and in doing so had alienated some of his parishioners. He would address the congregation from the pulpit and ask the well-dressed women sitting in the pews before him if they had come to church merely to show off their new hats or was it for the good of their souls. He would not marry a divorced person or allow his church to be used for anything other than divine service. He refused to christen or to marry if those who had asked him were not committed Christians and sincerely believed the vows they would be making around the font or at the altar. This, of course, set himself apart from many of his fellow priests who regarded him as something of a dour and distant character, someone who refused to move with the times.

'You're a bit like mi granddad, you know,' Danny told him. The vicar smiled. 'Really? In what way?'

'I mean,' continued Danny, ''e was never book-learned like you but 'e said yer should allus tell t'truth. "Tell t'truth an' shame t'devil", 'e used to say. Any road, he said that if you tell lies you're sure to be found out in t'long run, unless tha's gorra reight good memory.'

'He sounded a shrewd and thoughtful man, your grandfather,' said the vicar.

'When he was in t'ospital,' said Danny, 'he told me that 'e was goin' to die. It was t'worst thing I'd ever 'eard. I couldn't tek it in. I remember sittin' by 'is bed an' there were all these tubes an' bottles an' that 'ospital smell. "We've allus been 'onest wi' each other" 'e telled me. "I've never kept nowt from thee, allus telled yer t'truth." Then 'e said 'e was gunna die. I cried all t'way back to Dr Stirling's 'ouse an' stopped in mi room all day.' He bit his lip in thought and then tears blurred his eyes. 'I miss 'im a reight lot.'

'Your grandfather could have said he was going to get better and that everything would be all right, couldn't he?' answered the vicar. 'Had he said that it would have, at that time, made you feel happy. But then a short time later, when he died, you would have discovered that he was not being honest with you. You would have felt somehow cheated. So he was right not to deceive you.'

'I know,' muttered Danny, 'but all t'same, it were an 'ard thing to 'ear it.'

'There are many things in life which are sometimes hard to hear,' said the vicar, 'but it is always best to be honest.'

They sat there for a moment in silence, contemplating their fishing rods.

'I told a lie this mornin',' said Danny.

The vicar did not respond but continued to watch for a twitch on his line.

'We had a visitor to t'churchyard looking for a grave,' continued the boy. 'It were that big marble tomb what got smashed by t'falling branch. 'E were from America this visitor an' 'e'd come special like to see weer one of 'is ancestors were buried.'

The vicar lowered his rod and listened in studious silence.

'I didn't tell 'im that t'grave 'e was lookin' for was buried under that big pile o' rubble,' said Danny. 'I said I di'n't know an' I showed him to an old worn tombstone an' I said I reckoned that was t'one 'e was looking for. I di'n't want to upset 'im yer see. Was I wrong?'

'Yes, Danny, I think you were wrong,' said Mr Sparshott.

'Would you have told 'im t'truth?'

'I would. You see, as I have said, it is always best to be honest with people. Suppose that that visitor returns and discovers that he had been misled. Don't you think he would have been even more upset to have been so deceived?'

'Aye, I s'pose so,' replied Danny.

'There are, of course, lies and lies,' said the vicar, looking at the boy. 'Your intentions were kindly. They were not meant to hurt or cause any harm but, nevertheless, I think you should have told him the truth.'

They both fell silent.

'Thinking about your suggestion to make a rockery in the churchyard from the remains of the tomb,' said the vicar more cheerfully, after a while, 'I have had a word with Mrs Sparshott and she considers this to be a good idea. We could then place a small plaque near it with a dedication to Dean Steerum-Slack. We might put—' He stopped mid-sentence and put his hand on Danny's shoulder. 'I think you have a bite,' he said. 'Reel him in, gently.'

Mrs Pocock, on her way to catch the bus to Marfleet for

another psychic consultation with Mrs Wigglesworth, paused on the bridge and observed the two figures by the river bank.

She gave a slow smile of satisfaction.

At the moment when the vicar was debating the rights and wrongs of telling the truth with Danny, Mr and Mrs Ross were facing a most painful duty.

'Let's wait until after dinner, Hamish,' said Mrs Ross. 'It's always best to hear bad news on a full stomach.'

''Ow d'ya think t'lad'll tek it?' asked her husband.

'Hard to tell,' she replied, 'He's a deep one is Robbie. It's difficult sometimes to know what's going on in that head of his. Any mention of his mother and he closes up like a tulip in a shower. He just won't talk about it.'

'P'raps we should leave it for a bit,' said the farmer. 'I mean t'lad is still cut up abaat losin' t'pig.'

'There's never a good time,' said his wife. 'Best get it over and done with.'

'Aye, I reckon your reight,' agreed her husband.

'I think it might be best coming from you,' said his wife.

'Nay, Elspeth, I'm not t'one wi' words. Best if you tell 'im.'

That evening, as was their custom after dinner, Mr and Mrs Ross and Robbie sat in the parlour. It was an untidy, rather shabby room with an old settee, two threadbare armchairs, a faded brown carpet and an old dresser cluttered with crockery. On the mantelpiece were displayed various framed photographs of smiling children the couple had fostered over the years.

Mr Ross sat on one of the armchairs pretending to be reading the farming page in the local paper and wondering when they should broach the difficult subject with the boy. His wife, thinking the same thing, sat on the settee knitting. Robbie was curled up in the other armchair, his head in a book.

'What are you reading, Robbie?' asked Mrs Ross.

'It's a book my teacher gave me,' replied the boy.

'What's it about?'

'Pigs.'

'Pigs!' exclaimed the farmer, folding up the newspaper and putting it down. 'I don't reckon tha'll learn much abaat pigs from out of a book. Tha'll learn more abaat pigs by rearin' 'em. On t'job trainin'.'

'Hush up, Hamish!' cried his wife. 'It's good that the lad's reading.'

'I've never 'ad much time for books an' readin' missen,' said the farmer. 'I weren't much of a scholar at school, always gerrin into scrapes an' not doin' mi work. I 'ated sittin' behind a desk all day when I could 'ave bin out an' about an' 'elpin' mi father on t'farm.'

'I loved reading,' said his wife. 'I had a lovely teacher. She taught you as well.'

The farmer chuckled, 'Old Biddy Baxter in her thick tweeds an' bullet-proof stockings.'

'She was nice was Miss Baxter,' said Mrs Ross. 'She used to read us stories and lend me books. I read them all: *The Children of the New Forest, Ballet Shoes, Heidi, Swallows and Amazons, Little Women, Black Beauty, Peter Rabbit.*'

'If I see a rabbit on this farm, I shoot it!' exclaimed the farmer. 'They're a bloody nuisance.'

'Hamish!' exclaimed his wife. 'Language!'

'I'm sure t'lad's 'eard worse,' said her husband. He winked at Robbie. 'An' I reckon 'e's used a few choice words hissen in 'is time. Am I reight, Robbie?'

The boy gave a small smile. He had put down his book to listen. He liked it in the evening listening to Mr and Mrs Ross chattering on good-humouredly. It was something he had never been used to back home with his miserable, unhappy mother and his ill-tempered step-father. In the farmhouse parlour in the evenings Robbie felt comfortable and content.

'My favourite book was *Winnie the Pooh*,' Mrs Ross was saying.

'That's a daft title if ever I 'eard one,' said the farmer. 'Don't ya reckon, Robbie?'

The boy nodded.

'A. A. Milne, that's who wrote it,' said Mrs Ross. 'He was Miss Baxter's favourite writer. She had this quotation of his over her blackboard and I would read it every day. I can still see it now.' She looked over at the boy who was listening attentively. 'Something you might well bear in mind, Robbie,' she said. '"You must always remember", it said, "you are braver than you believe, stronger then you seem and smarter than you think".'

'Aye well,' said Mr Ross, 'there's some sense in that.'

They sat in silence for a while.

Mrs Ross put down her knitting and gave her husband a knowing look. 'Hamish and me want to have a word with you about something, Robbie,' she said.

The boy knew by her earnest expressions and the nervous demeanour that she had something serious to tell him.

'I did my best,' said Robbie, his head lowered.

'Abaat what?' asked the farmer.

'About the pig,' said the boy. 'I tried to make it better but it wouldn't eat and it wouldn't drink.'

'We know you did your best,' said Mrs Ross. She got up and sat next to him and squeezed his hand. 'Nobody could have done more. You were out there all hours tending to it.'

'It sometimes 'appens,' said the farmer, 'that nature tekks its course. It were a weak little runt an' di'n't 'ave much of a chance. It's allus sad when yer lose one but that's t'way o' things.'

'It died in my arms,' said Robbie.

'Aye well, yer did what yer could.'

'But why did it have to die?' the boy asked sadly.

'Because that's t'way o' things,' repeated the farmer. 'It comes to all of us in t'end, Robbie lad, some afore others.'

'Can I go to my room?'

'Not just yet, Robbie,' said Mrs Ross. 'There's something we have to tell you.'

The boy sensed the seriousness of what she was about to say in her tone of voice and the way she twisted her hands together. He looked at her, wary and stony-faced.

'Have I done something wrong?' he asked

'Gracious no,' exclaimed Mrs Ross. 'You haven't done anything wrong. Whatever gave you that idea?'

'And I can still stay here?' asked the boy.

'Look, lad,' said the farmer, 'I don't know 'ow many more times I 'ave to tell yer. 'Course you can stay. I don't say summat I don't mean an' I don't gu back on mi word. Tha should know that by now. I shall tell thee ageean, tha can stay 'ere as long as tha wants. It's summat else t'missus wants to tell thee.'

'What?' asked Robbie, a guarded look on his small face.

'If tha pins back tha lugs, tha might find out,' said Mr Ross.

'It's your mother, Robbie,' said Mrs Ross. 'She's ill, love, she's very ill. She's in hospital and it's likely that she won't be coming out.'

'You mean she's going to die?' asked Robbie bluntly.

'Yes, love, I'm afraid so,' said Mrs Ross.

Robbie thought for moment, his head down, and then jumped up and threw the book on the floor. 'I'm going to see the pigs,' he cried and ran out of the door.

'Robbie, love!' shouted Mrs Ross, getting up herself.

'Leave t'lad be,' said her husband. 'I reckon 'e wants to be by 'is sen for a bit.'

When it began to get dark, Mr Ross went in search of the boy. He found Robbie sitting hunched behind one of the sheds where the pigs were kept. His small shoulders were bunched as if a heavy weight was pressing down upon them. He was sobbing. The farmer sat beside him and put a hand on the boy's shoulder. Robbie wiped the tears away with his fists and sniffed.

'You cry, lad,' said the farmer, looking at the boy's stricken face. 'Tha's got good reason to.'

They sat there listening to the snuffling and squealing of the pigs and the hooting of an owl in the distant wood. Together they watched the shadows lengthen and the bats flutter above their heads like scraps of black cloth blown by the wind. An enormous cold moon hung over the fields. They gazed up at the stars which burnt bright and cold and for a long time they didn't exchange a word.

'You know, Robbie,' said the farmer after a while, 'some things in life do 'urt an' it's 'ard to cope. I think yer know that well enough. I'll tell thee summat now what I've never telled any o' t'kids what we've fostered. We lost a child, a little girl. 'Er name was Grace. She 'ad summat up with 'er breathin'. She were two when she were tekken. Missus an' me di'n't think we could go on, but we 'ave. We wanted another kiddie but nowt 'appened so we took up fosterin' an' thought we'd look after other people's. Ovver t'years we've fostered loads of young 'uns, mostly from homes where t'parents couldn't cope. It weren't because they didn't want their kids or stopped lovin' 'em, it were just that things gorron top of 'em', just like *your* mam. It's not that she didn't want you, Robbie. She still loves yer. She were caught in t'middle an' I know that when you went into care she felt bad abaat it, really bad. Do you understand what I'm tryin' to say?'

Robbie sniffed and stared ahead with a fixed expression. Tears shone on his cheeks in the moonlight.

'She's not too good at t'minute,' continued Mr Ross. 'Now I want you to do summat for me. I want you to come wi' me an' t'missus an' go an' see yer mam. Will you do that?'

Tears came to the boy's eyes again but he blinked them away. He sniffed and nodded.

'Good lad,' said the farmer, putting his arms around the boy and holding him close. 'Good lad.'

Danny was cleaning out the ferret hutch at the back of Clumber Lodge, whistling away as if he hadn't a care in the world, when Michael approached.

'You sound in a good mood.'

'Mustn't grumble as mi granddad used to say,' replied the boy. 'If 'e'd 'ave fallen under a bus 'e'd be sayin' that to t'ambulance men when they dragged 'im out an' asked 'ow 'e was. "Mustn't grumble", 'e'd say.' He chuckled.

'So everything's all right then, is it, Danny?' asked the doctor.

'Champion,' replied the boy. 'I've been givin' Ferdy a wash-an'-brush-up.'

He reached into his pocket and produced a little sandy-coloured, pointed-faced creature with small bright black eyes. He held the animal under its front chest, his thumb under one leg towards the ferret's spine and using the other hand he gently stroked the creature down the full length of its body.

'How's the fishing going?' asked Michael.

'That's champion an' all,' Danny told him. 'I caught this big fat rainbow trout last time we were down by t'river. Mr Sparshott said I should bring it back for our dinner but I purrit back in t'watter. It seemed a shame to kill such a beautiful fish. There were all these colours on its back.'

Michael had discussed with Elisabeth Danny's fishing trips with the vicar. It seemed very odd to him that such a stern and self-important man lacking in social skills should strike up a friendship with a young boy. He had promised her that when an opportune occasion arose, he would have a word with Danny.

'How do you find Mr Sparshott?' asked Michael.

Danny pondered for a moment and stroked his ferret. 'I suppose 'e's what mi granddad'dcall'd a bit of a funny onion.'

'In what way?'

'Well 'e comes across at first as bein' a bit serious like but when yer gets to know 'im 'e's really interestin' an' 'e's kind as well. 'E's given me a fishin' rod an' all t'tackle an' a book on coarse fishin'. Mi granddad used to say that some folks are better for knowing. Mr Sparshott's like that.'

'You seem to have taken to fishing,' remarked Michael, thinking how he might broach the subject he had discussed with Elisabeth.

'Oh I 'ave,' said the boy enthusiastically. 'I've allus wanted to fish. I used to catch little tiddlers in a net but this is like proper fishin'.'

Michael struggled to find the words. 'And does Mr Sparshott ask you to do anything for him, Danny?'

'Oh yeah,' replied the boy.

Michael was startled by the bluntness of the answer. 'He does?'

'Yeah.'

'What sort of things does he ask you to do?'

Well, 'e asks me to keep t'churchyard tidy, dig up t'weeds, 'elp 'im put some plants in, pick up litter, things like that. We're now workin' on mekkin a rockery from all that rubble.'

'And anything else?' asked Michael.

'How do you mean?' asked the boy innocently. He had a quizzical look on his face.

'Does he, er . . . ask you to do anything you feel uncomfortable with?'

'I don't know what you mean,' said Danny. He looked genuinely perplexed.

'Something you might want to talk to me about.'

'Such as?'

The boy was making it very difficult and Michael felt he

was getting nowhere. 'What I'm trying to say, Danny, is that when you go fishing with Mr Sparshott is that all you do?'

'Well, we do other things as well as fishin'.'

'You do? What sort of other things?'

'We talk a lot. 'E tells me abaat when 'e was a kid an' about t'books 'e likes to read, about 'is daughters an' 'is sons who are away at school.'

'Just talk?'

'Aye, nowt else.' Danny shook his head. He looked mystified. 'I really don't know what you're gerrin' at,' he said. 'What other things could we be doin' apart from fishin' an' talkin'?'

'It doesn't matter,' Michael told him, 'but just so long as you know that if there is anything you wish to talk to me about, anything at all, you just have to ask. All right?'

Danny looked at Michael, still with a puzzled look in his face. 'Aye, I will,' he replied.

'You promise me you will?'

'Aye,' Danny told him, confused by the topic of the conversation.

Mrs Sloughthwaite, the fount of all village information, folded her dimpled arms under her substantial bosom and leant on the counter. Her two regular customers had called in for the latest gossip.

'So it turns out Bianca wasn't poisoning him,' divulged the shopkeeper.

'Well I never believed she was,' remarked Mrs Pocock disdainfully, her mouth thinned with certainty, 'although, as I said, there's many that would like to. You know Fred Massey of old. Makes a drama out of everything.'

'Turns out he's a celeriac,' said Mrs Sloughthwaite.

'A what?'

'He can't eat anything with wheat in it. Dr Stirling's put him on a gluten-free diet.' Mrs Sloughthwaite chuckled. 'He's got to give up beer so you can imagine how that went down when he was told. He came in here like a bear with a sore backside moaning and groaning and complaining.'

Mrs Pocock gave a dry little laugh.

'I had that Mrs Stubbins in yesterday with her youngest in tow,' the shopkeeper announced. 'She was telling me she's taking the school to court for negligence.'

'Negligence!' huffed Mrs Pocock. 'She's a right one to talk. If there's any negligence it's on her part. She's always neglected them two lads of hers and that's why they've turned out as they have.'

'You're not wrong there,' agreed Mrs Sloughthwaite. 'Regular little tearaways they are. Nothing's safe on the counter when those two come in the shop and you've never heard the language they use. They were in here yesterday giving cheek left, right and centre. I don't know how the teachers cope with them.'

'"In every orange is a rotten pip", as my grandmother used to say,' remarked Mrs O'Connor.

Mrs Sloughthwaite sometimes found it hard to understand the meaning of her customer's words of wisdom but nodded sympathetically as if she did.

'So what's this about a court case?' asked Mrs Pocock.

'Her youngest, that Norman, fell off the wall bars in a PE lesson,' said the shopkeeper. 'Bruised himself he did and knocked out a tooth. Mind you, with teeth like the ones he's got it's not surprising it was the first part of him that got damaged. He could eat a tomato through a tennis racket. He's the spitting image of his father. Buck-teeth runs in his family like that lad's nose.'

'Well he shouldn't have been climbing up a wall,' said Mrs Pocock. 'Mind you, those lads of hers are enough to drive anyone up the wall. Their mother lets them run wild.

Out at all hours they are, hanging about the war memorial of an evening, making a racket and up to no good and dropping litter. They want a dose of good old-fashioned discipline.'

'Children have it too easy these days, so they do,' announced Mrs O'Connor. 'We never had all the things they have – toys and games and computers and I don't know what. We had to make our own entertainment. And as for all the jeans and trainers and fancy outfits they wear, I had to make do with my sister's patched hand-me-downs.'

'They do have it too easy,' agreed Mrs Pocock. 'I never ate in a restaurant when I was a girl or had one of these take-aways. We ate what we were given and it was precious little at times. I never went on a plane or a train and didn't go on foreign holidays like they do these days.'

'You were lucky to have a day out in Scarborough,' added Mrs Sloughthwaite.

'I had to walk two miles to school, there and back every day, sometimes in the pouring rain,' said Mrs Pocock, now getting into her stride, 'and if I was late I got the strap.'

'My mother, God rest her soul,' said Mrs Connor, 'cooked every day for all eight of us and when Da got home from work we'd sit at the kitchen table and if I didn't like what was on my plate I was made to sit there until I did like it.'

'We didn't have a telephone and there were no showers or inside lavatories,' said Mrs Sloughthwaite.

'We had to share the privvy in the yard with the neighbours, so we did,' added Mrs O'Connor, 'and instead of all that fancy toilet tissue they have these days, we cut up squares of news-paper to use.'

'I only had one bath a week,' said Mrs Pocock, 'and washed after my sister in a tin bath in front of the fire.'

'And I had all the washing to do,' said Mrs O'Connor, not wishing to be outdone on the deprivations of childhood. 'I had to scrub them clothes 'til my hands were red raw and then use a mangle.'

'But we were happy,' said the shopkeeper.

'Yes, we were happy,' agreed her customers.

The shop doorbell rang and Major Neville-Gravitas breezed in. He was dressed in a finely cut tweed jacket and matching waistcoat, green cord breeches and he sported a pair of bright-brown brogues polished like conkers. A heavy silver fob dangled across his chest. His face dropped when he saw the three women.

'Good morning, ladies,' he said with forced cheerfulness.

'Good morning, Major, said the shopkeeper. 'We were just saying how youngsters these days have it too easy.'

'Indeed,' said the major. 'National Service, that's what young men need. It would knock these lads into shape. Army discipline, there's nothing like it to build up the character.'

'I'm glad I've bumped into you,' said Mrs Pocock. 'I've wanted to have a word.'

'If it's about being in the governing body I have already told you that—'

'It's not!' she interrupted. 'It's about the litter.'

'The litter?' repeated the major.

'When are you going to do something about the litter?' she asked fiercely.

'What am I going to do about the litter?' he asked, looking her full in the face. 'I'm afraid I don't follow your drift.'

'The litter in the village,' said Mrs Pocock. 'What do you intend to do about it?'

A fleeting expression of annoyance passed across the major's features. *This dreadful woman finds fault with everything*, he thought. *No wonder her ne'r-do-well husband spends most of his life propping up the bar in the Blacksmith's Arms.* 'Pray tell me, what am I supposed to do about the litter?' he asked.

Mrs Pocock stared back at him belligerently and then stabbed the air with a bony finger. 'You're on the parish council,' she told him snorting with vexation. 'It's up to you and your cronies to do something about the state of the village. We don't elect you to sit on your backsides all day. There were plastic bags and broken bottles, sweet wrappers and paper bags, cigarette packets and tin cans all down the high street this morning.'

'Anything else?' muttered the major, thinking how very observant the woman was to have noticed such a variety of litter.

'It's a disgrace,' the customer told him.

'You can hardly lay that at the door of the parish council,' replied the major casually. 'The litter on the high street would, I guess, be the result of the weather. The squally winds we have been having will have no doubt blown the bins over and spilled the litter out. I can assure you it will all be removed in time.'

'When bricks fall from the skies,' said Mrs Pocock. 'It wants picking up now!'

The major was tempted to tell the woman that she might like to pick up the litter herself since it seemed to bother her so much but he resisted the temptation. He knew from experience there was no point in arguing with her.

'You are not suggesting, I assume,' replied the major, 'that I should do this myself?'

'I'm suggesting you frame yourself and get the council to do it.'

'And you want to get them to clean up the chewing gum that covers the pavements while you're about it,' said Mrs Sloughthwaite. 'That gets up my nose. I refuse to sell chewing gum and if I have complaints I tell the customer it's at the shop owner's discrepancy what I sell and what I don't.'

'It's dog mess I find hard to swallow,' remarked Mrs O'Connor, screwing up her face.

'And then there's the graffiti,' added Mrs Sloughthwaite. 'The bus shelter's covered in it. It wants cleaning off. I was waiting for the Clayton bus with Dr Underwood and the things that were written on the shelter would make a sailor blush.'

'And what about the broken pavements?' said Mrs Pocock. 'I nearly went full length last week on that piece of cracked paving by the butcher's. One of these days someone is going to trip up and then they'll be claiming compensation and the council will have to shell out.'

The major sighed. He had called in the store merely to purchase his cigars and was not expecting to receive a full-frontal assault.

'I recall when Miss Sowerbutts slipped in the supermarket by the frozen pizzas and broke an arm,' said Mrs O Connor, 'she got a fair old hand-out so she did.'

'Speaking of compensation,' said the shopkeeper, not missing the opportunity of gleaning some information, 'I hear that the school's being taken to court over an accident and the parent is claiming compensation.' She leant over the counter, smiled and tilted her head.

'I am afraid that I am not in a position to discuss the matter,' the major told her indifferently. 'Suffice it to say that the governors are firmly behind the head teacher and we are repudiating the allegation.'

'It was Mrs Stubbins, I hear,' persisted the shopkeeper.

'Yes, I believe it was,' said the major airily.

'Well that doesn't surprise me in the least,' said Mrs Pocock. 'She's out for all she can get is that one. It wouldn't surprise me at all if it was those two lads of hers who drop all the litter. She lets them run wild.'

'May I have a packet of Panatelas please?' asked the major, keen to be away.

'So are you going to do something about the litter then?' persisted Mrs Pocock.

'You will be pleased to hear that there is a meeting of the parish council tomorrow evening,' the major told her. 'I will raise the problem of the litter and the other complaints then.'

'Well make sure you do,' said Mrs Pocock, addressing the major as one might scold a disobedient child. 'Great bladder of wind,' she said when he had departed.

In the school office the following Monday morning, Elisabeth found the caretaker and the school secretary in earnest conversation.

'I still think we should get the vicar to exorcise it,' Mr Gribbon was saying.

'I don't think that will be necessary,' said Elisabeth coming into the room.

'Oh! Mrs Stirling!' exclaimed Mr Gribbon, 'you gave me quite a start. I was just saying to Mrs Scrimshaw we ought to get the vicar to sort out the ghost.'

'Yes, I heard you,' replied Elisabeth, 'and, as I said, I don't think an exorcism is necessary. I am sure that Mr Sparshott would find it amusing to exorcise a peripatetic sheep.'

'A sheep!' cried Mr Gribbon.

'A sheep,' repeated Elisabeth.

'Well I never,' said the caretaker, scratching his scalp.

'So there is your supernatural presence,' scoffed the secretary.

'Well it put the wind up you as well as me, Mrs Scrimshaw,' retorted the caretaker.

'Evidently the old ewe that grazes on the village green,' Elisabeth explained, 'discovered that the grass on the school field is greener than that where it usually grazes and, when the teachers and children have gone home and it's quiet, it has been in the habit of searching for juicier pasture. It has become quite adept at pushing open the gate. So there is your ghost,

Mr Gribbon, not some long-dead pupil in clogs haunting the place. I think it might be a good idea to secure the gate down the side of the school in future.'

'A sheep,' muttered the caretaker, shaking his head.

19

The young policeman with the red nose, colourful acne and greasy black hair leant back in the chair. His colleague, a pale-faced woman with her hair scraped back into a small bun and dressed in a business-like grey flannel jacket and a blouse buttoned up to the neck, sat beside him, stony-faced. They were in the rectory sitting room. It was now dark outside and there was a drizzle of rain.

'So what is all this about, Officer?' asked Mr Sparshott. He was standing by the widow.

'Perhaps you might like to sit down,' said the woman police officer.

'No, I prefer to stand,' replied the vicar. 'Now, how can I be of help?'

'We have had a complaint, sir,' said the young policeman.

'A complaint,' repeated the vicar.

'That's right, sir.'

'About me?'

'That's right, sir.'

'And what is the nature of this complaint, might I ask?'

'I'm about to tell you, sir, if you would just bear with me,' said the young policeman, sitting up and flicking through his notebook. 'I believe you know a young man called Daniel Stainthorpe?'

'Yes I do. He helps me in the churchyard.'

'And I believe you take him fishing?'

'Yes I do.'

'Just the two of you?'

'Yes, just the two of us. What is this about? Has the boy had an accident?'

'No, sir, he has not had an accident.'

The young policeman looked at his colleague. It was the cue for her to talk.

'Do you not think it might be considered rather unwise to spend your time, an adult, in the company of a young boy who is no relation to you?' she asked sententiously.

'Unwise? In what way is it unwise?' His voice was hoarse with indignation.

'People might get the wrong idea,' said the policeman. He touched the flare of red spots on his cheeks.

'Get the wrong idea!' exclaimed the vicar. 'What are you suggesting?' He clenched his hands behind his back and his face assumed a contorted look. 'Look, what is this all about?'

'We are not suggesting anything, sir,' replied the young policeman, giving a small smile and attempting to sound eminently reasonable.

'We're just following up a complaint,' added his colleague.

'A complaint that I have been doing what exactly?' asked the vicar. 'I was not aware that fishing is now a criminal offence.'

'It's not about the fishing,' said the woman police officer. She had a poker-face.

'One has to be very careful when it comes to the care and well-being of children,' said the young policeman. 'I am sure you are aware of that, sir. There have been occasions in the past when a neighbour has had their worries about a child's well-being ignored with unfortunate results. We do follow everything up when it comes to the welfare of children.'

'I am still at a loss what this has to do with me,' said the vicar.

'The person who contacted us said that you seem to be

spending a great deal of time in the company of the young boy and she felt concerned.'

'And why should she feel concerned?' asked the vicar angrily. 'What might I ask is so wrong with taking a boy fishing? Is there a law against it?'

'Some might consider it imprudent,' said the woman police officer.

'Are you implying that there is some impropriety here?' demanded the vicar. His face looked frozen.

'No, sir,' said the young policeman. 'We are not suggesting that but you will be aware, I am sure, having read the papers, that some adults who become friendly with children . . . how shall I put it . . . do so for less-than-innocent reasons.'

'I have never heard the like!' exclaimed the vicar, his voice trembling with anger. 'I find what you are saying highly offensive. You seem to be implying that I have some sinister ulterior motive in taking this young man fishing. It is quite unconscionable to insinuate such a thing.'

'We are not saying that there is anything improper in your relationship with this boy,' said the woman, 'but we do feel it is ill advised. This visit is just to make you aware that people might get the wrong idea and it is to advise you to discontinue these regular meetings with the boy.' Then she added, in what she imagined was in a conciliatory way, 'For your own sake.'

'Have you spoken to Daniel or to his parents?' asked the vicar, his face tight and angry.

'I don't think we need to go down that road, sir,' said the young policeman, snapping shut his notebook and getting to his feet. 'I think we will leave it at that.'

'Well I do not intend to leave it at that,' said the vicar angrily. He was shaking. 'I am outraged at the suggestion that my association with Daniel is anything other than entirely blameless.'

The woman police officer stood, smoothed her hands down

the front of her skirt and was clearly unmoved by the outburst. 'We have to follow up complaints,' she said officiously. 'We would not be doing our job if we ignored them.'

'I think you had better leave,' said the vicar, plainly shaken by the exchange.

'What was that all about?' asked Mrs Sparshott, coming into the sitting room when the police officers had gone. 'I heard raised voices.' Her husband, staring out over the rain-soaked garden with a face as white as plaster, turned to face her. The rain had started in earnest now and the window frames rattled, buffeted by a blustery wind.

'I need to go out,' he told her suddenly.

'What, at this time?' she asked. 'It's pouring down with rain.'

Ignoring her question, her husband hurriedly left the room.

Mr Sparshott stood at the front door of Clumber Lodge soaking wet and bedraggled and looking highly agitated.

'Mrs Stirling,' he spluttered when Elisabeth opened the door. 'Mrs Stirling, might I come in?'

'Yes, of course,' replied Elisabeth, startled by the drenched and dishevelled figure who stood before her on the doorstep.

The vicar came into the hall dripping water on the carpet.

'Here, let me take your coat,' she said. 'My goodness, you are soaked through. Go into the sitting room.'

'I'm sorry to call at this hour,' he said, the strain showing on his face, 'but I must speak to you and Dr Stirling on a matter which has caused me great distress.'

'Are you ill?' she asked.

'No, no, not ill, just very upset.'

'I'll fetch my husband,' she told him and left the room.

A moment later Michael came in with her.

'Do sit down,' Elisabeth told the visitor. She passed him a

towel. 'I'll put the kettle on. I am sure you could do with a cup of tea.'

'Or perhaps you might like something a bit stronger,' said Michael. 'You look as if you could do with a stiff drink.'

'A small brandy would be very acceptable,' said the vicar, perching on the end of a chair and wiping his face with the towel. 'Thank you very much. I don't normally drink but in the circumstances . . .' his voice trailed off.

Michael poured him a large brandy. He noticed the vicar's hand shaking as he took the glass.

'I must apologise for calling at this hour and unannounced, Dr Stirling,' said Mr Sparshott. He took a sip of his drink and coughed. 'But as I explained to your wife I need to speak to you both. I have had quite a shock this evening.'

Elisabeth and Michael didn't reply. Intrigued, they just waited for him to explain.

'I have had a visit from the police which has left me quite shaken,' the vicar told them. He took another sip.

Michael was tempted to ask him if he had been arrested for pawning the church silver but, seeing the man's tragic expression, thought better of it.

'Do go on,' he said.

'Two police officers called this evening,' continued Mr Sparshott, 'and said they had received a complaint, a complaint about myself.' He took another sip of his drink. 'This is very difficult and distressing. I really don't know how to put it. They wanted me to stop seeing young Daniel, not to encourage him to visit the churchyard and implied that my taking him fishing was somehow . . . somehow inappropriate, that my motives might be misinterpreted, that people might, as they put it, get the wrong idea. I was speechless. That anyone should imagine that I would . . . that there was something unseemly, something improper occurring is quite unthinkable. I am aware that you did not make any complaint because the police officers told me they had not been in contact with you or indeed that they had spoken to Daniel. Dr Stirling, Mrs Stirling I . . . I . . . want to assure you both that my actions have at all times been upright and proper and that—'

Elisabeth held up a hand. 'Let me stop you there, Mr Sparshott,' she said calmly. 'There is no need to assure us of anything. Some people, I am afraid to say, can be malicious and always seem to think the worse of others. I suppose if one were to put a charitable gloss on this, one might argue they were concerned about Danny's welfare. There have been occasions where the voices of vulnerable children have been ignored and predatory adults have taken advantage and we need to be vigilant. However, if the person who made this complaint had any worries in that direction they should have approached myself and my husband and not the police. We live in a world where, if someone has an accident through their own fault, it is blamed on others, a world where anyone who takes an innocent interest in children is suspected of some devious motive.'

'Thank you, thank you, Mrs Stirling,' said Mr Sparshott looking greatly relieved. 'That is most reassuring.'

'We know that your association with Danny is a perfectly well-meaning one,' she told him and then added, 'he would have said something if it was otherwise.'

'If you speak to Daniel . . .' began the vicar, 'I am sure that he will tell you—'

'There is really no need,' interrupted Michael, deciding to keep to himself the earlier conversation he had had with the boy. 'The thing about Danny, as you are probably aware, is that he is such an open, honest, straightforward sort of boy, he would have said something if he had felt uncomfortable. When I was his age I used to take shopping down the road to an elderly neighbour and spent a fair bit of time in his company. He was a most interesting old man was Mr Pritchard. He had fought in the war and was full of fascinating stories. No-one ever imagined that there was anything improper about me spending time in his house. My parents knew him and trusted him as we do you. So please don't upset yourself or give it another thought.'

'It is a great relief to hear you say that, Dr Stirling,' answered the vicar. He gulped down the rest of the brandy. 'A great relief. My taking Daniel fishing was meant as a thank you for all his hard work in the churchyard. He has been such a help. I never imagined that anyone would think . . . '

Danny burst into the room. 'I thought I 'eard yer voice, Mester Sparshott,' he said to the vicar. He looked at Michael. 'I'm not interrupting owt, am I?'

'No, no, we were just hearing what a great help you have been,' said Elisabeth.

'I've just bin readin' up abaat salmon fishing in that book yer gave me,' he said to the vicar. 'Mebbe we could 'ave a go at catching a salmon next time we go fishin'.'

'I think perhaps, Daniel,' Mr Sparshott replied, 'that for the time being we should—'

'The next time you go fishing with Mr Sparshott, young man,' Michael cut in, 'you make sure you bring back the fish and not put it back in the river. I could just fancy a nice piece of rainbow trout for my dinner.'

Danny gave a great beaming smile.

Sir Cosmo Cavendish Boys' Grammar School was built at the turn of the century, paid for by the wealthy wool manufacturer and philanthropist from whom the school had taken its name. It was a huge, ornate, ostentatious pile of a building with squat, black turreted towers and mullioned windows, long, cold corridors and dark, cramped classrooms. Dominating the main entrance was a pretentious bronze statue of the school's founder. Sir Cosmo stood on a large plinth, hands on his hips, legs apart and chin jutting out like a mastiff about to pounce.

It was the morning of Oscar's interview. His parents had applied for one of the few bursaries the school offered and, having passed the entrance examination with flying colours, their son was now being called for an interview with the headmaster.

Oscar pressed a buzzer on the reception desk.

'This place smells of cabbage and floor polish,' he remarked. 'Not a very good first impression.' If he was nervous he certainly didn't show it.

The frosted glass slid back and they were confronted by a thin, hawk-faced woman with small, cold, blue eyes behind large black-framed glasses. She gave them a stony stare.

'May I help you?' she asked. She had a face which would frighten the birds off the trees.

Oscar's father passed a letter through the opening. 'My son is here for an interview with the headmaster,' he told her hesitantly.

The secretary glanced cursorily at the letter. 'I shall tell Mr McCarthy you have arrived,' she said. 'Take a seat and he will be with you presently.' With a tight smile of dismissal she slid back the glass.

A few minutes later they were shown into the headmaster's study. It was an unprepossessing room. Ornate dark oak wainscoting covered the walls on which a number of portraits of stern-featured former headmasters were exhibited in their fancy gilt frames. A large well-polished desk was positioned before a tall arched window which overlooked the school playing fields. Around the room were heavy overbearing chairs, bookcases crammed with books and grey metal filing cabinets. On a small occasional table there was a marble bust of the school's founder.

Mr McCarthy, the headmaster, was a tall, fair,

good-looking man approaching middle age. He wore a well-tailored charcoal-grey suit with narrow chalk stripes, a crisp white shirt, college tie knotted tightly at the neck and he sported a pink silk handkerchief in his breast pocket. He looked like a successful banker.

'Good morning,' he said, smiling widely and shaking hands with the two parents. 'Do, do come in and take a seat.' He gestured to the three chairs facing his desk before sitting down himself. 'Thank you for coming.'

Oscar placed himself on the middle chair sandwiched between his parents and sat up very straight with his legs together and his hands resting on his lap. He lifted his head and looked around the room like a gun dog listening for a movement in the bracken. The headmaster observed the boy for a moment. Unlike the previous candidates, two shy, quiet, nervy boys who had shifted uneasily in their seats and looked like condemned men facing execution, this young man seemed completely undaunted by the situation.

Oscar turned his head and his gaze settled on one of the large oil paintings on the wall. It was of a cadaverous-looking man with sunken cheeks, greyish skin and a mournful countenance. With his long pointed nose and heavy hooded eyes, he resembled a melancholy bird. The figure sat, draped in a long black academic gown, enthroned in a heavy chair behind the same desk in front of which Oscar now sat, and stared from the canvas with great gloomy eyes.

'That is Dr Magnus, a former headmaster here,' the present headmaster told Oscar, following the boy's gaze and pointing at the portrait. He smiled. 'He looks a bit stern, doesn't he?' The question was rhetorical but Oscar nodded in agreement.

'He does,' he replied pertly. 'Not what you would call a fun-loving sort of person. He looks rather like an undertaker, doesn't he?'

The headmaster smiled tolerantly. He was going to enjoy this interview with such an obviously precocious child. Some adults found children like Oscar, often described as 'too clever by half', and 'old beyond their years', rather irksome but Mr McCarthy found them fascinating and something of a challenge. He was aware that some of the greatest minds, when young, were described as precocious and proved rather troublesome for their teachers. He, however, found such children thought-provoking and knew from experience that they added immensely to the life and work of a school. He opened a folder in front of him. 'So this is young Oscar, is it?' he asked, addressing the parents.

'Yes, this is Oscar,' said the boy's mother.

'And he is at . . . let me see . . .' Mr McCarthy referred to the folder, tapping it with a finger. 'He's a pupil at Barton-with-Urebank Primary School?'

'Yes I am,' said Oscar, before his mother could reply.

A fixed polite smile of amusement remained on the headmaster's face. 'Well, Oscar, you performed extremely well in the entrance examination and your reference from the head teacher at Barton-with-Urebank says you are quite a remarkable young man.'

Oscar nodded as if he had heard this many times before. He had known from a young age that adults thought of him as unusual. Like many a gifted child, he could not see why he was viewed as being different from others of his age, that he came across as outspoken and opinionated. He saw himself as ordinary and the world around him eccentric.

'Mrs Stirling says you enjoy school and work very hard,' said the headmaster.

'Yes, I do enjoy school,' replied the boy, 'and I do put in the effort.'

'Well now,' said Mr McCarthy, 'I am going to ask you a few questions. Don't be nervous. They aren't meant to catch you out. They are just for me to learn something about you and see if you will fit in with us here at SCCGS. '

Oscar leant forward expectantly. He didn't look in the least nervous.

'Now, would you like to tell me about yourself?' asked Mr McCarthy.

Oscar crossed his legs, looked up and pondered for a moment. 'I play the piano,' he said, 'and have just passed my Grade Six examination. I'm learning the flute. I enjoy reading and writing poetry . . . '

'He won the School Library Poetry Competition last year,' interrupted his mother.

'Mother,' said Oscar rather sharply and gave her a look which said 'let me do the talking'.

'I like public speaking,' the boy continued, 'and came runner up in the county Poetry and Prose Recitation Competition.'

'And what did you recite?' asked Mr McCarthy.

'Some verses from *The Ballad of Reading Gaol* by Oscar Wilde,' replied Oscar. 'Do you know it at all?'

It was unheard of for the headmaster to be asked a question by a candidate during the interview. 'I do,' he replied with a smile. 'It is a very fine poem.'

'It is, isn't it?' said Oscar. 'Of course, Oscar Wilde was treated very badly and put in prison. It was in Reading Gaol that he wrote the poem.'

'You enjoy reading?' asked Mr McCarthy.

'Yes, I read a great deal,' replied Oscar. 'A particular interest is geology and I have become quite interested in astronomy lately. I am at present also taking Latin lessons.'

'Latin?' Mr McCarthy sat forward in his chair and rested his hands on the desk top. 'You are learning Latin?' He exchanged glances with the boy's parents. They smiled and shrugged.

'The teacher at my school is teaching me,' continued Oscar. 'He studied Classics at university and I am enjoying it very much.' The boy looked again at the portrait on the wall. 'Doesn't "magnus" mean "great" in Latin?' he asked.

'Indeed it does,' replied the headmaster, 'and Dr Magnus was a great man.'

'If a little frightening,' added Oscar.

'We have a very fine Classics department here,' the headmaster told him. 'The subject is compulsory for the first two years.'

'Really,' replied Oscar, 'I'm very pleased to hear it.'

In his many years of teaching Mr McCarthy had rarely come across such a confident, articulate and quick-witted eleven-year-old. 'Could you translate this school's motto do you think?' he asked indicating an elaborate coat of arms displayed on a wall. '*Industria Floremus.*'

'It means "We Flourish by Industry",' replied Oscar.

'Good gracious me!' exclaimed the headmaster. 'That's quite amazing.'

'Well, not really amazing,' replied Oscar with a small smile. 'You see, I saw the motto at the top of your letter we received from the school and I asked my teacher what it meant.'

A glimmer of private amusement crossed the headmaster's face. 'So you like literature and music. What about sports?'

'I have to admit I am not too good at sports,' acknowledged Oscar. 'I am not one of nature's athletes nor am I a joiner of groups, although I do enjoy chess which is thought by some to be a sport.'

'We have a flourishing chess club at the school,' Mr McCarthy told him. 'One of our students won the county championship last year.'

'Really,' replied Oscar. 'Do you play chess?'

'I do,' replied the headmaster.

'It's a fascinating game, isn't it?'

Why was it, thought Mr McCarthy, that he had this feeling that it was he who was being interviewed and not the candidate sitting before him cross-legged and assured. This young man was intriguing.

'What is it about chess that you like?' he asked.

'It's a game of skill,' the boy replied. 'You face your adversary almost like facing the enemy on a battlefield. The aim is to destroy your opponent. That's why it's so exciting. Mr Hornchurch, he's my teacher, says chess teaches us some of life's most important lessons – concentration, how to appear trusting but really being on the ball. You have to think about what will happen many moves ahead. It's also about taking a few risks. I suppose it's all to do with tactics.'

The headmaster's smile broadened.

'My favourite piece is the knight,' continued Oscar. 'He is the queen's greatest enemy because he can leap across the board and over other pieces when you are not expecting him. Other pieces can't do this. The bishop can only move diagonally and can only move on one colour.'

Mr McCarthy glanced at Oscar's parents during their son's lecture. They looked back and shrugged again as if to say, we know exactly what you are thinking and we haven't any idea where he gets it from.

Following a few general questions which Oscar answered clearly and with great self-confidence, the headmaster brought the interview to an end.

'Is there anything you wish to ask me?' he said, looking at Oscar's parents.

'No, not really,' Oscar replied, 'we've read the prospectus.'

It was unheard of for the headmaster of the prestigious Sir Cosmo Cavendish Boys' Grammar School to make a decision on the bursaries at the interview. The submissions were so numerous and the competition so great that he considered all the applications after having carefully consulted his colleagues and the Chairman of Governors. On this occasion, however, he decided to dispense with custom and give a bursary there and then. Mr McCarthy knew that students coming to a school such as his were keen to fit in, not to question but to obey the rules. Schools were, after all, designed to reward conformity, curb unacceptable behaviour and impose a particular version of morality using various systems of rewards and punishments. He also knew that this non-conformist, creative, outspoken character who sat serious-faced before him might very well prove a handful but a child with these gifts would add immensely to the school. He looked at the bust of Sir Cosmo who during his lifetime was labelled outspoken, non-conformist and eccentric but who had gone on to be seen by later generations as a man endowed with great originality and vision.

'I have very much enjoyed speaking to you this morning, Oscar,' said the headmaster, 'and I should like to offer you a place at the school with the full bursary.'

'Thank you,' replied the boy, standing up and extending a hand. 'I have enjoyed our conversation too. I have a couple of other schools to look at before I make up my mind,' he said pertly. 'I want to keep my options open. We will be in touch.'

Mr McCarthy shook his head and laughed. 'I look forward to hearing from you,' he said.

'We won't stay too long, love,' said Mrs Ross. 'We don't want to tire your mum out.'

Robbie was at the hospital with his foster carers. He had been very quiet in the car on the way into Clayton and now walked slowly down the long corridor to the ward with his head held down. It had been arranged for Mrs Banks to be transferred to a hospice the following week but she was now too weak to be moved. It was clear to the doctors that she had very little time to live.

'Are you all reight, lad?' asked Mr Ross.

'Yeah, I'm OK.'

'I've never liked 'ospitals mi'sen,' said the farmer, making conversation. 'Don't like t'smell.'

'A bit nicer than the smell of your blessed pigs,' said Mrs Ross chuckling.

'You leave t'pigs alone. They're all reight our pigs, aren't they, Robbie?'

'Yes,' the boy said in a voice hardly audible.

'She's not too good at the moment,' said the nurse, taking Mrs Ross aside as they approached the ward. 'I shouldn't stay too long.'

Mrs Banks was in a corner bed in a private room surrounded by brightly coloured screens. It was clear that she was a very ill woman. Flesh seemed to have peeled off her bones and her papery-white skin hung loose. Her breath was laboured. Milky tired eyes were half hidden behind dark lids.

'Here we are,' said the nurse, pulling back the screens. 'We have some visitors for you, Rita.'

Mrs Banks opened her eyes and her face lit up when she saw Robbie.

Mrs Ross went over to the bed, sat down on the chair at the side and put her hand on the woman's arm and rested it there. The patient's skin was cold and clammy. 'Look who I've brought to see you,' she said, trying to sound cheerful.

'Hello, Robbie,' said Mrs Banks. Her voice was throaty. She gave a thin smile.

The boy stood there for a moment. He was appalled by the greyness of his mother's face and the white bony fingers which lay on the covers.

'Hello,' he mouthed. His voice, which had been hard and defiant when speaking to his mother in the past, was now flat and toneless.

'Come and give your mum a kiss,' Mrs Ross told the boy.

Robbie hesitantly approached the bed, bent and pecked his mother on the cheek.

'Now you come and hold your mother's hand,' she said, 'and you can tell her how you've been getting on.' She turned to her husband. 'Come along, Hamish, we'll go and get a cup of tea and let these two catch up.'

On their way to the hospital café Mr and Mrs Ross bumped into Fred Massey who was shuffling along the corridor with a sour expression on his weathered face. Like all who knew him, Mr and Mrs Ross did not like the man who constantly complained and who was tight-fisted and bad-tempered.

'Hello, Hamish,' Fred grunted.

''Eyup, Fred,' replied the farmer.

'What are *you* doing here?'

'Missus an' me are 'ere wi' one o' t'kids we're fosterin'. T'lad's mam is ill an' 'e's 'ere to see 'er.'

'You deserve a bloody medal for looking after other folks' kids,' growled Fred. 'I wouldn't do it, I'll tell you that. I have enough trouble with my own family. Our Clarence and that bossy wife Bianca and screaming baby of his are living with me now and it's hell on earth. I don't have a minute to myself.'

'Come on, Hamish,' said Mrs Ross, not wishing to endure listening to a catalogue of Fred's gripes. 'Let's go and get that cup of tea.'

'I could fancy a cup of tea myself,' said Fred. 'I'll join you.'

Mrs Ross pulled a face and breathed out noisily.

Not in the habit of paying for anything unless under duress, Fred had his drink bought for him. He settled down at the table, leant back in the chair and explained why he was at the hospital.

'I'm here for more tests,' he grumbled. 'I'm intolerant according to the doctor.'

'You don't need a doctor to tell you that,' said Mrs Ross pointedly.

'Intolerant to wheat. It's called gluten intolerance. I've been having these terrible belly aches. Took to my bed for a week. I thought that bossy Bianca had been putting stuff in my food, slipping in a Death Cap mushroom with my breakfast. I wouldn't put it past her. Anyway, it turns out it's wheat what causes it. I can't have anything with ordinary flour in – cakes and pastries and buns and pasties. I can't even have fried fish because of the batter and bread is off the menu as well. Worse than that, I can't drink beer. I'm having to sup cider from now on and I hate the stuff. Of course that's not the only thing what's wrong with me. I'm still having trouble with my foot after having caught it in the beet cutter and my arm's not been right since I broke it cutting down that branch in the church-yard and another thing . . . '

The unrelenting carping and complaints went on until Mrs Ross was unable to stand it any longer. She finished her tea and got up.

'We shall have to collect Robbie now, Hamish,' she said, giving him a knowing look.

'Aye, we 'ad better mek a move,' said her husband.

'If you're going back through Barton,' said Fred, 'you can give me a lift. It'll save me getting the bus. You wait hours for a bus and then they all come at once and you can never get a seat and they've put the fares up. I'll wait here for you in the café. You'll not be that long, will you?'

'We are—' began Mr Ross.

'We are not going your way.' Mrs Ross cut off her husband. 'We're taking the boy we're fostering for a meal and then the cinema to take his mind off things.'

'Oh I see,' mumbled Fred.

'We're taking him for pizza,' she said. Then, as a final riposte, she added, 'I don't suppose you can eat pizza any more, can you, Fred?'

When they arrived back at the ward and approached the

screens which had been pulled back around the bed, they heard Robbie's voice. Mrs Ross took her husband's arm and held him back. 'Just wait a minute, Hamish,' she whispered.

For a moment they eavesdropped on the conversation. Robbie was sounding unusually animated.

'Boars can be really vicious, you see,' he was saying. 'They have these tusks which they use to rip. Hamish, Mr Ross that is, he had this big boar once called Boris. He said it was a nasty piece of work – born bad. It would try and nudge him and then turn its head and try to use its tusks. You have to take off the tusks when they're young otherwise they can use them. They're really sharp. Hamish snapped one of them off with these kind of pliers but when he tried to do the other it saw him coming and was ready for him. He couldn't get near. In the end he had to shoot it. We don't have boars any more, just pigs for fattening.'

'My goodness,' said Mrs Banks.

'He gave me the tusk that he snapped off,' Robbie told her. He took it from his pocket to show her. 'It's my lucky charm,' he said.

'So you like it where you are?' asked the boy's mother.

'Yeah, I do,' said Robbie.

'Mr and Mrs Ross are good, kind people, Robbie.'

'I know.'

'Look, love,' said Mrs Banks, 'I'm sorry how things have worked out. I could have handled things better, I know I could. I should have stood up to Frank more. I'm sorry, love, I'm really sorry.' She began to cry.

'It's all right,' said Robbie.

He put the boar's tusk on the small bedside table. 'You can have my lucky charm,' he said.

'Now then,' said Mrs Ross, appearing from behind the screens, 'have you two had a nice chat?'

'Yeah,' said the boy. His eyes were pricking with tears.

'We've had a lovely talk,' said Mrs Banks, sniffing.

'Well your mum looks a bit tired now,' said Mrs Ross, 'so we'll be making tracks. Say goodbye, Robbie. We'll pop in again tomorrow.'

'Goodbye, love,' said Mrs Banks.

Robbie hugged his mother and they both began to cry.

20

'Nervous?' asked Michael.

He was sitting with Elisabeth at the breakfast table at Clumber Lodge. It was the day of the court action for negligence.

'I am a bit,' she replied. That morning she was not as calm about the court case as she had pretended to be when speaking to Mr Jolly. It would be her first time in a court of law. She had seen programmes on the television depicting bewigged barristers, urbane, assured sharp-witted, reducing witnesses to stuttering wrecks when ruthlessly cross-examined, and stern-faced judges, in red silk, staring down on the court. She felt both excited and daunted.

'There's really nothing to feel nervous about,' he reassured her, patting her hand. 'The case should never have gone to court and the judge is certain to throw it out.'

'That's what I've kept telling myself,' said Elisabeth, 'but there is this niggling doubt at the back of my mind that it might not work out like that. I've never been in a court of law before and from what Mrs Robertshaw has told me it's quite a daunting experience. She was on jury service a few years ago and said how these clever lawyers have a way of twisting the truth and tying you up in knots.'

'I can't see that happening to you,' chuckled Michael. 'Remember I've seen you in action. You are quite formidable when you want to be. I'm sure that when the judge hears your account of what happened he will agree and there will be no case to answer.'

'It's how Mr Jolly will cope that really concerns me,' Elisabeth told him. 'Yesterday he was in a terribly nervous state. You would think he was facing a murder charge. I worry that he will go to pieces in the witness box and admit the accident was his fault.'

'What's your defence lawyer like?'

'It's a Mrs Pickering,' Elisabeth told him. 'She's the county solicitor and seems very competent and feels there is no case to answer.'

'Well, there you are then.'

'But she did say not to count our chickens. Sometimes things do not turn out as expected.'

'She's got to say that,' Michael told her. 'She can't positively guarantee the outcome. It's a bit like me with a patient who is facing a serious operation. Of course I reassure them and say there is a good recovery rate and they have the very best surgeon but I never say that everything will be fine because sometimes it isn't.' He could see by his wife's expression that he was not setting her mind at rest and was, rather, sowing some seeds of doubt in her mind. 'This Mrs Pickering will know what she is about,' he assured her, putting on a cheerful voice, 'and has probably been through this sort of thing countless times. It will all turn out for the best I'm sure.'

'I suppose so,' said Elisabeth but sounding unconvinced.

'What time are you due in court?' asked Michael.

'This afternoon.'

'Well you've plenty of time. I've an afternoon surgery, so will drive you into Clayton.'

'Thank you but I'm going to call into school later this morning,' said Elisabeth. 'It will take my mind off things.'

'It will soon be over,' said Michael, taking her hand and squeezing it.

'It's a real nuisance is this,' said Elisabeth, getting agitated.

'This affair has taken up so much of my time and disrupted the whole school and there's been a cost. I have had to employ two supply teachers for the day to cover lessons and all over a silly accident which was caused by the child's own carelessness.'

'And that is what the judge will think,' said Michael.

'I hope so.'

'The boys got off to school all right?' he asked, keen to change the subject.

'Yes, fine,' she replied. 'That's another thing; I'm constantly thinking about how John is getting on at school – it's so hard to have him away from me for so long though I know he's in the best place for him. And I'm worried about how Danny is getting on at school.'

'Sweetheart, you know you're doing the right thing for everyone. John is doing so well and Danny seems to be happy enough,' said Michael.

'He's happy enough at home,' agreed his wife, 'but he's not doing a great deal at school from what I can gather. James tells me that the boys in Danny's class are rude and disruptive and never out of trouble.'

'Has Danny said anything to you?'

'No. When I ask him he just shrugs and says, "All right." I think he sees school as some sort of tedious business he has to put up with, a bit of an irrelevance. He's so different from James who loves school and is doing really well.'

'Well you know Danny, Elisabeth,' said Michael, 'he's a free spirit; he likes nothing better than to be outdoors. He's a country lad through and through. I suppose being stuck in a stuffy classroom behind a desk he feels confined, like a caged bird beating its wings against the bars, desperate to be flying free.'

'Being put in a bottom group can't be doing much for Danny's self-esteem and confidence,' said Elisabeth. 'I think the teachers care more for the brighter pupils like James rather than those who struggle with their work. Danny rarely gets any homework and I've never seen him with a book.'

'Ah, now that's where you are wrong,' Michael told her. 'Last week he had his head buried in a book.'

'Really?'

'A rather battered little book called *Fishing for Boys.*' Michael smiled. 'Quite an unusual title, don't you think? He was struggling a bit over some of the words but he was certainly interested in it.'

'Wherever did he get a book like that from?' wondered Elisabeth. 'I'm sure he didn't bring it home from school.'

'I gather the vicar has lent it to him.'

'Mr Sparshott?' she said. 'He's lent him the book?'

'So Danny said.'

'Well I never.'

'Perhaps we've judged the man too harshly,' said Michael. 'I know when we first met him he appeared a rather pompous and unsociable sort of chap but maybe that covered up for some insecurity. I mean, he can't have been over the moon to be told by everyone when he arrived how popular and respected was his predecessor and how wonderful his curate was. Anyway, Danny certainly seems to like him otherwise he wouldn't spend his Saturday mornings tidying up the church-yard or going fishing with him.'

Elisabeth nodded. 'Yes, you may well be right. I must say we saw a different side of Mr Sparshott when he came to see us. All that haughtiness had disappeared. You know, I felt quite sorry for him. '

'So it appears our new vicar does get on with some people, judging by the way Danny has taken to him,' said Michael.

The telephone in the hall rang.

'I'll get it,' he said, jumping to his feet.

He came back into the kitchen a moment later. He had a pained expression on his face.

'What's wrong?' asked Elisabeth, getting up from her chair.

'That was Mrs Scrimshaw,' said Michael. 'She asked me to tell you that Mr Jolly has phoned in sick. He won't be with you in court today.'

That afternoon Elisabeth appeared at the Clayton County Court as a defence witness in the care of *Stubbins versus the Local Education Authority*. She was dressed for the occasion in a tailored slate-grey suit, cream blouse, black stockings and bright-red shoes with silver heels. It was the outfit she had worn when she came for the interview for the head teacher's position at the village school. She sat, straight-backed and serious, in the witness box, her hands resting on her lap. She looked undaunted by the occasion but inside her stomach was churning.

The counsel for the litigant, a whey-faced young man with a long nose and flared nostrils approached the witness box.

'You are the head teacher of Barton-with-Urebank Primary School,' he stated in a thin, nasal voice.

'I am,' replied Elisabeth.

'And you were in school at the time of the unfortunate accident, were you not?'

'I was.'

'Would you recollect for the court please, Mrs Stirling, the events of the day in question?'

'Yes, of course,' she replied. 'I was teaching that afternoon and just before break time a pupil from Mr Jolly's class arrived at my classroom. She had been sent by her teacher to ask me if I might go to the school hall where there had been an accident. I dismissed my class since it was nearly playtime and went to the hall.'

'And what did you find there?' asked the barrister.

'I found one of Mr Jolly's pupils, Norman Stubbins, in a distressed state. He was sitting beneath the wall bars rubbing his shoulder. I asked his teacher what had happened and was informed that the boy had been climbing up the wall bars, lost his footing and fell.'

'And what did you do then?'

'I checked Norman and, although a little shaken, he appeared to have no serious injury. Then the school bell rang for afternoon break and I told Mr Jolly to dismiss his class. I asked the caretaker, who had joined us, to tell the school secretary to telephone the boy's mother, explain what had happened and ask her to collect her son. I intended to see Mrs Stubbins when she called at the school and suggest that, to be on the safe side, she should take her son to a doctor or the hospital to have him checked over. Unfortunately there was no reply at home or at the emergency number so I decided to take Norman to the A&E department at Clayton Royal Infirmary myself.'

'Where a doctor examined the boy,' interposed the counsel.

'That's right.'

'And I believe the doctor found the boy to have suffered extensive bruising and broken teeth.'

'No,' replied Elisabeth. 'The doctor said no bones had been broken, there was some bruising and a chipped tooth but, since the boy had not banged his head, there was no need for an X-ray. He said it would be fine to take him home. This I did but Norman's mother was still out. I waited until she got back, which was about five thirty, and informed her what had happened. She told me that her son was always having accidents and that—'

'That is of no relevance, thank you, Mrs Stirling,' interrupted the lawyer. He allowed himself a small, self-satisfied smile. 'Now tell the court, is it customary for young children to be climbing walls bars which stretch as high as the ceiling?'

'No it isn't.'

The barrister looked surprised by the answer. 'So young children should not be climbing wall bars then?'

'By young children I assume you are meaning infants – those below the age of seven,' said Elisabeth. She knew exactly what he meant but took exception to his sharp manner. 'These children are too young to climb on walls bars. They do, however, have climbing frames in the play area in the playground. It is important for them to have regular exercise. For juniors such as Norman, however, it is certainly very customary for them to use the PE equipment which includes the wall bars. That is what the wall bars are there for. Indeed, it is a statutory requirement that all children receive some opportunity for physical activity during the week.'

'I see,' said the lawyer. The irony did not touch him, or if it did he chose to ignore it. 'And am I correct in saying that children who use this equipment should wear suitable footwear?'

'No, you are not correct,' replied Elisabeth. 'The children who do PE have bare feet. It would be dangerous for them to wear plimsolls or trainers. They get a better grip with bare feet. I believe that some gymnasts prefer to perform in bare feet. It's safer.'

'I am indebted to you, Mrs Stirling, for enlightening the court on that point,' said the lawyer in a patronising tone of voice. 'Now tell us, is it the case that children undertaking PE should be made fully aware of the potential dangers of using equipment such as wall bars?'

'Yes it is.'

'And if the children are not warmed of the possible dangers, that this would be considered negligent?'

'Yes it would.'

'And further, if the children undertaking PE are not suitably supervised this too would be considered negligent?'

'Yes it would.'

'I put it to you, Mrs Stirling, that the children in the lesson where the boy fell were unaware of the potential dangers of using this equipment and that they were not adequately supervised.'

'As to the first point, I can assure you all the children in the school are fully aware of the potential hazards of using the equipment. In the school's curriculum policy document it states very clearly that at the start of every PE lesson the teacher will stress the importance of the children being careful when using the equipment. As to the second point, the teacher was in the hall for the entire lesson when this accident occurred. With a class of children he could not be expected to watch every individual child for all of the time.'

'That is what Mr Jolly, who is unfortunately not with us this morning, asserts,' said the lawyer.

'Yes he does.'

'Why is the teacher who supervised the children not present?' asked the district judge.

'I am told he is ill, your honour,' replied the lawyer.

'Very well, continue,' the judge told him.

'The young man who fell states he was unaware of the potential dangers of climbing wall bars,' said the lawyer.

'Perhaps he wasn't paying attention,' said Elisabeth. 'He is a child who does have some difficulty with concentrating on what he is doing and listening to what the teacher tells him. Certainly the other children in the class—'

'If I may finish,' cut in the lawyer. 'Norman Stubbins says that at no time did the teacher tell the class to be careful and that when he fell the teacher was busily occupied at the other side of the hall.'

'As I said,' Elisabeth told him, 'the teacher cannot watch every individual child and it was possible he was supervising other children at the time.'

'That will be all, Mrs Stirling,' said the lawyer dismissively.

Elisabeth turned to the judge. 'May I say something, your honour?' she asked.

'If it is relevant to this case,' replied the judge.

'Following the accident,' said Elisabeth, 'I interviewed the teacher who was in charge of the class at the time and am satisfied that there was no negligence on his part.'

'Your honour,' said the lawyer approaching the bench, 'perhaps this witness should be reminded that it is for the court and not she who needs to be satisfied.'

'One moment, Mr Pennington-Padgett,' said the judge. 'I should like to hear what this witness has to say. Do continue, Mrs Stirling.'

'In addition to speaking to Mr Jolly, I interviewed each child the day after the incident. They all stated that the teacher had explained at the start of the lesson the potential dangers of using the equipment and told them to take care. They also were all of the same mind in saying that the boy who fell was acting the fool, swinging from the top bar like a monkey and that his fall was the result of his own carelessness.'

'This is hearsay,' interrupted the lawyer.

'Well I guess you could call the children to testify,' replied Elisabeth. 'I am sure they would verify what I have just said.'

'Do continue, Mrs Stirling,' the judge told her.

'I should just like to say, your honour, that in my experience children do have accidents. They tumble out of trees and break bones, they fall off their bikes, bang their heads playing rugby and sprain ankles playing football. It is all part and parcel of growing up. This, to my mind, was an accident caused by the boy's own lack of care.'

'Thank you, Mrs Stirling,' said the judge. He turned to the lawyer. 'Are there any more questions Mrs Pennington-Padgett?' he asked.

'No, your honour.'

'Then in that case,' said the judge, 'Mrs Stirling, you may stand down.'

In summing up, the district judge made it clear that he felt the action should never have come to court.

'I regret the fact,' he stated, staring fixedly at Mr Pennington-Padgett, 'that more and more lawyers are adopting what I term "the proactive approach to litigation" and I lament the increasing tendency of people to resort to the law for quite unjustifiable reasons. What I would call "bad luck" seems to have gone out of the window. Schools cannot be expected to be hazard-free zones where children are protected from every possible injury. Teachers are not under a duty to safeguard children against harm under all circumstances. Such a position would defy common sense. The relevant question here is whether this injury was caused as a result of negligence or breach of duty on the part of the school and the Local Education Authority. In this case, did the school provide a reasonably safe and secure environment bearing in mind that children, as the head teacher stated, are prone to accidents and inclined to lark around? A judgment in favour of the plaintiff could prompt all schools throughout the county and indeed the country to remove wall bars. Clearly the young man who had the accident got up to mischief. It was unfortunate that he suffered some injury but such things happen. As the head teacher has explained so eloquently and elegantly, accidents are part and parcel of growing up. Such are the vicissitudes of life. I have to add that there have been far too many claims for compensation for accidents coming through the courts. We seem to live now in a blame society. It is always someone else's fault. The case should never have come to court and I have no hesitation in dismissing the action.'

'Ah, Mrs Stirling,' enthused Mr Nettles, approaching Elisabeth outside the court. He had a smug expression on his face and was rubbing his hands together vigorously. 'I think we can be very well satisfied with that verdict.'

'I'm surprised to see you here, Mr Nettles,' she said coldly. 'I thought you would be too tied up to spare the time.'

'I thought I might be asked to be an expert witness,' he replied.

'Well, if you will excuse me, I have to get back to school. This action has caused a deal of disruption.'

'As I said, I think that this was a most satisfactory outcome,' he said, walking with her. 'Had the judgement gone against us this would have been very unfortunate in setting up a precedent. It would have opened the floodgates for claims for compensation and—'

'Mr Nettles,' interrupted Elisabeth, stopping to face him, 'if you recall your suggestion was to settle out of court.'

'Ah yes, but—'

'I can't say that your support in this matter was very forthcoming. Had I followed your advice this would have had a dire effect not only on the reputation of the school but upon Mr Jolly who has been most distressed over this whole matter. In fact, it has made him ill. Now I must get back to school.'

Elisabeth left the education officer standing on the steps to the court. Heading for her car she caught sight of Norman's mother waddling down the street before her. She caught up.

'Might I have a word, Mrs Stubbins,' she said.

The woman looked embarrassed on seeing the head teacher. 'It weren't a matter of the money you know, Mrs Stirling,' she dissembled. 'It was the principle.'

'I am pleased that common sense prevailed,' Elisabeth told

her. 'I do hope in future, Mrs Stubbins, that should anything like this happen again you will come in to see me before taking such action. In this case, had you done so, it would have saved a great deal of inconvenience and upset.'

'I was propositioned, Mrs Stirling,' said the woman.

'Propositioned?'

'Solicited.'

'You were what?'

'In Clayton, this man came up to me and asked if any of my family had had an accident and I told him about Norman. It wouldn't have occurred to me if he hadn't approached me. He said there was a clear case to answer and his firm of solicitors would represent me – no win, no fee. I wouldn't have bothered if I hadn't been solicited.'

'I see,' said Elisabeth. 'Well, as I have said, I would appreciate it if you would see me if you have a problem concerning Norman. Now, I noticed when I called into school this morning on the way to the court that he was absent. Is he all right?'

'Yes, he's fine,' replied Mrs Stubbins. 'I've kept him off today because he's had a bit of an accident. He fell out of his bunk bed this morning.'

The following morning Ms Tricklebank arrived early. On her last visit to the school the previous year, Mr Gribbon had observed a dumpy, red-faced woman with a rather intense expression on her face standing by the school gate watching the children as they filed up the path and he had mistaken her for Mrs Pugh, the new part-time cleaner. Before Ms Tricklebank could inform him that she was the Director of Education, the caretaker had rattled on non-stop (accompanied by the jangling keys) complaining about the amount of work he had to do, all the dusting and cleaning, polishing and floor buffing, before he moved on to the problem of the cockroaches which came out from under the skirting boards at night. That morning when he saw Ms Tricklebank, whom he now recognised, walking up the path to the school, he straightened his nylon overall, jangled his keys and went to greet her, his face wreathed in a broad smile.

'Good morning, Ms Tricklebank,' he said in a most ingratiating manner.

'Good morning, Mr Gribbon,' she replied.

One of the strengths of the director of education was her capacity for recalling the names, titles and faces of people she had met. Those she had come across only once were most impressed and flattered that when she came across them again she remembered what they were called and what was their job of work.

The caretaker opened the door to the school in a flourish, stood back and bowed obsequiously. 'A lovely morning, Ms Tricklebank, if I may say so,' he said, still maintaining the treacly tone of voice.

'It is,' she agreed.

In the entrance she complimented him on the clean, bright state of the building. He went pink with pleasure and considered mentioning the need for a part-time cleaner but thought better of it. It could, he thought, raise the spectre of Mrs Pugh which might have reached the director's ears. Best not push his luck.

'May I escort you to Mrs Stirling's classroom where she is awaiting you?' he said, kowtowing.

'Thank you,' she replied, smiling tolerantly.

'A most satisfactory conclusion to a most taxing affair,' Ms Tricklebank said later. She explained the reason for her visit: to congratulate Elisabeth on the outcome of the court action, learn how the amalgamation was going and see if the redeployed teachers had settled in and were proving satisfactory.

'I must say I found the experience in court rather intimidating,' admitted Elisabeth.

'The county solicitor, with whom I spoke yesterday after- noon, didn't think you looked intimidated. Quite the reverse, in fact. Mrs Pickering said you made the case for her most eloquently. I gather there was little she had to do to argue the local authority's defence after you had left the witness box. She said you acquitted yourself splendidly.' Ms Tricklebank paused and tilted her head. 'It is a pity the same cannot be said of Mr Nettles. Mrs Pickering felt he had not been at all helpful in this matter.'

'No, not really,' said Elisabeth, 'but it is water under the bridge now.' She had made her feelings plain to the education officer and wished to leave it at that.

'I shall be having a word with Mr Nettles myself this after- noon,' said Ms Tricklebank, 'and see what he has to say for himself. Anyway, how are the teachers we redeployed getting along?'

'Miss Kennedy and Mr Hornchurch are excellent,' Elisabeth told her. 'They fit in well, work hard, are enthusiastic and relate well to the children.'

'And Mr Jolly?'

'Mr Jolly less so but he is making an effort. I feel sorry for him, to be honest. He is aware that he is not an inspiring teacher compared to his colleagues and has been through a tough time lately with the court action.'

'I did say,' said the Director of Education, 'when we discussed the staffing of the new school that Mr Jolly is perhaps not the best teacher in the world but that I was confi- dent that with your guidance and encouragement he would improve.'

'I hope so,' said Elisabeth.

Mr Jolly returned to school the following day. He arrived early in order to see Elisabeth and perched on the end of a chair in the staff room, facing her with a look of anxiety and pain on his dull-reddish face. He swallowed nervously.

'I'm sorry I never made it to court,' he said in a voice barely above a whisper. He looked at his feet, unable to raise his eyes to meet those of Elisabeth's. 'I just couldn't face it.'

'I understand that,' replied Elisabeth. 'I appreciate how distressing it could have been for you. In the event, as I mentioned to you on the telephone yesterday afternoon, everything turned out for the best, as I knew it would. The case was thrown out and you have been completely exonerated.'

Clearly these reassuring words did not have the desired effect, for the man still looked wretched and miserable. He ran a hand through his lank thinning hair, looked up and stared ahead with a haunted look.

'And how are you feeling?' she asked.

He looked edgy and ill at ease. 'To be honest, I'm not feeling all that good. I've not been able to sleep and I've had this headache for some time now.'

'Perhaps you ought to go and see the doctor,' suggested Elisabeth, 'or take a few days off until you feel better.'

Mr Jolly stared forlornly at the floor again. It was apparent he was not listening. 'Over the last couple of days,' he said, 'I've had time to think about things.' His voice was as emotionless as the blank look on his face; his hands were knotted together on his lap. 'I have decided to resign.'

Elisabeth received the news without undue surprise, dismay or pleasure. She had witnessed in the run-up to the court case how tense he had become, remaining in his classroom at breaks, hardly speaking to his colleagues and disappearing from the building at the sound of the home-time bell. It was clear to her that he was a stressed and deeply unhappy man.

'I think you are being hasty,' she said. 'You need to give the matter more thought.'

'I know I'm not a very good teacher,' he told her candidly. 'I've always known it, to be honest. At Urebank I just about managed and I got by but I can't say I was very effective. Here in this school it's become more evident. I've observed how the children flourish in Mr Hornchurch's class, how keen they are in his lessons and I've seen the quality of the work they produce. He's a born teacher. I'm not. By comparison, my lessons are dull indeed. At the parents' consultation evening, as you are no doubt aware, there were complaints about me with some of the parents asking if their children could move into Mrs Robertshaw's class and—'

'Look, Donald,' interrupted Elisabeth, 'I will be frank with you. I had strong reservations when I knew you were to teach here. I imagined that you would be uncooperative and resentful and go out of your way to be difficult but I was wrong. You have made an effort to fit in and I think in time all this bother about the accident in the hall will be water under the bridge. This is what I said to Ms Tricklebank when she came in to see me yesterday.'

'The director came in to see you?' he asked, looking alert for the first time.

'Yes she came into school to congratulate us on how we handled ourselves in court.'

'At which I never appeared,' he said with an expression of pained regret. 'I guess she wasn't overly satisfied by the way I have behaved in this whole sorry affair.'

'It was never mentioned,' Elisabeth told him. 'Now I want you to put any idea of resigning out of your mind and we will talk again in a few weeks when things have got back to normal.'

'No, no, I've made up my mind,' he said. 'I was offered early retirement before the amalgamation. I shall get in touch with the Education Office and see if it is still open to me.' He held out a hand. 'I want to thank you, Mrs Stirling, for your support. It is much appreciated but I think it is for the best for all concerned if I tender my resignation.'

There was a loud knock and Mr Gribbon poked his head around the door. 'You had better come, Mrs Stirling,' he said with a long, weary sigh. 'That stupid Stubbins lad has been stung by a bee.'

21

Mr Ross found Robbie sitting atop a five-barred gate watching a herd of black and white cows. The 'beeasts', as the farmer called them, illuminated by a bright moon, huddled by a water trough and stared back at the boy with elaborate indifference, swishing their tails slowly and chewing methodically.

The farmer stopped in his tracks and considered the words he might use. He looked at the figure perched on the gate. Small and skinny with his cropped chestnut hair and gangly legs, he looked like a little monkey.

''Eyup, Robbie,' he said, approaching the boy.

'Hello,' replied Robbie softly.

A wedge of geese flew overhead, honking. Somewhere in the distance came the indignant call of a magpie.

'It's a grand neet,' said Mr Ross, leaning against the gate and placing his leathery hands on the top. He cleared his throat several times and then swallowed nervously.

Robbie looked down at him with curiosity. He sensed the farmer had something to say.

'Is something wrong?' he asked.

'Aye, lad, there is,' replied the farmer.

'Is it my mum?' Robbie asked.

Mr Ross nodded and looked down at his hands.

There was a short silence. 'She's dead, isn't she?' Robbie said, his voice choked.

'Aye, lad, I'm afraid she is.'

The boy said nothing but just stared ahead. 'There are

things I should be doing,' he said after a while, 'lots of things. Jobs to be done. I meant to look in on the pigs, see if they had enough water and feed.' There was a tremble in his voice. 'I have to check on the hens and there's other things but I just can't remember what they are. I just can't remember.' His small body was shaking.

'Thas'll remember 'em,' Mr Ross said gently. 'There's no rush.'

'I said some horrible things to her, you know' said Robbie, rubbing his eyes with a fist. 'I said some horrible things. I didn't mean any of them.'

'We all say things we shouldn't 'ave an' then later when we've 'ad a think abaat it, we regret what we said,' the farmer told him. 'Yer not alone in doin' that.'

'I told her I hated her,' Robbie said, biting his lip to stem the tears. 'I said . . . I said . . . I wished she was dead. Now she is.' He began to cry softly.

Mr Ross sighed, then climbed up on the bottom rung of the gate until his face was level with the boy's. He put an arm on Robbie's shoulder. 'She knew tha din't mean it.'

'Did she?' asked the boy piteously. He looked as if he was filled with genuine remorse.

''Course she did. She was yer mam an' knew young un's say things in t'heat o' t'moment when they're angry an' feel 'ard done by. She were so pleased to see yer at t'hospital. Yer made yer peace wi' 'er an' I'll tell thee summat, if it's possible to die 'appy, yer mam did.'

'I'm no good,' murmured the boy.

'Hey, hey!' cried the farmer. 'Don't you let me 'ear yer say that.'

'It's true,' sobbed Robbie. 'I'm always in trouble. I'm no good.'

'Now you just listen to me, Robbie 'Ardy,' said the farmer, 'an' you listen well. Don't you go talkin' like that, it'll mek me angry. We all mek mistakes an' say 'urtful things an' some-times do things what are wrong but I've fostered a lot o' kids an' I know for a fact that there was good in every single one of 'em. An' yer a good lad at 'eart. Tha dun't need to be perfect tha knaas, to be loved. An' yer mother loved you. There's no doubt abaat that. An' as for allus bein' in trouble, it's a fact that t' wildest colts make t'best horses.'

Robbie began to cry and shake with the force of it.

The farmer's hands wrapped around him and he held him close. 'And just remember what my missus told thee, "yer braver than yer believe, stronger then yer seem an' yer smarter than yer think".'

Elisabeth's son sat on the grass in the garden at Clumber Lodge, fascinated by the wasps which were buzzing madly around the fallen fruit. Danny, with a contented look in his face, was leaning back on a bench stroking his ferret which stretched out on his lap. James sat beside him reading.

John's second visit was proving much more successful than the first. This time his teacher had accompanied him and after a bit of coaxing the boy had emerged from the car and settled down in the garden.

'He does get a bit flustered,' explained Mr Campsmount, 'particularly when he is out of his comfort zone and sees lots of new faces. He seems pretty happy now though.'

John looked around as if he were aware they were talking about him. He blinked and smiled.

'It's so good to have him here,' said Elisabeth. 'He's doing so well. And thank you for giving up a Saturday to be with him.'

'Let's hope this is one of many visits he will be making,' said the teacher. 'I guess it won't be long before he will not want me coming with him.'

'You know you are always very welcome,' she replied. 'You

have worked wonders with John. I can't believe he's the same boy he was when I first moved here.'

Michael came into the garden.

Elisabeth walked to meet him and linked her arm through his. 'I'm so happy,' she said, reaching up and kissing him on the cheek. 'I have the best husband in the world, three lovely children, a great job and a wonderful home. I don't think I have ever been as happy. Thank you for arranging John's visit again, Michael. It was sweet of you.'

'And I've never been as happy,' he replied.

'Really?' she said.

He bent and kissed her on the lips.

'Ugh!' groaned Danny and James in unison.

'You wait until you boys are a bit older,' said Michael laughing, 'and you start taking an interest in girls. You might feel different about kissing then.'

'No chance,' cried Danny. 'I prefer mi ferret to lasses any day.'

'And I like my books,' added James.

'Come and join us,' Elisabeth said to Michael.

'I'd love to but I can't,' he answered. 'I've had a call from Bianca up at Tanfield Farm. Evidently Mr Massey isn't too well. He's taken to his bed moaning and groaning as if he's on his last legs. I just came out to tell you that I'll be back in time for tea and there's a Mrs Ross wishing to speak to you. I've put her in the sitting room.'

'Oh dear,' she sighed. 'I guess it's about Robbie.'

Elisabeth found her visitor standing at the small table by the window. She was looking at the photographs in the silver frames.

'That's my husband's first wife,' said Elisabeth, coming into the room.

'She was very beautiful, wasn't she,' said Mrs Ross.

'She was,' Elisabeth agreed. 'She died in a riding accident.'

'I hope you don't mind me calling on you at home like this, Mrs Stirling.'

'Not at all. Do sit down. Would you like a cup of tea?'

'That's very kind, but not for me thank you. I don't want to keep you and anyway, I have to get back. I wanted to see you. It's about Robbie.'

'Oh dear,' sighed Elisabeth, 'has he had one of his outbursts?'

'No, no, nothing like that. He's behaving himself but he's pretty down at the moment. I thought I'd call round to let you know that his mother died yesterday in the hospital at Clayton.'

'I see,' said Elisabeth. 'How very sad.'

'She was very ill,' continued Mrs Ross, 'and it was just a matter of time. I gather that if she had been to see her doctor earlier they might have been able to do something for her but she just ignored what she had. We took Robbie to see her earlier in the week and he was as good as gold. I think they made it up with one another.'

'I'm so pleased. How is he?' asked Elisabeth.

'He's very upset, of course,' Mrs Ross told her, 'but he's coping as best he can.' She looked thoughtful. 'He has to, doesn't he, poor lad? You know, some children have the best the world can give them and others have a rough time of it. We've fostered many a child who didn't have much of a chance. Anyway, I just wanted you to know that he won't be at school on Monday and when he returns he might be a bit . . . well you know.'

'I understand,' answered Elisabeth. 'I'll keep a close eye on him. And are you still determined to adopt Robbie?'

'We are,' said Mrs Ross. 'That's what we promised his mother. I guess it won't be all plain sailing but Hamish and me have taken to the lad. We like him, Mrs Stirling, and he likes us. He needs a home, some stability and lots of love and someone to take care of him. We talked it through with Robbie last night and he's happy that he can stay with us. We're to see Miss Parsons first thing on Monday.'

'Ashley!' exclaimed Emmet.

She stood on the doorstep at Limebeck Lodge.

'May I come in?' she asked.

'Of course, come through,' he said, turning on the light.

'I'm not disturbing you, am I?'

'No, not at all.'

'If it's not convenient . . .'

'It's fine.'

'I didn't think you were in,' she said. 'The place was in darkness.'

'I was sitting in the dark,' he told her. 'I sometimes do that to think about things.'

'I see.'

'The place is in a bit of a mess in here I'm afraid, as you can see.'

'You should see my cottage,' she said.

'There's still quite a lot to do,' he told her, 'but once we've got the new kitchen fitted and put up some bright curtains and hung a few pictures on the walls it will look a bit more like home. I've also promised Roisin that eventually we will have a long case clock. She likes the one you have at Wisteria Cottage and is always going on at me to—'

'Emmett,' interrupted Ashley, 'I need to talk to you. Could you stop talking for a moment?'

'Yes, of course,' he replied, sensing the depth of feeling in her voice.

Ashley took a deep breath. 'Could you sit down, please?' she said. Her mouth felt bone-dry.

'This sounds ominous,' he said, moving some papers off a chair. He sat leaning forward, a worried expression on his face.

She sat across from him and looked into his dark eyes. 'I don't really know where to start,' she said after an awkward pause. 'Emmet, have I said something or done something that has upset you?'

'No, of course not,' he said. 'Why do you ask that?' His gaze was earnest and steadfast.

'It's just that when I saw you last, when we were talking about the window to put in the church, you seemed so distant. It was as if a cloud had come between us and all the brightness of the day had gone. I've never known you to be so aloof. It seemed as if you didn't really want to speak to me, that you were glad to see me go. I thought that I had somehow offended you.'

'Offended you! Of course you've not offended me,' he cried.

'I just thought—' she began.

'Look, I'm so sorry if I gave you that impression,' he told her. His face was sharp with anxiety. 'I didn't mean to be unfriendly. I . . . I suppose I was thinking about all the work that needs to be done at the big house. My mind was on other things I guess.'

His mind had certainly been on other things. It had been on the woman who now sat before him looking tense. He was torn between compulsion and desire; compulsion to tell her how he felt and desire to hold her in his arms and kiss her. He was in love with her, he was sure of that, and the thought of her with another man had made him feel despondent. Of course he knew she was too good for him. How could he compete with someone with a first-class honours degree, a man from her sort of privileged background, Oxford educated and middle-class, someone she had known since university? He had once hoped that given time she might feel something more than friendship for him, but now . . .

'Is that all?' Ashley asked.

'I'm sorry?'

'Is that the reason for you being distant with me?' she said.

'Yes, of course,' he lied. He noticed her hands were trembling.

'I don't believe you,' she said quietly. 'There was something else that troubled you. Emmet, I've known you long enough to recognise that.' There was another, longer pause. She looked away from him, her eyes pricking with tears.

He reached out and gently touched her hand. 'Hey, Ashley, what's wrong?' His voice was solicitous and kindly.

'I've thought long and hard about what I might say to you,' she said, scared of catching his eyes. Her voice was heavy with emotion and her heart began to quicken. 'In the end I've decided that I should be honest and get it off my chest. You need to know.'

He swallowed. 'Know what?'

'This is so embarrassing,' she said taking a breath. 'I wanted to tell you that . . . I . . .'

Emmet leant further forward and stared at her intently. He reached for her hand and squeezed it. 'Please, Ashley, tell me what it is,' he said gently.

'I . . . I don't know where to start.' She stood up suddenly, raised her hand which was trembling and pushed back her hair. 'I think I have to go,' she said suddenly. 'This was a mistake. I should never have come.'

As she made for the door, Emmet took her arm. 'Tell me, please,' he said. 'I can't bear to see you like this.'

'Emmet . . .' she started.

'What is it?' He gazed at her steadily.

She swallowed hard. 'I think . . . I think . . . I'm falling in love with you,' she said, looking into his dark eyes. 'No, no, I'm not falling in love with you. I love you. I think I've always loved you. There . . . I've said it.'

Emmet felt a catch in his breath. He looked stunned and his

eyes, large and dark, widened. 'What did you say?' he whispered.

'I'm in love with you, Emmet O'Malley,' she repeated. Her breath came shallow and quick.

His mouth fell open and he blinked several times. He couldn't take his eyes off her face; it was as if he was looking at her for the very first time.

'Well say something please, even if it's to tell me how silly and forward and embarrassing I am.' She looked down with tears in her eyes.

He lifted up her face, wiped away a tear and then he seized her hand and pressed it to his lips.

'I think of you all the time,' he said. 'I've loved you, Ashley Underwood, since the first time we met. You're the loveliest, kindest person I know. I've always loved you.'

'You have?' There were more tears in her eyes.

'You are in my thoughts all day, every day,' he told her. 'You are the reason why I live and breathe.'

'You never said,' she told him.

'How could I? I thought there was someone else in your life. I was told that by Elisabeth.'

'Oh, Emmet! It was you,' she said. 'It was you. It's always been you. Did you not know that?'

'But I saw you at the bus stop,' he said. 'I thought you and that teacher at the school were going out together.'

'Rupert Hornchurch,' she said laughing. 'Rupert is gay, Emmet. He's just a friend, that's all, just a friend.'

'I didn't know,' he said. 'I'm such a fool, aren't I, jumping to the wrong conclusion? I was so jealous. I wanted to tell you how I felt about you but couldn't bear the thought of being rejected, making an eejit of myself. To hear what you say now is like the sunshine appearing after a long time in the cold and rain.'

'The Irish blarney,' she said, wiping her wet cheeks.

'This is no blarney,' he said. 'It's God's own honest truth.' He put his arm around her, his hand in the small of her back. Then he was kissing her, lightly on the lips.

As Mrs O'Connor's Grandmother Mullarkey might have remarked, 'A day lasts until it is chased away but love and happiness last until the grave.' With the approach of that very special season, when peace and goodwill are in the air and people feel well disposed to one another, there were many happy faces in Barton-in-the-Dale and not a little love as the year drew to its close.

To Elisabeth's delight, John became a regular visitor to Cumber Lodge and continued to make progress at school. Lady Wadsworth viewed the newly installed stained-glass window in St Christopher's dedicated to her brother with great satisfaction and pride. Watson, her long-suffering butler, was given his long-awaited pay rise and his cold, damp, draughty room in the East Wing of Limebeck House with the peeling wallpaper, threadbare carpet and noisy pipes was given a complete overhaul. The Venerable Atticus, Archdeacon of Clayton, much to his wife's gratification and his own apprehension, was elevated to become the new suffragan bishop. Mrs Scrimshaw was elected unanimously as President of the Barton and District branch of the Women's Institute and Mr Gribbon was granted his wish for the appointment of a part-time cleaner to start the following term. Mr Jolly, granted early retirement and given a generous severance package, opened a heath food shop in Whitby and spent the days ahead happily selling nuts and dried prunes.

And as the night drew in and the shadows lengthened, the curate and the Irish traveller snuggled up on the sofa in Wisteria Cottage before the crackling fire and talked of the life they would lead together.

'There are sure to be a few raised eyebrows,' said Emmet.

'Oh, I think we will be able to cope with that,' replied Ashley.

'I wonder what the archdeacon will say,' he said.

'He'll be delighted.'

'And the bishop?'

'Him too.'

'And what about your mother?'

'Emmet, my darling, I am really not bothered what people will say, least of all my mother. I love you, you love me and that's all there is to it.'

'I wish it were as simple as that,' he said thoughtfully.

'It is,' she said. 'Now, as Mrs Sloughthwaite might say, "stop your mithering" and give me a kiss.'

And what of Robbie? After much prayer, patience, dedication and love he developed confidence in himself and was able to imagine a more hopeful future. Soon to be the adopted son of Mr and Mrs Ross, he became something of an expert on pig rearing and, dressed for the part in a waxed jacket, flat cap and green Wellington boots, he entertained the farmers at the auction mart with his knowledge. And the Reverend Mr Algernon Sparshott, Vicar of Barton-in-the-Dale, referring to his Bible and thinking of the theme for his homily for Sunday worship, decided that the lesson that week should be on the subject of love. 'For love,' he read, 'bears all things, believes all things, hopes all things, endures all things.'

ACKNOWLEDGEMENTS

Tremendous thanks to my editor, Francesca Best and my literary agent Luigi Bonomi for their continued patience, support and encouragement. A special thanks goes to Alban Wood Esq., gentleman farmer of Hinderwell, North Yorkshire, for his invaluable advice concerning pigs.

How it all began – the first charming instalment in
the *Little Village School* series

GERVASE PHINN

The Little Village School

She was wearing red shoes! With silver heels!

Elisabeth Devine causes quite a stir on her arrival in the
village. No one can understand why the head of a big
inner city school would want to come to sleepy little
Barton-in-the-Dale, to a primary with more problems
than school dinners.

And that's not even counting the challenges the mysterious Elisabeth herself will face: a bitter former head
teacher, a grumpy caretaker and a duplicitous chair of
governors, to name but a few.

Then there's the gossip. After all, a woman who would
wear red shoes to an interview is obviously capable of
anything . . .

Out now in paperback and ebook

HODDER

Book Two in the *Little Village School* series

GERVASE PHINN

Trouble at the Little Village School

Elisabeth Devine certainly rocked the boat when she
arrived in Barton-in-the-Dale to take over as head
teacher of the little primary school. Now it's a new term,
and after winning over the wary locals, she can finally
settle in to her role. Or so she thinks . . .

For the school is hit by a brand-new bombshell: it's to
be merged with its arch rival, and Elisabeth has to fight
for the headship with Urebank's ruthless and
calculating headmaster.

But add in some gossip and a helping of scandal, not
to mention various newcomers bringing good things
and bad to Barton, and that's not the only trouble that's
brewing in the village.

Out now in paperback and ebook

HODDER

GERVASE PHINN

Out of the Woods But Not Over the Hill

For Gervase Phinn growing old is not about a leisurely walk to the pub for a game of dominoes or snoozing in his favourite armchair. As this sparkling collection of his very best humorous writing shows, he may be 'out of the woods' but he is certainly not 'over the hill'.

Looking back over more than sixty years of family life, teaching, inspecting schools, writing and public speaking, Gervase never fails to unearth humour, character, warmth and wisdom from the most diverse of experiences, whether they be growing up in Rotherham with the most un-Yorkshirelike of names or describing why loud mobile phone users get his goat.

Brimming with nostalgia, gently mocking life's absurdities, never shy of an opinion, this is Gervase Phinn at his wittiest, twinkly eyed best.

Out now in paperback and ebook

HODDER